"A true communion of place, character, and plot. Waters of the Dancing Sky is a complete vision, one with reverberating depths and serious surprises." Laura Kasischke, Author of *The Life Before Her Eyes*

"A complicated tale of brokenness and renewal. Kay weaves together a story with themes of shame and violence, redemption and forgiveness. Beautifully written, this is a brilliant tale of second chances and building a better stronger life." Melissa Levine, Independent Professional Book Reviewers

"An elegantly told story filled with twists and turns, pain and tenderness, conflict and resolution. Touched by spirits of Native Americans long since passed from this world, emboldened by the majesty of the North Woods, this is a story about the universality of life – a book about the magic of the human spirit and the often wisp-like will of the human mind. Highly recommended reading for lovers of life everywhere." Don Bacue, Executive Editor, International Features Syndicate

"Beautiful Rainy Lake and its surrounding wonders and seasons become the focal setting and center stage for Waters of the Dancing Sky. Basking in the beauty and wonders of nature almost cause one to forget the heartaches, broken promises, and losses which occur. It is here that Beth finds peace, security, and an anchor as she derives strength to weather the storms of life." Dorothy Barron, Author of *Slinging Stones*

"The hero seeking light in the fog of an unsettled past, in the swirl of a disturbing present, and finding courage to embrace the unknown future ... all elements of a true mythic story. Waters of the Dancing Sky is a soul journey that unfolds like a plot of a Hallmark Channel movie." Frank Zufall, Spooner Advocate

Waters of the Dancing Sky

by **Janet Kay**

"The past is consumed in the present

and the present is living only because

it brings forth the future."

James Joyce

Dedication

*For my loved ones who have passed on
to the other side of life
but whose spirits
live on forever:
for Carol & Wally,
Joe & Virginia,
Nannie & Elmer,
and Allen.*

Acknowledgements

It takes a village to create a novel. *Waters of the Dancing Sky* has been bubbling around in my head for years, becoming a life force that needed to be released on paper. I have many people to thank for helping me turn this vision into reality.

I must begin with the communities of Rainy Lake, Minnesota, a place I've fallen in love with and have used as the setting for my novel. A special thank-you to Mike Williams, historical boat tour guide and Rainy Lake resource, for introducing me to the lake and its fascinating history; to Ed Oerichbauer, Director of the Koochiching County Museums, and Voyageur's National Park staff for assisting me with my research; and to all who shared their fascinating stories with me.

Thank you to Steve Henry (www.HenryImages.net) for the use of his amazing photo of the Aurora Borealis; to Rainy Lake artist, Bernie "Spike" Woods for allowing me to use several of his hometown sketches of Ranier; and to Anna Martineau Merritt (www.mistypinephotography.com) for the use of her stunning seagull photo and my portrait which she took at a special place on Rainy Lake. I also want to thank the *Waters of The Dancing Sky Scenic Byway* organization for allowing me to use their slogan in the title of my book.

A heartfelt thank-you to Randi Anderson of Seeley Lake, Montana, for her valuable editing assistance. I also greatly appreciate the support and feedback from the members of the St. Croix Writers of Solon Springs, Wisconsin and the Alpine Artisans Writing Group of Seeley Lake, Montana. To Mary Beth Smith, Agnes Kennard, Sarah Reeves, Randi Anderson, Mike Williams, Peggy Roeder, thank you for reviewing and providing input on my first draft.

A very special thank you to my children - Shannon and Will Graber, Shane and Sandi Jenson, and Sherry Jenson for reviewing and commenting on my manuscript - but most of all, for their encouragement and love. I have ten special *little people* that I must also acknowledge - my grandchildren - Derek, Malachi, Milton & George Jenson; Madelaine, William, Abigail & Andrew Graber; and Audrey &

Jared McLochlin. Thank you for your hugs and laughter - and for keeping me in touch with that *inner child* that writers need to create their fictional worlds.

Janet Kay

". . . a true communion of place, character, and plot . . . This is a carefully constructed novel, but lush in its evocation of a time and people. As in all the best fiction, there is not a detail here that could be removed and leave the rest intact. *Waters of the Dancing Sky* is a complete vision, one with reverberating depths and serious surprises."
                    —Laura Kasischke, author of *The Life Before Her Eyes*

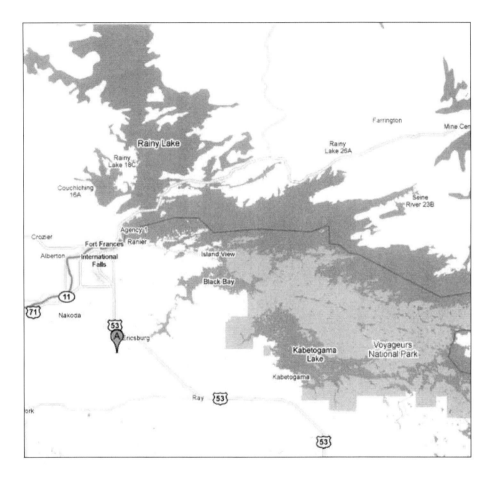

"I'm nobody! Who are you?"
Emily Dickinson

Chapter One

"*J*ust go to hell and leave me alone!" she sobbed, hurling a crystal goblet dripping with vintage French Beaujolais into the flames of their massive fieldstone fireplace. Distorted images of Rob's sneering face seemed to leap from the flames, taunting her, refusing to let her go.

She was alone…as she'd been most of her life. Tonight, she sat on the floor of their Chicago high-rise surrounded by views of Lake Michigan crashing against the pier far below. Pounding almost as loudly as the fear and humiliation surging through her veins. Wearing a tattered bathrobe that she'd had forever, the one Rob hated, she was surrounded by remnants of their life together—photos of their wedding, their social life, exotic travels. Like a madwoman, she compulsively shredded tear-stained pieces of the past, tossing them into the raging fire. She laughed, then cried, as the flames consumed twenty years of misery, lies, and abuse. A marriage disintegrating before her eyes.

Flipping through page after page of old photos, Beth Calhoun decided that photo albums were nothing more than twisted versions of reality. All the smiling faces. The happy times. Where were the *real* times of their lives—the tears, the hostile words, the bruises? Where were the *other women* who had haunted their marriage over the years?

She was startled upon discovering a photo dated 1986. A smiling, young Rob Calhoun stood in their bedroom, in his shorts, proudly displaying a breakfast tray of his homemade waffles topped with strawberries and whipped cream. One perfect red rose bloomed in a cut-glass vase that sparkled with sunlit diamonds streaming in through the window. Sometimes a little love note would be tucked beneath her plate of waffles. He brought her breakfast in bed on Sunday mornings back then—the only leisurely day they had to spend together. He was in law school, studying night and day for his bar exams. She was pregnant with Emily, trying to become the wife Rob wanted her to be.

She'd long forgotten those Sunday morning breakfasts in bed—and what usually followed—until she became too big and uncomfortable to do much more than lie there like a beached whale. He began to stay out later and later at night—with his college pals, of course. It wasn't long before their Sunday morning breakfasts drifted into a hazy past. He didn't have time. All she could think about was the life growing within her. She dreamed of the wonderful life they would be able to provide for this child—dreams that were sometimes shattered by cold gusts of reality.

Tonight, twenty years later, she sifted through fading photos depicting a perfect marriage, one that had never existed. Her mind began to fill in the blank pages with the ugly memories, the ones that had never been captured on film. Why, she wondered, did life seem to shift back and forth like the tides of the sea? The tide moved in, gently depositing pebbles of hope on sun-drenched beaches. Then, it moved out, taking the pebbles away. Sometimes the sea churned into a blind rage that destroyed all life in its wake. The cycle repeated itself over and over again. Why, she wondered, did change seem to happen so gradually, so subtly, that you never saw it coming...until it was too late?

There were no photos of the first dinner party that Beth threw for her new in-laws. Painfully aware that Rob's parents felt she was not worthy of their only son, she had tried her best to prepare a gourmet dinner that would please them. Never mind that Rob's mother, the vivacious and promiscuous Nora, had never prepared a meal in her life. Nora hired, and fired, the best chefs in Chicago. Beth had fretted for days, researching and trying out recipes, buying china and crystal, a floral centerpiece for the table, the right wine to complement the main entrée. This was a far different world from the one Beth had grown up in. She had been raised by her grandmother on a wilderness island in Rainy Lake on the Minnesota/Ontario international border. It had been a simple life, just the two of them, after Beth's mother had drowned in the big lake many years ago...

She had not been prepared for her first dinner party in Chicago. By the time dinner was finally served that evening, Beth was exhausted. She was eight months pregnant. Rob was angry that she hadn't set the table properly. The napkins weren't even folded correctly. The Beef Wellington was overdone, thanks to Nora, who had arrived an hour later than her husband. Nora seemed flustered as she tottered in on spiked alligator heels, wearing a slinky leopard-skin dress that clung to her curves. Her black hair was tousled, her makeup smeared. She made a feeble excuse although nobody seemed to be interested. Her husband and son ignored her—as if this was a common occurrence that they had learned to live with. As if she didn't really matter. The focus shifted to Beth's dinner, to ways she could learn to improve her skills.

The final straw, according to Rob, was when Beth plopped a plastic tub of margarine on the table. Where were the flowered swirls of real butter, floating on a bed of ice chips? He was humiliated, he told her later, disgraced before his parents. His eyes had hardened into sheets of steel, his mouth drawn into a tight line that promised revenge. Beth had never seen him like this. She did not know what to think.

The moment that his parents left, she discovered another side of her new husband. He grabbed her wrists, backing her slowly toward the wall. "Stop!" she cried. "You're hurting me, Rob. What's wrong?"

His grip tightened as he pinned her against the wall with the weight of his body. "Can't you do anything right?" he exploded, as her tears began to fall. "My parents are right, you know. You're nothing but trash—white trash. You don't belong here. You never will. My God, I can't believe you're going to be the mother of my child, the poor little bastard…"

She would never forget those stinging words. A slap across the face would have been much kinder. Nor would she forget lying rigidly beside him that night, drenched in fear. She listened for the welcome sound of his snoring, but it never came. They lay side by side, awake most of the night. Just before dawn, he pulled her into his arms and stroked her head. "Oh my God…Beth, honey, why do you make me do these things? If I didn't love you so much, I never would have gotten so upset. You know I love you. I could never live without you. Please, Beth, please forgive me…" He told her about his childhood and how it had created these doubts and insecurities within him. His father was a workaholic who had ignored him as well as his mother. And his mother…well, she had a steady stream of lovers to keep her busy. Her behavior had been humiliating for a young boy to deal with. But that was history, he told her. Now, he had a wife to love, the only one who could make it all better for him. He promised that he would never hurt her again. She forgave him that morning, the first of many times, as the sun crawled sleepily over the horizon, hesitating at the uncertainty of the day unfolding on the planet below.

From that day forward, Beth now realized, there had been good days—and bad days. Days when she struggled to decide what kind of a day it had actually been. Their marriage became an emotional roller coaster. She held on bravely through the ups and downs, telling herself that no marriage was perfect. They had to learn to adjust to each other.

She was confident that her love would somehow provide the missing ingredient in Rob's life. If she loved him enough, she believed that she could change him and transform their marriage into one they could both be proud of—one that would provide a happy home for little Emily. This became her mission in life.

Sometimes she felt like she was winning the battle. Rob would come home with tickets for a weekend in Paris—just the two of them. He would hold her in his arms and promise to love her forever. He adored Emily, showering her with baby dolls and books—until her crying drove him away from home for some well-deserved silence. He was, after all, a hard-working attorney by now, consumed with his rise to power within his father's prestigious law firm.

Then there were the bad days. Beth would never forget the nights that Rob didn't bother to come home. The pre-dawn mornings when he stumbled into their bed with the scent of another woman's perfume ground into the pores of his skin. She sobbed for days the first time it happened. Crushed at his betrayal, she soon learned that the pain of confronting him was far worse than pretending to ignore the obvious. He spent hours detailing all the things that she did wrong—as if that justified his transgressions. He told her that she was a hindrance to his career, a bad wife, an incompetent mother. She was uneducated and therefore, an embarrassment to him. But when she tried to enroll in college classes, he refused to let her attend. When she tried to get a job, he insisted that no wife of his would work outside their home.

She felt trapped, dependent upon her husband and his constantly changing opinion of her. There still were days when he told her what a good mother she was, raved about the dinner she had prepared, or expressed his pleasure with the way she had decorated their home. But little by little, Rob's negative messages began to dominate her thoughts, to gnaw away at her shaky self-esteem. Little by little, the abuse seemed to escalate. She learned to tread lightly when Rob was home, afraid to trigger another episode of some kind.

On her darkest days, while the baby napped in her crib, Beth daydreamed about leaving him. As if he could read her mind, he would come home early on those evenings with Chinese take-out food instead of a briefcase full of legal briefs. "I think you can use a break, honey," he'd say, pulling her into his arms. "Relax. I'll take care of Emily." With that, he'd change the baby's diapers and settle down on the floor to play with her. Tickling her, hugging her, making those silly noises that babies seem to bring out in adults. He was good to Emily. She loved her daddy—at least she did in those days. As Beth watched them together, she remembered why she stayed. It was for Emily, of course. Emily would not grow up without a father.

Beth pulled herself back to the present, back to this horrible night that had changed her life forever. Once again, she grabbed her scissors, slicing Rob's smiling face into fragments of the past. Slashing memories of their shared history into smaller and smaller pieces before committing them to ashes of the past. As if Rob never existed—never had, never would again.

Why, she began to chastise herself, had she allowed him to come over earlier this evening, despite the fact that he had moved out and filed for divorce two months ago? He had needed his freedom, he told her then, so he could move in with his twenty-two-year-old, pregnant girlfriend. This was just the latest in a series of affairs that had destroyed her self-esteem and, finally, her marriage.

Somehow, in a brief moment of regret and guilt over the failure of her marriage, Beth had toyed with the idea of forgiving him one last time. Perhaps it had something to do with the red roses that he'd had delivered to her this morning. Her favorite. He knew that. Yes, Rob had always known exactly how to play the game, which buttons to push at any given moment. How to get his own way.

In her loneliness, Beth had actually looked forward to spending an evening with Rob tonight. She hoped he had come to his senses after a two-month absence. Perhaps he realized what he was about to throw away, along with a good share of his assets. More importantly, he might have discovered that he still loved her and was willing to change in order to preserve their marriage. How many times, she wondered, had he told her that he couldn't live without her? Perhaps it was not too late to try to find a way back to each other.

She had to admit that she'd missed him in some ways. He had become a habit, good or bad. She wondered if it was possible to love someone whom she also hated. She'd never been with another man. It had always been Rob, only Rob…from that first night on the beach at Sand Point Island on Rainy Lake: the night that had resulted in the birth of their daughter Emily, who was now nineteen years old.

Humming along to classical music, she had slipped into the little black dress that Rob had always loved, dabbing his favorite French perfume behind her ears. Her long auburn hair flowed freely over her bare shoulders. The final touch was the pear-shaped emerald necklace and earrings that she retrieved from her jewelry vault. A gift from Rob— years ago. "They match your haunting green eyes," he had whispered in her ear, caressing her gently, then more urgently.

But that was long ago, she sharply reprimanded herself. Still, it didn't hurt to dress up once in a while, to make him think about what he was foolishly throwing away. Beethoven played softly in the background. Candles were lit on the glass table beside the vase of red roses. A bottle of vintage wine chilled beside a plate of sushi. Yes, tonight they would find their way back to what they once had together…whatever that was. There must have been something…

Her daydreams, however, soon turned into a nightmare. Rob had casually sauntered into their penthouse suite wearing a crumpled white shirt, his tie undone. He bent to give her a lingering kiss, his eyes hope-ful. He reeked of whiskey. She stiffened and pulled away from him. "Rob, we need to talk," she stood her ground. "You can't just walk in here and act like nothing has happened. My God, you left me—for your pregnant girlfriend! You've filed for divorce."

His blue eyes turned to steel as he leered at her, undressing her with his eyes. "Not now. We can talk later," he mumbled, grabbing her roughly.

"No, Rob. You've been drinking. Please leave."

"It's my house. You're my wife, and I'll do whatever I damn well please." He shoved her down into the plush cushions of the sofa as she struggled to free herself.

"Stop! Leave me alone! Please, Rob!" she pleaded, fighting him off with all her strength. But the harder she fought, the more agitated he became, the harder he gripped her arms. "You're hurting me," she cried, tears wetting her cheeks.

Fury streaked through his eyes as he slapped her across the face, leaving a painful imprint upon her left eye. She was shocked, terrified. He raised his hand again, threatening her, as she felt blood trickling down her chin. "Are you done fighting, bitch? Guess you want it rough, huh?" he snarled as if she were a stranger, one of his whores. As she cowered, he fell on top of her, shoving her dress up to her waist. Tear-ing her black lace panties in two, he forced her legs apart and penetrated her roughly with his fingers.

"Stop! Please stop! No, Rob!" she pleaded, bracing herself, trying to pretend this wasn't really happening to her. Crying, hysterical, she closed her eyes, trying to block him from her mind. She felt the pulsating heat of his body, smelled the whiskey on his breath. She was about to be raped by her own husband.

He unzipped his pants. Then suddenly, he zipped them back up again. He released her and stood up. "You're pathetic, Beth," he glared at her, towering above her. "Why would I want to make love to you? You aren't woman enough to satisfy any man, you know that? I sure as hell don't need you when I can have any other woman I want."

Make love? The words echoed wildly through her mind. As she lay there, partially naked, trembling with fear, she knew that it was finally over. Her feelings were dead beyond resurrection. He had finally crossed the line beyond which there was no return. Not ever. She did not move, did not respond. Please God, let him go, she prayed silently.

He stood there silently, watching her, as if he wanted to say something. Instead, he walked slowly toward the door, his head hanging. Finally, she heard the door slam behind him. Pulling herself to her feet, she stumbled to the door and locked the deadbolt, activated the alarm system, and shoved a heavy leather chair in front of the door.

Then she collapsed in a hot bath, trying to wash the filth from her body. Trying to erase the brutal memories. Trying to understand what had just happened to her, and why.

Fragmented thoughts raced through her mind. *Could this be partly my fault?* she wondered. She had, after all, dressed up for him and allowed him to come over tonight. She had even thought about a possible reconciliation. Had she, in any way, given him false expectations that he had acted upon? *No, no*, she chastised herself, *I do not deserve what he did to me tonight.*

She thought about calling the police but was afraid that nobody would believe her story. It would be her word against his. And he was so convincing—a highly respected attorney, a well-known advocate for human rights. Few people had ever seen the dark side of Rob Calhoun, she realized. It would be just too humiliating to file a police report. If she pressed charges against him, she'd have to face him in court. That was not something that she was willing to do. She'd watched him performing in the courtroom, devouring his opponents. She feared that she would be portrayed as the crazy one, the bitter, soon-to-be ex-wife.

Maybe she was crazy…crazy to have gotten herself into a situation like this. She had no friends, no real friends. No one to talk to. He had seen to that, isolating her throughout their marriage. He picked their friends, who were more like social acquaintances. Besides, it was difficult to have real friends when you lived with secrets that you could share with no one. Secrets of his infidelity, his emotional abuse. At first it had been an occasional slap across the face, but gradually, the abuse had escalated, interspersed with the good days that made her doubt her own perceptions. Shame ensured her silence.

As her self-esteem had deteriorated, she pretended it didn't matter. She focused on the one good thing in her life—their daughter, Emily. Tears welled in her eyes once again as she thought of Emily. She missed her talented, enthusiastic daughter, who was now touring and studying art in Europe. God, how she missed her. Life without Emily felt like a black hole that could never be filled. Of course, she was pleased that Emily was seeing the world, getting an education that would enable her to have a much better life than her mother had been able to achieve with her father.

Sometimes she worried about the things that Emily had surely seen or overheard at home. The arguments and the tension certainly spilled through the closed doors of their bedroom. It was difficult to hide the way Rob treated her, the rumors of his affairs, her angry silence. There was an occasional bruise that supposedly happened when clumsy Beth stumbled into the table or a wall. These were the family secrets that were not spoken of. Not ever. Beth had learned to pretend that everything was wonderful, for Emily's sake. And Emily soon learned to play this dysfunctional game…for her mother's sake. Looking back, Beth recalled times that Emily had watched her closely with lingering questions clouding her huge eyes. Beth had turned away to a sink full of dirty dishes, hiding her tears, pretending that all was well.

Beth dreaded telling Emily of the pending divorce and had put it off for two months now. She didn't want to hurt her. But she realized it was time to break the shattering news—now that there was no longer any possibility of going back. Not after tonight. Still, there was no way that she could tell Emily about the things that Rob had done to her tonight, or many of the other ugly details of the past. That would not be fair to Emily. Beth had always believed that a mother had a duty to protect her daughter from things that she should not have to worry about. Now, she began to wonder if she had an obligation instead to teach her to stay away from men like her father.

Conflicting images of the past swirled slowly through Beth's mind as she stood before the full-length oval mirror holding an ice bag over her swollen eye. Who was this pathetic creature staring back at her with a vacant look? It was nobody, she assured herself. Nobody that mattered. Nobody that she cared to know. This helpless person had no identity. She was no longer a wife, no longer the mother of a growing child who needed her. She no longer had a mother. She'd never had a father. No job, no education, no financial security. Soon to be homeless…

You're nobody, the stranger in the mirror reminded her—hollow words reinforcing the messages that Rob had carefully implanted within the withering cells of her brain over their years together. *Nobody…*

"Deep into that darkness peering, long I stood there, wondering, feeling, dreaming dreams no mortal ever dreamed before."
Edgar Allan Poe

Chapter Two

"It's a dream…only a dream." A small voice from someplace deep down tried to wake Beth as she thrashed about in restless sleep that night. It was a voice she had trained over the years to awaken her whenever *the dream* returned. But tonight there was something different about the dream that had haunted her for so many years. The voice could not wake her.

The dream always begins with six-year-old Beth rowing her old wooden rowboat in circles on Rainy Lake. She watches her reflection in the mirror-like surface of the lake and waves to her grandmother, who watches from the dock of their island home. She giggles as the loons call out to each other, diving playfully beneath her boat. But suddenly the loons begin shrieking in terror as a northeasterly wind rips through the narrows, blowing the little girl farther and farther out into the big lake. The lake begins to bubble and boil as whitecaps pound the little boat from all directions. Black rain begins to drip, then pour from the sky as dense sheets of fog roll across the lake. She can no longer see the familiar shoreline of her island.

"Mommy, help me!" she screams into the shrieking wind. But the relentless winds drive her farther and farther into the big lake and over a treacherous waterfall that drops thousands of feet into a saltwater sea. This is where the ancient creatures of the deep live, where they prey upon foolish little girls somersaulting over the falls. Curled up in a fetal position in the bottom of the boat, she sobs, her tears flowing into puddles of black rain that are filling the leaky boat. She wants her mommy back.

"I'm here, Beth, over here," her mother's raspy voice echoes hauntingly through the layers of fog. Cautiously, the little girl looks out into the storm-tossed seas, shrieking in terror at the ghostly image floating in the water. Her mother's tangled auburn hair spreads around her like the tentacles of an octopus. She is draped in seaweed, her face bloated and distorted.

"Mommy, mommy!" Beth screams, reaching out to her, trying to save her. But the waves turn black, converging into a whirlpool that hisses and howls, suddenly sucking her mother's body down into the depths of the sea.

Beth cannot stop the dream tonight. The little girl sucks her thumb, drifting through the eye of the storm where she lives alone, numb, lost in time that no longer seems to exist. Distorted faces surround her, taunting her with singsong chants that echo louder and louder. "You don't have a mother…you never had a father," the voices cry out. One by one, their faces blow up like balloons, exploding into the air and disappearing.

Her little boat suddenly lurches up into the air and attaches itself onto the back of a mysterious creature that swims forcefully through the screaming waves. She wonders if she is going to be saved so she won't drown like her mother, so she can go home to Nana. But a huge tentacle slithers out from beneath one side of the boat. It looks like an octopus winding through the water. A large head at the end of the tentacle springs from the lake with a thunderous splash. A suddenly older Beth recognizes Rob's head, Rob's face. He is smiling at her, his eyes reflecting a love that she had never before seen in them. Frozen, she watches as hands begin to sprout from the tentacle, reaching out for her. His eyes hold hers as his hands move in slowly, caressing her back, her shoulders, comforting her. Just as she begins to relax, to close her eyes, another head explodes from the other side of the boat, streaking through the water like a missile. It is Rob's face again…but this face is cold and cruel. It snarls at her like a mad dog before it begins to roar in laughter. As the nice Rob slinks back into the depths of the lake, the evil one begins to sprout hands and gnarled fingers of ice that move in closer and closer, threatening her, piercing her. Blood oozes from her heart. Everything turns black.

Finally, the dream shifts back to its usual ending. Little Beth is back—back in Nana's cozy kitchen on the island. "Blueberry pie, honey?" Nana hands her a big piece of pie across the table. "Uncle Jake picked the berries for you this morning." Beth's mother, Sarah, glows outside the kitchen window, watching wistfully, no longer a part of this world…

With a jolt, thirty-nine-year-old Beth bolted upright in bed, finally emerging from the dream that had held her captive for so many years. Her heart pounded wildly. She was drenched in sweat. *It's only a dream,* she reminded herself. But Rob had never before been able to penetrate her nightmares. He had no right to be there. She knew then that she had to get away soon…before he destroyed her.

Taking deep breaths to calm herself, she glanced at the clock on her bedside table. It was only six o'clock. Still dark. Too early to get up, too early to face the tough decisions that she knew she had to make. It would be so much easier to bury her head beneath her pillow, a strategy that she'd used for years as she had hoped and prayed that the ugliness would just go away. But it was just too scary to stay in bed this morning. She had to get away before the dream returned.

Wrapping herself in her tattered robe, the one that had belonged to her mother, she stumbled into the kitchen to put on a pot of coffee. Flicking on Illinois Public Radio, her everyday companion, she settled into the plump pillows on the window seat. Twenty-one stories below, the windy city of Chicago was already waking up.

Surrounded by glass, she could see the city lights illuminating the architectural wonders of the historic Wrigley Building. Soft, old-fashioned lights cast reflections across the waters of the Chicago River, highlighting the flower beds and walking trails winding along the river as it flowed toward Lake Michigan.

Lake Michigan fascinated her more than anything else in Chicago. She spent hours perched up here, watching the tall ships coming and going, the old lighthouse guarding the harbor, Navy Pier jutting out into the great lake. She was exhilarated by the storms that blew in over the lake, and by the foghorn calling out from another time, another place. In some ways the lake reminded her of home, of Rainy Lake, where she had grown up in the mist that shrouded bittersweet memories of her past.

She realized that she was in for a spectacular sunrise this morning. As much as she enjoyed watching the lake from her window seat, she sometimes felt like a prisoner in a glass castle in the sky. Sometimes she had to get out and walk, to feel the breeze caressing her face, to smell the lake, to watch the seagulls circling above her stifling world. Sometimes she had to escape from her problems, to tuck them away as if they didn't really exist…

Lake Michigan seemed to call to her, to comfort her, when she needed it most. Today was definitely one of those days—a beautiful day in the magical city of Chicago, according to the radio. She was not sure how many more days she would spend in the Windy City. Not sure where she would go, what she would do…only that it was time for her to move on soon.

Rob would be in court today. Last night would not change that. Nothing would. She knew she'd be safe walking down to Navy Pier. He would never confront her in public.

Most mornings Beth started off with a swim in the pool downstairs and a vigorous exercise regimen at the fitness center. This morning, however, she was not about to show her naked face. She took pains to conceal the cut above her lip, the bruise that was spreading like a purple web around her left eye, and the telltale red hand mark splashed across her cheek. She wore oversized, dark glasses and a straw hat with a large, floppy brim.

Thankfully, she had the elevator to herself today, all the way down to the lobby. While she thought she had covered the damage pretty well, she was still self-conscious. And having to make conversation with anyone today was the last thing that she wanted to do.

As she emerged into the lobby, she glanced around nervously and walked quickly through the quiet elegance of the lobby with its rich, hand-carved woodwork, ornate fresco ceilings, and marble floors. Overstuffed European sofas were clustered around fireplaces. Vases of fresh daffodils seemed to sway to the soft music that filled the lobby. Several elderly residents relaxed by the fire, reading the *Wall Street Journal* or the *Chicago Tribune*.

Fourteen Hundred North Lake Shore Drive was one of Chicago's finest high-rise residences. Built in the late 1920s in the city's historic Gold Coast District, it was now listed in the National Registry of Historic Places. It was well-known as a prime example of old European craftsmanship. Three residential wings loomed twenty-one stories into the sky and were separated by two secluded courtyards filled with ornate fountains and waterfalls, rose gardens, benches, and gazebos. The building was self-contained and included a beauty salon, dry cleaner, florist, restaurants, liquor store, gift shops, several exclusive clothing stores, library, café, bakery, and a little grocery/drug store. It was possible to live here without stepping out the door.

As always, James, the doorman, was waiting as she approached the heavy, gold-trimmed, glass doors. "Good morning, Mrs. Calhoun," he greeted her, as he had almost every day for the past twenty years. "Good morning, James," she replied as always. Today, she did not look directly at him. From beneath the brim of her hat, she glanced sideways to catch just a glimmer of pity in his eyes. Professional as always, James averted his glance and wished her a good day.

Taking a deep breath, Beth stepped out onto the sidewalk, feeling the warmth of the early-morning sunshine. She fell in step with the flow of human traffic marching toward Lake Michigan. As much as she loved the culture and the excitement of Chicago, she had never liked the crowds of people. It was only May and the tourist season had not yet begun. Still, there were too many people. Certainly too many cars, buses, and taxis.

The Chicago Harbor glistened as a light breeze gently nudged sleepy waves toward the breakwater wall. A flock of seagulls circled over the Chicago Harbor Lighthouse. The earliest lighthouse on Lake Michigan, it stood proudly on a massive rock at the harbor's entrance. Its white, cast-iron, conical tower loomed forty-eight feet above the Chicago skyline. Since 1893, its original Fresnel lens had flashed a red beacon of light from its black lantern in the sky, beckoning ships to safety. A beacon of hope through the uncertain storms of life. For Beth, this old lighthouse represented safety, security, and permanence— things she had always longed for but never managed to achieve…

Her spirits began to lift as she walked slowly along the three-thousand-foot-long Navy Pier. Breathing in the fresh air, the aroma of coffee drifting along the pier from several outdoor cafés, she embarked upon a journey back in time. Blocking out the other early-morning visitors, she marveled once again at the old wooden-masted schooners anchored at the pier, the 148-foot-tall Ferris wheel, the seven-story Shakespeare theater complex with its English-style courtyard and pub. At the far end of the concrete pier was a 1916-era brick and terra-cotta auditorium with twin towers jutting up into puffy cotton clouds that floated across the azure sky. Beth had always been fascinated with the grand ballroom and its high, half-domed ceiling. Old Chicago had dined and danced in this magnificent structure at the end of the pier for decades. They had listened to the big bands here, accompanied by the eerie sounds of the foghorn blasting from the big rock.

Beth found herself a lonely bench at the end of the pier. Gazing out at the lighthouse, lulled by the sound of the waves lapping against the wall, she slowly sipped a mocha latte. As always, she was mesmerized by the seagulls as they soared effortlessly through the brilliant blue sky, diving into the sparkling water, circling slowly through her troubled mind. She wondered why these chattering white birds had such a calming effect on her. Perhaps she simply wished she could fly like a seagull, soaring above the fray of her life. Perhaps they reminded her of the seagulls surrounding her childhood home on Rainy Lake. Or the wooden seagull that Uncle Jake had carved for her years ago…not long after her mother had drowned in the big lake.

Uncle Jake had been an important part of her life growing up on Rainy Lake. After she married and moved to Chicago twenty years ago, he had come to visit them every year for Thanksgiving. While she and Emily had enjoyed his visits, Rob had never been very hospitable to him. The visits had grown more and more strained. Uncle Jake always encouraged her to come back to Rainy Lake for a visit, but of course, Rob strongly discouraged her from doing so. Once he took her car keys away to keep her from leaving. As the fighting wore her down, her visits home became less and less frequent.

Beth's thoughts drifted back home to Nana, the grandmother who had raised her on their rocky island near the international border. She wondered how Nana was doing—and how they could have grown so far apart. Over the years, Nana had reached out to her, inviting her home for the holidays, sending her chatty letters. They talked on the phone—but only when Rob wasn't home. Beth had tried to stay in touch, tried to reassure Nana of all the wonderful things happening in their lives. She'd sent pictures of Emily—the center of her family's volatile universe. But as the bad days began to zap Beth's energy, casting clouds of gloom that overshadowed the good days, it became harder and harder for Beth to call or write. It was easier to hide from the truth. As Emily trotted off to kindergarten, eventually to high school, and as Rob became preoccupied with his career and his extramarital obsessions, Beth had slowly retreated into a world of her own.

It had been almost three years since she'd been able to sneak a brief visit back home to see her grandmother. Maybe it was time to go home again. Of course, that also meant facing the demons that had driven her away in the first place—the gossip and rumors over the identity of her missing father. She was an illegitimate child and the world had never let her forget it. As a child, she had plugged her ears and finally decided that she did not need a father anyway. She had Nana and Uncle Jake. She convinced herself that she did not want to know anything about the stranger who had deserted her and her mother. All she had wanted was to get away from Rainy Lake and start a new life without the tragic shadows of her past.

As the sun rose higher in the sky, Beth walked the pier in a daze. Her weary mind shifted back and forth, trying to decide what to do. She could hardly believe what Rob had done to her last night. In fact, a part of her began to wonder if it had happened at all. Had she imagined the whole thing? Was she losing touch with reality, as Rob had told her over and over again? Catching a glimpse of her reflection in a window along the pier, she realized that she could no longer deny the truth. Last night had happened.

If she left Chicago, where would she go? How could she just slither back home to Rainy Lake, her tail between her legs, and move back into her childhood home with Nana? She had no idea how she would support herself up there—or anyplace else. She could not imagine any-one wanting to hire a thirty-nine-year-old woman with no work experience aside from waitressing at the Thunderbird during high school. As for any support or alimony from Rob, she was afraid that he would do everything possible to stall the process. It could be years be-fore she got any equity out of their home. Rob knew all the tricks and he would use them against her.

Beth knew that she had a hard time making decisions. Rob had, af-ter all, made most of her decisions for years. It was terrifying to think about making a big decision like this one. There were roadblocks in all directions. She needed more time to think, she decided. But she also knew that the clock was ticking like a time bomb. She had to do some-thing. Soon.

Dreading the thought of returning home to her high-rise prison, she impulsively decided there was enough time, before Rob was out of court, for an early dinner at Riva. This was her favorite restaurant on the pier. She would treat herself, one more time, to Riva's signature dish of Swordfish Oscar, smothered with crabmeat and Hollandaise sauce.

Seated alone at a corner table in this cozy Italian restaurant with its open kitchen and seductive murals of the Italian Riviera, she gazed out at Lake Michigan and Chicago's magical skyline. She and Rob had di-ned here together many times over the years. She remembered the times they'd indulged in one too many glasses of vino, the times they'd found a private place on the pier to make love as they made their way back home. She also remembered the times that the evening had accel-erated into a nasty fight—usually brought on by his perception that she was flirting with the waiters. Maybe it wasn't a good idea to come here after all…there were too many memories. She ate in silence, her face hidden beneath her wide-brimmed hat.

Glancing at her watch, she realized that it was time to get home—before Rob got out of court for the day. She needed time to secure the place so she would be safe—at least for one more night.

"Life is a succession of lessons
which must be lived to be understood."
Ralph Waldo Emerson

Chapter Three

"*B* aby, it's me…I don't know what to say except I'm sorry for what happened last night," the first voicemail message began, dripping with Rob's most apologetic tone of voice. "I just lost it after you told me to leave, as if you didn't give a damn about me anymore. You know I love you. We can work this out. Call me back right away."

Stunned, Beth impulsively deleted the message after returning from her day at Navy Pier. Why, she wondered, did he always have to twist things around? For God's sake, he almost raped me last night, she shuddered to herself. How could he even suggest working it out?

Her thoughts were interrupted by a knock at the door. Tensing up, heart racing, she peered out through the peephole of the heavily barricaded door. It was just Danny, the local florist's delivery boy. His smiling baby-face peeked out through several dozen red roses. From Rob, of course, along with a sickeningly sweet note declaring his undying love for her. She accepted the roses graciously, then stuffed them into the trash can.

The answering machine continued to blink with unheard messages. Against her better judgment, she decided to play them out.

It was Rob again, one hour later. "Where are you, Beth? You haven't called me back. You know we need to talk. I need you, honey, you know that, don't you? Call me on my cell. I'm in court but I'll check for your message. Love you."

Then, two hours later, "Beth, where the hell are you? You haven't called me back. I hope you're not out in public making a spectacle of yourself. It's not my fault that you banged your head on the table, for Christ's sake! Call me back—immediately."

There was one final message from Rob. "OK, Beth, I don't give a damn what you do anymore. Just remember that nobody walks out on me, do you understand? If you're stupid enough to try, just remember that you deserve anything that happens to you. You really are pathetic, you know…" End of message.

Trembling, she shut off the answering machine, reinforced the barricades around the doors, and checked to be sure that the alarm system was activated. She thought once again about calling the police, but she was afraid they would not take her seriously. Most of the cops knew and respected Rob Calhoun. Rob would be angrier than ever if he found out that she'd called the police. Her best bet would probably be just to get away, as far away from him as possible.

The answering machine continued to blink red with more messages, but Beth did not have the courage to listen. She retreated to her bed, pulling the downy quilt over her head, hiding from a world that had gone wrong. Tomorrow she would have to make some decisions. Tonight she desperately needed some rest so she could think straight.

It was another fitful night of tossing and turning alone in her king-size bed. She fought hard to keep the dream away. As she finally nodded off in exhaustion, the phone began to ring, over and over again. Holding her breath, she strained to hear the message. It wasn't Rob this time. Instead, it was a familiar voice from the past, her Uncle Jake. Glancing at the alarm clock beside her bed, she grew fearful. It was three o'clock in the morning. Something must be wrong.

"Beth, this is urgent. You need to call me back right away. It's Nana…" Jake spoke in a solemn voice laced with fear and sadness.

"Jake? It's me…What's wrong?"

Skipping any preliminaries, Jake cut to the quick once he heard Beth's sleepy voice on the other end of the line. "Beth, you must come home immediately. Nana's in the hospital. It's her heart…she's asking for you, Beth. She needs to see you again." His voice choked up as he paused to regain his composure.

Beth clutched the phone as fear surged through her body. "Oh my God. Oh my God. How bad is she?"

"She's dying, Beth. They say she doesn't have long—maybe not more than a week or two. God only knows. You just need to come now. Meet me at the Falls Hospital. I have to run." His voice trembled and trailed off as tears spilled down the crevices of his weathered face.

"Jake, I'm coming. Tell her I'm coming. Tell her I love her," Beth cried into the phone as Jake abruptly replaced his phone in its cradle. The big man buried his head in his hands, hidden in the semi-darkness of the hospital's waiting room.

He had to get back to eighty-seven-year-old Nana, to hold her hand and tell her that Beth was coming. He was the only source of support that the old woman had left in her shrinking world, the only one at her bedside as she prepared to leave this world. Although he was not even related to her, he had grown to love this gentle and independent spirit over the years of their friendship.

Now, as Jake O'Connell sat helplessly at Nana's bedside, he understood that she was preparing to join her loved ones on the other side. Her loved ones…including her lovely daughter, Sarah, Beth's mother, who had been a victim of Rainy Lake at the age of twenty-eight. More tears, more pain. *Damn it all*, he thought to himself, *why was life so unfair? Why her? Why not me?*

Jake had assumed a caretaking role for Nana in recent years. She was a widow living alone on her island. Beth, her only granddaughter, had disappeared into her own world in Chicago. Now, as Jake listened to the steady hissing of the machines in Nana's hospital room, he thought about the things that he should have done, years ago perhaps. He should have insisted that Nana move off her beloved island and into the River's Edge senior housing facility that was located, ironically, adjacent to the hospital where she would draw her last breaths. He wondered if it would have made a difference. Many of her old friends lived there now, beside the Rainy River. Nana would have enjoyed sitting on the deck overlooking the manicured lawns that sloped down to the river. She would have loved watching the flowers grow, looking out across the water at her Canadian neighbors. She could have spent hours reading, and rereading, her favorite books in the gazebo. The home even took its residents on boat trips down the Rainy River and into Rainy Lake, perhaps past Nana's island. He had tried, again and again, to convince the stubborn old woman to leave her island.

⋄⋄

As Jake pondered the should-haves and the should-nots of his life, Beth was reeling with her own regrets as she threw her suitcases onto her unmade bed. *Oh my God! How can this be? Nana can't die. I owe her my life. I have so much to make up for. Hold on, Nana. Please hold on. I'm coming.* She repeated these phrases silently, over and over again, as she began tossing essential items into the suitcases.

As she walked through the great room for the last time, pulling her suitcases behind her, she realized that once again the big decision had been made for her. She would not be coming back to Chicago, not ever again. She was leaving behind her husband and her lifestyle of the past twenty years. She would not be back to pick up the pieces or reclaim her property. And it really didn't matter anymore…

Beth impulsively grabbed Uncle Jake's hand-carved seagull off the shelf and stuffed it into her bag as she slammed the door behind her. As the first blush of dawn peeked over the Chicago harbor, Beth backed her SUV out of the parking garage and headed north.

Only 645 miles to go, an already sleep-deprived Beth reminded herself, over and over again. Please, God, she prayed silently, let me get there in time. Jake had said she had about a week or so, but what if…what if something happened before she was able to get there? Maybe she should have flown instead. But with a four-hour layover in Minneapolis/St. Paul before a flight to Duluth, and another commuter flight into International Falls, flying would have taken longer than driving.

As she prayed for Nana, she nervously watched through her rearview mirror for any sign of Rob. It was unlikely that he'd be roaming around this early in the morning…but she was leaving the city, and if he caught up with her…what would he do? She shuddered, just thinking about a recent article that she had read in the newspaper. A young woman had been killed by her ex-husband. He had stabbed her, over and over again, with a butcher knife, as she tried to get away. She left two little children behind.

White knuckles clutching the steering wheel, she maneuvered her Lexus SUV toward Interstate 90 where she set the cruise control on eighty miles per hour and began to relax just a bit. Her cell phone was on, just in case Jake needed to get ahold of her, just in case there was any change in Nana's condition. Somehow, her adrenaline seemed to kick in to fight off her exhaustion. Each time she stopped for gas, she bought a large cup of coffee to go. She sipped slowly as she listened to classical music on the radio, trying to calm herself.

Each mile was one step closer to Nana, one step farther away from Rob. She breathed a sigh of relief as she crossed the Wisconsin state border. She'd always liked Wisconsin, especially the northern region with its pristine lakes and woods, little towns and villages where life seemed to be so much simpler. She was cruising along on Highway 53, passing the growing community of Rice Lake, when her phone rang. It was Jake.

"Beth, she's hanging on. She's awake and she knows you are coming. She is waiting for you…so drive carefully and take a break when you need it. Have you eaten yet today?"

"Well, no, not exactly…I just wanted to get there fast. And I wasn't really hungry," she replied, realizing that her stomach was actually growling as she spoke.

"Stop and eat," he ordered her. "In fact, you may want to stop at that White Birch restaurant in Solon Springs for a fast meal and to stretch your legs. There is time. They say it's not quite as urgent as it seemed at first. She's not going anyplace until she's had some time with you. You know how she is…"

Beth sighed with relief. Yes, she did know how Nana was. Nana would be the one who decided exactly when it was her time to leave this world.

"Ah, Beth, I'm sorry if I was a little short with you when I called earlier," Jake continued. "I was afraid that maybe Rob would object to your coming…"

"That's no longer a problem," she replied softly, letting the thought hang heavily in the air between them.

Jake wasn't sure what to make of her remark but decided not to pursue what sounded like a relatively fresh wound surfacing. There would be time to talk later, hopefully more time than they'd had in a very long time. He couldn't help feeling pleased that she was coming alone, without her husband.

Beth took his advice as she neared Solon Springs, Wisconsin, cutting off toward the White Birch, a cozy little restaurant with tulips and daffodils starting to bloom in the window boxes. She sat at a corner table by the old stone fireplace. A fire blazed, warming the rooms on this chilly spring day. Its flames danced to the soft background music. She'd eaten here once before with Jake. They'd had an excellent prime rib dinner, she remembered. They had driven down from Duluth, after a doctor appointment, to attend an outdoor symphony in the park at the nearby Lucius Woods Performing Art Center. It had been a memorable experience, one of the few they'd shared together over the past twenty years…a warm summer night relaxing on lawn chairs beneath majestic towering pines, listening to the Duluth Symphony Orchestra as a full moon danced and played across the rippling waters of Lake St. Croix.

After a quick bite to eat, she was back on the road, concentrating on the scenery to relieve her anxiety. Before long, she crossed the Minnesota state line over Duluth's expansive Bong Bridge winding high over Lake Superior. She was going home—home to Nana, home to the lake and woods she had always loved. Almost always.

As she passed through the little town of Cook, she wished she had time to stop at Zup's Food Market for some of their homemade sausage. Jake always used to stop here to pick up Swedish sausage for Nana. Nana loved it since she was Swedish and had vivid childhood memories of the Swedish sausage that her mother used to make. There was no time today, however, Beth realized. Besides, she was already getting low on cash. She knew that she'd have to find a way to get some money out of their joint bank account soon, without Rob being able to trace her whereabouts. Jake might have some ideas on how to accomplish that. He was a successful real estate broker with a good understanding of business and banking.

Eighty miles to International Falls, the highway sign advised her. Hang on, Nana, she thought to herself, I'm almost there.

"For everything there is a season
and a time for every matter under heaven:
a time to be born, a time to die;
a time to weep, and a time to laugh;
a time to mourn, and a time to dance."
Ecclesiastes 3:1-8

Rainy Lake

Chapter Four

*N*ana opened her eyes, wondering if she'd been dreaming—or if she had already departed this life and was floating somewhere, suspended in another world. She knew there was something important she had to do…someone she was waiting for…she struggled to remember as she lapsed in and out of consciousness. Oh yes, it was her granddaughter, Beth. A soft smile spread across her face. Beth was coming home at last. She would be here soon, Jake had assured her. Nana's weary mind drifted in and out, trying to differentiate between yesterday, today, tomorrow. Between this world and the next.

Tossing and turning in her hospital bed, Nana was unaware of the maze of tubes connected to her veins, the steady clicking and hissing of the machines surrounding her. She found comfort in the presence of Jake, who sat silently at her bedside holding her hand. Jake, always there when she needed him most.

She gazed out the window at the Rainy River that flowed gently past her hospital room. Appropriately shrouded in mist, it was the river of her life, feeding her lifelong existence on Rainy Lake. She had spent sixty-seven of her eighty-seven years living on the island that she so dearly loved. Living in the log house that her husband, Pete, had built in the summer of 1941 shortly after they were married. They had moved in just before the Japanese attacked Pearl Harbor and the United States entered World War II. Together, they had made many happy memories there…until that fateful day in 1954 when her husband's young life was snuffed out by the big lake.

Their only daughter, Sarah, was born and raised on their island—until she also became a victim of the big lake. Nana's eyes filled with tears once again. How she missed her only child and her husband. In all these years, the pain never really went away. Yes, her life had been marked by multiple tragedies and hardships. But somehow, she'd developed an inner strength over the years. She had found ways to survive, to cope, to find pleasure in the simple things of life. It was the lake, always the lake, that comforted her despite the fact that it had taken away two loved ones who meant more to her than anything in this world. She could feel their spirits now, patiently waiting for her to cross over to the other side. She could feel their love swirling around her, through her. They were eager to welcome her home…

∽§∾

As Jake held her frail hand, images of the past flashed through her mind…

She was a young girl again—living on the family farm on Jackfish Bay, not far from the Village of Ranier. She was exploring the lake with her brothers, swimming, picking wildflowers and blueberries. Searching for arrowheads and hidden treasures along the shore and in the woods. Their young imaginations soared wildly. At the sound of the cowbell, they ran home to help with the chores. Nana gathered eggs from the chicken coop, helped Mama bake pies and breads. Her mother taught her to knit and to play the old upright piano. Nana learned to make Swedish family recipes from the old country.

She saw herself helping Papa milk the cows early in the morning before he bottled the milk and began his daily delivery route by horse-drawn carriage. She was tending the garden, weeding, picking produce. Drawing water from the pump and hauling it home in the wood bucket. Bringing in armloads of firewood that her father and brothers had cut and split.

She remembered the Great Depression. Ration vouchers for sugar and lard. Relying on what her family could grow, trap, or hunt. The whole family would gather around the radio to listen to President Roosevelt's fireside chats. Their crackling radio became their window to the world.

She recalled family visits to the old Indian camps on Birch Point. They would trade their goods for maple syrup, blueberries, and wild rice harvested by the Ojibwe. She had been entranced with their birch bark canoes, wigwams, babies tightly bundled on cradleboards in traditional papoose style. As a little girl, she had hidden behind her mother's skirts when their drumming and colorful ceremonial dances began. She remembered peeking through the willows with her friends, watching daily life unfolding at the White Birch Indian campsites. She'd been curious, frightened at first. But she had grown to appreciate the Indian culture, learning about the wonders of nature from her young Indian friends. She never did understand what all the fuss was about these days over the word *Indian*. Most of her friends still cherished this title and saw it as a sign of respect for their traditional culture. Times were always changing…

Nana's mind flashed further back to the stories her father, Olaf, had shared as the family huddled around the wood-burning barrel stove on cold winter evenings. Olaf had immigrated to this country from Sweden in 1895 at the age of ten. At that time, Sweden was experiencing severe droughts interspersed with devastating floods. Crops were destroyed and starvation imminent. Olaf's father had, in desperation, brought his struggling young family to America on a crowded ship. They came to find a better life and to stake out a homestead claim where they could eke out a living from the soil. Olaf's family had been drawn to the Rainy Lake region where other Swedish families had already settled. They had traveled by stagecoach to Crane Lake, where they boarded a steamboat with all of their belongings, including an old trunk. That trunk had been stored in the attic of Nana's island home for years. It was still there, full of the family's history and more recent secrets that had lain dormant for many years. Secrets that she needed to reveal to her granddaughter...

Nana's mind drifted back again to the fireside of her youth. Her father had captivated them all with tales of the Rainy Lake region. It was, according to her Papa, the last frontier—wild, untamed, with no roads, no doctors. Clearing the densely forested land was hard work. There were muskeg swamps and bogs to cross, bothersome bugs, and hungry bears lurking in the woods. Growing seasons were short, and crops that they relied upon were frequently destroyed. Papa told them about one winter when his pioneering family survived on a diet of dry bread, salt pork, snared rabbits, berries they had gathered and dried in the fall, spoiled potatoes stored in the old root cellar, and venison that his father shot. They used dogsleds, homemade skis, and snowshoes to navigate through the heavy snow. Sometimes it was impossible to get through and they were stranded for weeks at a time.

Nana remembered visiting the rustic farmhouse that her grandfather had built in 1896. It was crudely crafted of hand-cut spruce logs. Her grandfather had peeled the bark, assembled the logs, and stuffed the cracks with a mixture of mud and dried moss. As the logs dried and the house shifted on its boggy foundation, new cracks emerged and had to be filled on a regular basis. In the winter, the wind blew through the crevices of the walls and mice moved in, out of the cold. In the summer, they put cheesecloth over the windows and built smoky fires in a smudge pot to keep the army of mosquitoes from attacking. They even slept with mosquito netting over their beds.

On the lighter side, Nana smiled as she remembered Papa's stories about the home brew they made from cracked corn with a few raisins, a little sugar, a bit of yeast, and a few potato peelings. For entertainment they had rolled up the rug, played the fiddles and violins they brought from the old country, and danced the night away. In the spring, the growing community turned out on the banks of Rainy Lake to watch the lumberjacks drive logs from their camps to the mills at International Falls. In the summer, they watched the Lady of the Lake steamer, loaded with affluent tourists, cruising through the lake. Once a road was cleared to International Falls, pioneer families hitched their horses to their buggies and traveled to the Falls for entertainment. Nana had loved trips to the circus, vaudeville acts, performances of the Koochiching Orchestra. She'd never forget the first silent moving picture show she saw with her family.

ৰ৵৽

Her thoughts fast-forwarded to her grade school days at Ranier. She could still picture the big, two-story, frame schoolhouse where she first met Pete Peterson. He was an islander who boarded with relatives in Ranier during the school year. She would never forget school fire drills when they slid together down the winding fire escape chute, laughing hysterically, connecting more deeply than she understood at that time in her life. During recess, they sledded down the hill on homemade toboggans to the frozen creek below. They spent carefree afternoons skating on the ice.

Pete and his family had attended Ranier's old Gospel Mission Church, as her family had. She remembered Christmas Eve services in the frosty, white, wood-framed structure. She had stared in awe at the Christmas tree, adorned with simple white candles. Their flames danced in the breeze as the winds of winter drifted in through the crevices of rotting old windows that the church could not afford to replace. She and Pete had grinned at each other across the aisle as their families filed out of the building into a winter wonderland filled with brilliant stars dancing across the black universe. Looking back, she realized that she'd been in love with Pete since second grade. She had married him when she was twenty, and was widowed at only thirty-three. She was still in love with him…always would be. There had never been another man in her life.

Memories of Pete flooded her aching heart. They had honeymooned at Kettle Falls, smack-dab in the middle of Rainy Lake. They had picnicked beside the roaring falls where he told her about summers he had spent working at the old Kettle Falls Hotel. Stories of catching and filleting fish that proprietor Ma (Lil) Williams served to hotel guests; loading and unloading visiting boats; hauling water, ice, and wood; cleaning out the saloon—and pretending not to notice the "ladies of the night" who mysteriously descended upon the island each time the lumberjacks did. It was the Roaring Twenties, complete with fast dancing, moonshine, bootleg whiskey, and portable stills that Pete helped to hide in the woods every time the Internal Revenue squad showed up.

Their antique-filled honeymoon suite had delighted Nana. She had danced closely with her new husband to Duke Ellington records playing on the hand-cranked Victrola in the sitting room. They'd gathered with other guests around the upright piano and sang songs. They'd lounged in willow rocking chairs on the vine-covered veranda, reading, holding hands, drinking lemonade, and gazing out at the pristine beauty of the wooded Kabetogama Peninsula. In the background, the fancy new nickelodeon in the saloon played the tunes of the times. They talked. They made plans…so many plans for their future together…

Oh, Pete, the old woman sighed. She still remembered the sound of his chuckle, the way his eyes danced and crinkled. She could almost feel his strong but gentle hands, could almost see him cradling an injured bird in one hand or bottle-feeding the fawn whose mother had died.

Pete had grown up as the son of a commercial fisherman, working side by side with his father. After Pete's father died and Nana had given birth to Sarah, Pete took on other jobs around the lake. He was a fishing guide for tourists staying at local resorts. He was a caretaker for summer island residents, mostly those living on Grindstone Island. And he became a boat captain transporting mail, passengers, and supplies back and forth from Ranier to Kettle Falls. He'd stop along the way to pick up and drop off mail and passengers on various islands. The islanders all knew and loved Pete, one of their few contacts with the outside world.

He was also appointed by the U.S. Coast Guard as the Rainy Lake Lamplighter. That meant that he was responsible for maintaining four twenty-foot-high, white wooden light towers that were strategically positioned around the lake to ensure the safety of international boaters. Pete brought her along sometimes while friends took care of Sarah. She sat in the boat, holding her breath, while he climbed to the top of the towers to replace the batteries that kept the lights flashing. She liked to tag along with him in the spring when he put floating buoys out into the channel that ran from Ranier to Kettle Falls. In those days, the buoys were made of steel and weighed about a hundred pounds each. They were attached with heavy chains to concrete anchors in the lake. In the fall, when it was time to pull the buoys out before freeze-up, the weather sometimes turned blustery and threatening. Pete refused to let her come along on those days. He went alone while she worried at home, waiting for him to finally burst through the door with the wind howling at his back. Those were the times that Pete felt more alive than ever. He was invigorated, bursting with a sense of accomplishment. He'd survived. Pete Peterson had to live on the edge of life. A well-read, self-educated man, he could have gotten a job anyplace. But he wouldn't leave Rainy Lake. "This lake is a part of me," he always told her.

"Oh, Pete," Nana whispered, squeezing Jake's hand as she lapsed back in time to that tragic day in September of 1954—the day Pete met his fate transporting a boat loaded with fish across the Brule Narrows. It was a freak storm that came out of nowhere, a northwesterly wind ripping down the twenty-seven-mile length of the narrows. Helpless witnesses told of giant whitecaps pounding and washing over the boat as the winds drove sheets of sleet and ice across its bow, capsizing the large vessel. By the time the rescue boat was able to respond, all that remained was splinters of wood, fish crates, and debris floating on the water. It was too late for Pete Peterson. A week later, his body drifted up on shore.

��

Brushing the tears away, Nana's mind shifted to Sarah, her free-spirited little girl. Memories of the miracle of her birth. Of baking cookies and blueberry pies together. Exploring their island and discovering the wonders of nature. Playing Scrabble by the fire on cold winter nights. Reading stories, cuddled up together in the window seat in Sarah's upstairs bedroom. Picking blueberries. Homeschooling her on the island after Sarah's Papa died so they could stay there, close to his memory, instead of moving into Ranier. As Sarah grew up, she became a poet and a writer, with a promising future ahead. At the age of twenty-two, Sarah, unmarried, had given birth to a daughter whom she named Elizabeth Ann. They called her Beth. Sarah and Beth lived on the island with Nana—until—until Sarah's young life had been taken by the lake. Beth had been only six years old.

"Sarah, Sarah, oh, my darling daughter," Nana gasped, writhing about in her hospital bed, reliving the worst nightmare of her life. She began to sob uncontrollably as Jake gripped her hand tightly in his own. How could God have let this happen? Sarah had been so happy, so much in love, such a wonderful mother, so excited about the camping trip she was taking with a dear friend. But she'd never returned. "Oh my God," Nana began to wail in her tiny, frail voice.

"It's OK, Nana," Jake held her close, trying to reassure her. *Damn it, it isn't OK,* he thought to himself as tears filled his eyes. *It never was, and it never will be.* "I'm so sorry, Nana, so sorry. But Sarah's here, you know…and you will be with her soon." He wanted to say more but could find no words.

Nana relaxed in her old friend's arms. Beth, her only granddaughter, emerged from the depths of a lifetime of memories. Nana had raised her alone on the island after Sarah's untimely death. Looking back, she realized that raising Beth had been a bittersweet experience. Without Beth, Nana wasn't sure how she could have survived her daughter's death. Without Beth, she wasn't sure how she could have gone on, day after day. Beth was the reason she got up each morning.

As time had marched on, Nana remembered how badly Beth had wanted to fit in with the kids at school, with the rich summer residents who led exciting lives far from Rainy Lake. As Beth grew up, she became embarrassed by the simple, old-fashioned lifestyle that they led on the island and had become a bit rebellious. She rebelled because her mother had died, because she was fatherless. Her mother had never publicly revealed the identity of her mysterious father. Nana's heart went out to her. She understood. She knew that no amount of grandmotherly love could make up for that. Despite these difficulties, Nana had loved raising Beth. It had been a good life—until Beth had gotten herself pregnant by that young playboy from Chicago, married him, and left the island in a cloud of disgrace. What was his name again? She couldn't remember and really didn't care. She'd never liked him. But she deeply regretted the fact that Beth had rarely visited Rainy Lake over all these years. And she'd never really gotten to know Emily, her great-granddaughter. Nana suspected that Beth's supposedly glamorous life in Chicago was not all that she pretended it to be.

It was time, Nana now realized, to make sure that Beth learned the identity of her father. She had always planned to tell her, of course, but there never seemed to be a right time. As Beth grew up, she'd learned to brace herself against the rumors swirling through the small-town grapevine. At that time, Beth had no interest in learning the truth about her father. He had left her, after all. In her mind, he did not exist. As the years passed, Nana had been afraid that it was too late to reopen a healing wound. Soon, it was too late.

⊰❧

Pete and Sarah seemed to hover over Nana's bed, arms outstretched, beckoning her to come home with them. Nana's mind spiraled toward a brilliant light —until she heard the shuffling of Jake's bedside chair. Someone had just entered her hospital room, someone whom Jake was tearfully embracing in the doorway of her darkened hospital room.

Eyes closed, breathing slowly, Nana felt the touch of a familiar hand grasping hers, holding tightly. She began to come back to the present, bidding the future to hold on until it was time for her to cross over to the other side of life. She had unfinished business here. "Beth, is that you?" Nana opened her eyes as her long-lost granddaughter fell into her outstretched arms, sobbing.

"Nana, I'm so sorry. I love you. I should have been here for you. I'm so sorry…can you ever forgive me?"

"Of course. I love you, child. You're here now. That's what counts. Now, let me get a good look at you. It's been so long," Nana sighed, tears of joy filling her eyes.

Beth leaned in closer, still hiding behind her big, ugly sunglasses.

"Those glasses—take them off and let me look into your eyes again."

Reluctantly, Beth removed them. She positioned one hand near her left eye in an attempt to hide the ugly bruise.

The old woman gasped. "Oh, my dear. My dear. He did this to you?" She held Beth's hand tightly in her own, stroking it with her thumbs. Suddenly, she understood the long absences, the phone calls that had grown less and less frequent.

"Nana, it's OK. I've left him. You don't need to worry, I promise you." She heard Jake swear under his breath, promising revenge, as he left the room. "I've finally come home where I belong. But…but, I came home to be with you, to help you, to make blueberry pies together like we used to do. Remember, Nana?"

Nana's eyes fluttered and closed as she drifted off, still clutching Beth's hand.

"Tell me it's not too late. Please, Nana." Beth's tears flowed freely, dripping softly onto the pillowcase where her grandmother's head lay. Nana's thin white hair curled softly around her face, framing it in pin-curled shadows of the past. She slept peacefully. Beth waited, watching her breathing, praying that she would open her eyes again.

And she did. Searching for Beth, Nana gazed intently into her eyes. "Beth, I don't have long. You need to find the old trunk…" Her heavy eyes began to close again. Beth leaned in closer as Nana continued weakly, "In the attic…our island…things you need to know…" Beth waited, feeling that there was more coming, if Nana could stay in this world long enough. "Things I should have told you long ago…" Her tiny voice disappeared into a whisper.

As Beth stroked her veined hand, Nana drifted back into another world. Beth watched the monitors bleeping in the background to assure her that Nana was still with them. She was just sleeping, dreaming, wasn't she? Jake stood in the shadows.

Days passed as Nana floated between this world and the next. Beth and Jake took turns at her bedside. They were startled each time that her breathing stopped abruptly, afraid she was leaving them. Over and over again, she would gasp, coming back, opening her eyes, and squeezing their hands. Sometimes a faint smile seemed to curl the corners of her lips. Or was it just their imagination?

"Nana?" Beth shook her gently one evening when her eyes flickered open once again, focusing upon the ceiling of her hospital room. "My father? Who was my father?" Beth pleaded. Although she had never wanted to know the truth in the past, she now realized that Nana may be the last living person who knew the truth. Would she take this secret to her grave? Even if she, Beth, could care less about the bastard, Emily might someday need to know who he was and what his medical history was.

Nana did not respond. Jake suddenly felt the need to move in closer. As Nana's frail hand fell limply to her bed, her face suddenly lit up with joy, eyes wide open, focusing someplace above her bed. " Papa, Sarah!" she exclaimed as she went to the light.

Her eyes closed—for the last time—as Beth and Jake held her in their arms, their tears mingling in the stillness of the night.

"The bittersweet tears shed over graves
are for words left unsaid
and deeds left undone."
Harriet Beecher Stowe

Houska's Point, Ranier by Bernie Spike Woods

Chapter Five

*N*ana's wish was to have her ashes buried on the island beside Papa and Sarah—except for a small jarful that she wanted scattered over Kettle Falls, just as her late husband's ashes had been. All she'd wanted was a simple burial ceremony following a memorial service at the community center in Ranier. Since Ranier's old Mission Church had closed in the early 1970s, she'd had no church home. Occasionally, when she was able to get to the mainland and into International Falls, she had enjoyed attending services at the old stone St. Thomas of Aquinas Church. In recent years, she had taken to watching Dr. Robert Schuller's services on television. She had been inspired and comforted by his messages of hope and loved to sing along with the hymns flowing from the Crystal Cathedral into her snowy television.

Jake quietly made the funeral arrangements from his real estate office in Ranier. His old log office was located on Houska's Point. It was
strategically positioned on a mound of ancient Precambrian bedrock
laced with streaks of quartz that glistened in the early-morning sunlight.
A scraggly jack pine, twisted and gnarled with age, stood guard at the
end of the rocky point overlooking Rainy Lake.

Forty-five years ago, when Jake and Evelyn had married and moved
to Ranier, they had purchased this old landmark cabin and lovingly renovated it into their first home. New plumbing, new electricity, big
country kitchen, a master bedroom with French windows overlooking
Rainy Lake, and a big office for Jake. He would have been content to
live there forever.

It hadn't been long, however, before Evelyn insisted on moving into
International Falls, three miles west of Ranier. Using her own money and
resources to finance the place, she had purchased a two-story colonial
home on Riverside Drive. It had a beautifully landscaped yard surrounded by a white picket fence, roses climbing trellises in a secluded
old English garden, a wraparound porch with a wooden swing. The
house had four bedrooms, three bathrooms, a library, a sitting room, and
a formal dining room for entertaining. Jake had reluctantly consented to
the move, provided that he was able to keep his office in Ranier. That
had become his escape, his refuge from a distant and unfulfilling marriage that droned on uneventfully year after year after year.

Today, Jake planned to pick Beth up at the Holiday Inn where she
was staying and bring her to his office so they could talk about final arrangements for Nana. He was the executor of Nana's estate and needed
to convey some information to Beth. He wasn't sure how she would take
it…what she expected…what her plans were for the future. He wasn't
sure that he was prepared to answer some of the questions that she might
have. As thrilled as he was to have her back home again, he wondered
how she'd feel if and when she discovered the truth about her past.

✦✧✦

A gentle rain drizzled on the morning of Nana's memorial service,
nurturing sunny daffodils and scarlet tulips that seemed to spring up
everywhere throughout the historic little village of Ranier. Nana would
be pleased, Beth thought to herself, especially when the sun broke
through the clouds to expose tear-shaped drops of rain that glistened on
gnarled branches like diamonds of hope. Hope…wasn't that what Nana
was all about? She'd never given up hope, Beth realized.

She and Jake sat together in the front row, dressed in traditional black, taking comfort in the presence of the other. Several of Beth's cousins, whom she hadn't seen in years, sat behind them with an assortment of children, husbands, and wives. Emily had been unable to get home from Europe in time for the funeral. Beth had not encouraged her to come, not yet. As anxious as she was to see her daughter and talk with her in person, she preferred a visit once she'd settled in and made some plans for her future. As it was, her life was in a shambles. Yet, in the face of Nana's death, her problems were, in fact, rather insignificant.

The pastor, at Beth's request, read "The Great Spirit Prayer," a poem that Nana had framed and hung above her kitchen table. Beth remembered seeing it there ever since she'd been a toddler. She clutched Jake's hand for support as the pastor read these words, words that Nana had lived by and found strength in despite the trials that she had faced throughout her lifetime:

OJIBWE PRAYER

Oh, Great Spirit, whose voice I hear in the winds
And whose breath gives life to all the world,
Hear me.
I come to you as one of your children;
I am weak…I am small…
I need your wisdom and your strength.
Let me walk in beauty, and make my eyes
Ever behold the red and purple sunsets.
Make my hands respect the things you have made,
And make my ears sharp so I may hear your voice.
Make me wise so that I may understand
The things you have taught my people and
The lessons you have hidden in each leaf and rock.
I ask for wisdom and strength,
Not to be superior to my brothers, but to be able
To fight my greatest enemy…myself.
Make me ever ready to come before you
With clean hands and a straight eye,
So when life fades away as a fading sunset,
My spirit may come to you without shame.

Despite living alone on her island, Nana had more friends than Beth realized, friends who packed the historic Ranier community center, built in 1939. After the service, they clustered together on the porch with its white picket railings, gazing at the flag waving in the breeze above the pines and flowering shrubs. Here, they offered their condolences and shared their memories of Nana with the others. There were church friends, quilting friends, other islanders, and mainlanders who had stopped at her island for a cup of coffee along with a piece of her famous blueberry pie.

❧❧

A smaller group of mourners then walked silently down Spruce Street, past the historic brick building on the corner with its arched stained-glass windows and wooden benches nestled amongst pots of flowers. They crossed over the railroad tracks and past the expansive white-framed Ranier railroad depot, the last stop in the United States before internationally-bound trains lumbered over the ninety-five-year-old cantilevered bridge into Canada. They passed Grandma's Pantry, the old Spruce Street Landing shops, Woody's Pub, and Tara's Wharf on their way to the Sand Bay marina.

A light breeze rippled the waters of Rainy Lake as they boarded an assortment of boats that would take them out to the island. Beth boarded Jake's boat along with the pastor, his wife, and the funeral director, who carefully carried Nana's urn of ashes. Evelyn was not there, as usual.

This would be the first time that Beth had been home to the island in several years, she realized, hating herself for her weakness, for not standing up to Rob. Now, it was too late…and it was all her fault.

Waves of remorse soon gave way to resignation as she lost herself in the gentle waves, the fresh breeze, and calming scent of Rainy Lake. This lake truly was a magical place, a place unlike any other. Anticipation set in when she caught the first glimpse of the rocky, crescent-shaped island surfacing on the horizon. With the sunlight sparkling and dancing through forests of pine, the island took on an emerald glow. The sky merged into the lake as if they were one, diamonds of light glittering across the shimmering surface of the big lake. As the boat pulled up to the sagging wharf, she knew that she was finally home. Home where she belonged. She'd left as a rebel, hating everything that the island stood for. Today, she wondered how she could have been so wrong, so foolish. *Nana was right*, she admitted to herself, *the other pasture is not always greener.*

37

The funeral party proceeded up the well-worn path that meandered through a sea of spring-green ferns and delicate moss roses. They were accompanied by the songs of the birds, the chattering of squirrels, and a gentle wind sighing in the white pines. Lost in their own thoughts, they passed Nana's old log house and veered left toward the gazebo at the far end of the island.

Just beyond the gazebo, on a rocky point overlooking the lake far below, lay the family cemetery. Two gravestones stood side by side. One was inscribed, *Pete Peterson, beloved husband and father, born 1916, died 1954.* The other, *Sarah Peterson, beloved daughter, mother, and special friend, born 1946, died 1974.* Someone had mowed and weedwhacked the little graveyard for the occasion. It was surrounded by lilacs that Nana had planted after Papa's death. It was fitting that they were blooming today, filling the air with their sweet fragrance. Today, the day that Nana's ashes were returned to the earth. Nana would be pleased…

Beth rocked with the waves, teetering on the brink of reality. She barely heard the pastor's words as he spoke quietly at Nana's gravesite. He talked about Nana's love for Papa, for Sarah, and for Beth—the granddaughter she had raised alone on this island. Beth wanted to scream, "But I did not deserve her love! Look what I've done!" The pastor droned on about Nana's independent spirit, her faith that had helped her to transcend the tragedies in her simple life. Beth ground her foot into the dirt, digging deeper and deeper, thinking that she was the one who deserved to return to dust. Some way, someday, she must find a way to make it up to Nana. But Nana was gone. *Dear God, what can I do to make this right?* She searched the heavens above for an answer. All she could hear were Rob's angry words, "You deserve anything that happens to you, Beth…you're pathetic!"

A man with long black hair stood alone in the long shadow of the gazebo, quietly remembering Nana, his friend and neighbor. He watched her granddaughter closely, absorbing the pain that seemed to gnaw at her soul.

As the mourners began leaving the island after paying their last respects, Beth and Jake stood silently at the dock. It was time to go…but where, Beth wondered. On a sudden impulse, she announced to Jake, "Go ahead. I'm staying here."

"You're what?" Jake thought he had heard wrong.

"I just want to be here. I don't want to go back to the hotel tonight. I'll be fine, really." She attempted a weak smile.

"Beth, you can stay with us until we figure all of this out." He was already taking on responsibility for her…the least that he could do. "Please come home with me?"

"You know as well as I do that Evelyn will not be happy if I show up on her doorstep." She tried to force another half-hearted smile. Taking a deep breath, she counted slowly to herself. One, two, three…one, two, three. This was a trick that she'd learned over the years. It was her way of trying to control the fury, the shame, and the tears that threatened to erupt from someplace deep within her soul. Here, in this secret place, Beth had buried her feelings and painful memories of the past. It was like a steel vault, protected by layers of ice that could not be penetrated. But there were times when the rumbling within shattered the ice and threatened to burst forth like the Fourth of July fireworks. Fireworks that she feared would scorch and destroy her. Lately, there were times when the vault seemed to be leaking, when buried feelings from the past seeped into her consciousness. This terrified her. One, two, three…

Jake knew she had a point. But he felt the need to do something, anything, to comfort her. "I really don't care what Evelyn thinks. I don't want you out here alone, not today, not after we've just buried Nana, for God's sake."

"Well, I'm not leaving," Beth announced quietly but defiantly. She surprised herself as the words spilled from her mouth. She had actually made a decision on her own, an important one at that. "This is where I belong. I'm sorry, Jake. I'll be in touch, OK?" She softened her tone as she headed up the trail toward the big house. Looking back over her shoulder, she watched Jake shaking his head, arms folded across his chest. He had aged since she'd last seen him. His hair was gray, but still thick and wavy. His skin was tan, weathered by the sun and the lake. His eyes were not as bright as she remembered them. They weren't smiling today. He looked tired, worn out. But then, he had to be well over seventy by now, she realized. Today, he was a man in mourning, one of her grandmother's best friends. She was not sure that she understood the unusual relationship that the two of them had shared for so many years—but thank God he had been there for Nana. She, Beth, had not.

Impulsively, she turned and walked back to him, giving him a kiss on the cheek. He hugged her tightly. "Call me if you need anything, anything at all," Jake wearily conceded, realizing that she probably did need to be alone. He could understand that. In fact, he planned to spend the night at his office instead of going home to face Evelyn. She wasn't happy about Beth being back in town.

"Jake…thanks for everything, for all you've done for Nana. Let's talk tomorrow?"

"Tomorrow…I have a closing in the morning. The old Anderson place on Grindstone Island has been sold. But I'll be here sometime in the afternoon. We need to get your things out to the island—if this is where you really plan to stay?"

"I do," she smiled, "tomorrow then." Once again she headed back up the trail to her childhood home. *Nana won't be here to greet me this time*, she reminded herself, as her tears began to fall once again, as memories of her grandmother crowded into her broken heart. *She's not here*, she whispered to herself, *not today, not ever again.*

"The leaves of memory
seemed to make
a mournful rustling
in the dark."
Henry Wadsworth Longfellow

Nana's Island Home

Chapter Six

*B*eth felt like she was stepping back in time as she approached the clearing in the woods. The rustic log structure that her grandfather had built stood facing south on a rocky knoll perched above Rainy Lake. The lake lapped gently on the shore far below the screened porch that wrapped around the front and sides of the house. The willow-branch rocking chairs that she remembered from her childhood still rocked in the breeze on the porch. The hanging porch swing was still there. She'd spent many hours here as a child swinging, reading, watching sunsets and storms moving in…and later on, planning her escape from the island. An assortment of tangled vines climbed peeling logs that supported the suspended porch. Wild ferns crowded empty flower pots that surrounded the sagging wooden steps leading up to the porch and main entrance. Nana hadn't had time to plant her red geraniums in the pots this year…

The heavy wooden door was unlocked as always. It creaked and groaned as she slowly pushed it open and stepped into the main room. The last rays of the day's sunlight filtered in through dusty window-panes, across the hardwood floors and the flowered Victorian rug that lay beside the stone fireplace. Papa had built that fireplace with rocks that he had hauled home from neighboring islands. It was the focal point of the room, surrounded by wall-to-wall bookcases that were filled with hundreds of books accumulated over the years. Reading had always been an avid interest and pastime for her family, especially during the long winters they spent on the island. The library included some of the school books that Nana had used to homeschool Beth's mother on the island. *My mother*, Beth sighed. It was hard to remember her anymore…

❧ ❧

She wandered through the house, touching things that Nana had touched. Her bag of knitting that sat beside her favorite chair in front of the fireplace. An assortment of knick-knacks and souvenirs that represented highlights of her life. Framed photos of the past were scattered around the room—Nana and Papa beside Kettle Falls on their honeymoon, Sarah as a baby, Sarah as a beautiful young woman sitting on a big rock surrounded by water, Beth as a baby and growing up on the island, a mother-daughter pose of Beth and Emily. There were no pictures of Rob.

The old desk that Papa had built long ago of hand-sewn boards supported by crisscrossed log legs stood beneath the French glass windows. Beth could almost see Nana sitting at the desk, stroking the wood that Papa had sanded and varnished, as she gazed out toward the gazebo on the rocky point. Several antique kerosene lamps sat on the desk. She remembered Nana lighting them every time the electricity went out.

The big country kitchen was exactly as Beth remembered it. Still painted light yellow, Nana's favorite color, still full of Nana's violets and house plants—some of which were badly in need of watering. The family-sized, hand-hewn wood table stretched out beneath an expanse of French windows with a view of the vegetable garden and the woods beyond. Beth had eaten her meals here while watching deer grazing at the edge of the woods. She and Nana had laughed at the silly little spotted fawns scampering and playing in the field. Together, they had watched the birds coming to the feeder in the winter, the squirrels trying to chase them away.

The "Great Spirit Prayer" still hung on the wall above the table. Open shelves along the kitchen walls were filled with dishes, bowls, pots and pans, flower vases, canned garden produce, and homemade jelly. A corner curios cabinet displayed Nana's treasures—an antique copper kettle, depression glass, Swedish Jell-O molds, glass canning jars, old bottles, and vases. The freezer held blueberries, venison, wild duck, chickens. Beth wouldn't starve here, she realized. Checking out the refrigerator, she realized that she'd have to throw most of the food out. Nana hadn't had time to clean it out for a while…

Peeking into Nana's bedroom, just off the main room, Beth saw an unmade bed and a pile of dirty clothes in an overflowing laundry basket. Dust had accumulated on the dresser top, which was stacked with old photos that Nana had apparently been sorting through during her last days. The adjoining bathroom needed cleaning. There were stains and built-up scum on the claw-foot tub, smudges on the mirror over the sink, an overflowing wastebasket. This was not at all like Nana's usual meticulous housekeeping.

She needed help…she needed me, Beth collapsed into Nana's chair in front of the cold fireplace. "Why didn't anyone tell me?" she cried aloud, her shaky voice echoing through the empty house. "Why wasn't I here for her?" she corrected herself. "It's all my fault." *You're pathetic, Beth,* Rob's words pierced her heart. Maybe he was right…at least as far as the way she had treated her loving grandmother.

Hot tears began to flow like a river bursting through the dam. Tears of sorrow, of regret for all the things she should have said and done. It wasn't Nana's fault that her mother had drowned. It wasn't Nana's fault that she had no father. Yet, Beth realized, she'd blamed Nana in some ways. There was nobody else to blame. She'd taken out her frustrations on the one person who had loved her and been there for her over the years. Beth rocked back and forth, clutching Nana's furry blue slippers, the ones she always kept beside her rocking chair.

As darkness fell upon the island, a chill filled the air. Shadows of the past seemed to swirl through the room where Beth continued to rock. Her tears were spent. She stared into the past, consumed with memories bubbling up from the vault where she'd buried them long ago. Perhaps it was time to face the past that she'd hidden from for so many years. She was shivering. She hadn't eaten since breakfast. It didn't matter. Nothing mattered.

The house was cold and dark by the time an exhausted Beth found the flashlight in its usual place on the fireplace mantle and climbed the familiar staircase to her old bedroom. Her footsteps echoed eerily in the silence of loneliness. The house itself seemed to miss Nana. Nothing was the same without her.

At the top of the stairs, Beth entered the room that she had shared with her mother for the first six years of her life—until the lake had taken her mother away from her. They'd called it their "eagle's nest" since it was perched above the main floor of the house with shuttered windows on all four sides of the room. Memories flashed through her mind. Memories of her mother reading stories to her on the window seat as they looked out at the world, listening to the sounds of nature. Memories of cuddling up beside her in their big bed at night. Of playing imaginary games together, watching the clouds floating in the sky, picking wild daisies, braiding chains of clover. That was so long ago, Beth sighed, realizing that she needed to learn more about her mother, about her life. Until she filled in the missing pieces of her past, she would never be complete. She would never know who she really was. She would never be free.

Beth had been alone in the eagle's nest after her mother died, after the first few weeks that she'd spent sleeping downstairs with Nana. She'd decided then that she must move back upstairs. She wanted to be there, waiting in bed, when Mommy came back home. But Mommy never came home again. Still, she sometimes visited Beth in her dreams…

In later years, Beth found refuge in this room. It became her sanctuary, a place where she could sit on the window seat gazing out at the world. Watching the trees shimmering in the sunlight, moonbeams dancing across the hardwood floor. Listening to the lake, the wolves howling, the cry of the loons. Thinking and dreaming…

It had been twenty years since Beth left the island, pregnant with Emily. In some ways, it felt like yesterday. In other ways, it felt like forever. Her room had not changed. Nana had kept if exactly the way she'd left it—as if she expected her to come home again someday. Beth had forgotten the incredible views from their eagle's nest. Tonight, she threw open the shutters to let the evening breeze flow through the room. Sheer lace curtains fluttered into the room, dancing in intricate patterns illuminated by the full moon. Taking a deep breath of the fresh lake air, she suddenly realized how exhausted and emotionally drained she was. Somehow, she felt safe here. She would sleep tonight in her old four-poster bed, snuggled beneath the down-filled quilt that Nana had made for her so many years ago.

"Good night, Nana. Please forgive me. And always remember that I love you," Beth whispered silently, as she crawled into bed in her funeral clothes.

"There are no facts,
only interpretations."
Friedrich Nietzsche

Chapter Seven

"That's simply not possible!" Beth challenged the Chicago bank manager over the phone first thing the next morning. "According to my records, I should have $6,282.50 in this account. That's my household expense money. There must be some mistake."

"I'm sorry, Mrs. Calhoun," a curt voice on the other end of the line repeated his previous words. "This was a joint account and it was closed out yesterday. Your husband had the right to do so."

"All right then," she held her breath, beginning to realize what was happening to her. "I will need to make a withdrawal from my money market account."

She clutched the phone, waiting for a response. As she feared, it was the same situation all over again. Joint account. Closed. Rob had taken the money and closed all accounts that she had access to.

Her attorney, who was waiting to be paid for the last bill that he'd sent her two weeks ago, wasn't encouraging. "It's going to be a long and bitter fight, Mrs. Calhoun. We will go for a temporary support order. And you will eventually get your share of all assets, rest assured. But you need to know that your husband is stalling and refusing to cooperate. It may take some time before you receive any support. You may want to consider looking for another source of income, perhaps a job, to see you through?"

Beth felt as if she'd been slapped across the face. She wondered if she could trust her own attorney, if he was on Rob's side or hers. What was she supposed to live on while she waited for Rob to quit playing games? She hadn't worked since she was a waitress at the Thunderbird Lodge on Rainy Lake's mainland over twenty years ago. Not since she became pregnant with Emily. It was hard to imagine that anyone would hire a middle-aged woman with no experience whatsoever, no education. Not unless she was destined to spend the rest of her life flipping burgers at McDonald's—assuming there was a McDonald's someplace on the mainland. She shuddered at the thought. If she stayed on the island, she couldn't rely on getting into the mainland for work during the winter. She had no idea how much she would need to live a simple life here, far removed from her old lifestyle in Chicago. She realized that she may have to sell or pawn her diamonds, even the emerald necklace, if she was destitute…something she hated to even consider. They should go to Emily someday. Thank God she'd remembered to take her jewelry from the vault when she left Chicago.

As she mulled over her rapidly deteriorating situation, she began sorting through Nana's file of important papers. Maybe she'd find something that could help her out…maybe Nana had left something for her, her only blood relative. She assumed the island would pass to her. At least she'd have a roof over her head.

What she found shocked her. There was a signed and recorded quit-claim deed signing Nana's island over to Jake. Jake had owned this island since 2000. How could that be? Working herself into a frenzy, she searched through old bank account statements, looking for a substantial deposit representing the proceeds of the sale of the island. There was none. Nothing out of the ordinary—except that Nana's savings account had been changed to a joint account, also in 2000. A joint account with Jake. There was a balance of $2,768. Jake was a successful and well-respected real estate broker, specializing in the sale of island property. He knew the value of Nana's island.

None of this made any sense to Beth. She loved Jake and had totally trusted him. Yet, everything she found seemed to imply that he had taken advantage of an old woman. He stole her inheritance. It seemed to be a dirty little secret that she had discovered by staying out here on the island—before Jake had a chance to remove the incriminating evidence. No wonder he didn't want her to stay here last night. Beth's thoughts raced. She became more and more suspicious, convinced that she was, once again, a victim of betrayal by those she loved. She'd trusted Rob, and look what he had done to her. Now Jake? Men could not be trusted, she decided. She'd never trust one again. Not ever.

Yet, a small voice within quietly reminded her that Jake had been the one who was here for Nana. She, Beth, had not bothered to come home. Maybe she didn't deserve the island or anything else. Still…this just wasn't right. Jake was wealthy…he owned prime real estate throughout the Rainy Lake region. He didn't need Nana's island.

The pristine beauty of a dewy morning on the island was lost on her as she paced back and forth around the kitchen, still wearing her crumpled, slept-in funeral clothes from yesterday. Her hair was uncombed. Gulping cup after cup of black coffee to fortify herself before Jake showed up on *his* island, she waited.

She heard his boat pull up at the dock. From the porch, she watched as he unloaded her suitcase and the contents of her vehicle. He had groceries for her and a big can of boat gas that he left beside Nana's boat at the dock. Nana hadn't driven it in years, but Jake had seen to it that it was in good working order. Beth would have transportation back and forth to the mainland.

Jake whistled as he hiked up the path toward the big house, as if everything was just fine. He looked happy, not at all apprehensive about what Beth may have discovered. How, she wondered, could he be so calm after what he'd done?

His whistling stopped abruptly as he felt the chill in the air. It was coming from the porch where Beth stood, arms folded across her chest, no hint of a smile upon her face. No greeting. She looked like hell. It must have been a rough night for her, as he'd feared it would be. A questioning frown spread across his face as he watched her staring at him silently.

"You OK, Beth?" he finally asked.

"Just great," she replied icily. "Thank you for sharing *your* island with me, Jake."

"Oh shit," he blurted out. Somehow, she already knew what he had come to tell her. Maybe she had found the deed to the property. But she had no way of knowing what was behind this transaction—or what the future would hold for her.

"It's not the way it looks," he began, as he unloaded several big boxes onto the floor of the porch and settled his large frame into one of the rockers. "Sit down. We need to talk."

She remained standing, arms folded. "Oh, it's just fine, Jake. You were the one who was there for her, right? It's yours. I really don't need a place to live…" Her words gushed out sarcastically.

"Calm down, Beth. Listen to me instead of jumping to conclusions, will you?"

Reluctantly, she slid into the other rocker, rocking furiously, trying to control her tears.

"Yes, I own this place, technically. Yes, Nana deeded it to me. Do you know why?"

She shook her head.

"Several reasons. One, she could no longer afford to pay the taxes as the value of her island skyrocketed. I've paid her real estate taxes for many years. Two, we decided it was best to get her property out of her name in case she had to go into a nursing home someday—something I've tried for years to get her to do. Most importantly, we wanted to protect the island for the future…" his voice trailed off.

"Whose future, Jake—yours?"

"No, Beth, your future. What you don't know is that I've already executed a quitclaim deed back to you. It's locked in the safe in my office until the time is right to make the transfer to you. It's your island—it always has been."

Feeling somewhat guilty for the horrible thoughts she had harbored against him, she was still puzzled. "So why wasn't it passed directly to me?"

He sighed patiently. "Because if it had been, your husband would be able to claim his half of your island. Nana and I never expected your marriage to last, Beth. We wanted to be sure that Rob couldn't get his hands on what belongs to you. You should also know that we've protected her money by adding my name to her accounts—joint accounts. Rob won't be able to get his hands on any of that, either."

Tears welled in her eyes. She felt foolish, ungrateful. Yes, she had jumped to conclusions. This was Jake that she was dealing with, not Rob. "I'm so sorry, Jake. I should have known better. It's just that it looked like…well, it's been a horrible day. Rob has closed all my accounts. I have no money. When I found Nana's papers, it seemed that I had no place to live either. Nothing."

"You're forgiven," he smiled gently as he patted her hand. "I can only imagine what it looked like, as upset as you've been over your pending divorce and now, Nana's passing."

After putting the groceries away and hauling the rest of her belongings from the boat to the house, they talked more. Jake referred her to a local attorney, a good friend of his who would represent her interests. He insisted on writing her a check, from Nana's account, for $2,000 that she could use to set up an account at the local bank. It was a start, and he offered to help her out further with his own funds if needed.

Beth unpacked, took a long shower, and changed into clean clothes while Jake fixed the sagging steps of the porch. Always something to fix on an old place like this. He'd been Nana's handyman for years. Somehow, it helped to ease the painful losses of the past.

❧❧

"You do clean up nicely," he grinned when Beth finally emerged wearing an elegant black outfit contrasting with silver designer jewelry. Her auburn hair gleamed in the sunlight, her emerald eyes reflecting its penetrating rays. For now, she could afford to dress like this. That could change soon…

Beth whipped up a quick Italian spaghetti dinner that they shared out on the porch with a glass of red wine as the sun set over the big lake. They talked and reminisced, exchanging stories about Nana. This was one of the most comfortable relationships that Beth had ever known, despite the fact that she and Jake had had very limited contact over the past twenty years. They seemed to be able to pick up where they left off so many years ago. Beth felt a connection here that she savored, one that seemed to last unconditionally. If there was anyone in this world that she could trust, she realized that Jake was the one.

She walked him down to the dock when he left, hugging him warmly and once again apologizing for her mistrust and her outburst. It was water over the dam, he said, no big deal. He invited her for lunch at the historic Kettle Falls Hotel on Sunday afternoon. She had vague recollections of previous Sunday afternoon boating excursions across Rainy Lake to Kettle Falls—with Jake, her mother, and Nana. Now Jake was inviting her back into the past. This could be a good time to do more reminiscing, to learn more about her past.

Beth accepted his invitation, then inquired, "What about Evelyn? Will she be coming?"

Jake shrugged his shoulders in resignation. "She's in New York again for a few weeks."

"New York? Doing what?"

"The usual. Shopping. Broadway plays. Art museums. Fancy dinners. Time with her old girlfriends. More shopping. Did I mention shopping?" His eyes twinkled, then became serious. "Time away from Rainy Lake—and from me…that's what it's really all about."

As a silver sliver of a moon materialized in the darkening sky, Jake boarded his boat, waving to Beth who stood on the dock waving back at him. As he fired up the engine, a shadow of doubt flickered across his face. He had survived the first round. There would be more, and they would be more difficult. He hoped with all his heart that their relationship could survive the unveiling of long-held secrets from the past. Secrets that would be disclosed soon.

"Whoso loves,
believes the impossible."
Elizabeth Barrett Browning

Chapter Eight

B eth's first week on the island was a busy one, filled with cleaning the house, unpacking, organizing, and planting red geraniums for Nana. She worked hard hoeing, weeding, and clearing the crusty over-grown garden patch so it would once again produce fresh vegetables. She repaired the holes in the fence, trying to keep the deer and rabbits out.

Drawn to the aging gazebo beside the family burial plot, she spent hours sitting on the sagging steps of the structure, thinking about her mother and her grandmother. And she thought about Papa, the grandfather she'd never met, the one who lived on in her memory simply because of Nana's colorful stories about him. She wondered how their lives would have been different if he had not drowned so many years ago... Now, they were all buried together on the island they had loved. It was her turn to love the island, to care for it as they would have wanted her to. She would start by restoring the old gazebo to its original glory, complete with flowers and a little bench overlooking the lake. She planned to spend some time here reading, thinking, trying to put her life back together again. Trying to discover who she really was and who she was meant to be.

Every day she wandered into Nana's bedroom, just soaking it all in. She'd made her bed and cleaned the room, as if Nana would be coming home again. Otherwise, she had not touched a thing. It was like a sanctuary. Someday, she'd go through her drawers and the closet, trying to recapture Nana's life. She wasn't ready yet.

One morning she started Nana's classic wooden launch, a 1950s Chris Craft runabout, on the first try. Jake had taken good care of Papa's boat over the years, polishing the mahogany wood until it gleamed in the early-morning sunlight. It had been her grandfather's pride and joy, or so she was told. He'd named it *Misty of Rainy Lake*. The name was in-scribed in bold gold script across the stern of the boat. She backed it out of the boathouse and skimmed across the mirror-like surface of the lake, heading toward the mainland for supplies. Her hair flying wildly in the wind, she maneuvered the powerful boat through the familiar channels and bays. It was a route she'd taken countless times with Nana. Once she was old enough to drive the boat by herself, she had used it to go back and forth to work at the Thunderbird Lodge. That's where she was headed today, where her car was parked. From there, she'd drive into Ranier or International Falls for groceries, more plants and flowers for her gardens, and white paint for the peeling gazebo.

As she skirted Grindstone Island, the Thunderbird Lodge loomed on the horizon. Suddenly, she was consumed with memories. Memories that she must now face. Until she did, she knew that she would never escape from a past that continued to haunt her.

Rob's youthful face seemed to be everywhere. This was where she had met him over twenty years ago. Rob, the handsome, rich playboy with the fancy houseboat, the party boat. Rob, who at that time represented everything that she thought she wanted. She had been sick of living in isolation, far from the excitement of the big city. She desperately wanted more than a simple lifestyle trying to make ends meet. She wanted to party, to have fun, to drink life in. As much as she loved Nana, she was just too old-fashioned for her then. Nana didn't understand what it was like to be young—to have big dreams far beyond Rainy Lake.

Beth would never forget the day when it all began. She was seventeen, late for work, securing her boat at the marina's dock. As she ran up the pier toward the Thunderbird Lodge, she almost ran into a young man standing on the deck overlooking the lake. He playfully blocked her, flashing an irresistible grin, perfect white teeth gleaming against his well-tanned face. Obviously one of the rich kids, she thought to herself as she tried to dart around him. She'd noticed that they had a certain air about them, a strong sense of confidence, sometimes an arrogance. They were used to getting what they wanted, when they wanted it.

"Hey, what's the hurry?" he beamed at her, a beer in his hand. He was barefoot, shirtless, and incredibly handsome. His gaze penetrated hers. She could not move, could barely breathe. "Don't I know you from someplace?" he asked in a deep, sexy drawl.

"I…I don't think so," Beth stammered, knowing she had to get to work, not wanting him to know that she was a working girl.

His arm slipped casually around her shoulders. She shivered in the heat. "Come on, baby," his eyes held her captive. "Let's get a beer and sit out here by the lake for a while. If I don't know you yet, I need to…I really need to get to know you…"

"I can't. I…ah, I promised to waitress tonight. A good friend of mine needed a favor, and…"

"Oh, you work here. Hey, that's cool. My friends and I were just going to come in for dinner."

With that, he followed her into the dining room of the lodge and seated himself at a table by the windows overlooking the lake. His friends soon joined him. They drank, ordered expensive steak dinners, laughed, had a ball. But his eyes followed her everyplace she went. They were hungry eyes, eyes that knew exactly what he wanted. This wasn't the first time that a guy had hit on her. But somehow, this was different. There was no way to simply dismiss this man. She wanted to get to know him. She wanted to be a part of his exciting world…instead of the little waitress serving him and his friends.

When they left, he tucked a hundred-dollar bill into her hand, stroking her palm. "I'll be back," he whispered in her ear, sending shivers up and down her spine. Something unexplainable was happening to her, something she could not control. She stood by the window for a moment, trying to regain her composure as she watched him board his houseboat with his friends and disappear into the mist of Rainy Lake.

She didn't even know his name. She knew nothing about him. Still, she dreamed about him at night. She thought of him during lazy summer days that seemed to drag on forever. She looked for him every night at the Thunderbird. As lonely days turned into endless weeks, she shuffled through life without a drop of enthusiasm. Sometimes she scolded herself…telling herself that it was foolish to think he was coming back. Why would someone like him want to date a poor waitress from the North Woods? As the weeks crawled by, she created an image of this stranger in her mind that was impossible for her to resist. She was seventeen.

One early fall evening, Beth walked into the lodge for her shift at work. Her eyes scanned the room hopefully as they always did. Her heart almost stopped when she recognized him sitting alone at a corner table for two. He brooded silently, tapping his fingers impatiently against his water glass. As if he was waiting for something, for someone.

Cautiously, she advanced to his table, trying to mask her reeling emotions. He wasn't smiling this time, wasn't joking. "I don't even know your name," he began, "all I know is that I haven't been able to think of anything but you for the past month…"

She melted, as he had expected her to. "I'm Beth," she whispered, extending her hand. He held her hand in his, stroking her palm in tiny circles. "I'm Rob," he gazed intently into her eyes, "and I've been waiting a long time for you." She quickly agreed to meet him after her shift ended at 10 p.m. His friends were having a bonfire out on Sand Point Island. He would pick her up in his boat.

For a brief moment, she hesitated. Sand Point Island was actually in Canada, just across the international border line in the midst of Rainy Lake. It was about four miles away by boat. Nana won't like this, Beth thought to herself. But this is *my* life, not hers, she rationalized. *This could be my only chance to find love and happiness*. Sometimes a person had to take a few risks in life, right? She had no intention of spending her life alone, like Nana, chained to the past. Life was meant to be lived…and Rob had already awakened something within her that she'd never felt before. Reluctantly, she dialed her home phone to tell Nana that she'd be late and not to wait up for her.

Nana was not happy. "A party on Sand Point? Beth, who are these people? Do we know them?"

"Please, Nana," Beth spoke quietly so others wouldn't hear her, "I just have to go. I can't pass this opportunity up. They're really nice kids, kids that I've gotten to know here this summer. I'll be fine. You need to trust me, OK?"

Nana sighed, "I do trust you, Beth, but I still don't like this. I worry about you and I don't want you to go. You could invite them here instead, you know…I'd like to meet your friends."

Beth was aghast. She couldn't imagine what Rob would think of their simple home, so different from the fancy house that he must live in. "I can't do that. I'm sorry. I need to go," her voice hardened. "Good night, Nana, love you." She hung up the phone.

Her shift droned on forever that night. When she finally walked out to the marina after work, a full moon throbbed above the horizon. Rob was waiting for her in his boat, a beer in his hand—one of many that he'd already slugged down that evening.

She climbed into the seat beside him, her heart pounding, feeling wild and carefree. A star-studded universe seemed to open before her, welcoming her into a world that she'd only dreamed of. Rob put his arm around her as he gunned the boat, flying across the lake toward Sand Point. As they docked at the beach, Beth was shocked to see a nude couple running across the beach into the shimmering waters of the lake. Here, they merged into a shadowy image of two lovers locked in an embrace beneath the light of the moon. Rob blared the boat's horn at them, laughing. Maybe Nana was right, she thought to herself—then quickly shoved her doubts into the back of her mind. She was not going to ruin this night.

Beer flowed freely around the campfire on the beach of Sand Point Island. Music blared from a portable cassette player. A group of ten to twelve teenagers were gathered on the beach. Beth did not recognize any of them. She averted her eyes away from several couples who danced together suggestively, clad in low-cut bikinis and clinging trunks, touching at every possible opportunity. As the effects of the booze, the music, and the mystical light of the moon overpowered them, couples began to disappear into the darkness of the surrounding woods.

She and Rob sat together on a log beside the bonfire. He brought her a beer from a cooler in the woods. Silently, they gazed into the glowing embers of the fire. She wanted to get to know him better, but small talk didn't seem to be one of Rob's priorities tonight. She learned he was from Chicago, that his father was a lawyer and that he was on track to become a partner in his firm. His family had vacationed on Rainy Lake for many years, usually living in their houseboat. He didn't ask many questions about her life, which she was grateful for. She remembered how he held her hand. He moved closer, inching his restless fingers up her thigh, releasing feelings within her that she never knew she had. Moving her further and further toward a place she'd never been before.

Beth looked deeply into the shadows of his face—searching for the sun, the moon, the stars…for all that she'd ever wanted in life. Searching for a man to love her, to always be there for her. After a few beers—something she was unaccustomed to—she thought she could see the love in his eyes, a love that was reflected in her own. Their eyes locked together intensely. When Rob suggested a walk in the woods so they could be alone to talk, she gladly stumbled along beside him. She was feeling a little wobbly, a little strange. She'd never been with a man before.

They reached a clearing in the woods where the orange light of the moon flickered through the trees to expose a soft bed of old pine needles. Here, he laid her down, stripped her of her clothes, and began to caress every inch of her body. She moaned softly, consumed with new-found pleasures, wanting more, wanting everything that a woman in love could possibly want.

Finally, he unzipped his pants and fell on top of her. She quivered with fear of the unknown as he kissed her tenderly, telling her that he loved her. He entered her gently at first, then more urgently, thrusting deeper as he became lost in his own desires. Years later, she still remembered the sharp pain—pain punctuated with quivers of ecstasy. When he was done, he rolled over onto his side and fell asleep as she clung to him—for reassurance that she had not just made the biggest mistake of her life.

"God, you can't be a virgin!" he exclaimed in disgust when they woke together before dawn in a puddle of blood. Tears welled in her eyes. Of course she was a virgin. She had waited to find *the right one*. She thought she had found him. A light drizzle began to dampen her spirits as they walked silently back to the boat.

Nine months later, Emily was born.

Beth would never forget Rob's reaction when he learned that she was pregnant with his child. He was not pleased. "How could you be so stupid?" he'd blurted. He and his parents had at first insisted upon an abortion. Rob's parents had offered to pay her a generous amount of money to comply with their wishes. After all, their son had a brilliant future ahead of him as a partner in his father's law firm. He had already been accepted into a prestigious law school. A wife and a baby simply did not fit into their plans for him. And while they never put it into words, it was obvious they felt that Beth was not of his social class. She was not the wife for him—not now, not ever.

Beth had refused his parents' offer. She wanted this baby. She wanted Rob. Nana supported her decision, knowing from experience how important it was to have a father for your child. After all, she had raised both her daughter and her granddaughter on her own, without the support of a man.

Surprisingly, Rob stood by her. He was madly in love with her…just as he was, in later years, madly in love with the endless string of women with whom he had affairs…

Rob had defied his parents' wishes and insisted upon marrying Beth at once. Looking back, Beth had often tried to figure out why he had been so adamant about marrying her and providing for his daughter. Perhaps it had been to spite his mother, Nora, the glamorous socialite who had humiliated him throughout his life with her blatant affairs. While his father had been a workaholic, obsessed with building a multi-million-dollar legal firm, his neglected wife had resorted to promiscuity.

Beth clearly remembered one night on the beach with Rob, cuddling by the campfire, talking about their respective families. Rob had clenched his fists as he recounted episodes of coming home as a young teenager to find his mother in bed with some strange guy who was years younger than she was. The kids at school even talked and laughed about his mother. He had hated her in some ways. His father never seemed to care—as long as he was free to pursue his own dreams.

Beth had held him close against her swelling stomach that night, understanding his pain. She had grown up without a father. Although she had deeply loved her mother, she still had to live with the rumors, the taunts from others. She'd overheard the vicious gossip... "What kind of a woman would become pregnant and have a child without a father?" "Who and where was Beth's father?"

⁂

Twenty years later, she still didn't know who her father was. Until now, she hadn't wanted to know. Looking back, she wondered if being fatherless had anything to do with the course her life had taken. Perhaps it was the reason she'd fallen in love so easily, gotten herself pregnant, and tried to escape from the echoes of her past.

Shoving the memories aside, Beth tied her boat to the pier at the Thunderbird marina. Taking a deep breath, she decided that it was time to move beyond the past that had haunted her for so many years.

Beyond the marina, the Thunderbird Lodge stood, proudly displaying a large thunderbird symbol on the front of the expansive building. A deck with umbrella tables stretched comfortably along the length of the wooden structure. A cozy dining room overlooking the lake offered spectacular views of the bay, the houseboats and fishing boats skimming across the waters. The Thunderbird had been well-known for its elegant dining for years. Yet, the atmosphere was casual and a pot of coffee was always on. It was a place where locals and tourists alike hung out.

Beth waved at several strangers relaxing on the deck with mugs of steaming coffee. They were smiling and animated as they admired her classic boat. Yes, this was a fresh start for her, she decided, seeing the old place through new eyes of opportunity. She actually began to hum an old tune as she walked toward the parking area to find her car.

There it was…but what was that on the windshield? Scrawled in angry red letters were the words, "Go home, bitch!"

Oh my God, she panicked, stopping dead in her tracks. Rob had found her! He'd been here…he could still be here lurking in the shadows, watching her, waiting to catch her alone. He could have tampered with her car, cut the brake line. Her thoughts raced, spiraling out of control. Nervously, she glanced around her. People casually went about their business—hiking down to the marina with their fishing gear, out for a walk on a beautiful morning, heading into the lodge for breakfast. Maybe that's what she needed to do…go where the people were so she wouldn't be alone and vulnerable.

Forcing herself to breathe slowly and deeply, she counted one-two-three, one-two-three, over and over again as she cautiously walked back to the lodge and into the dining room. She needed to be alone. But she needed to be near people as well—just in case he was here somewhere. "You deserve anything that happens to you, Beth," Rob's words rang in her ears.

One-two-three, she repeated silently as she settled into a chair at a table by the windows. She could see her launch rocking gently at the dock. She could see the people on the deck, still admiring her boat. The friendly waitress brought her a cup of coffee and took her order. The background blurred with the chatter of families and friends enjoying breakfast together and planning their day on the lake.

Beth was alone. Trying to calm herself. Trying to think clearly, to decide what she needed to do next. She would call Jake, of course—perhaps the Sheriff's Department as well. Lost in her thoughts, her hands wrapped tightly around her mug of coffee, she did not notice the stranger standing beside her table.

"Excuse me…" he cleared his throat.

She startled, looking up into the ruggedly handsome face of a stranger. He had long black hair that cascaded carelessly against his dark skin, strong facial features chiseled in the American Indian tradition, and dark chocolate eyes—eyes that seemed to draw her into their depths. He radiated an aura of kindness, honesty, sincerity. She wasn't afraid, only curious. Why was he approaching her?

"You're Beth, aren't you?" he spoke softly, not wanting to frighten her.

She could only nod, trying to remember where she'd seen or met him before.

"I'm sorry. I should introduce myself properly and tell you how I know your name, right?" He grinned. "Mind if I join you?"

She nodded toward the seat across from her, feeling uncommonly comfortable for some strange reason. There was something about his eyes...

"I'm Seth—your neighbor, your only neighbor," he tried to lighten the mood, sensing that this young woman was in need of some company, yet terrified of something. He wondered what was wrong. Whatever it was, he felt an overwhelming need to be here for her, just as he had while watching her at Nana's burial ceremony on the island. Her anxious eyes stirred his soul. He looked away to catch his breath.

Of course, Beth suddenly realized. This must be the artist Jake had mentioned, the one who lived on the island just across from the rocky point where her gazebo stood. As a child, she had rowed her boat over to his island to pick blueberries. She had explored the remains of an old cabin there, finding remnants of someone else's life—even a journal documenting one man's life on the island in the early 1900s.

Seth studied her intently, waiting for a response, feeling a kindred connection with this struggling spirit. She fidgeted nervously across the table from him—playing with her napkin, her water glass, her spoon. Finally, she smiled back at him. She could not do otherwise.

"Look, I don't mean to intrude, Beth. You have things on your mind," he began cautiously. "I just wanted to tell you how sorry I am about the loss of your grandmother. She was a special lady, one I was honored to help out now and then."

"Thank you—and ah, thanks for being there for her," she lapsed back into blaming herself for not having been there, twisting a lock of her auburn hair around her little finger.

He was startled for some reason, trying to clear his head. "I also want you to know that I'm here, close by, in case you ever need anything. Highly recommended, by the way, by Jake...your uncle?"

"Yes. Thanks, Seth. I do appreciate your offer. I'm sure I'll be just fine here. But...just in case, do you have a phone by chance?"

He hurriedly scribbled his name and phone number on a napkin and handed it to her, their hands brushing softly over her plate of Eggs Benedict. An electric spark seemed to sizzle between them. She pulled back abruptly.

What was that all about, Beth asked herself as she watched Seth depart. A part of her desperately wanted him to stay. Another part, equally as desperate, wanted him to go away—and to stay away—forever. Men were not to be trusted. She wanted no part of this man or any other. She compulsively tore his name and phone number into tiny pieces before his boat was out of sight. She did not need anyone, not now, not ever.

All she needed was to stop Rob, to keep him away from her. Jake responded to her phone call immediately, before her breakfast had cooled.

"We need to establish where Rob has been over the past six days," he told her. "That was when I parked your SUV here. I'll check with the Thunderbird staff. You need to call Emily and anyone else you can think of who might know Rob's whereabouts within the past week."

Her daughter, Emily, she decided, would be her first contact, after Jake escorted her back home to her island and determined that nobody was hiding out there. He offered to stay, knowing that she was too independent to allow him to do so.

Forgetting the time difference between Minnesota and Paris, France, where Emily was currently living, Beth woke her sleepy daughter in the middle of the night.

"Mom, is that you?" Emily grasped the phone beside her bed. "Is everything OK?"

"God, I forgot, once again, that it's the middle of the night for you, honey. But this is important. I need to know if you've heard anything from your father recently…"

There was a pause at the end of the line before Emily summoned up her courage to reply. "Mom, I don't want to upset you…but Dad was just here visiting me. He showed up with that stupid girlfriend of his. I couldn't believe he would have the guts to bring her to my place! What am I supposed to do? He is my father, after all, and he is supporting me. So, do I just slam the door in his face? It's not like I didn't want to, you know…" she rambled on.

Beth drew a long breath, trying to control her fury, before she could respond. "Is he there now?"

"No, they're traveling, thank God. They stopped here and took me out for dinner one night last week."

"What day, Emily? It's important."

"Hmmm…it was one week ago exactly. Why?"

Beth tried hard to focus on the reason she had called. So Rob had been in Europe when this incident occurred—with his *girlfriend*... She wondered if he would have hired someone else to deface her car. If not, who wanted her to leave Rainy Lake, and why? They talked more as Beth finally revealed the reason she had called. She was surprised when Emily announced that she did not believe her father was responsible for the incident. Nor did she believe that her mother needed to worry about any more threats or repercussions from her father.

"I know you're stressed, Mom, but this is ridiculous," Emily sounded almost defensive. "Why do the two of you have to act like children? Why couldn't you have worked this out a long time ago, before it came to *this*? Like, before you ran away from home? Before he made such a fool of himself that I'm embarrassed to introduce him and that little tramp of his to my friends?"

Beth bristled. "Listen, young lady. You have no idea what he has done to me over the years. I never wanted you to know, but it sounds like you're blaming me now. This is *not* my fault!"

Emily sighed as the phone connection crackled. "OK, I'm sorry. I'm not blaming you, Mom. I grew up wondering why you put up with him, why you didn't leave. But now that you've left, well, I'm like mad as hell. And I don't know who to be mad at. Does that make any sense?"

"I guess it does," Beth had to admit. "You're not the only one who is mad as hell, Emily. Just remember that he filed for divorce two months before I left. And the reason I left, if you want the truth, is that he attacked me. He hurt me. That's why I'm living in fear, afraid that he will find me and make good on his threats." There, it was finally out in the open.

"Oh my God!" Emily cried. "Are you OK, Mom? What happened? I can't believe he would do something *that* bad..."

"You don't know your father very well, I'm afraid. Yes, I'm OK. I really can't discuss the details right now. But I wanted you to know why I need to know his whereabouts."

"Are you sure you're OK?" Emily's voice quivered.

"Yes, please don't worry. This is exactly why I never wanted you to know. But I can't have you blaming me, Emily. I just can't handle that."

"I don't." I just don't know what to think anymore. I just wish things were different, that's all. They will be back to visit again in three days, Mom, before they fly back to the States."

"Did he say anything about the divorce?" Beth pried, hoping her daughter would level with her. She knew that she was bound to have conflicting loyalties, and she didn't like to put her in the center of things. But she had to find out.

Emily paused, choosing her words carefully. "Well, he says that he wants to get the divorce over as soon as possible so he can move on with his life. He has no interest in *pursuing* you, as he put it. And Mom, you need to know that he knows where you are... like *he* figured it out. *I* never told him."

Emily's words sent a chill up Beth's spine. This was her worst nightmare, although she should have known he would figure it out. Where else would she go?

"Mom? Are you there?"

"Yes, go on, what else did he say?"

"He hoped that since you have a place of your own, you won't need as much support from him. As he put it, living expenses up there are so much cheaper than in Chicago that he should be able to get by with less alimony. He said he just wants to get this over with and he wants you to get on with your own life as well." Emily didn't like the position that she had been put in, balancing one parent against the other. But she felt her mother needed to know. She was the victim, after all.

"I wish I could believe that," Beth whispered as she started to tell her daughter good-bye.

"Mom, I don't know if I should tell you this...but there's more," Emily hesitated. Her mother had enough to deal with, she realized, but she had to share this shocking news with someone. It had been building inside her, gnawing at her, for the past week. She needed to tell somebody before she exploded. But she'd been too humiliated to do so.

"What is it, Em?" Beth held her breath.

"This is going to be a shocker for you, but I *think* it's possible that Dad's little friend *might* be pregnant." Emily tried to tone it down. It was obvious that the little bitch was pregnant. The two of them had the guts to proudly announce her pregnancy during dinner. Wanda, or whatever her name was, hung on him, smiling up at him with adoring eyes. She idolized him. He treated her like the child that she was. Emily had felt like she was going to faint or vomit—or slap her father's beaming face. It had been an evening from hell. Now, she was trying to spare her mother the gory details.

"I know," Beth replied weakly, wondering why it should still bother her.

"*You know*?" Emily couldn't believe it. "*You know*? Is that what this is really all about?"

"It's why he left, Emily," she replied numbly, remembering how badly she once wanted another child. A little brother for Emily. Rob had adamantly refused. Now, he was having a baby with a girl who was not much older than Emily.

"Oh my God, Mom. How could he do that to us?" She began to sob. "Like I could just die, I'm so humiliated! This is so sick! It's like…she's a child, a little slut, and she's having my father's baby?"

Beth tried to calm her down, wishing she could just hold her in her arms like she used to do. As she hung up the phone, she realized that she was relieved that Emily finally knew the truth. The tension in the air between them seemed to have faded into the past, a past that they were both trying to put behind them.

Meanwhile, back at the Thunderbird, Jake was having her vehicle checked out to be sure it was safe. He met with the sheriff's deputy and took a few photos of the angry words scrawled child-like on the windshield. It wasn't paint, he realized as he began removing the ugly words. It was red lipstick. Somehow, that didn't seem like something that Rob or any other man would use… If not Rob, who, he wondered, and why?

He took the car for a test drive to be sure that it was safe. As he got out, he noticed a small object glittering in the sunshine. A discarded tube of Brilliant Red Revlon lipstick. He tucked the incriminating evidence into his pocket.

"A soft liquid joy like the noise of many waters
flowed over his memory and he felt in his heart
the soft peace of fading tenuous sky above the waters,
of oceanic silence, of swallows flying
through the sea dusk over the flowing waters."
James Joyce

Kettle Falls Hotel

Chapter Nine

*N*ana's remaining ashes accompanied Beth and Jake on their Sunday outing to Kettle Falls. They would be scattered over the falls after lunch, just as Nana had scattered Papa's ashes there over fifty years ago.

Beth was determined, as she climbed into Jake's boat, that this would be a day for Nana and Papa, for reminiscing about their lives, for enjoying all that Rainy Lake and Kettle Falls had to offer. It would not be a day to worry about lipstick smeared on a car window or her pending divorce. That could wait. She worried too much lately—about everything. She had to let some of it go…

Rainy Lake itself tended to wash away one's troubles on a day like this, to make them pale in significance against the backdrop of endless miles of open water flowing gently around thousands of pristine, pine-studded islands. Islands borne of ancient Precambrian bedrock—granites, schists, and greenstones laced with streaks of quartz. Beth lost herself in the company of some of the oldest rock formations in the world. They were a part of the Canadian Shield that was created 2.7 billion years ago when the earth's crustal plates clashed together violently enough to build mountains and rearrange the seas of the planet. Then the continental glaciers bulldozed their way through this region, forming Rainy Lake and its many islands.

Jake maneuvered his big boat along the familiar route, through the sometimes treacherous Brule Narrows, where Pete had drowned. They passed deserted old commercial fishing camps and swung through picturesque Andersen Bay, where an eagle swooped overhead. Seagulls soared through brilliant blue skies. An occasional loon dove playfully beneath the sparkling surface of the lake.

Kettle Falls was located on the eastern tip of the Kabetogama Peninsula, now a part of Voyageur's National Park. Accessible only by water, this wilderness retreat was often referred to as "the jewel of the forest." Obviously an emerald, Beth thought to herself, as they pulled up to the Rainy Lake landing. They were greeted by a forest of pine shimmering in the sunlight, creating an aura of multiple shades of iridescent green.

Several deer stood gracefully in the woods, watching them in silence as they hiked up the gravel path. They crossed a rustic wooden bridge spanning a large bog and headed up the trail to the clearing in the woods where the historic Kettle Falls Hotel stood majestically. As many times as Jake had been here, it never failed to thrill him when the old hotel seemed to magically appear in what seemed to be the middle of nowhere. It was an expansive, white, frame structure with a red roof and red-and-white-striped awnings. They crossed the lawn with its horseshoe pits, picnic tables, fire pit, and volleyball net. A fox stood guard just beyond the clearing—looking for leftover crumbs from someone's picnic lunch.

Baskets of cascading petunias hung from both sides of the stairs leading up to the hotel's screened-in veranda. Guests relaxed in wicker rockers, chatting and gazing out through vine-covered windows. Golf carts transported guests, luggage, and supplies from the boat landings to the old hotel.

Jake steered Beth to a glass-covered bamboo table in the dining section of the veranda. They toasted Nana and Papa, clinking glasses filled with Chablis, before ordering the walleye shore lunch. In the background, they could hear tunes tinkling from the antique nickelodeon in the barroom. The historic hotel had been built in 1913 on a bed of clay, without a foundation. Heavy rains would periodically wash away the soil beneath the building. As the walls sank, the floors sloped and slanted in various directions. The sloping floor of the old bar room became a landmark. When the building was renovated by its new owner, the National Park Service, the rolling bar floor was preserved in honor of the hotel's historic past.

"Ah, there is magic to this place, isn't there?" Beth sighed, more relaxed than she'd been in weeks, perhaps months…even years.

With that, Jake was off, telling her stories about the history of Kettle Falls. Stories of bootleggers like Moonshine Joe, of the infamous "ladies of the night" who had haunted this place—and still do from their "girlie" photos prominently displayed on the walls of the bar. Stories of lumberjacks from neighboring camps who came to visit the girls.

"Did you know that Robert Williams bought this place—and the old Ranier Saloon—from timber baron Ed Rose in 1918 for a thousand dollars and four barrels of whiskey?" Jake went on enthusiastically. "What a character Williams was… They say he was a gambler, a bootlegger. You see, it was prohibition time. Whiskey manufactured in Canada was shipped through Kettle Falls to the notorious Chicago gangster, George 'Bugs' Moran. In fact, the old-timers here swear that Bugs spent some time up here, hobnobbing with the local outlaws."

"What a history this place has. Did you know that my grandfather used to hide moonshine in the woods when the feds came? It was part of his job when he worked here as a boy," Beth laughed.

"Yes, Nana told me. You know, the feds confiscated trainloads of moonshine in Ranier, coming in across that old wooden bridge from Canada. The guys at Woody's Pub still laugh about the time the feds hacked open kegs of moonshine on the ice in the harbor there. Well, the alcohol settled in pools on top of the solid ice. So the locals showed up with ladles and buckets to help out—and dispose of the moonshine themselves."

"Those were the days, huh?" Beth sighed.

"And the fish stories," Jake continued. "Did you know that some-one caught a 236-pound sturgeon right here by the falls? The Indians speared sturgeon here for hundreds of years. Can't you just see it, Beth?" He paused dramatically. "It's an early spring evening, almost dark. The sturgeon are spawning at Kettle Falls. The Indians are slowly descending upon the falls, twenty birchbark canoes lashed together, torches lighting their way. An Indian stands in the bow of each canoe holding a long-handled spear and a wood mallet made of birchwood. The canoes pass slowly, silently, upriver, paddled by squaws in the stern. As the sturgeon is attracted to the light, the spear is cast. After a short flurry, the great sturgeon is speared and hauled to the edge of the canoe where its struggles end with a whack of the mallet."

"OK, Jake, I have a fishing story for you," Beth jumped in, remem-bering one of Nana's favorite stories about Papa. "One of my grandfather's jobs was to catch fish that were served in the dining room. When guests arrived and ordered walleye for dinner, the cook handed Papa a one-dollar bill and told him how many fish he needed to catch. Well, Papa would grab his trusty Prescott spinner and head for the dam. They say he never failed to catch as many fish as needed—always in time for dinner."

Jake chuckled, "He must have been quite the fisherman. I wish I'd known him…"

"I wish I'd known him, too," she sighed. She felt like she'd learned so much from him, just by listening to Nana's recollections. If only she could apply those lessons to her own life…

Jake continued sharing colorful stories of the past as Beth laughed so hard that tears spilled down her cheeks. He knew what she needed…a good laugh to help put her life back into perspective again.

His final story, as they finished their walleye, was about the friend-ly ghosts who still enjoyed paying an occasional visit to the historic Kettle Falls Hotel. Sometimes in the middle of the night, lights would flicker on and off, and the old nickelodeon in the bar would begin to play. Some guests reported hearing footsteps on the stairs—and finding nobody there. Were these ghosts of the past here to relive old memo-ries, Jake wondered? Were they looking for company, or for recognition that they had once existed?

Beth wasn't sure that she believed the local ghost stories…but she enjoyed hearing them.

∞§∞

It was time to hike down to the falls to fulfill Nana's last wish. Casting aside their previous frivolity, the two of them walked in silence toward the sound of the roaring falls. Climbing up the path toward the overlook deck above the falls, they wound through patches of staghorn sumac and red berry bushes. Blushing pink moss roses and wild white daisies sprung from the crevices of the moss-covered bedrock.

Standing side by side on the deck, they looked south across the falls into Canada—from the United States. This erratic international boundary line had been created to honor the historic route of the Indians and, later, the French-Canadian voyageurs who had paddled through this waterway over two hundred years ago. It was fascinating to think that if they had stood in this spot then, they would have seen colorful brigades of birchbark canoes, loaded with fur pelts, as the voyageurs made their annual three-thousand-mile journey along this river of commerce. Eventually, the furs ended up in Europe where they were made into fashionable fur coats and beaver hats.

Beth and Jake stared silently into the roaring falls that cascaded into boulder-filled pools churning with white froth. They were lost in their own thoughts. Beth could almost see Nana and Papa sharing a honeymoon picnic on the slab of rock jutting out from beneath the newly constructed deck.

"Are you ready?" Jake asked her solemnly. She nodded, holding out the urn. They each threw a handful of Nana's ashes over the falls. A light breeze scattered them across the falls that devoured them, washing them away, far away.

"God bless you, Nana. Papa, too," Beth said softly, tears filling her eyes.

"God bless us all," Jake whispered. "And Sarah…" he murmured as a seagull swooped silently over the falls, lighting on the deck railing beside him. He pulled Beth into the comfort of his aging arms, holding her close as she cried.

They sat together on a bench for a while. Beth could understand why this place had meant so much to Nana and Papa. It felt as if spirits of the past lingered here by the falls, as if she could almost reach out and touch Nana. She wondered if it was possible for Nana's spirit to be here today, watching her ashes disappear into the falls. That's probably just wishful thinking, Beth reminded herself.

Suddenly, she remembered the story Nana had told her so many times about one of their last picnics at Kettle Falls. She needed to share it with Jake.

As Nana told the story, she, Papa, and seven-year-old Sarah were picnicking at the falls one summer day shortly before Papa's fatal accident. Papa had been preoccupied, lost in his thoughts, as he gazed into the churning waters. He had not responded to questions posed by his inquisitive daughter, nor engaged in the usual conversation.

"What are you thinking about, Papa?" Nana had gently probed, squeezing his hand.

He had sighed deeply. "Just…about life and what it all means," he'd replied contemplatively. "When I look deeply into the falls, I become a part of them. I feel their power, their strength. I feel like I can flow freely through life. Splashing against the boulders at times, perhaps. Drifting out into the deep waters of life, toward the sea of immortality. It soothes my soul… Someday, I know that I will become a part of the lake again…I will be free as a seagull to soar over the roaring falls, to dip down and feel the spray of life, to feel your love…always."

Nana had been puzzled at the time by this eloquent and philosophical observation by a simple man who never expressed such thoughts. But she never forgot his message.

"Today, this story is finally beginning to make some sense to me," Beth confided to Jake, "I think…"

"I'm not afraid of storms
for I'm learning to sail my own ship."
Louisa May Alcott

Chapter Ten

*B*eth had always been intrigued by the battered old trunk in the attic of her grandmother's island home. It had been padlocked, totally off limits to her, as far back as she could remember. She'd been told that her great-grandfather Olaf, Nana's father, brought this trunk over to America on the boat from Sweden. As a child, she'd imagined all kinds of things hidden in this forbidden world of the past. Perhaps pirates' treasures, valuable coins, photos of Sweden and of relatives she had never known. As she grew older, she felt as if her deceased mother's life was somehow mysteriously locked away in that trunk.

Now, she was free to open this window into her past. Nana had, on her deathbed, told her to do so. Beth had replayed her dying grandmother's words over and over again in her mind since then: "Things you need to know…things I should have told you long ago…"

While she was anxious to discover what the trunk contained, something kept holding her back. She had pulled down the folding staircase leading up into the attic, climbed up with a flashlight, and stood staring at the trunk at least ten times since she'd moved back home to the island. But something always stopped her.

It was time to fill in the missing pieces of her past…but could she handle what she might discover? Was it better not to know the truth about some things? Perhaps, then, she could write her own history, or rewrite it the way she wanted it to be. She would not need to face the ugly skeletons that might be buried in that trunk—skeletons that could open up old wounds or create new ones that were even worse. Someone once said that "ignorance is bliss," she remembered. Perhaps it was true…

She wondered if the identity of her father was also hidden in the trunk. She still wasn't sure that she wanted to know the truth. Should I, or should I not, she asked herself one more time, flashlight in hand, peering down at the threatening trunk. It stood beneath a cobweb-framed dormer window in her grandmother's attic. She watched a black spider hard at work spinning silky threads. Maybe the phone would ring to save her…or the flashlight would die…or the oven timer would go off, signaling that her dinner was ready. No such luck.

Just do it, she told herself sternly. With one whack of the hammer, she smashed the rusty padlock. It fell to the floor in pieces, signaling that it was indeed time to face the past.

Cautiously, she lifted the heavy lid, barely breathing. A chill swirled through the stifling air, as if spirits of the past had suddenly been released from the dusty vault that had held their secrets for so long.

With trembling hands, she succeeded in lighting a kerosene lamp and began carefully extracting items from the trunk. *Oh my God…* Beth's great-grandfather Olaf's immigration papers, dated 1895, when he and his family had arrived at Ellis Island! A lovely handmade, white, lace wedding dress with a note carefully pinned to it: *Wedding dress of Emma Peterson, betrothed to her beloved husband Pete Peterson on September 16, 1941.* She recognized Nana's familiar handwriting. Nana and Papa… Beth sighed. Beneath stacks of old scrapbooks and photo albums, she found the treasure—her mother's diaries and notebooks filled with her poems. Clutching them closely to her breast, she began to sob, unaware of the storm that was brewing outside the windows of her island home.

A bolt of lightning suddenly flashed just beyond the attic window as thunder boomed across the lake. Sheets of rain pelted the house as fierce winds bent majestic trees to their knees. Climbing down the ladder, she found herself in darkness. The electricity had been severed. The temperature had dipped at least thirty degrees. Shining her flashlight ahead of her, she made her way down the stairs to the main level. She started a fire in the fireplace and lit all the kerosene lamps that Nana had scattered around the great room. How many times, she wondered, had she and Nana done this together over the years? Losing power was a frequent occurrence for islanders who relied upon an underground electric cable to provide power to their homes. If only Nana was there with her now…but then, maybe she was…

She decided to retreat to her swing on the enclosed porch where she could watch the summer storm churning across the lake, crashing against the boulders that supported the cabin. She enjoyed the storms of Rainy Lake, always had, although she had no inclination to be out on the lake when one hit. Swinging in the dark, watching the lightning crackle and light up the sky, Beth thought about how the lake's storms had taken away the grandfather she'd never known, and her mother.

Despite her losses, these storms somehow had a soothing effect upon her. Perhaps, she mused, it had something to do with energy levels…with the fact that the turbulence raging within her soul found its match in the wild energy of the storm. They were one and the same. In the midst of a storm, she was no longer painfully aware of the disparity between her internal pits of darkness and an external world that glittered with sunshine and clouds of pure fluff.

From her porch swing, Beth heard the sound of a boat pulling into the pier below. Who in the world would be out on the lake at a time like this, she wondered. Had to be someone in trouble. Grabbing Nana's old yellow rain slicker and her flashlight, she carefully opened the porch door. The howling wind and relentless rain pelted her from all directions, making it difficult to proceed along the path. Lightning flashed across the skies, sizzling, producing bolts of thunder that roared across the lake. The trees along the path swayed in the wind. Step by step, she splashed her way toward the pier below.

"Beth!" a voice shouted through the fury of the storm. "Stay there! I'm coming. Just shine your light along the path." It was Jake's voice. Thank God!

Jake was soaked by the time he made it up the hill to the cabin and collapsed in a rocker on the porch. He knew better than to attempt a trip like this when bad weather was supposed to be moving in. He had been determined to pay a visit to that little Canadian island in Pound Net Bay…the one that he returned to again and again over the years. A place where he could be alone to relive the memories. A place where *she* lingered on. He'd sit on their favorite rock overlooking the lake. Here, he rewrote history, over and over again, in his own mind. This time, he never made it to their island. The storm had moved in so quickly that he decided to take shelter at Beth's.

Beth gave him a towel and dry clothes, then seated him before the wood fire in the great room with a snifter of brandy. She stoked the fire and settled into the rocking chair beside him. The storm continued to rage outside as they sat together silently, safe and warm, lost in their respective thoughts. Finally, when he had drifted off to sleep in the rocking chair, she woke him and steered him into her grandmother's bedroom where she covered him with extra blankets and tiptoed out.

Tomorrow, she would tell him about the trunk in the attic, about the discovery of her mother's diaries. Tomorrow, she would ask him to tell her more about her mother. Over the years, Jake had shared so many wonderful stories about Sarah. He had known her perhaps better than anyone else alive. But Beth needed to hear more, much more, as she ventured into the personal journals that her mother had written over thirty years ago.

≈§∾

"Nana?" Beth bolted out of bed early the next morning. It was the smell of coffee percolating and bacon frying that triggered an instant memory of Nana making big breakfasts for her every morning of her life here on the island. "Most important meal of the day," Nana always told her, "rise and shine!" Now, Nana was gone, she remembered…it was Uncle Jake who was already up and about. She had to smile at the thought of Jake making breakfast for her.

The storm was over. The electricity was back on. She realized that she'd slept like a baby cradled in the eye of the storm. The first traces of sunlight flickered through her windows, shimmering over clusters of raindrops huddled together on leaves of green. She wrapped her mother's old robe around her and went down the stairs into the big kitchen.

"Breakfast is served, ma'am," Jake bowed, his eyes twinkling, as he handed her a cup of coffee.

"Jake, you're too good to me," she laughed, pleased to have his company. Sometimes it was nice *not* to eat alone…and he could even cook. He served up two plates filled with scrambled eggs, bacon, and whole wheat toast spread lavishly with Nana's homemade strawberry jam. Together, they devoured their food as they watched several spotted fawns scampering through the yard. A doe stood guard, trying to nudge her silly children back into the woods.

"Oh, before I forget, I need to extend an invitation to you for dinner next Sunday," Jake broke the silence. "At our house in the Falls. Evelyn insists."

Beth almost choked on her coffee. This was totally out of character for Jake's mysterious wife. "What? Why?" she stammered.

"I'm not sure. All I know is that when she called from New York the other day and heard about the episode with your car, she seemed to have a change of heart. She felt bad, she said, and thought it was time to extend a 'welcome home' to you."

"I don't know what to make of this…she has never before wanted to have anything to do with me or my family. She didn't even come to Nana's funeral. It was always as if we weren't good enough for her or something…is that it?"

"I have no idea," he sighed, "and it's not worth worrying about at this point. You know she has always been…well, different. I don't understand her and I never will."

"Still, you have always been such a close family friend—my *Uncle Jake*. But your wife…she was never involved. Never. So why now?"

He smiled gently. "Maybe she's mellowed in her old age," he joked. "Will you come—and not worry about *why now*?"

She agreed, somewhat reluctantly. At least Jake would be there to run interference if problems surfaced. She'd always been curious about Evelyn…intimidated by this formidable woman who seemed to have the power to destroy anyone who got in her way.

As they sipped their coffee, Beth finally shared her exciting news. Her wide eyes sparkled with joy, reflecting just a hint of fear of the unknown, as she blurted out, "I've found my mother's diaries, Jake!"

"You've what?" He almost dropped his cup of coffee, hands trembling. His face suddenly turned pale, as if he'd seen a ghost.

"My mother's diaries! Isn't it wonderful? Now, I can finally discover who she was, what her life was like. Oh, Jake, this is the best thing that could ever happen to me…I think…"

Jake was silent, trying to regain his composure. Sarah's diaries? They still existed after all these years? Oh my God…oh my God!

"What?" She was puzzled at the strange look on his face, his inability to speak.

He abruptly got up from the table and headed out the kitchen door toward the cliff overlooking the lake. There he stood silently, staring into the past. Breathing deeply. Still trying to regain his composure.

She followed, her tattered blue robe fluttering in the breeze that was already coming in off the lake. "Jake, are you OK?"

He nodded slowly, unable to hide the tears in his eyes from her careful gaze. She wrapped her arms around him, comforting this old friend who obviously still cared deeply about her mother. Somehow, this had been a shock for him. They sat down together, side by side, on the edge of the cliff, legs dangling over the waters lapping beneath them. She waited until he was ready to speak.

And finally he did, cautiously. "Yes, I'm shocked, Beth. It's like a beloved ghost from the past has come back. You know I loved your mom…she was the best friend I ever had. I've never forgotten her. You're so much like her…"

"Thanks…I take that as a serious compliment," she tried to lighten the mood.

"I'm just afraid…" He struggled for the right words. "I'm just afraid that those diaries could stir up a lot of things for you—things that you may not want, or need, to know. It's going to hurt, Beth. Damn it, it's going to hurt!"

"I've thought about that. I almost decided *not* to open that trunk, but remember how Nana told me that it held our family secrets? Don't I have an obligation to find these things out? Maybe it's finally time for me to find out who my father is…"

Jake sighed deeply. "Beth, I think you already know. Deep in your heart, you've always known. It's just that you've run from the truth all your life. You didn't want to know before. And I understand why…the truth was buried in those ugly rumors. People can be cruel."

Perhaps, Beth realized, her father's identity was buried deep down in that secret vault of hers, the one where she hid things that were too painful to face. She thought about what Jake had just told her. Did she already know the truth?

Jake finally went on, "And how do you feel about finding out the truth, Beth?"

"I'm not sure," she absentmindedly stripped petals from the wild yellow daisies growing beside her. "I guess my first thought is, why should I care about finding the bastard who left my mother pregnant and alone? The one who didn't have the guts to acknowledge his own daughter? Someone who wasn't interested in being a part of our lives? I can't understand how a father would not want to know his daughter…how he could go through life never supporting her or being there for her. How could my mother have fallen for such a loser?" Taking a deep breath, she was surprised to notice the pile of mutilated yellow petals at her feet.

Taking a deep breath himself, Jake finally responded. "I'd be mad as hell if I were you. I understand that. But you need to understand that there could be another side to this story. There may be more here than you know…things that could even change the way you feel…"

"Not likely! You know who he is, don't you? And it almost sounds like you are defending him in some way...can that be? Jake, why haven't you told me before?" Angry tears began to flow freely down her cheeks, tears that had bubbled and sometimes boiled beneath the surface for so many years. Tears that she had rarely allowed herself to shed. Now, she was so close to the truth. And she was scared, scared to death, at what she might discover.

"Yes, I know...of course, I know," he began slowly, his eyes locked on the horizon. "I was always going to tell you, but there never seemed to be a right time. I tried, you know, but you didn't want to hear it then..."

She held her breath, clutching the sides of the rock that she was perched upon, waiting for him to finally reveal the truth about her father.

Instead, he changed the subject. As they sat side by side, focusing on crystals of sunlight bouncing across the lake, he reverted back to Sarah's diaries. "You know," he reflected, "your mother used to spend hours sitting in that gazebo on the point. She wrote in those diaries of hers, and she wrote beautiful poetry. She was so talented, a born writer. Who knows what she might have become if..." his voice trailed off once more.

Beth released her death grip on the rock. This was apparently not going to be the moment of revelation. She listened to Jake and tried to imagine her mother writing in the gazebo. "That's where I'll read her diaries—in the gazebo," she decided. "Maybe I'll even publish some of her poems someday, Jake, as a tribute to her. First, I need to understand who she really was, and why..."

"You will, when the time is right. I have no doubt of that," he smiled at her tenderly as he patted her hand. "It's all about timing. Life is all about timing. The problem is that we don't always understand the concept of time and how important it is."

Jake glanced at his watch, realizing he had to get back to the office to meet a client. As he stood to leave, Beth couldn't help asking, "Is there anything more that you want to tell me before you leave? About my father, I mean."

"Please, Beth. Let your mother speak first. She deserves to be the one to tell you. After you've read her diaries, *then* we will talk. I promise. All I can tell you now," he hesitated for a moment, "is this: please try not to judge until you've heard the whole story. I will also tell you that your father loved your mother more than life itself. And he has always loved you, from afar. You need to understand that life is messy sometimes, Beth. Complicated. And people aren't perfect. Sometimes we make mistakes, bad mistakes." He was afraid he'd said more than he should have. "Now, just let your mother speak…"

As Jake pulled away from the dock, he saw her waving good-bye, a trace of a smile upon her face. His heart ached for her, for what she would soon be facing in the pages of her mother's diaries. He hoped she would be able to understand, to forgive.

"When one door of happiness closes, another opens,
but often we look so long at the closed door
that we do not see the one which has opened for us."
Louisa May Alcott

Chapter Eleven

Jake's words played over and over again in Beth's mind as she hiked back up the trail. Her father had loved them…but he'd made mistakes, Jake told her. *But…if my father loved us, why? Why?* Despite her curiosity, she was having second thoughts about delving into her mother's past. There must be some sordid secrets hidden in the pages of those diaries. Why else, she wondered, had this been hidden from her for so long?

After throwing on a pair of faded jeans and a T-shirt, she hiked the trail to the gazebo with her notebook and a cup of coffee. Here, she threw herself into making a to-do list—of all the things she must accomplish before she returned to the diaries. To-do lists had always served a purpose in her life. They helped her to focus on trivial chores so she could avoid dealing with big issues. They kept her busy, feeling productive as she compulsively checked completed items off her list. Items like *pick up the dry cleaning*—something she no longer had to worry about.

She did, after all, have some business to take care of now. She began scribbling items on her list: call attorney re: status of divorce/alimony settlement; balance checkbook; weed garden; check on dates for Emily's visit; to mainland for supplies; paint gazebo; and so on.

Yes, before she began her journey into the past, it was only fitting that she would finally restore her mother's gazebo to its original glory. This would be a beautiful day to begin, she decided. Armed with Papa's old hammer, a handful of rusty nails, paint scraper, and a crow bar, she tackled the project with a vengeance. Hard work should help to drive her problems away, not the least of which was the lingering memory of the lipstick threat smeared on her windshield.

She was so busy hammering that she did not at first notice a boat approaching her island. Someone was waving at her, coming in closer, now idling, with a big smile upon his face. It was Seth, the neighbor she'd met that traumatic day at the Thunderbird.

"Hello, neighbor," he called out cheerfully. "Looks like you've got yourself a project there," he observed.

"Hello," she stammered, "ah, yes, I'm, ah, just fixing up the old family gazebo." Relaxing a bit, she couldn't help returning his magnetic smile.

"If you need a helping hand or anything else, you know I'm just across the bay," he began carefully. He was well aware that this woman was easily frightened. He wondered what she was hiding from, why she had come home to Rainy Lake—alone. Jake had always hired him to cut and stack a winter's supply of firewood for Nana. He wondered if he'd be doing that for Beth now.

"Thanks," she replied softly, her eyes carefully avoiding his. She remembered the eerie connection she'd felt the moment she met him. As if she'd always known him. It had unsettled and confused her.

"The reason I stopped by is that I'm on my way to the mainland to pick up a few supplies. If there's anything you need…or if you care to go in with me…" He paused for some kind of a response from her.

Beth pondered his offer. She was planning to make a trip to the mainland for white gazebo paint. After the lipstick threat incident, she was feeling a bit apprehensive. Still, she wasn't about to risk going in with Seth, nice as he may seem. Too nice, perhaps…they were the ones to watch out for.

He waited patiently. "I don't bite, you know," he grinned at her. "Besides, your Uncle Jake even likes me!"

"I'm sorry. I've got a lot on my mind and some things I really need to do here. But…"

"But?"

"I could use two gallons of high-gloss white exterior paint—if it's not out of your way," she finally blurted out, shocking herself. That would mean, however, that he'd need to pull up to the island to get her money, and again, to bring the paint back. She almost wished she could take her words back, but it was too late to do so without appearing to be incredibly foolish.

"No problem. I'll be back with the paint in several hours." He waved, hit the throttle on his boat, and roared away from her island.

True to his word, he was back at her dock in several hours. She ran a comb through her wind-tossed hair when she heard his boat coming in, and met him at the dock with cash in hand. It would have been neighborly to invite him up for a cup of coffee or a glass of lemonade, but she could not bring herself to do so. In fact, she was careful not to touch his hand as she handed him her money. She reminded herself that it was important to keep a respectable distance between them. It was, however, nice to have a neighbor close by, someone she could call upon for help. Just in case Rob ever showed up here…or a bear broke into her place…or she had an accident.

Beth thanked him, adding, "I owe you a favor, Seth. I mean, if you ever need anything when I go in to town, or something…" Why did his dark, lingering gaze rattle her into foolish stammering?

"Hmmm," he hesitated, "now that you mention it, your grand-mother always used to make me a blueberry pie with berries I'd picked over on my island. The berries are ripening already, looks like a good crop this year. Bet you can't bake blueberry pies like she could!" He stood casually in his boat rocking on the waves, eyes sparking with mischief.

His lighthearted banter relaxed her enough to tell him about her childhood days picking blueberries on his island. And yes, she had spent many summers at her grandmother's side learning to make her famous pies. They laughed together, enjoying each other's company— from a safe distance.

"Then we've got a deal, eh? I'll let you know when the berries are ready. If you feel like picking with me, you're more than welcome. Got to harvest the crop, you know, before the bears do."

With that, he was gone, careful not to overstay his welcome. Per-haps, he thought, she was simply a loner like he was—craving solitude, space, time to think, to create, just to be. Nevertheless, he knew that even loners needed a little company once in a while. Not too much, just a little…

She watched his boat skimming across the channel and into the bay that flowed between their wilderness islands.

❧❧

Over the next few days, she scraped and painted the gazebo. She planted and watered a sea of colorful flowers that flowed around the perimeter and cascaded from hanging pots. She loved the smell of the earth, the feel of soil slipping through her fingers as she tenderly placed the young plants in the garden. As she planted, she thought of Nana and of Mama. They'd be pleased, she smiled to herself, as she admired her work. Jake had delivered a flat of plants for her yesterday. He'd chosen mostly yellows—Nana's favorite color. A parade of sunny marigolds now swayed in the breeze beside stately white and yellow daisies, golden begonias, and cascading white petunias. Beth also planted several Fire Island hostas in the shady nooks. They had brilliant yellow leaves accented by light red petioles.

As she worked, she could see Seth's boat anchored on his island. Sometimes she caught a glimpse of him down by the dock. If she ever needed help, she figured that she could flash a light from her gazebo. He would surely see it across the water. And somehow she knew beyond a doubt that he would be there for her.

By Saturday night, the gazebo was ready—ready for her to move in with her mother's diaries. She'd found an old wicker rocking chair that she'd cleaned up and painted, along with a trunk that served as a table. A battery-operated lantern hung from the peak of the ceiling. That night as the sun slipped into the lake, she watched it from her gazebo, celebrating with several glasses of red wine. It was a peaceful summer evening on Rainy Lake. Loons called to each other across the lake, their wails and tremolos echoing in the distance. The rhythm of the waves splashing against the rocky shoreline below mesmerized her. She watched the stars emerge in the blackening sky, shining more brightly than she had remembered. A shooting star streaked across the horizon. The only other light that she could see was a soft glow emanating from Seth's cabin across the lake. She wondered what he was doing tonight…probably sitting down on his beach gazing up at the stars just like she was. And she wondered why she wondered…

As she hiked back to the house under a canopy of glittering stars, a wolf howled in the distance. She breathed deeply, absorbing the fresh scent of the sleeping lake. Life was almost beginning to feel manageable again.

≈∽

Beth's sense of tranquility was soon shattered, however, as she fell into a deep sleep that night.

Once again, she is a little girl plucking delicate petals, one by one, from a field of wild daisies. Yellow daisies flutter through the sky, cascading into her lap. Falling like a gentle rain…like a child's tears. "She loves me…loves me not," a tiny voice from long ago whispers mournfully. Carefully, she removes each silky petal, holding her breath, telling herself that it doesn't really matter. She can keep on picking petals until she someday finds the answer that she seeks.

Little Beth cautiously gazes up at billowy clouds of iridescent cotton. They float through an azure blue sky, changing shapes, teasing her. She remembers the times that she and her mother lay together amongst fields of daisies, watching the clouds overhead. They saw faces, wild horses, ghosts. But Beth is alone now, searching for her mother's face within the shifting cloud formations. She desperately needs to see her mother beaming down upon her, telling her that it's OK, that she still loves her. Perhaps she still has a mother after all, like all her little friends do. Somewhere…but where?

"Loves me, loves me not," the little girl continues to chant. *But she left me! She went away—without me!* Scalding tears begin to flow, mingling with piles of daisy petals scattered around her shrinking frame. She squashes the golden heart of the daisy like a bug, stomping it into the ground. Glaring at the heavens above, she decides that God must have gone away, too. "Loves me *not!*" she cries out, mutilating another daisy heart. And another, and another.

A loud voice suddenly booms from above as a gust of wind churns piles of daisy remnants into a cyclone that swirls around the angry little girl. "Damn it, girl! She always loved you. She still does," the voice echoes across the darkening sky as bolts of lightning slash through the heavens.

"Loves me?" a small voice whimpers as the lightning dances around her in narrowing circles. She curls up on the ground, wrapped snugly in a cloak of daisies. The dream fades into total blackness.

Beth thrashed about all night—still picking daisies. Still searching for answers, for love, for someone to hold what was left of that little girl.

❦

Snuggling deeper beneath her quilt, clutching her pillow, she had no desire to get up and face the day. Not today. A gentle rain drizzled on her world, past and present. The future didn't look so promising either. It seemed that each time her life began to improve, something brought her back down again. If it wasn't Rob, it was a memory from the past, or a black hole that threatened to suck her in and consume her. That old cycle of good days followed by bad days seemed to follow her around like a plague wherever she went. Today, she had foolishly agreed to go into town for Sunday dinner with Jake and Evelyn—the last thing in the world that she wanted to do. Why wouldn't people just leave her alone? Why couldn't she just hide from the world in her cozy bed, cuddled up with a good book and a cup of tea?

"Damn it, girl!" she recalled the voice from her dream. "Get out of bed and quit feeling sorry for yourself," she scolded herself as she padded downstairs to start the coffee. She'd need her raingear for the trip to the mainland, and a thermos of hot coffee. Probably wouldn't hurt to throw an overnight bag into the boat—just in case the early morning drizzle turned into something worse.

The life of an islander, she reminded herself. She'd been well-trained in wilderness survival as a child. She'd hated it then, she remembered. Was it so different now, she wondered? She thought she'd grown to love the island and all that it stood for. Or was that just another illusion, like so much of her life? *What was real—and what was not? Who was to be the judge of that?* Perhaps she viewed her world through a different lens than others did…was that wrong? Did it really matter?

Gray skies dribbled outside her kitchen window. Minnesota Public Radio crackled with interference from the weather. Beth could almost feel the reassuring presence of her dear grandmother sitting across the table from her. This morning, Nana would have patted her hand reassuringly, telling her that it was just a dream. Some things never changed… Perhaps she would never really be alone, Beth realized—not here on this island where she was blessed with so many memories of her family. Good ones. Bad ones. Horrible ones. Yet, a common thread of belonging seemed to weave through all those misty memories of the past. A thread to hang on to as she struggled to find herself.

> "Things do not change,
> we do."
> *Henry David Thoreau*

Chapter Twelve

$\mathcal{J}$ ake paced back and forth along the front porch of Evelyn's house in International Falls, waiting for a glimpse of Beth's vehicle coming down Riverside Drive. Evelyn's house—that's how he always thought of it, although he did live here part of the time. He enjoyed strolling through the vine-covered English gardens that came to life under her magic touch. He didn't belong here, however—not in a house full of fragile antiques and porcelain cups and saucers that she collected from her trips around the world. It was a beautifully decorated house to show off to the world—but too formal for him to live in comfortably.

No, he didn't belong here…certainly not living with this woman who happened to be his wife of forty-five years. Forty-five years, my God, he thought to himself. *I've wasted most of my life living a lie.* After all these years, he still didn't know her. He didn't want to. And he sure as hell didn't like being here. He belonged in his rustic cabin on Houska's Point in Ranier. Rainy Lake was his life, his love, flowing with memories that gave him the strength to go on alone in this world.

Puffing on his trademark hard-carved wood pipe, he stared into the light drizzle. What was he *thinking*, he scolded himself, when he encouraged Beth to accept his wife's invitation to Sunday dinner? He should have known better. He wondered what the real reason was for Evelyn's insistence on bringing Beth into her home after all these years. She was already into her second Brandy Alexander—at four o'clock on a Sunday afternoon. She'd started shortly after she returned from church, after giving the cook final instructions for the fancy dinner that she'd planned.

❧

Beth was running a little late. Her boat trip to the mainland had taken longer than usual. She'd decided to take a longer route through sheltered passages that would provide some protection from the wind and rain. After docking at the Thunderbird, she ran into the ladies' room to comb her hair and reapply the makeup that had washed away in the rain. She stripped off her rain gear, exposing white capris and a light pink summer blouse that set off her auburn hair. Yes, she decided, she looked presentable enough for her Sunday dinner with the mysterious Evelyn. It was going to be a good day, she tried to tell herself, especially once she knew that her vehicle was fine. No lipstick threats this time. No flat tires.

As she pulled up to the curb of the impressive white colonial mansion, she was reassured to find Jake on the porch waiting for her. But as she got closer, she noticed lines of tension in his tan, leathery face. "Is everything OK, Jake?" she asked after giving him a hug.

"I hope so. Just be careful what you say, Beth. Evelyn seems to be, well, a little under the weather. She can't handle her booze anymore. I hope to hell this wasn't a bad idea…"

The main door suddenly flew open, framing a perfectly coifed, white-haired woman with bright red lips. She was dressed elegantly in an expensive white linen suit set off with gold jewelry. "Oh, do come in, my dear," Evelyn gushed, reaching out to give her a welcoming hug, as if she'd known her all her life. Stepping aside, she wobbled a bit in her high heels as she led them into the library where they would visit before dinner. Evelyn seated herself in an ornate Victorian loveseat facing the fireplace, gesturing to Beth to sit beside her. Jake stood by the fireplace, fidgeting with his pipe.

"Darling?" Evelyn swirled her empty glass in the air, ice cubes clinking against glass. A sign apparently that she was ready for another drink.

Darling? Jake chuckled to himself. Since when had she ever called him "darling"? She called him many other things—most of which should not be shared with company.

"I said, *darling*," she flashed an exaggerated smile at her amused husband. "I think we all need a little drink here to toast Beth's homecoming, don't you?"

Jake shuffled slowly toward the leather bar, afraid of what another drink would do to his wife's behavior. She was up to something, he realized, and it probably wasn't good.

"How about a glass of wine?" he suggested.

"Brandy Alexander for me, sweetheart," Evelyn sang out. Beth and Jake each opted for a glass of Chablis. As Jake mixed his wife a weak drink and poured their wine, he listened to their conversation in amazement.

Beth was also puzzled as Evelyn raved on and on about what a wonderful husband Jake had been to her over the years, how much they still loved and cherished each other. That certainly wasn't the picture that Jake had painted of their marriage, nor the impression that Beth had developed.

"Enough of this, Evelyn. Let's talk about Beth. She's our guest," Jake interjected as he passed out the drinks and settled himself very carefully within the delicately carved arms of a cherrywood Queen Anne chair, circa 1750. God only knew what she'd paid for this extravagance. Not that it mattered.

"Here, here," Evelyn giggled, raising her glass into the air. "I propose a toast to Beth. Welcome home, my dear! Such a pleasure to have you visit your old home again—although I'm sure you will be anxious to leave once you've had your fill of this...this, how can I say it...dreadful place..." she sighed with disgust. She was beginning to slur her words, Jake noticed.

"Here, here. I can do better than that," Jake interrupted his wife before she tumbled down any further into her destructive train of thought. "I want to wish Beth the very best in her new island home! It's wonderful to have you back. We're here for you, you know, anything that you need."

"Thanks," Beth mumbled, feeling trapped in the middle of something that she didn't understand. "I am happy to be home. I love it here, and I intend to stay!" She raised her glass into the air, unaware that she'd just dropped a bombshell into the room.

A moment of shocked silence followed Beth's announcement. Evelyn's smile turned hard, twisted into a snarl, as she gulped her drink. Trying to compose herself, she turned on her synthetic smile once again. "My dear girl," she began slowly in her best candy-coated voice, "you cannot be serious about staying out there on that dreadful, isolated island. Why, Jake and I would be worried sick about you out there all by yourself. We simply cannot allow it, for your own good, you know. You've been through so much, poor child...you won't find what you need here. I can tell you that from personal experience." Her smile was fading fast.

"I think that is entirely up to Beth. We can't make that decision for her," Jake interrupted.

"But...but you need to know that Jake and I may have other plans for that island," Evelyn blurted out her real concern to Beth, ignoring her husband. The liquor was seeping through her façade, down into the depths where her ulterior motives usually remained hidden from the rest of the world.

Jake and Beth were both stunned. Somehow, Evelyn knew that Jake legally owned that island, and she was not about to let it go. She, of course, had no way of knowing that paperwork was already in place for Jake to quitclaim the island back to Beth. Perhaps the sooner the better, Jake realized, before Evelyn tried to stake a claim on it by virtue of their so-called marriage.

Jake's green eyes flashed with anger. This was too much—more than he was going to tolerate from this woman, more than he would allow Beth to be subjected to. "It is Beth's island, Evelyn," his voice was firm. "It is hers to live on forever or do whatever she damn well pleases. And *that* is final." He rose from his chair, staring silently, defiantly, into the dying embers of the fire.

Evelyn laughed harshly, swinging her drink carelessly through the air as she tried to focus on Beth. "Now, isn't that just like my *loving* husband? Always taking care of others—instead of the one he should be thinking of. Always looking out for the underdog... You have no idea how much time he's wasted running back and forth, back and forth, to that damn island to help your grandmother, the poor dear, God bless her soul," she rambled on stupidly.

Beth drew her breath in sharply, as if she'd been slapped in the face. She was shocked at the audacity of this woman. *Underdog?* So that's what she thought of her family. They weren't good enough for her, just as Beth had suspected. She realized that Evelyn was drunk, but that didn't excuse her behavior. It was useless to even respond, she decided.

"Enough, Evelyn!" Jake reprimanded her sharply, to no avail.

"But," she sloshed her drink onto the plush carpeting, addressing Beth once again, "but, if you decide to stay on that godforsaken island over the winter, my dear, you have no idea what you're in for. You'll be alone—stranded. Nobody to help you. Don't expect old Jake, the big hero here, to rescue you. You know, he's too old for much of anything anymore..." her voice trailed off.

Ignoring his wife's remarks, well aware of Beth's growing discomfort, Jake jumped into the one-sided conversation. "Beth, have you had a chance to meet Seth, your neighbor?"

"Yes, I have," Beth replied, relieved to have him steer the conversation into a safer direction. "Seems like a nice man. It's nice to have someone close by—you know, in case I ever needed anything."

"Seth!" Evelyn exclaimed loudly. "You mean that lazy Indian who lives on that blueberry island? Doesn't even have a job. Sure wouldn't trust one of his kind. You know what they say…"

"What *who says,* Evelyn?" Jake shot back at her. "I know him well, and I can tell you that he's a wonderful young man—an artist who sells his work over the Internet. He loves nature and has a great deal of respect for the traditions of his Ojibwe people. I'd trust that man with my life. And I have no doubt that he'd be there in a heartbeat if Beth ever needed help."

"You're such a fool," Evelyn roared. "You really think he's going to…going to…save her from a winter like—what year was that? You know, that winter when the islanders were all stuck on their islands, starving, because the lake was un-impasse…hell, you know what I mean."

Beth vividly remembered that winter of 1978. She was ten, living on the island with her grandmother. They'd been stranded for two months, unable to even snowshoe across the lake. An unusually heavy snow load had blanketed the lake early that year, causing massive amounts of slush that would not freeze. The ice roads on which they all relied to get back and forth to the mainland weren't yet plowed. The ice wasn't thick enough to support the plow trucks. It was impossible, Beth recalled, to even attempt crossing the lake by snowmobile or ski-plane.

"It was 1978," Beth plunged into this rapidly deteriorating conversation. "I was stranded on our island, alone with my grandmother. It was an adventure that I'll always remember. We got along fine. We didn't starve because we had friends who supported us. I remember one good friend who flew over our place, dropping red onion bags full of groceries, supplies, and mail from his airplane. You know, there are lots of good people here, Evelyn. People who care. That's what Rainy Lake is all about—good friends, good neighbors."

"Bullshit!" The prim and proper Evelyn Carter O'Connell ended the conversation with a loud hiccup.

"Maybe it's time for me to go?" Beth whispered to Jake as the cook came in to announce that dinner was ready to be served. At that instant, a bolt of lightning slashed through the summer sky as rain and hail began to pelt the windows of the library. The electricity suddenly went off as the city's severe weather warning sirens began to wail. Jake found a flashlight and lit kerosene lamps throughout the house. Another summer storm in the northland. Obviously not a good time for Beth or anyone else to leave.

"Dinner's ready," he calmly announced. "Let's eat while it's still warm." And they did—by candlelight as the storm raged on. Silence permeated the dinner table as they listened to updated weather reports squawking over the battery-operated weather scanner. There was no way for Beth to return to her island home in this weather. Jake would not, however, allow her to drive to the Holiday Inn where she planned to spend the night. It was not safe out there in this storm to go anyplace. He insisted that she stay with them, in the guest room upstairs. Evelyn had nothing to say. She slumped over her dinner plate, tears clouding her eyes, trying to figure out what she'd done wrong.

"Will you be here?" Beth asked Jake quietly before she headed up the winding wood-carved staircase, flashlight and overnight bag in hand. "Yes, I'll be in my room upstairs," he assured her. "First room on the left, just down the hall from yours. I'm sorry, Beth, so sorry…"

"It's OK," she sighed wearily, "it's not your fault. I just need some sleep." Such a beautiful home, she thought to herself, as she flopped down on the bed in the antique-filled guestroom. Such a tragedy that nobody here was able to appreciate all that it had to offer.

Despite the storm raging outside her window and the nastiness of the evening, Beth fell into a deep sleep within minutes. She wasn't sure how long she'd slept, or where she was, when she was jolted out of a deep sleep by angry voices filtering up the stairway. Jake and Evelyn, she realized, in her sleepy state of mind. It didn't help to pull the pillow over her head. Besides, she needed to know what was happening here—obviously something worse than she had imagined, something that she was somehow involved in…

"You bastard!" Evelyn's voice was accentuated by the sound of breaking glass—possibly a glass being hurled into the wall.

"Go to bed *now*," Jake ordered his wife. "You are goddamned drunk and you made a fool of yourself tonight, Evelyn. How could you do this to Beth? How could you?"

"Beth?" she screamed hysterically. "What about me? What about *me*, Jake? You have humiliated me—made a fool of me all my life. You've tarnished my family's name, ruined my life with your foolishness."

He ignored her outburst as he had so many times in the past.

"Don't you dare ignore me! You listen to me, Jake! Just look what you've done—you're a liar, a cheat—and you're going to burn in hell, you know. You're not even sorry, are you? After all you've done, you don't even give a shit, do you?"

"I have no regrets," Jake mumbled under his breath, "none, except that you have kept me from spending my life with the only woman I've ever loved."

"What? Did you say something?" she stared at him with wild, red-rimmed eyes.

"I have nothing to say to you, Evelyn," his voice was cold as ice.

Within seconds her rage tumbled down into grief and self-pity. "What happened to *us*, Jake?" she began to sob uncontrollably.

"*Us*? There never was an *us*, Evelyn. I tried. God only knows how hard I tried. It never happened. You never let it happen. What the hell did you expect?"

"Lying bastard!" More breaking glass. Then silence.

Beth heard his footsteps slowly ascending the stairs and disappearing into the first room on the left. The only remaining sound was the sobbing of the woman downstairs. The sound of an intoxicated woman screaming into the stormy night, "Why don't you love me anymore? Goddamn it, Jake, why don't you love me?"

∾ô↔

Why don't you love me? Jake repeated her words, shaking his head in disbelief. How could anyone love this vicious drunken woman, he asked himself? It was hard to believe that she was the same woman he had married forty-five years ago. She'd been beautiful then—in fact, dazzling. She was elegant, well-educated, and had traveled the world extensively. She was the daughter of a wealthy, prominent family from New York—a family that Jake's father had desperately wanted to create a business merger with...and he had, shortly after their marriage. Both families had strongly encouraged their marriage. And Evelyn had been anxious to marry him.

Had she loved him then, he wondered? Had he ever really loved her? He had to think long and hard before he could honestly answer that question. Perhaps he'd been attracted to her then, he had to admit to himself. An old memory floated into his mind—one of their wedding day. It had been an elaborate affair, and Evelyn had been a stunningly beautiful bride. He'd beamed with pride as his wife-to-be came down the aisle on her father's arm. Her face was radiant as she looked adoringly at him, promising to love him forever. Yes, he probably did love her then, he realized. It all depended on how you defined the mysterious word *love*. Then one day, years later, he accidentally discovered what real love was all about… Still, he had to admit that he and Evelyn did have some happy days together during the first few years. They'd traveled to exotic places, danced beneath the stars on a beach in Hawaii, toured King Ludwig's castles in Germany. Then things changed…

He remembered a heart-to-heart talk he'd had with his father shortly before the wedding. Jake was having second thoughts about going through with it, consumed with nagging doubts that something was missing. This was a lifetime commitment, and that scared the hell out of him. How could a person know what lay ahead years down the line? How could he promise to love and honor her forever, whatever that meant?

Jake had cornered his father in the library where his father spent most of his time alone, working at his desk and drinking. Jake had been careful to approach him early in the evening before he'd had too much scotch. His father had listened, tapping his foot impatiently, anxious to get back to more important business. "This wedding will *not* be cancelled, son, just because you've got cold feet!" his father growled. "We will *not* let the Carter family down, do you hear me?"

"But what if I'm not sure that I love her the way I should? Is this going to last?"

John O'Connell shook his head in frustration. "Love is not the issue here. What the hell is *love*, anyway? Nothing but a temporary illusion. Believe me, it changes over time. Always does. What counts is if you can get along, raise a nice family together. That's all anyone can expect, Jake…" his father sighed as he stared into his own past. Jake now wondered if there had been something missing in his father's life, just like there was in his. Maybe that's why he drank—why he'd been abusive at times.

"That's it? That's all there is, Dad?" Jake sounded disappointed.

"Believe me. Besides, Evelyn will be a wonderful mother for your children, my grandchildren," his father winked at him.

You were wrong, Dad, so wrong, Jake silently chastised his deceased father. *There is more…I found it, too late. And children? What children?*

A lonely tear slid down his cheek as he thought back to the baby that he and Evelyn had conceived together during the second year of their marriage—the one she had aborted without his knowledge, certainly without his consent. He'd been furious when he found out. They'd always planned to have two or three children. She knew how badly he wanted children. But she'd deceived him all along. At the time of the abortion, she finally informed him that she had no intention of becoming a mother—not ever. As she put it, "I don't even like kids, and I am not willing to be burdened with a snot-nosed brat." Shortly thereafter, the ice queen had retreated to her own bedroom for the duration of their marriage. She told him that as a good Catholic, she didn't believe in using birth control. In all those years, she had rarely joined her husband in bed or showed him any affection. Jake clenched his fists as he sat on the edge of his bed in the dark. What the hell did she expect?

For years, he'd looked upon their marriage as a financial arrangement that had benefited both sides of the family. The business merger had made millions for both families, including Jake and Evelyn. Jake had used his stock dividends to invest in recreational real estate and had done very well for himself over the years, amassing a small fortune through his clever dealings. Evelyn had spent lavishly and traveled the world.

The money never bought them happiness, however. There were too many strings attached, too much family interference. In fact, it was the family business that had blocked Jake's one chance for happiness, as he saw it. Forty years ago, he had begged Evelyn for a divorce from their loveless marriage. She had refused, determined to punish him for perceived wrongs by preventing him from finding love elsewhere. She'd convinced both sides of the family to apply pressure on Jake to stay in the marriage. If he persisted, he was informed that he would be stripped of his inheritance—and he would be held accountable for Evelyn's suddenly fragile health. She'd conveniently suffered several nervous breakdowns—at least that's what she called them. This would happen every time Jake threatened to leave. Reluctantly, he stayed, at least temporarily, until he could find a way out of this deteriorating situation. Later, it no longer mattered. Nothing mattered.

⚬⚬⚬

Down the hall, Beth could not stand to hear any more. What, she wondered, could Jake have possibly done to deserve such wrath from Evelyn? Or was she simply delusional and drunk? All Beth wanted was to escape to her island as soon as possible. She would leave this mansion of horrors by daylight, before Evelyn emerged from her drunken sleep…even before a weary Jake awoke to face another agonizing day. This was not her responsibility. She pulled the pillow over her head, trying to drown out the wails from the woman below. Total silence from Jake's bedroom down the hall.

Before dawn, Beth tiptoed quietly out the door, turned on the headlights of her SUV, and headed for the Thunderbird to retrieve her launch. She was out on the lake in time to see the sun rising over Rainy Lake.

"There's a whisper in the night wind,
there's a star agleam to guide us,
and the wind is calling, calling – "let us go.""
Robert Service, Alaskan Poet

Chapter Thirteen

It was Sarah's turn to speak—finally. She had waited from beyond the grave for thirty-four years now. Waiting for her beloved daughter to finally discover long-held family secrets that were buried within the old trunk in the attic.

Beth's hands trembled as she retrieved her mother's diaries and carried them to the gazebo. It felt like a funeral procession to the family graveyard. Maybe it was... She opened the first journal, instinctively rubbing her index finger over her mother's handwritten words. This was a part of her mother that she needed to feel, to absorb, to hold onto.

May 25, 1964
Dear Diary,

I've just graduated from high school, ready to embark upon my journey in life. I've thought long and hard about the next steps in my life...I love writing, have written poetry all my life. A part of me would love to attend college and major in creative writing. I want to write novels someday, to become a published author! Mama has even encouraged me to go to college, especially after the high school counselor told her that I had potential and could get scholarships to attend. The problem is that I don't think I can leave Mama alone on the island, not after all she has done to raise me here. Since Papa drowned, it's been just the two of us. I'm all that she has. How can I just leave her?

As for Mama, she will <u>never</u> leave this island—not until she's hauled away in a pine box! This is where she belongs—with Papa and her memories of him. So sad...they loved each other so much. Why did God choose to take him away so soon? I pray to God that someday I will find a man like Papa to marry and have children with. Where will I find <u>my</u> man, though, when I rarely get off the island? Perhaps it will happen someday...when the time is right.

Anyway, I've decided to get a job instead of going to college. Jake O'Connell, a real estate broker with an office in Ranier, has just hired me as his secretary. It sounds like a very interesting job with decent pay. Mama likes Mr. O'Connell and feels he will be a good person to work for. I start next week—my first job!

Mama and I are going into Ranier today to find a little cabin for me to rent near the real estate office. When the weather is bad—and especially once winter sets in, I will need a place to stay on the mainland. I can go home to stay with Mama on the weekends. One of her friends, Ethel, has a group of cabins that she rents out. Ethel lives in the big house on the hill overlooking the cabins. So she's close by if I ever have a problem. I don't need a babysitter, however, so I hope Mama doesn't expect Ethel to keep an eye on me. That would be just too humiliating! I think Mama's having a hard time letting me go.

Beth sighed deeply, thinking about Emily and how hard it had been—still was—to let her go. She gazed out at the seagulls circling over the lake below. It felt almost surreal, yet so comforting, to hear her mother speaking through the words that she had scrawled so long ago. *It feels like she's writing to me, for posterity,* Beth thought to herself. The diary included details, names, and places that future generations needed to know. Beth read on, unable to pry herself away from the pages of her mother's life.

July 1, 1964
Dear Diary,
Where have I been for the past month? Busily settling into my new life—my new job, my very first home. And I love it! The job is exciting and very rewarding. Mr. O'Connell—Jake—is a wonderful boss. He's busy listing and selling real estate so he's gone a lot. I'm in charge of the office and am being given more and more responsibilities. I thrive on challenges. He's even letting me write the real estate ads and is very pleased with what I'm doing. My goal is to create a written picture of the property, one that entices readers to call us and hopefully buy the property. I try hard to write ads that present a lifestyle that will appeal to homebuyers. That's what we're really selling—a lifestyle. Jake has promised to take me along on some of his listings so I can take photographs with the new camera that Mama bought me for my high school graduation. When I think about it, this job fits me perfectly—I'm writ-

ing and taking photos. And when I go back to my little cabin at night, I still write poetry and study my writing books. It's a wonderful life!

Let me tell you about my home, dear diary. It's a tiny white clapboard cabin perched on a rocky ledge that overlooks Rainy Lake. The cabin and its little porch are anchored on a haphazard pile of ancient, moss-covered rocks that were tossed into strange formations by a glacier thousands of years ago. I can climb down the boulders to my very own secluded beach that is sheltered by two rocky points jutting out into the lake. As I look out across the big lake, I see Canada on the other side. I see the church steeple of the Canadian Mission Church piercing the blue sky above. At night, the steeple glows, changing colors amidst some of the most glorious sunsets I have ever seen.

My one-room cabin is rustic and furnished simply. An old wood trunk sits below the large window that spans the entire front wall of my little cabin. There's a built-in corner cabinet with glass doors where I stash my dishes and groceries, a little wood table with two chairs, a small stove, a mini-refrigerator, and a three-tiered bookshelf full of my books and writing materials. Ethel has decorated the cabin with eagle feathers, birchbark baskets, and Indian artifacts that were found along the beach. (There once was an Indian village just down the shore from my home.) Small paintings of loons, white pelicans, and eagles adorn the walls. Someday, I will sketch a seagull that I will add to the collection. Oh, as for Ethel, she's very nice. She's there if I need her, but she doesn't interfere in my life or watch me through her binoculars!

One of the things that I love about my tiny home is that I can lie in bed at night, snuggled in my down-filled quilt, and watch the northern lights. I wake up in the morning to the sunrise streaming in through the big window. At night, I can look out at the stars and listen to the waves. I never close the curtains at night—I want to let the wonders of nature into my home, not shut them out. I need to be as close to the lake as I can possibly be! It's a lot like living on the island. But here, I can just walk across the dirt road to Jake's real estate office on Houska's Point. I can walk to the beach, to the store, or to Grandma's Pantry for breakfast or lunch.

Speaking of breakfast, I need to run. Jake is taking me out for breakfast this morning, Saturday morning, to celebrate a big sale we just closed. He says that my ad played a big part in attracting the wealthy New York family that purchased this exclusive Rainy Lake island estate. After a hike around the village this morning, I'm ready for a platter of blueberry and wild rice pancakes.

Beth reluctantly closed her mother's diaries, lost in the past, a past that she needed to learn much more about. It would be a good day, she decided, to run into town to pick up her mail at the post office. After that, she could begin retracing her mother's footsteps—the ones she left behind thirty-six years ago in the little village of Ranier, Minnesota. Perhaps she'd pay Jake a visit if he was in his office.

The big lake was calm today with just a whisper of a breeze ruffling the feathers of a sultry summer day. Sunbathers lounged on the deck of the Thunderbird, sipping chilled drinks, cooling off in the lake. Beth tied her boat up in its usual place at the pier and headed into the lodge for a glass of lemonade. She was becoming a regular, warmly greeted by the staff and other regular customers who hung out here. It felt good to be a part of this little world once again after so many years. She could think of worse fates than working here again during the summers, if she had to get a job someday.

Soon she was on the road to Ranier. This village made her feel at home. It was small, friendly, a place where dogs ran loose and every-one knew their names. A place where people didn't need to lock their doors. An old-fashioned main street was lined with vine-covered, brick-and-wood-framed storefronts preserved from another era. It was the kind of place that stirred a deep sense of nostalgia for a simpler life with fewer expectations. Yet, it was also a place with a colorful history going back to prohibition days, when bootleggers smuggled whiskey from Canada into the United States across the ninety-five-year-old can-tilevered railroad bridge. The railroad still played a major role in the local economy, with many trains crossing the old bridge that spanned two countries each day. The historic railroad depot remained a focal point for the community—a bridge between past and present, between yesterday's illegal whiskey runs and today's intensive homeland secu-rity efforts.

First stop, Beth reminded herself, was the post office. Mail delivery to the islands had ended the year she was born, 1968, when the last Rainy Lake supply boat ceased operations. However, she had fond rec-ollections of mail drops by air during her childhood on Nana's island. A family friend with an airplane would disrupt the tranquility of idle summer days on the island by buzzing the cabin—flying low overhead to alert them of a mail drop. Beth would run out into the yard, waving wildly to old Frank Bohman as he circled back and tossed a brightly colored bag of mail as close to the porch as possible. With a big grin, he would tip his wings and shoot his little plane back up into the blue sky. Beth and Nana would tear the bag open to find an assortment of letters—people actually wrote letters in those days before email or reliable phone service. They were always anxious to devour the latest edition of the *Rainy Lake Chronicle*, Ranier's own homespun weekly newspaper. It included the latest village board controversies, local gossip, and Ted Hall's poetic *Drumbeat* column. It was a sad day for islanders and mainlanders alike when Frank's untimely death in 1981 brought his generous mail drop program to a halt.

Tearing herself away from the memories, Beth opened her post office box to find a long-awaited letter from Emily, postmarked Paris, France. She settled on a bench outside the post office where she eagerly opened the letter. Immediately, she was drawn into the world of her adventurous and artistic daughter. Sometimes it was hard to believe that they lived in the same world, she thought to herself, as she began to read about Emily's latest adventures in Europe.

"Mom, you simply have to come over and see this place!" Emily gushed, enthusiastically describing the highlights of the infamous city on the River Seine. She had fallen in love with the Louvre, where she had spent most of the past week in awe of the Greek, Roman, and Egyptian antiquities, including the second-century-BC sculpture of Aphrodite. She had marveled at the Mona Lisa and the paintings of Leonardo da Vinci, Michelangelo, Rosso, and others. And she had strolled through the pristine Tuileries and Carrousel gardens, admiring the nineteenth-century sculptures that accentuated little lakes, fountains, and terraced gardens. Steeped in ancient history, the Louvre had transformed her understanding of the world, she said, and her respective place in it. *"Where art and history merge,"* Emily wrote, *"my world comes alive, providing meaning above and beyond this tiny lifetime of mine."* Beth was amazed at the deep, poetic words of her daughter. She'd certainly broadened her perspective on life since she left home… Still, there were times when she reverted back to being a typical nineteen-year-old who struggled with parents who simply didn't understand her.

Emily went on describing this "city of lights" that she adored. She told her mother about the magnificent Champs-Elysees winding its way toward the River Seine where the Eiffel Tower stood guard. She claimed to feel at home in the little outdoor Parisian cafes, especially those where artists and writers hung out. She was painting and beginning to display her work. Life was wonderful. She wasn't sure she wanted to live back in the States again…not after her eyes had been opened to the rest of the world. An old world that was rich in culture and history—so much older, so much deeper than life in the United States.

Beth read on, tears clouding her vision. She wasn't sure if they were tears of happiness for her daughter—or of apprehension and sadness for herself. What if Emily decided to stay in Europe, to live there? It was so far away…and Emily was all she had left in this world.

Beth had always hoped to live close to her daughter. But in some respects, their visions were as far apart as Paris and Rainy Lake were. While Beth craved solitude and a wilderness setting, Emily longed for excitement and a cosmopolitan city steeped in art and ancient history. Perhaps they were simply in different phases of their lives. Beth remembered the lure of the big city, the desire to escape from the islands when she was Emily's age. Now, she was back home and feeling that this was where she belonged after all. She wondered if Emily would also return to her roots someday. Emily's roots, however, were far different from Beth's. Emily had grown up in an affluent Chicago neighborhood near the Magnificent Mile, where she got her first taste of art and culture. Emily and Beth had spent countless hours together at the Chicago Art Institute. There, Emily's passion grew into a lust for broader experiences in the arts. She must follow her own dream, Beth realized. She must make her own decisions, even if that meant living in Europe. Decisions are not, after all, cast in stone…maybe she'd come home someday soon.

At least Emily was planning a visit over the Christmas holidays—a fact that delighted her mother. It would be an old-fashioned Christmas on the island, just the two of them. Jake would probably come, too—certainly not Evelyn. There was time to plan all of that. Emily was coming for Christmas!

৵৹

Tucking Emily's letter into her purse, Beth decided to walk down to Jake's office on Houska's Point. From there, she would try to determine where the tiny cabin was, the one her mother had lived in. As she crossed the railroad tracks and passed the prominent old railroad depot, she noticed Seth coming out of Grandma's Pantry, the village restaurant where her mother once had breakfast with Jake. Perhaps more than once.

Seth immediately saw her, his dark eyes lighting up as he approached her. "Beth, I was just going to get ahold of you. The blueberry crop is ready to be harvested. I could use your help if you have time?"

She smiled back at him, pleased to see a familiar face. There was something about those eyes, about the way he looked at her... Of course, she made sure to keep a respectable distance between them. And he was careful not to overstep the boundaries.

"Would this afternoon work for you?" he continued.

"Why not?" she surprised herself as her words seemed to gush from her mouth without even thinking this through. Too late now to backtrack, she decided. Besides, it can't hurt to make a friend.

"Should I stop by and pick you up, say about two o'clock?"

"I think I'll just kayak over to your island. It's a beautiful day to get out on the water."

"Good! I also love to kayak. It's about the silence, I think, about losing myself in the sounds of nature. I can almost feel myself becoming a part of the waves, of nature itself. That's how it is for me anyway." His voice trailed off, his mind drifting deeper.

"That's a lovely way to put it, Seth. I feel it, too. It's one of the reasons I decided to move back home. I needed to reconnect with something greater than myself and my problems." She reluctantly shifted her eyes away from his, reprimanding herself for sharing too much, too soon, with someone whom she barely knew.

He nodded, deciding not to pursue the subject. This was not the right time. She was like a frightened bird, ready to take flight when others got too close. He understood. But why, he wondered, did he have this strange compulsion to care for this wounded spirit? She was so different from all the other women he'd ever known.

"Two o'clock then?" he spoke softly.

"Two o'clock," she met his gaze once again, "see you then, Seth."

⚜

Taking a deep breath, Beth glanced at her watch. She had several hours to spare before blueberry picking—enough time to follow her mother's early footsteps through this quaint little village. She hiked down the main street to Woody's Pub where she turned down the alley that ran past a deserted old marine repair shop, past Ranier Beach to Jake's office, which sat proudly on Houska's Point jutting out into Rainy Lake. This was where her mother had worked, where she first met Jake.

Beth had not spoken to Jake since the dinner episode at their home. He had left a voice mail message apologizing again. She had not yet returned the call. She was confused, not sure how much more she wanted to know. She felt sorry for Jake. She even felt sorry for Evelyn in some ways. Beth had enough of her own problems to cope with. Yet she feared that her own problems were hopelessly entwined with those of Jake and Evelyn. As if the three of them were stuck together amongst the intricate strands of a deadly spider's web. Unable to unravel a single thread without releasing the poison that would destroy them all.

Today, after reading her mother's first journal entries, she hoped to see Jake, to ask him a few questions. A part of her also hoped that he wasn't there. And he wasn't. She left a note on the door—"Jake, sorry I missed you. See you soon. Beth."

She walked around the house, Jake's office and refuge from the world, admiring the view of Rainy Lake on three sides of the peninsula. Jake's boat was tied to the pier. A large deck wrapped around the house. It was old and weather-beaten but offered incredible views of the lake, the village, and Ontario, Canada, just across the bay. One lonely rocking chair claimed the deck's best view obviously the place where Jake spent a considerable amount of his time. Probably escaping from his wife, lost in his own world. Beth climbed up onto the deck and sat in his chair, rocking back and forth, trying to imagine what it was like for Jake.

As she rocked, she tried to imagine her teenaged mother working here for Jake over forty years ago, writing ads, taking photos, loving her job. Walking home across the gravel path to her cabin. Beth followed her trail, across the drive, to a group of cabins now known as *The Lakeview, A Summer Residence on Rainy Lake*. Chills ran up and down her spine as she approached the closest cabin at the edge of the lake. It was tiny all right. *Cabin #5*, the sign above the door read. She froze in her tracks, recalling her mother's vivid description of her first home away from home. This had to be it, although a deck overlooking the lake had been added in recent years. This had to have been her cabin! She walked closer as if in a trance and was startled by someone approaching.

"Can I help you?" a pleasant-looking older woman asked. Her thick gray hair flowed gently around a kind, round face. She used a cane and walked slowly.

"I...I think my mother may have lived here once," Beth stammered. "A long time ago, about 1964 or so..."

"Oh, I didn't own the place that long ago. But I grew up here and I've always known the place, the people," the woman smiled at her. "Left it pretty much the way it was when I bought it twenty years ago. There's a lot of history here."

"Could I, if it's not too much trouble..." Beth questioned.

"Of course. Come on in and take a look."

And she did. It was almost exactly as her mother had described it in her diary. She could almost see her young mother writing at the table, reading in bed, looking out at Rainy Lake as she had described it. The old trunk was still there, the eagle feathers, the corner cabinet. She gasped as she noticed a framed sketch of a seagull hanging on the wall above the bed. Looking more closely, she made out the faint signature at the bottom—*Sarah Peterson, 1965.*

"Oh my God, that's my mother's work!" she gasped. "She painted her seagull after all!"

"Your mother? Sarah was your mother?" the woman's tone of voice suddenly changed. As if she knew something, some secret of long ago. Sarah's daughter was back? What did this mean, she asked herself.

"You knew my mother?"

The woman collected her thoughts, veiled them, and closed down. She was not about to discuss small-town gossip with a stranger who claimed to be the product of one of the village's best-loved scandals. She hated gossip and tried her best to stay away from it. Evelyn O'Connell, however, had spent years entertaining everyone at the local beauty shop with gossip and speculation about Sarah Peterson and her untimely demise. For unbeknown reasons, Mrs. O'Connell had not liked Sarah Peterson and had been committed to destroying her reputation via the Rainy Lake grapevine. It made no sense to the Lakeview's new owner to perpetuate the gossip. She tried to live her life according to an old saying that she'd picked up years ago from childhood friends at the nearby Birch Point Indian Village: "Do not judge others until you have walked a mile in their moccasins."

"I knew *of* her," the woman fidgeted with her cane. "A lovely and talented young lady, I'm told. So sad what happened to her—to your mother. I'm very sorry. And your grandmother—such a wonderful and independent woman. I'm also so sorry to hear about her passing. I was out of town and missed her funeral."

"Thanks. I'm Beth Calhoun," she extended her hand to the nervous woman. "And I'm back home, living on my family's island. I'm trying to learn more about my mother. You see, I never really got to know her…"

"Welcome, Beth," the woman squeezed her hand. "I'm Dorothy…I'd like to help you if I can. I can only imagine what it's like for you to come back into your mother's old world. But, you see, I didn't know her personally."

"Do you know who her friends were, anyone I could talk to?"

"Hmmm," the woman paused carefully, leading her back outside to sit at the table on the deck. "You may want to talk with Jake, the local realtor who lives over there on the point. Your mother worked for him and I believe they were good friends."

"Oh, yes, I know Jake well. He's also a very good friend of mine. Anyone else you can think of?"

A hint of surprise flickered across Dorothy's eyes as she cleared her throat. She liked this young lady. In fact, her heart ached for her, knowing some of the things that she would most likely uncover here and have to deal with. How much of it was true, she didn't know. Who really did, after all these years? Who…except for Jake O'Connell?

Beth waited as Dorothy retreated into her private world, watching one of her pet chipmunks scampering around her feet. "Chippy's hungry. I give him treats sometimes. He's my friend," she smiled, eager to change the direction of this conversation.

"He's cute."

"Yes, he is. He can do tricks, too. But you're not here to talk about my chipmunks, are you?" she chuckled.

"That's OK. I'm enjoying just being here where my mother lived. She loved it here, you know. I've found her diaries and am starting to read them. She described this little cabin almost exactly as it is today."

"Wait here," Dorothy interrupted as she gripped her cane, carefully stood up, and hobbled back into the cabin. She came out proudly holding the seagull sketch in her weathered hands. "I want you to have this." Her eyes crinkled with joy as she handed the sketch to Beth.

"Oh, thank you so much!" Beth's eyes misted over as she held her mother's sketch close to her heart. "This means so much to me. You are so kind."

"You have a difficult journey ahead, Beth. It's not going to be easy. If you ever need a friend, I'm here. It gets lonely sometimes… I'd like it if you stopped in for a cup of tea now and then. Perhaps you'd enjoy staying in your mother's old cabin sometime when you're here on the mainland?"

"I'd like that very much. And I will stop by again." This kind old woman reminded her of Nana. Regretfully, she hadn't been here for Nana in her last years. Maybe she could at least be here now for Dorothy in some small way.

Their eyes connected as if making a promise to stay in touch.

Beth suddenly remembered her blueberry picking appointment as she glanced at her watch. "I'm sorry but I need to run. I'm late."

The old woman reached her arms out for a hug from her new friend, someone who had been a stranger to her an hour before. Dorothy wanted to help her new friend through the inevitable rough waters ahead. If she'd had a daughter, she thought to herself, perhaps she would have grown to become a woman just like Beth. If… So many *ifs* in life. It wasn't meant to be.

Beth hugged her warmly and began to walk away as Dorothy called out to her. "One word of advice for you from an old woman who's been around a long time: do not believe everything that you hear. There are some local busybodies around who have nothing to do but gossip. You finally end up with stories that bear no resemblance whatsoever to what really happened. And some things…we never do find out the truth…especially when over forty years have gone by."

"Thanks," Beth called out with a wave, as she hiked down the path. *Do not believe everything that you hear,* she repeated the words silently. The old woman was warning her of the skeletons she was about to dig up. Of the ghosts from her mother's past.

Do not believe everything that you hear…

> "I have, as it were,
> my own sun and moon and stars,
> and a little world all to myself."
> *Henry David Thoreau*

Rainy Lake Island

Chapter Fourteen

*B*eth slid her red kayak into the lake, settling into the cockpit with her blueberry bucket, bear spray, and insect repellent. She didn't have time to worry about the fact that she was spending the afternoon picking blueberries with a man whom she was obviously attracted to. She was late. Dipping her paddle from side to side, she methodically sliced the glassy surface of the channel winding out into the bay where Seth lived. She ducked beneath gnarled tree branches reaching out over the channel, marveled at boulders stacked in strange formations, and wondered how trees could sprout and grow in pure rock. A pair of otters playfully thumped their tails at her before diving down into the lake.

Rainy Lake was as blue as the sky today, with fluffy cotton clouds shimmering in its depths. She was a part of it all—the lake, the sky—gliding along just inches above the waterline. With each stroke of the paddle, she let go of one more worry, one more fear.

She put the day's exciting discoveries behind her. All that remained in her mind was the image of her mother's sketch, reinforced by the squawk of seagulls soaring through the sky above her kayak.

Seth sat on a weathered bench at the end of his dock, waiting patiently for his guest to arrive. He had few guests—didn't encourage it. He thrived on his solitude and did not like to be interrupted when he was deep in thought, meditating, reading, or immersed in his painting. That's why he lived on an island, after all…so he could be alone.

This was different somehow. Beth was different. He looked forward to spending the afternoon with her. It wasn't a big deal, didn't mean anything, he told himself. She was just a friend, that's all. Still, he couldn't help grinning to himself as he watched her skimming across the water toward his island home. He wanted to show the place to her, wanted her to see his paintings. Few locals had ever been invited to do so. He sold his art, via his Web site, primarily to people from far-off places like New York, Chicago, and London. They paid well. Enough to cover his basic needs and enable him to send money to his people who lived on the Nett Lake Indian Reservation. He could have painted more, gone into mass reproductions. But that would have defeated the whole purpose and thwarted his artistic ability. He did his best work when something stirred his heart and soul, refusing to let go until he unleashed the force onto canvas. His fingers, his paints and brushes, seemed to be an extension of a magical force that flowed through him.

"Welcome to Blueberry Island," he said, extending his hand, gripping hers to help her out of the kayak. She let him help her, grinning back at him as she scanned the setting. The island had been wild when she'd picked blueberries here thirty years ago. The remnants of the dilapidated old cabin that she'd explored here as a child were long gone. Today, a path from the sheltered beach landing had been cleared up to a rustic log cabin with a big porch. "Where did that come from?" she asked him.

"It's my home, my studio. I bought it from the National Park Service back when Voyageur's National Park was created. Skidded it across the ice that winter. It's home—all I need in this life. Come on, I'll show you my wilderness retreat."

He led her up the path through wild ferns and berries, up onto the porch, and opened the massive wood door with a flourish. Stepping back, he gestured for her to enter. He watched her reactions carefully, wanting to see his life through her eyes.

She stopped abruptly just inside the entrance to his large one-room cabin. She felt something here that she had not felt in a long time, perhaps had never felt. The feeling of the place was almost spiritual, as if she was entering a sacred place. A place of belonging, a connection with the natural world that seemed to flow into and throughout the log-framed room. This was Seth's private world, she realized.

Her eyes were immediately drawn to his artist's corner where the walls were filled with paintings that captured the scenic beauty and the raw essence of Rainy Lake. There were also some visionary pieces depicting traditional American Indian culture. Beth was captivated by one large painting of an elderly Indian woman sitting on the ground beside a birchbark teepee, cradling a baby in her arms. Her face was lined with age, with hardship and weariness. But something inside glowed through her leathery face, softening its lines as she gazed lovingly at the infant in her arms. The woman's dark eyes radiated love and a powerful sense of hope. Hope for this child, for the future. She seemed to be preparing to leave this world, passing her unfulfilled hopes and dreams onto this child. Empowering him to create the future he deserved, but reminding him to always remember where he came from and who his people were. Beth choked up. She could not speak. She just stared, lost in the powerful feelings that his work evoked within her.

He waited quietly until she finally turned back to him, tears glistening in her eyes. "I am speechless, Seth. Your work is incredible! I can't even describe it, but I can feel it. This one of the old woman and the baby…it's overwhelming," she stammered.

"Thank you," he humbly lowered his gaze to the colorful rug on the floor. It was a family heirloom, handwoven by his great-grandmother. "I'm pleased that it gives you pleasure, Beth. That is the greatest reward for me, to see the look in your eyes."

"I'm shocked that a local artist living out here on an island can create something like this. Where have you studied?"

"I haven't. It comes to me when I am in flow with the land that I love, when I hear the thoughts of my ancestors who have lived here for thousands of years. It happens when I show respect for all that the Great Creator has given us, for nature itself."

Beth couldn't help turning back to the painting of the old woman. It seemed to speak to her, to empower her to rise beyond the hardships that she had endured in her own life. Who was this wise and powerful woman, she wondered? The painting almost seemed to live and breathe, as if the woman had once existed, as if her spirit lived on. Beth shivered. "Is this one for sale?" she whispered, holding her breath.

Seth could not respond at first. When she turned back to him, she saw tears welling in his dark chocolate eyes. Finally he spoke. "No, I'm sorry. I could never sell that painting. It means more to me that I can put into words. You see…" his voice trailed off into the past. "You see," he continued, "that woman is my grandmother, holding me on the day I was born—the day she died."

Beth's mouth gaped open. "Oh, I'm so sorry. It's an incredible painting, a wonderful tribute to your grandmother," she murmured as her eyes melted into his across the room. Some strange force seemed to be drawing them together. The old woman on the wall seemed to be watching, almost smiling, in approval. He moved closer to stand beside her, their shoulders touching. Silently, they gazed up at his grandmother, acutely aware of the other's presence. Suddenly, she blinked, emerging from an almost trance-like state. What was she thinking?

"We have blueberry picking to do," he stated calmly, covering up the rare emotions that were bubbling within him. He wasn't sure what had just happened. There was a powerful connection here, he realized, something he'd never felt before. But it made no sense. He barely knew this woman. And she obviously needed time and space. He would respect that. He glanced up at the painting of his grandmother, almost feeling her hand in this. Was she trying to tell him something? Clearing his head, he grabbed his bucket and headed for the door, badly in need of some fresh air.

She stood there a moment longer, catching her breath, scolding herself for her foolish reactions to this man. Perhaps she should not have come. She scoped out the rest of his abode before leaving. A work table splattered with paint, covered with an assortment of tubes and jars of paint, brushes of every size. A blank canvas stood on a large easel in the corner, waiting for his next inspiration.

On the other side of the room, a big four-poster bed was covered with a colorful Indian blanket. Bookshelves overflowed with an assortment of books, with more books stacked on the floor beside his bed. She glanced at the titles, wanting to spend some time thumbing through the books that filled his life. Handmade baskets hung on the wall over a rustic chest-of-drawers. His jacket hung from a hook on the wall.

In the opposite corner, there was a little kitchen with a rickety wood table, old appliances, and an antique sideboard that housed his dishes, pots, and pans. His computer and printer were set up on one end of the table. A lone placemat dominated the other end of the table, beside the salt and pepper shakers. A cast-iron pot-bellied wood stove stood in the center of the cabin, flanked by several old rocking chairs. A plump sofa with fluffy pillows faced the stove. She could almost see him stretched out on the sofa by the fire on cold winter nights, lost in one of his books.

Taking a deep breath, she stepped out onto the porch where Seth was waiting for her as if nothing had happened between them. Well, nothing *had* happened, not really, she assured herself.

"I see you are prepared," he flashed his big smile at her, "even bear spray, eh?"

They headed down the path into the woods where the blueberries grew. Together, they picked lush ripe berries, filling their buckets over and over again. It was not necessary to speak, a relief for both of them. It felt both strange—and relaxing—to spend time with someone else in such a comfortable state of silence.

No bears today, although Seth told her about the female bear and two cubs who resided on his island. They roamed the island freely, preferring to stay away from humans, as they should. Bears needed to remain wild, not dependent upon people. It was one of the laws of nature. The other night, however, he woke to the sound of his trash can being slammed around. Armed with his flashlight, he'd gone out onto the porch to find the mother bear tearing his garbage apart. He must not have secured the lid well enough. Two young cubs played nearby. He had reluctantly shooed them away, admiring the bear and all that she represented to his people, the Anisinabe or Ojibwe. The bear stood for courage, teaching man to have the mental and moral strength to listen to his heart, to be proud of his ancestry and the way of life given to him by Gitchi Mani-doo, the Great Spirit. The next morning he had a mess to clean up.

❧

This year's blueberry crop was exceptional. The sun hung low in the western sky by the time they decided that they had more than enough blueberries to last the winter. The bears would enjoy what was left.

"I'm starving," Seth suddenly announced. "How about you?"

"Me, too. I've enjoyed the day, Seth, but I guess it's time to paddle my way home."

"Wait. I have my famous rabbit stew all ready to heat up over the fire pit on the beach. I can make fry bread to go with it. What do you say?"

"Well, it sounds tempting..."

"I have one of the best sunset views here of any place on this lake. Go on down and enjoy it while I get dinner. I'll bring you a glass of wine if you like—red?"

How could she resist? "You've talked me into it. I can start the fire." She glanced at the sun blazing its way lower and lower across the horizon, gauging how much time she had to spare. She wanted to get home before dark.

"I'll paddle back with you later, in my canoe, with a few torch-lights," he seemed to be reading her mind. "Besides, we will need more than your little kayak to haul all of your blueberries home." With that, he headed off down the path to the house to begin making his fry bread. She followed, retrieving a glass of wine before she retreated to the beach and started the fire in the pit. It was already laid, as if he had been planning to cook on the beach, as if he was expecting company for dinner.

She sat on the beach beside the glowing fire, nursing her wine, as shades of pink began to streak across the sky, shimmering down into the rippling surface of the lake. A pair of loons called out to each other. Across the bay, she could see her little gazebo perched on the rocky point. She sighed, content just to be here and anxious for Seth to return so he could enjoy the sunset with her.

Moments later he appeared, balancing a kettle of stew with a pan of fry bread. A bottle of wine protruded from one pocket, an extra glass from the other. He carefully hung the kettle over the fire and propped the fry pan on a large rock slab beside the burning logs. Then he settled down on the beach beside Beth, refilling her glass and pouring one for himself.

"You're right. It is spectacular," she sighed as the glowing ball of fire sank lower and lower in the darkening sky. Brilliant pink flames now danced across the horizon, turning gold as the moon began to rise above the opposite shore.

He watched her silently. "Sharing it with you is the most spectacu-lar of all," he finally spoke.

She felt soft and warm inside as she looked up into his eyes—smiling eyes that radiated sincerity and admiration. Catching her breath, she looked away. It was time to set the record straight. It didn't matter what she felt. She knew from past experience that it was not safe to act on your feelings. You could not trust your feelings, not ever. "Seth…" she began slowly.

"I'm sorry if I've upset you with my words. You have my deepest respect. I will never do anything to hurt you. I just enjoy your company, that's all. Friends?" he extended his hand.

"Friends," she clasped his hand, feeling his warmth spreading throughout her. His hand was strong, yet gentle. An honest hand. The kind of hand that she'd like to hold on to—if she ever decided to do so again. But that was not an option, she reminded herself. She owed him an explanation, she decided. "Look, I'm sorry. It's just that…I do enjoy spending time with you. But that's all it can be. I'm going through a tough divorce right now…"

"I'm sorry. I understand. If I can just be your friend through this difficult time, I will be honored. No strings attached. No expectations. I understand."

"Thank you," she sighed. "I do value your friendship, you know. I just can't trust myself—or anyone else…not now, perhaps not ever. I don't even know who I am, if that makes any sense to you. All I know is that I've messed up my life and I'm not feeling very good about myself these days." She stopped, shocked that she was revealing so much to this man.

"Someday you will. Someday you will learn to appreciate the wonderful person that you are, to trust yourself again. But for now, let's eat!" he changed the subject as he began dishing up their plates.

The food was delicious. As they ate, he told her more about himself. He'd never married and, frankly, did not think he ever would. He loved his solitude, his privacy, his life on Rainy Lake. A few good friends, not many. What more could he possibly want? This was all quite reassuring to Beth. The more she learned, the more she valued this emerging friendship. She found herself sharing a little bit about her mother, about discovering her diaries. He listened quietly.

Her mind drifted back to the painting of his grandmother, wondering how he could have painted it if she really died the day he was born. That made no sense. Was he telling the truth?

"A penny for your thoughts," he broke into hers.

"I was just thinking about that painting of your grandmother," she began, not sure how to phrase the question without offending him.

"Of course," his eyes crinkled, "you're wondering how I could have painted her when she died the day I was born, when I was too little to remember her?"

Beth nodded sheepishly, twisting a strand of hair around her index finger. As she did, an odd sense of déjà vu consumed Seth. He stared at her, stunned.

"What?" she puzzled.

"Sorry, I'm afraid I drifted off someplace... Now, back to my grandmother." He smiled wistfully. "This may be difficult for you to understand, Beth, but I've always felt my grandmother's spirit beside me. There's a special connection, a bond, between us. One night I woke with an obsession to paint her, to paint her holding me in her arms as I'd been told she did on that day. Of course, I'd always had a physical image of her in the back of my mind..."

"You'd seen pictures of her?"

"No, never—not until after I painted her portrait and shared it with my relatives on the reservation."

"What happened?"

"My mother cried. She told me I had painted her mother—exactly the way she looked when she held me that day. My mother then found a faded old photograph of my grandmother..." He choked up for a moment.

"And?"

"She cried again, tears of happiness. There was no doubt that I'd captured the woman in the photo."

"Wow, that's an incredible story," she touched his hand, trying to understand how something like this could really happen.

⋙⋘

They paddled across the lake together as a full moon rose in the sky. They paddled quietly, side by side, their boats loaded with blueberries. Seth rigged a torchlight in her kayak and one on his birchbark canoe. He had made the canoe himself, spending countless hours building it in the tradition of his ancestors who had been expert canoe makers.

They laughed together as they lugged the bags of blueberries up the path to her cabin. Moonlight shimmered through the trees, illuminating their path with lacy patterns of light. Once they'd completed their mission, they stood together on the porch.

"Thanks for a wonderful day, your fabulous dinner, and the blue-berries," she smiled up at him, offering her hand.

He grasped her thin hand between both of his, returning her warm smile. Then he left, calling out to her, "Don't forget my blueberry pie!"

She stood on the porch for a long time, smiling as she watched him paddle back to his island by the light of the moon. As he faded into the night, she could still see the soft glow of his torch bobbing gently on the waves.

> "Life isn't about how to survive the storm,
> but how to dance in the rain."
> *Author Unknown*

Chapter Fifteen

Wrapped in warm memories of a special day, she went inside to find the red light blinking on her answering machine. Back to reality—a worse reality than she had expected. It was her attorney, advising her that there was another delay in the divorce proceedings. Rob was playing legal games—again. Stalling for time. Refusing to comply with the alimony settlement that the attorneys had previously negotiated verbally. It would be at least several months before she could expect to receive a check. In addition, their home was still on the market waiting for a buyer who could afford to purchase it. Her share of the equity was still tied up.

"Damn him." She deleted the curt message, tears welling in her eyes. She was running out of money and had depended on a payment by the end of the month. How was she going to cover groceries, the electric bill, gas for the boat and car? It was simply too humiliating to think about having to sell her jewels—Emily's inheritance. No, she decided, she could not bring herself to do that. There had to be another way...

Beth tossed and turned in bed that night, trying to figure out how she could survive financially for the next few months—possibly longer. Her garden was already producing lettuce and broccoli. The beans, tomatoes, and beets would be ready soon. This, along with the venison in the freezer—and all the blueberries—would cut down on her grocery bill. She could make fewer trips to town, perhaps even hitch a ride in with Seth now and then. Maybe her old attorney was right—she might need to think about getting a job on the mainland. She might need to figure out a way to support herself instead of relying on a man to support her. Finally, exhausted, she lapsed into a fitful sleep, thrashing about once again in the subconscious world of her dreams.

❧❧

This time she is lying in Seth's arms in the bottom of his canoe, drifting peacefully across Rainy Lake. Bobbing on silver-crested waves. It's a pitch-dark night. Slivers of moonlight rain down upon them. The flaming torch on the bow of the boat dances slowly to the rhythm of the wind. Together, they drift off to sleep, wrapped in Seth's Indian blanket. Suddenly, they are awakened by explosions of light coming at them from all directions, streaking across the lake, screeching like witches' whistles on the Fourth of July.

"Who's there?" Seth calls out, trying to conceal his fear as flaming rockets shoot across the black water, over their heads. The lake is now on fire, hot and angry. "Get down," he orders Beth, covering her with the blanket in the bottom of the canoe while he frantically tries to paddle away. But where can he go? The fire is getting hotter, sizzling like bacon in Nana's frying pan. He hears Beth crying, calling for him. He crawls beneath the blanket with her, holding her close. Beth's sobbing is soothed by his presence. Will they survive this attack? Perhaps they could swim for shore…but where is shore? They'd slept for hours, floating in the big lake. They have no idea where they are. If they'd drifted into the Brule Narrows, and if a northeasterly wind came down, their fate would be sealed. They would drown—just like her grandfather and her mother had…

"Just hold me, Seth," she cries as her eyes begin to adjust to the darkness beneath the big blanket. Searching for his eyes, she suddenly screams in terror. Seth is no longer there! It is Rob lying beside her, his evil eyes piercing her soul. "Leave me alone, please leave me alone," she pleads as Rob's icy fingers once again begin to penetrate her. "Please," she sobs, "I'll do anything, give you everything. Just leave me alone! Leave Seth alone! Please!"

"Seth's gone—for good. Why don't you jump overboard and die with him?" Rob laughs hysterically. "Your mother is also waiting for you, you little whore, in the bottom of the lake. Go to her—*now*." He begins to shove her out of the canoe into the wild, black waves. The torches are gone. The lake is no longer on fire. All is black, pitch black. She has no idea where she is, where Seth is, where land is. "Help!" she screams, over and over again, as she surfaces from her plunge into the icy water. She hears Rob's evil laugh growing fainter as he paddles the canoe away from the watery grave that he has planned for her. Exhausted, she begins to swim, to float on her back, to swim some more—hopefully in one direction so she can eventually find land. "Seth," her cries echo into the night, over and over again. No response. The moon hides behind the clouds as cold rain begins to fall. How much longer can she survive? There's no land in sight, no boats in sight—not until she almost runs into a dark houseboat anchored in her path. "Help," she musters up the last bit of her energy to try to get the attention of whoever is sleeping on the boat.

"Why should I help you?" Rob's familiar voice hisses like a snake from the deck of the boat. He extends his hand to rescue her from the sea. "I'd rather die," she whimpers, slipping beneath the waves. But he reaches down, grabs her, and pulls her up onto the deck where she collapses in a puddle of vomit. She pretends to be dead—maybe she is and simply doesn't know it yet… But she can hear him standing over her, talking at her.

"You're coming back with me—to court. You owe me. I don't owe you a damn thing anymore. Let Seth take care of you—if he comes back to life, that is."

Oh, God—Great Spirit, Creator, whoever you are, please spare Seth's life, she prays silently to herself. *Where is Seth?*

"Besides that, you're going to jail, bitch. You didn't pay your electric bill. You owe the gas station. You haven't paid your taxes. You're going to jail, and I'll be the first one to laugh all the way to the bank. You won't need money from me in jail now, will you?" His laughter fills the surreal night, echoing across the lake.

Where's Seth? she continues to shriek into the night as Rob's evil laughter rings in her ears—loud enough to awaken her from the terror of her latest nightmare.

"Love is a canvas
furnished by nature and
embroidered by imagination."
Voltaire

Chapter Sixteen

B eth's hands were still shaking with the lingering effects of last night's dream. She knew that she was fighting her growing attraction to Seth. The dream seemed to be a warning to stay away from him before she ruined his life as well as her own. Sometimes she felt cursed—as if her presence cast an evil spell that inflicted pain upon others. Maybe she was doomed to be alone so she wouldn't hurt or lose any more of her loved ones. Despite her own problems, she was driven back to her mother's diaries. She could not stay away. It was a diversion from her own life. More importantly, those diaries might hold the key to putting the pieces of her own life back together again—bloody fragments, torn and twisted into a complex puzzle that would not be easily solved.

Armed with a thermos of coffee, she headed out to the gazebo shortly after dawn, her mother's diaries tucked under her arm. After a quick glance across the bay to Seth's island, she flipped through the first journal to begin where she left off several days ago.

October 15, 1965
Dear Diary,

I am in love, so much in love that it has brought out the poet in me, I'm afraid. I cannot quit writing about him, poem after poem, when I retreat to my cabin after work. I am walking on air, floating through life, happier than I've ever known it was possible to be. It is all because of him. I've found my soul mate, something I never knew existed. He loves me in a way that I never knew was possible. He listens to me, sends me little love notes. He knows me almost better than I know myself. He understands my fears, my hopes, my dreams. When we're together, I am so content, so happy. I can't quit smiling.

At night, he's with me in my dreams. To be honest, he is now with me in my bed some nights as well. It just happened between us one night a few weeks ago. We were sitting together on the beach below my cabin late one night, talking quietly, cuddling beneath the silver sliver of a newborn moon. The waves lapped gently over our bare feet. We were alone, absorbing the magic of the universe when the northern lights began to flash in opaque curtains that lit up the sky—shimmering spikes of blue and green. We held each other close. "Waters of the dancing sky," he whispered, breathing softly in my ear as his hand wandered beneath my blouse, setting off an explosion of fireworks between us. We made love for the first time that night, on the beach beneath the northern lights. They danced wildly, erupting in spikes of passionate red as he gently introduced me to the wonders of love.

I know that we are destined to be together forever. As wonderful as our relationship is, there are a few complications that I don't care to go into right now. Still, I know that we will work through them together. A love as powerful as ours is meant to be. It will prevail and I have no doubt that we will spend our lives together.

Gotta run, dear diary. I'm cooking a romantic candlelight dinner for him tonight—Italian spaghetti with meatballs, garlic bread, a bottle of red wine. The table is set with Mama's good china and a vase of wildflowers I picked myself. I can hardly wait to be in his arms once again!

Beth closed the diary in frustration. Who is *he*? *My father?* She wondered about the complications that her mother didn't care to share—not even with her diary. It was hard to believe that her own mother had been so young—so blindly in love, so foolish… *Oh, Mama, how could you?*

She was starving, having read well into the afternoon. Deep in thought, she hiked back home to make herself a sandwich. Glancing back at the gazebo, she could almost see her young mother sitting there, sunlight dancing in her auburn hair, as she poured her heart out over some man…a man without a name, one who probably didn't deserve her love. Or maybe she wrote that entry at her little cabin in Ranier, looking out at the cove where she made love to *that man* beneath the northern lights. Beth shuddered—realizing that her mother hadn't been much older than she had been when she'd foolishly given in to Rob on the beach of Sand Point Island. Perhaps she had no right to judge her mother's actions after all… *Beth, how could you?*

✥✥

The phone was ringing as she walked into the house. "Beth?" Jake's slightly hesitant voice came softly across the telephone line. "Sorry I missed you yesterday. How are you doing?"

"Fine, Jake, I think. A little confused, however. I'm reading my mother's diaries…"

"Anything interesting?"

"Well, she's now madly in love, but I have no clue who *he* could be. I need to keep reading and doing more research, I guess. I met Dorothy yesterday, the lady who owns the cabin where my mother lived when she worked for you…"

"Oh yes, Dorothy, my neighbor. Nice lady. Did she have any information for you?"

"She told me to talk to you, that you were a good friend of my mother's. And…she told me not to believe everything that I hear."

"Good advice. You and I will talk, I promise you. But I do want you to read your mother's words first."

"Yes," she sighed impatiently, "later."

"Beth, I need to fly to New York tomorrow on business. I just wanted you to know that I'll be away for a few days. You can reach me by cell phone if you need me."

"New York? Well, have a great trip. I'll be fine. I have Seth close by if I need anything. He's becoming a good friend, a good neighbor."

"Glad to hear that. I like him. He's a very nice man, a gentleman. By the way, I'm leaving the key to my place under the doormat—just in case you need a place to stay here on the mainland."

"Why, thank you. That's very kind of you."

"Make yourself at home. I know you're bent on spending some time here in Ranier retracing your mother's life. So I thought that you'd at least have a place to stay while you're here."

"You're too good to me, you know."

"You deserve it. Take care, and I'll see you soon."

✥✥

The more she thought about it, she decided to take Jake up on his offer. After all, her mother had spent several years working there in his real estate office. It would be fun to spend some time there as she did a little more sleuthing around the village, trying to find someone who knew her mother. But first, she simply must get back to those diaries…

December 24, 1965
Dear Diary,

It's a quiet Christmas Eve on the island—just Mama and me. The lake froze over just in time for me to ski home to the island this morning. I'd been worried about Mama stranded out here alone until freeze-up. No use even trying to talk her off this island. She stocks up on supplies in the fall, including everything she needs for her traditional Swedish Christmas feast. I'm stuffed tonight with lutefisk, Swedish meatballs, rice pudding, and her homemade spice Pepparkakor cookies with sugar sprinkles. Delicious as always. Tomorrow morning, we will have our traditional Yule Kaka Christmas bread.

We hung our old stockings on the fireplace like we do every year—the ones Mama knit for us all years ago. We still hang a stocking for Papa. When I was little, after he drowned in the big lake, I'd write him a note or draw a picture that I would tuck into his bright red stocking. I always hoped that it would be gone the next morning—that he'd come to get it in the middle of the night, almost like Santa Claus. Finally, I gave up. He wasn't coming back. Still, his spirit always seems to be here with us for the holidays. Maybe it's just our memories of him. It's all so bittersweet...

Speaking of bittersweet, this is a bittersweet Christmas for me. While I enjoy spending the holiday with Mama and would never dream of doing anything different, I am spending my first Christmas (since I fell in love) without my beloved. My empty arms ache for him as I write tonight in my big bed, all alone. Mama is sleeping downstairs. I'm gazing out my window as huge snowflakes flutter against the windowpane, illuminated by a full moon. I hear the wolves howling in the distance. They sound lonely, too, their cries echoing through the wilderness. Do they also yearn for something they cannot have? Sometimes I wonder if happiness really exists. Or is it just a figment of our imaginations, a temporary state of insanity...like love?

I'm afraid that happiness cannot exist without sadness. You need one to appreciate the other. Well, dear diary, I simply don't feel like being happy tonight. I'd rather wallow in my loneliness, in my bittersweet existence. To be fair, he did give me an exquisite gold cross necklace for Christmas last night, a day early. It has a diamond set in the middle—a symbol of our love, a promise of our future together. I will wear it always, proudly, lovingly. Still—he's tied up for the holi-

days—*tied up with obligations from the life he had before he met me. I try to understand. That's not always easy. So…I think I will write him a little poem tonight to let him know how I really feel. I may, or may not, give it to him after the holidays. Here goes…*

BITTERSWEET (A little poem for Pooh Bear from Sarah)

As I gaze into your eyes,
I am drawn instantly, deeply
into another world…
a magical place
of warmth and beauty
that transcends
the cruel boundaries
imposed upon us by
the "real" world.

Within your eyes,
I feel my heart and soul
melting softly into yours,
eyes clinging to each other
as waves of passion
suck us deeper and deeper
into a churning whirlpool
of desire.

As the wind whips the whitecaps
into fierce breakers
clashing against the
rules of the real world,
I draw you deeper,
deeper within…

Here in this secret place
of fantasies and dreams,
there are no boundaries,
no rules.
There is only love.

Breathlessly, I emerge
from the depths of your eyes
back into the real world...
trembling with desire
my soul ignited by
the touch of your hand,
I float into the warmth
of your embrace.

But suddenly
the door of real life
flings itself open
with a vengeance—
cold air gushing in,
penetrating
like a knife,
tearing us apart,
shattering our dreams.

In the real world
we do not belong
to each other.
It is only in our hearts,
in our dreams,
that "we"
even exist—trapped
in a bittersweet world...

Beth pulled herself back to the present, wiping the tears from her eyes. Her heart ached for her mother. Yes, *bittersweet* seemed to be an appropriate way to describe her short life. But *Pooh Bear? Who was Pooh Bear?* And why, she asked herself, did his obligations prevent him from spending the holiday with her? He could be divorced with kids from a previous marriage. Or maybe he had an elderly parent depending upon him. Another nagging thought surfaced in her mind, one that she kept stuffing away, refusing to consider. *No*, her mother could *not* have fallen in love with a married man. *Not her mother!* As she closed the diary, trying to shut out her growing suspicions, her thoughts drifted back to the horror of last night's dream.

"Without darkness nothing comes to light
as without light, nothing flowers."
Mary Surton

Chapter Seventeen

Beth stopped at Seth's island the next morning on her way in to Ranier. She wanted to drop off a blueberry pie, fresh from the oven, as she had promised him. She found him painting at his easel, lost in his work, but pleased to take a break for a cup of coffee with his new friend.

"Is everything OK?" He immediately sensed a hint of fear and apprehension in her.

"Just a bad dream. I don't want to talk about it."

"All right," he waited, guessing that she really did need to talk about whatever it was that was bothering her. She fidgeted with a strand of her long auburn hair, wrapping it slowly around her finger, a gesture that once again stirred his soul. She paced around the room, finally slumping into a chair at the far end of the kitchen table. He sat across from her, sipping his coffee, watching her. Waiting.

"I'm not sure that I should be spending time with you, Seth. I had a horrible dream. It was almost like a warning for me to stay away…to stay away from you so something bad doesn't happen to you…"

"Do you want to talk about it, tell me about the dream?"

"No, I can't," she trembled, shuddering at the thought of reliving the horror.

"Well then, I'll tell you what I think…I think you're afraid because of everything that's going on in your life right now. That's what your dream was all about. Nothing bad is going to happen to you or to me—unless you decide not to be my friend anymore…"

She couldn't help smiling back at him. "I really hope you're right. Sometimes it feels like there's a black cloud of doom that follows me around, raining on everyone around me…"

"That's not the way I see it. I see sunshine all around you, flowing through you, trying to break free from the clouds of your past. You will too, someday soon."

He had a way of brightening her day, of calming her fears, of helping her put things back into perspective. "Thanks, Seth," she touched his hand gently across the table. He held her hand, briefly, in his strong but gentle hands, trying to give her some of his own strength.

She sighed, reluctantly pulling her hand away to focus on drinking her coffee. She had desperately needed to feel the warmth of his hand stroking hers. But now, as her emotions flipped from one extreme to another, it frightened her. His touch felt so good, too good. It was time to put a stop to this foolishness.

Breaking free, she told him that she'd be spending the next few days at Jake's office in the village, doing more research on her mother. It was reassuring to her to have someone like Seth who was close enough to check in with. A good neighbor who already seemed to be keeping an eye out for her.

He wished her the best, walking her down to the dock to see her off. It felt like she was beginning to trust him. That pleased him—more than it should have.

≪⊗≫

As Beth maneuvered her boat around the islands on her way to the mainland, kicking up a powerful wake behind her, she felt her worries disappear into the wind that tousled her wild hair. Sunlight bounced off the rollicking waves. She waved to the fishermen she passed, to guests on the National Park Service's tour boat making its regular trek to Kettle Falls.

She tied her boat up at the Thunderbird marina, hauled her overnight bag to her SUV, and glanced into the mirror before starting the vehicle. She needed a haircut…how long had it been since she had bothered with her hair? Not since she left Chicago three months ago. The old days of weekly beauty shop appointments at one of Chicago's exclusive salons were over. Maybe she'd stop at the beauty shop in Ranier for a haircut and styling before settling into Jake's place.

"Walk-ins welcome," read the sign on the door of the quaint little shop. The historic brick building was covered with vines and surrounded by planters filled with colorful flowers. The beauty shop did have an opening. Several older women chattered comfortably amongst themselves as their hair was cut, permed, and colored. Beth didn't recognize any of them—why would she? Nana had always cut her hair to save money. She would certainly not be recognized here, and that was fine with her. She was more interested in listening, in learning. They

125

paid little attention to her, a stranger in these parts, as they resumed their conversation.

"Did you see the hideous dress that Selma wore to the fundraiser?" one prune-faced woman with frizzly grey hair whispered loudly. "She could barely fit her big ass into it, bulging at the seams. And that plunging neckline? I mean, *really?*"

"They say she may be getting a little on the side—at least looking for it. Old John would kill her," the second woman gleefully jumped into their lifelong game of trying to outdo each other with the juiciest gossip.

"Say what?" the third said loudly, cupping her ear. "Can't hear your mumbling. Speak up!" Her hearing aid had been placed on the beautician's table for safekeeping. The others were more than happy to comply, raising their voices in unison.

Beth found it amusing, grinning inwardly as she was placed under the dryer. Even the blowing of the dryer, however, didn't drown out their rising voices. Flipping through a dog-eared Cosmopolitan magazine, she was suddenly startled to hear her mother's name spill from the acid tongue of the prune-faced woman.

"You remember Sarah Peterson, that girl who drowned in the lake so mysteriously years ago?"

"You mean the one with the illegitimate child? That one—they lived on one of those islands just beyond Jackfish or Stop islands?"

"That's the one. Well," Prune-Face boasted, pausing for dramatic effect, "well, they say that her daughter is back in town. What do you think of that?"

"No!" the others cried in unison. "Whatever for?"

"Well," Prune-Face gloated, "they say she is trying to find out about her mother, about what really happened to her."

The mouths of the others flapped open, flabby jowls hanging in quiet disbelief as they began reliving the scandal they'd heard about so many years ago.

"Poor thing. How would you like to find out that your mother was, shall we say, a *party girl,* to put it nicely? Why, they say she entertained so many men that nobody ever had a clue as to who the father of that baby was."

"Oh, there were clues all right, Bertha," the other interrupted. "I heard from a very reliable source that he was a wealthy man from New York, *a married man!*"

"Yes, I heard that, too. They say he dumped her and never admitted to being the father. She didn't like that, *oh no*. She tried to blackmail him for years, they say, trying to get money for the little girl. And then, Sarah mysteriously disappeared on a canoe trip, the last adventure of her life. Some think that she went with *him*, that guy from New York, that he had come back to get rid of her so she wouldn't blackmail him any longer."

"That may be, but maybe he wasn't the father. It could have been anyone, you know."

"Did you say New York?" The one without the hearing aid leaned in closer.

"Yes, New York," Prune-Face raised her voice impatiently.

"How would she ever find someone from New York up here on Rainy Lake? Doesn't make a lick of sense to me."

"You know," Bertha confided, "she used to work in Jake O'Connell's real estate office. He always had those rich clients from New York flying in to buy island property. And little Sarah may have entertained them, if you know what I mean."

"Do you really think so?" Bertha's stylist dropped her curling iron on the floor. She was relatively new in town and had not yet heard about this village scandal.

"That's what they say," Prune-Face concluded smugly. "We heard it from a very reliable source, right here in this beauty shop. No reason for her to lie."

"Heard it from whom?"

"Now, I don't want to cause trouble. I'm not one to gossip, but she is a highly regarded member of this community. And," she paused, "she of all people had inside information. She had to know the truth."

The tinkling bell above the door suddenly announced that someone was coming in, intruding on their personal conversation. They drifted into silence, cautiously glancing at Beth beneath the dryer. Thankfully, this stranger would not have been able to hear them. Village secrets were meant to stay within the village where they belonged.

Oh my God, Beth wailed silently, trying to show no outward emotion. Trying to pretend she had heard nothing. She closed her eyes as if she had dozed off under the heat of the dryer. A married man from New York? More than one lover? That was not possible—not her precious mother. *She was not a party girl!* Still, if there wasn't some terrible secret in her past, why had the truth been hidden from her for so long?

"Don't believe everything that you hear," Dorothy had warned her. And she wouldn't. But she *would* check out every last detail. She would search through Jake's real estate files this weekend, searching for clients from New York whom her mother may have met forty years ago. Would Jake still have those old records? Knowing Jake, she suspected that he would. He was not one to throw away or let go of pieces of the past.

In a daze, she drove through the village to Jake's place. The place where her mother had worked, where she may have met his clients from New York. *Lies, all lies,* she tried to assure herself as the cruel words of the beauty shop ladies rang in her ears. She wandered through Jake's home, through his office, not really seeing, too upset to even notice the panoramic views of the lake from the endless expanse of windows. She slumped down at his massive rolltop desk, an antique showing years of wear. The tears finally began to flow, to spill down her cheeks, harder, faster, until she was sobbing. Exhausted, she finally fell into a deep sleep on the sofa.

Hours later she woke with no recollection of where she was, why she was there, or what time of day it could be. She felt sluggish, feverish, as if she'd been drugged. Not sure if she wanted to face the day. Perhaps it was best to sleep on forever, peacefully, instead of being tortured with painful images and haunting questions from the past. Why was it, again, that she had embarked on this insane truth-finding mission? Was it too late to turn back?

Slowly, she regained control of her body and her thoughts. It must be Wednesday evening, she realized, as she heard the weekly sailboat regatta race taking off from the Sand Bay landing just across the bay. She'd slept away a good part of the day, something she never did normally.

She needed some fresh air and a good glass of wine. Jake had stocked several bottles of her favorite merlot before he left. She poured herself a glass and took it out onto the porch, where she settled into Jake's comfortable rocker. Breathing deeply, she absorbed the smell of the lake as she watched the sailboats skim across Rainy Lake. Rocking, gently rocking to the rhythm of the waves, going with the flow—from her mother's arms to Jake's well-worn rocking chair.

Still rocking, she watched the blue sky transform itself into fluffy pink swirls of cotton candy. As the horizon began to shimmer with spikes of gold drifting down into the black lake, she heard the ringing of Jake's phone in the background. She was not about to answer it. She did, however, listen at the door as Evelyn's voice boomed from the answering machine.

"Where the hell are you, Jake? I need to talk to you." Her words were slurred. She was drunk—again. "You're going to be busted if you don't start cooper—ah—cooperating with me. I'm just trying to help, you old fool. Call me."

What was that all about, Beth wondered. The black spider seemed to be spinning her web tighter and tighter.

Beth had work to do, half a century of files to search through. It would be a long night. She lit the kerosene lamp on Jake's desk, then opened the shutters to invite the breeze off the lake to keep her company. Turning on Jake's Bose music system, she fell under the spell of his CD selections. There was Frank Sinatra's *Strangers in the Night*, Tony Bennett's *Shadow of Your Smile*. These were the songs of her mother's era, the love songs she would have listened to back in 1965 and 1966 when she was so deeply in love with the mysterious Pooh Bear.

◈◈◈

By the time the sun rose the next morning, a bleary-eyed Beth had a list of her potential fathers. All from New York. All real estate clients of Jake's who had come to Rainy Lake during the timeframe of October 1965 through May 1968, when Beth was born. A second, smaller list provided names of any New York clients who had been here in September of 1974, when Sarah had mysteriously drowned. Only one client, a Dr. Phillip McSweeney, appeared on both lists. He'd spent a month here in the fall of 1965 when Sarah's diaries spilled over with her love for a nameless man. He'd been here again about the time that Beth was conceived. And most importantly, he'd returned to close a real estate transaction at nearby International Falls in September 1974, coinciding with Sarah's fatal canoe trip. Over the years, Dr. McSweeney had returned to Rainy Lake to tour Jake's island listings and had purchased several pieces of investment property from him.

Dr. Phillip McSweeney? *Pooh Bear?* Beth did a quick Google search on her laptop and found him. He was a prominent doctor out east who had done extensive research on Alzheimer's disease. He was seventy-two years old now, ten years older than her mother would have been. Digging deeper into his census records, she located a wife—the same wife—listed in 1960, 1970, 1980—all the way up to the last cen-

129

sus in 2000. Same name, Mary McSweeney. Dr. McSweeney was and had for years been married with children. *Oh my God,* Beth reiterated her growing sentiment. Maybe the ladies in the beauty shop were right, at least partially right. Perhaps her mother had fallen in love with this Dr. McSweeney. Perhaps *he* was her father. She copied down his address and phone number, anything else that she could find out about him. She didn't know what she would do with this information…not yet.

Elizabeth Peterson McSweeney Calhoun…was that who she really was? It was time to get back to her mother's diaries. There had to be more—some clues, something to help her figure this out.

"The willow tree weeps
alone she walks in sorrow
moon light shines on tears."
Kay Karras, Poet Laureate, Solon Springs, WI

Chapter Eighteen

September 16, 1967
Dear Diary,

I have no one to turn to but you, my silent and trusted friend. I cannot tell my terrible, yet wonderful, secret to anyone else. Not even Mama. I cannot humiliate her like this or cast my shame upon this household. The problem is that I'm pregnant! I'm scared to death and I feel so alone... Sometimes I pretend it's not real. God only knows that we did not intend for this to happen. I'm old enough to know better—I'm twenty-one. But I'm not sure that I'm prepared to be a mother—especially without a father for my child. He's older—thirteen years older than me—and yes, he also should have known better. How could he have let this happen? Part of me is furious with him—especially because of the circumstances. He can't marry me, not yet, although he swears we will be married as soon as possible. So what am I supposed to do as my belly grows larger every day? I can feel my baby moving sometimes. I already love her—yes, I think it's a girl, just a feeling I have. I want a little girl to love and care for. No matter what the circumstances are, I would never think of giving her up. She's mine—conceived in love, a love so strong that it spun out of control. Why didn't he control himself until the time was right for us? Why, dear God??

Sometimes I'm angry, sometimes sad. Sometimes I just need to feel his arms around me telling me that this will all be OK. But how can it possibly be OK? The problem is that the love of my life, my soul mate, is married this time around. I'm not proud of myself for falling in love with a married man, believe me. And I'm not proud of him either right now. He is locked into a loveless marriage that he has tried to escape from for a long time. He just needs to find a way to get out of it, and that will take a little time. More time than we have before the baby is born. All I know is that he loves me very much and he will be here for me always. In fact, when I told him that I was pregnant, his reaction told me so much. He was thrilled! He wants this baby as much as I do. He's trying to get a divorce. But right now, his wife is refusing to give him one. Why won't she let him go? They have lived separate lives for years, long before he met me. Does she just want to punish him, to make sure he can't find happiness with someone else? Does she suspect that he's in love with another woman? She doesn't know about me, I hope, or about our baby. Or, maybe if she knew…would she let him go?

I don't know what to do. I'm lost, terrified. I wear baggy clothes and Mama worries about my nausea and why I can't get over the "flu." I pray every night that God will help me, help Jake and me, to get through this. We need to be together as a family NOW. Our baby deserves this. How can I be patient when I'm going to have a baby? Dear God…what am I going to do?

❧❧

Oh my God! *Jake? Jake and me?* Beth dropped her mother's diary onto the floor of the gazebo, unable to read another word. She felt sick to her stomach. Jake O'Connell, their trusted family friend…her surrogate uncle for all these years…*my father? Oh my God!* How could he have done this to her mother, who had loved him beyond life itself? How could he have allowed gentle Sarah to be cast in the role of the *other woman* with no father in sight? He will pay for this, Beth resolved. He will also pay for the hell he'd created for her, his illegitimate child, for so many years. She still remembered how the kids had teased her because she had no father, how others had looked down upon her. How could that man have deceived her all these years and never acknowledged her as his child? What the hell was wrong with him? How could her mother have been so blind? As she collapsed in tears on the ground beside her mother's grave, a small voice filtered through her consciousness. *Deep in your heart, you've always known.*

Maybe that was true, she finally admitted to herself. Maybe she hadn't wanted to know, hadn't been open to hearing what others were trying to tell her. Sometimes the obvious was just too obvious, so close to home that you didn't even see it. Sometimes the truth could be so unsettling that it was easier to hide from it. So much for Dr. McSweeney. What, she wondered, were all those rumors at the beauty shop about?

If only she could find her original birth certificate, the one that had been missing all her life. Maybe Jake would be listed as her fa-

132

ther. She'd have proof. When she'd gotten married or applied for a passport, she'd had to request copies from the county records office. It had been embarrassing to see a blank where her father's name should have been listed. Deep down, she'd always wanted to fill in that blank, although she wasn't about to admit that to anyone else. But if she could just find the original certificate—maybe her mother or Nana would have written in the name of her father. Pulling herself to her feet, she ran back to the house. Slamming the door, she ran up to the attic where her grandfather's trunk held the family secrets. She dug furiously through papers, photos, old letters. Her heart was pounding. It had to be here someplace. At the very bottom of the trunk, tucked away in the far corner, she retrieved an official-looking manila envelope. Holding her breath, she carefully removed the contents. Her hands shook as she held her long-lost birth certificate. A tiny footprint. A newborn photo. Her eyes searched for her father's name, fearful that it would be blank. And it was. Her heart sank into the hollow pit of her stomach.

Reeling, she stumbled back down the stairs and settled in the rocking chair on the porch. She could hear the wind picking up outside, the waves slapping against the rocky shoreline. The sun disappeared beneath clouds of grey, almost as bleak as her world had suddenly become. She felt numb inside until the red-hot heat of her suppressed anger began to shoot through her veins. Damn him! How could he have done this to her? Impulsively, she picked up the phone and dialed his number. He answered on the first ring.

"How could you?" she sobbed into the phone. "My *father*? Oh no— you'll never be *my* father. I want you to just get out of my life, do you hear me?" With that, she slammed the phone down, poured herself a glass of wine, and began to pace back and forth around the room like a caged animal.

"Beth?" Jake spoke into the dead phone. She'd obviously found the truth in the pages of Sarah's diaries. She was furious, and he didn't blame her. He knew this would be ugly. He knew that he had to find a way to make things up to her. A six-figure inheritance wasn't going to cut it. This was about love, about relationships, about mistakes that should have been resolved long ago. It was all about being a coward, he thought to himself. What should he do now, he wondered—just stay the hell out of her life as she told him to? Or was it time for him to face the music and try to talk to her?

❦❧

It took only moments before he decided to make a trip out to the island. It was getting windy and rain clouds were brewing on the horizon, but that didn't matter right now. He grabbed his rain gear, fired up the engine on his boat, and headed out across the big lake.

Raindrops were beginning to fall as he arrived at the island and hiked up the trail, trying to decide what he should say to her. He cautiously opened the door of Nana's cottage to find Beth pacing up and down the length of the room. A fire blazed in the hearth on this late-summer evening, but it was unable to penetrate the chill in the air. She spun around when she heard his footsteps, surprised to see him. She had just told him to get out of her life, hadn't she?

"Pooh Bear?" she spat the words into his face the moment he entered the room. He stopped, stunned to hear Sarah's pet name for him exploding from the rigid lips of their daughter. He could not speak, but his silence told her all that she needed to know.

"How could you?" She glared at him, clenching her fists. "I thought I could trust you, my good old *Uncle Jake*! Now, I don't know who the hell you are! Look what you did to my mother, and to me. You've lied and deceived us all these years. You were married, for God's sake—you still are. You're a liar, a cheat, just like my husband! My God, how could you?"

"I know you're upset and I don't blame you. But you need to listen. Please, Beth. I am more sorry than you know—sorry that I wasn't able to find a way to tell you sooner. I tried, you know. You didn't want to hear it. Sorry that I made the biggest mistake of my life. All I ever wanted was to find a way to be with you and Sarah, to be together as a family like we'd always planned. Then," his voice choked up, "it was too damn late."

"I don't give a damn! You screwed up! You ruined our lives, Jake O'Connell. Oh my God, how could you?" she wailed as her long-repressed fury finally found a target. "Do you have any idea what my life was really like? While Nana and I struggled here alone, the kids made fun of me, Jake O'Connell. I was the kid without a father! And you—you just went about your life as if I didn't exist. Pretending to be my uncle—oh my God. How could you?"

"Beth, I am sorry…"

"Sorry? Is that all you can say? It's bad enough what you did to my mother. But me—what about me, Jake? Why did you leave me? Why?" She began to sob as she collapsed into Nana's rocking chair.

He longed to hold her in his arms, to kiss away her tears like he used to when she was a little girl. When he was the Uncle Jake that she adored. "I tried to be here for you as much as I could," he began.

"That's not good enough," she cut him off. Why didn't you take me and raise me like any decent father would have? Why did you refuse to admit you were my father?"

Like any decent father would have... Her words pierced his heart. He deserved it. He'd struggled for a long time after Sarah died, trying to decide what he should do about Beth. Trying to figure out what was best for his daughter under the circumstances. He'd thought about going through with his divorce, taking Beth and raising her at Houska's Point. But what about Nana? There had been no right answer, no way not to hurt somebody else. He had hurt his little girl instead! Watching her now, he was filled with guilt. Perhaps he had, once again, made the wrong decision. *Damn it, Jake, can't you do anything right?* His father's words rang in his ears. Maybe the old man had been right about him after all.

"Answer me, Jake. I deserve an explanation—not that anything you say could ever make up for what you've done." She began pacing around the room again.

"Yes, you do deserve an explanation," he began slowly, trying to find answers that she would understand. Why should she understand? He still didn't. "Maybe I should have taken you and raised you myself. Maybe that's exactly what I should have done. But how could I take you away from Nana? You were all she had left in this world. You loved her dearly, Beth. It was bad enough that you'd lost your mother. How could I take you away from the grandmother you'd lived with all your life, from the island where you belonged? Put yourself in my place once. What would you have done?"

"We could have all lived here together. That's what Mama would have wanted. You know that. But you were married, damn you, and you still are! You're no better than my cheating husband. Does Evelyn know about this, or are you lying to her, too?" She turned her back on him, staring out the window into the rain.

"She knows, of course. She refused to give me a divorce back then so I could marry Sarah. I always planned to leave when the time was right." He hung his head, speaking softly, lost in memories of the past. "Do you know how thrilled we were to have you, Beth? We had so many plans for our future together, trips we would take as a family.

Disneyland. The ocean. But then, after your mother died…" he choked up, sickened by the look of disgust flowing through his daughter's watery eyes.

"Then, what? Then you walked away from your own daughter, right? As if I didn't exist. What the hell is wrong with you, Jake? Why?"

"There's more, more than Nana pleading with me to let her raise you. This is painful for me to tell you this, but I want you to know the whole truth. After Sarah died…every time I looked at you, I saw her face. It tore me apart. I was drowning in despair, so devastated that I couldn't function. Every time I looked at you, I blamed myself for…for not being able to save your mother, for taking her away from you. I wish to hell that I'd been the one who drowned that day, not the love of my life," he clenched his fists.

"So do I!" she exploded, shocking herself.

"Well, then we agree on one thing, don't we?" he tried to mask the wound she'd just inflicted upon him.

She did not respond as she resumed staring out the window, carefully averting her gaze from the framed photo on the desk beneath the window. In the photo, a smiling Beth was celebrating her fifth birthday, admiring the fancy doll cake that Mama and Nana had made for her. Jake and Sarah stood behind her, their arms around her.

"Look, Beth. If you want to know the truth, I felt that I did not deserve you. I thought you'd be better off with Nana and I could just spend time with you both on the island—like an uncle. I thought that was the right thing to do for you. I really did."

"Well, you were wrong!" She settled back into the rocking chair, staring down at the flowered Victorian rug. Her puffy eyes traced and retraced the wine-colored vines that meandered across the floor in all directions. An endless trail filled with detours and dead ends—just like life, she thought to herself.

Why did she have to make this so damn hard? He'd always wanted her to respect him, to look up to him. But now he had no choice but to reveal secrets that could make her think even less of him. He took a deep breath and went on. "OK, here's the rest of the story, the other reason why I wasn't able to take you then, Beth…"

She looked up, her eyes challenging him to come up with something that would make some sense out of this disaster.

Jake cleared his throat and plunged in, reliving the miserable life he'd led after Sarah had drowned and left him alone. "I would not have been a good father to you then. I was so crushed that I couldn't manage my own life, much less take care of a child. I didn't have the energy to get through a bitter divorce. For what? Your mother was gone. I blamed myself for that, damn it, and I still do. I sunk into a deep depression. In those days, I drowned my sorrow by drinking too much. Way too much. Trying to kill the pain, trying not to think about what had happened. Trying to pretend it was all a bad dream. I couldn't even work that first year. My business was going to hell and I really didn't care—until I realized that I needed money to support you and Nana. It was the least I could do. Finally, I weaned myself from the bottle and began to escape into my work. I went from alcoholic to workaholic."

"So to hell with Beth, right?" she snapped, sick of his excuses.

"Look, I always thought that I'd find a way to come back for you, to be a real father to you," he hesitated, "but I had to work through my pain first and get my act together so I could be the kind of father you deserved. But the years wore on and we all seemed to settle into a pattern, I guess. You grew up, and I didn't want to rock the security of your world."

"*Your* pain, Jake? What about *my* pain?"

"You had Nana, and you were happy here together. She was doing a much better job raising you than I ever could have, especially with the long hours I was working."

"So you just cast your own daughter out of your life, is that it?" she bolted from her chair to confront him face to face.

"No, Beth," he finally raised his voice in frustration. "Goddamn it, I never cast you out of my life. I was here with you a lot over the years. You can't pretend I was never here for you. Think about it. Remember our fishing trips? Swimming at the beach? Making s'mores together over the fire? The bedtime stories I read you every time I came out to the island? Things my own father sure as hell never did for me. I tried to be the best father I could be. How can you accuse me of casting you out of my life?"

"I don't care! I just want you *out of my life—now! Out!*" She flung the door open, gesturing for him to leave.

"Please, Beth. There's more that you need to know. I'll tell you everything if you will just calm down. We need to talk. Please sit down."

Beth's eyes flashed with the fury that she'd stored up over the years. Fury that she never dreamed she'd have to unleash upon her Uncle Jake, of all people. She could not speak. She stood rigidly beside the open door.

"You need to know one thing—I love Sarah very much. I always have and I always will. And I love you, Beth," his eyes pleaded with her, trying to make her understand, to forgive him. If only she'd just give him a chance.

"Love?" she snorted. "What do *you* know about *love? Just get out of my life, Jake. Now!*" She grabbed a vase from the table beside the door, swinging it wildly through the air.

Jake hesitated a moment before deciding that this was not the right time to deal with this situation. At least he'd tried. He'd come back another day. He retreated out the door into a cold, drizzling rain, his head hung low. He heard a crash inside the house. Someday—yes, someday, he would find a way to make her understand. He would make it up to her. He slunk down the trail to his boat. He deserved her wrath. He was a coward, a despicable coward.

"Oh, Sarah," he whispered, focusing as hard as he could, "please help her to understand, to forgive."

৵৩৻৶

Beth kicked the remnants of the broken vase out of her way and bolted out the door. She could see the lights of Jake's boat receding into the distance. Jake, *her father?* She needed to get away, off the island, away from his blatant betrayal of her and of her mother. Raindrops seeped through her blouse, chilling her. She really didn't care. She backed the launch out of the boathouse, gunning it at full speed. She didn't know where she was going—just away. It was late, pitch dark. The moon hid beneath a dense layer of clouds, peeking out occasionally to tease the world below. Across the bay, she saw a light in Seth's cabin. It beckoned her, drawing her closer and closer to a place where she knew she did not belong.

Blinded by her tears, she ran up the trail to Seth's cabin, stumbling on the protruding rocks in the path. She pounded on his door as if someone was in hot pursuit. She didn't know why she was here on Seth's island, of all places…but there was no place else to go. Seth threw the door open, standing there in his shorts. She gasped.

"Come in. Let me get dressed," he mumbled, half asleep. Then, seeing the terror in her eyes, he pulled her into his arms, wanting to comfort her. She was wet, dripping onto the hardwood floor as she clung to him like a life raft. Her tears tumbled freely down his tan, muscular chest. He stroked her head, murmuring softly in her ear, "It's OK. You're OK."

She snuggled against him, unable to let go, holding him closer and closer. But the heat of her tears caressing his bare skin was more than he could handle. He had to break away. Holding her at a safer distance, he searched her eyes. He could feel her pain reflected in their depths. "Beth, what is it?"

"It's Jake," she replied, her voice shaking.

"Has something happened to Jake? Is he OK?"

"He's *my father*! I just found out that my *uncle* is really my *father*! My mother's diaries…and Jake, he admitted it. I can't believe it. I mean, how could he have deceived me all these years? He was married, Seth, a married man. And he never had the decency to marry my mother, he…" She couldn't go on.

"I know." He looked down at the floor, unable to look her in the eye.

"You know? Am I the only one in the dark here?" There was a hint of accusation in her voice, as if he should have told her, as if someone should have told her.

He sighed, turning away from her to pull on a pair of jeans and yesterday's shirt. "Yes, I know," he began slowly. "Look, your father made some big mistakes, Beth. Mistakes that he deeply regrets. He wasn't perfect. He married the wrong woman to begin with—Evelyn, I think that's her name. Then he fell in love with your mother and he couldn't stay away from her. All I know is that he loved your mother, and he has always loved you. I think a great deal of him, to be honest. In my book, he's a kind, decent man—despite the mistakes he has made in his life."

"Decent? You must be joking. He's deceived me all these years. And he never made an honest woman of my mother. Kind and decent?" She shook her head in disbelief.

"Yes, he should have told you. But maybe it wasn't easy to find the right time to tell you—especially after your mother died. He was afraid to tell you, to upset you. You know, it's always easy to look back and wish we'd done things differently. If only your mother had lived, Beth, he would have found a way to marry her, to be with you both…I have no doubt of that."

"And how would you know these things?"

"Because we talked, sometimes while we put up a winter's supply of firewood for your grandmother or hauled blocks of ice in for her. We talked because his heart was heavy and he needed to share his feelings with someone. I am honored that he trusted me enough to speak to me freely, from his heart, from the depths of his soul."

She searched his eyes, wanting to believe him, finally realizing that he spoke the truth. His eyes, however, were deep and dangerous, drawing her into them. She felt a drowning sensation as she melted into his arms once again. He held her close, heart pounding, then abruptly broke away from her embrace. He turned away, trying to hide his growing desire. Only the Great Spirit knew how much he wanted her, more than he'd ever wanted any other woman. But this was not the time or the place. He respected her too much to take advantage of this situation.

"Seth?" she pleaded softly with him, her arms outstretched. She became a child-woman at that moment. A woman needing the warmth of a man, this man, only this man. Yet, a little girl crying out in the dark, *Mama, can I sleep with you?* A lost child searching for the comfort of the father she'd never known.

He found a towel, used it to dry her hair, then draped it around her quivering shoulders. Then he grabbed one of his clean flannel shirts, handing it to her as he turned away. When she'd dried off and changed, he silently led her to the sofa. "You can sleep here," he said. He covered her with a blanket, tucking it around her like her mother used to do, like Nana used to do. "I'll be here if you need me," he bent over her, running his fingers across her forehead, down the side of her face, pausing at her uplifted chin. Almost touching her parting lips. Almost.

"But…" a bewildered Beth stammered as he withdrew his trembling hand. She was no longer able to think about anything except her need for this man. *Stay with me,* she pleaded silently, *I do need you.*

He held her hand, standing beside her, watching her. His heart ached, absorbing her pain. If only he could comfort her, love her the way she wanted him to. He waited silently as her eyelids began to close. "Sweet dreams, Ninimosche," he whispered tenderly as he tiptoed back to his own bed.

"Ninimosche?" she smiled softly to herself as she finally drifted off to sleep beside the glowing embers in his pot-bellied stove. She didn't know what it meant—probably an old Ojibwe word—but it filled her heart with love.

◈◈◈

She was already gone when he woke the next morning, as he knew she would be. He had watched her sleeping late into the night, her face bathed in pale moonlight streaming in through the window. Hugging her pillow like a little girl. He wanted to paint her someday.

Turning on his computer, he was alerted of a new message. From Beth. *"Seth, I just want you to know how sorry I am for my behavior last night. I was upset and I made a fool of myself. I think I need to be alone for a while to sort out my feelings—feelings about a lot of things. I'm really not fit for company right now. But I will get through this. You have given me the strength to know that I can. Thank you. Sincerely, Beth."*

He'd figured as much. She was humiliated, and she was retreating into her private shell. He wondered if he could have done anything else, anything different, to make it better for her. At least he hadn't given in to his desires, as difficult as that had been. He knew that would have ruined everything—forever.

He hit the reply button. *"Dear Beth, there is no reason to apologize to me. I understand. Just remember that I'm here for you. I think the world of you and I'm honored that you came to me last night. Yes, you will get through this. Take care and come on over anytime. Friends always, Seth."*

She opened his email message the moment it appeared on her screen, grinning to herself. He had a way of making her world a little brighter. *But…*even if *he* could forget and forgive her lapse in judgment last night, she was not ready to forgive herself. *What was I thinking? I threw myself into his arms, like one of Rob's whores! What would have happened if Seth hadn't had the decency to back off?* Rob's words came back to haunt her once again: *You're pathetic, Beth. Pathetic…*

Yes, she needed to be alone for a while. The last thing in the world that she needed was to get involved with another man. Seth was too good to be true…there had to be a dark side lurking someplace deep down, just like all men. She decided that she had to stay away from this man—the one that she could not quit thinking about. She was not ready, not now, probably not ever. It made no sense to make friends with anybody until she found herself, until she understood who she was and what she wanted in life.

And then, there was the matter of Jake, her father…

Chapter Nineteen

I t was time to return to Sarah's words. This time Beth was apprehensive as she trudged back to the gazebo. How much more could she stomach? How much worse could it get? Still, she needed to know the truth. Her mother may have been naïve and foolishly in love, but she *was* her mother.

June 15, 1968
Dear Diary,

Emily Dickinson "dwelt in possibilities." As for me, my possibilities have just begun with the birth of our darling baby daughter, Elizabeth Ann Peterson. Someday, she will be known as Elizabeth Ann Peterson O'Connell. Jake and I are so anxious for the day when we will all be together as a family.

Beth was born May 8, 1968, at the Falls Memorial Hospital. Jake was there to hold my hand, to stroke my back, to reassure me that it would be OK. I am content just to hold her in my arms, hour after hour. We are both in awe that we have been blessed with this beautiful child. She has her daddy's eyes and my hair. When her eyes open wide and look into mine, I fall in love with her over and over again.

The circumstances of Beth's birth are not perfect… Jake is not yet divorced. His wife recently suffered a nervous breakdown designed to keep him from leaving her. Her wealthy family, and his, have descended upon them threatening to eliminate them from the family business. This would mean financial ruin to all concerned. I, frankly, do not care. All I want is to become his wife. Jake is still somewhat hesitant to disobey the father who has controlled him for years. He worries about financial security if he pulls out and is disinherited. Again, I don't give a damn about money. It's useless if you can't be with the ones you love.

Timing is everything, they say. Someday, when the time is right, we will be together without having to hide our love for each other. This is my prayer, my wish for our future. God grant me the strength to perse-vere until we can make our dream come true!

For now, Jake is playing the role of dear family friend, Beth's Un-cle Jake, as we call him. He can't seem to stay away from us, always making excuses to come out to the island to see us. Mama loves him as well and doesn't question his involvement. He is totally spoiling little Beth—always bringing her a little toy, pretty dresses that I could never afford to buy. And he gives me money each month to support our little girl—more than we need. I save some for a rainy day.

Mama takes care of Beth sometimes so Jake and I can go for a walk or a boat ride alone together. I love spending time with him, wrapped in his arms. We have to be careful about being seen together too much…I don't like that. But I guess it's true that no relationship is per-fect. There are always problems to resolve. I would never trade my relationship with Jake, married or not, for marriage to any other man. Not ever! What we have is something so special that I struggle to find words to express it. If there's such a thing as reincarnation and past lives, I have no doubt that Jake and I have shared a number of past lives. It's as if we have always known each other. It's beyond us to un-derstand why we can't be together completely this time around…at least not yet.

Beth paused to reflect, feeling the intensity of her anger subsiding a bit. Her mother had obviously been happy with him, despite the cir-cumstances. And he *had* been there for them both, in his own way, the only way that he could at that time in his life. They apparently accepted their circumstances. Did she, Beth, have the right to pass judgment upon them, to refuse to accept the arrangement they had chosen?

Still, she wondered if either of her parents had bothered to consider the impact of their arrangement upon their daughter's life. Would things have been any different if Sarah had lived? Seth seemed to think so…yes, Seth. Life, she realized, was not always black or white. Just shades of grey. Perhaps we each created our own reality, based upon the lens through which we viewed our world.

"The woods are lovely, dark and deep
and I have miles to go before I sleep,
miles to go before I sleep."
Robert Frost

Ranier Waterfront by Bernie "Spike" Woods

Chapter Twenty

*T*here is a time to live, a time to die…a time to laugh, a time to cry. Jake contemplated his choices as he trudged down the alley toward Woody's Pub for a few beers. Hands stuffed in his jacket pockets, head down, he braced himself against the wind that was howling off the lake. It was going to be an early fall. He could feel it in the air. In his weary bones.

He passed Ranier Beach, just steps beyond his office on Houska's Point. Whitecaps whipped across angry grey swells, splashing against the wharf that protruded from the deserted beach. He hoped that Beth had the sense not to venture out onto the lake on a day like this. She knew better, of course, but he still worried about her in her distraught frame of mind. And she didn't even know the rest of the story…not yet. Would she ever forgive and accept him as her father? Could she find it within her heart to understand that he was not perfect but had done the best that he could?

Beth's shrill words of yesterday seemed to echo in the wind. "What about me? Why did you leave me? Why?"

Because I'm no damn good, he chastised himself, using the words he'd heard so often as a child. *Can't I do anything right?* He never could measure up to his father's standards, no matter how hard he tried. He'd even tried football just to please the old man. He'd hated it and he really was no damn good at it. He already knew that—why did the old man have to bellow these cutting words across the field in front of everyone? While his father thrived on competition, Jake wasn't into competitive sports or competition at any level. He had preferred solitary sports and activities, especially fishing and skiing. He was pretty good at both, but his father belittled anything he accomplished. He made it clear that he was not about to waste his precious time sitting out on a lake with his son.

Jake remembered how the old man would call him into his office in the evening after he'd belted down a few too many whiskies. That always meant trouble. That's when the tirade would begin. No matter what Jake did, it was always wrong. There was no way to please the man. He wasn't always mean, Jake remembered. He was usually too busy to pay any attention to him at all. He never attended any of his school functions, not even the time he played the leading role in his high school play. In his father's eyes, he didn't exist—except for those times that he was called into the office and brought to tears by his father's stinging words. Crying wasn't acceptable, however. "What kind of a pussy are you?" The old man would shake his head with contempt. "Get a grip, boy. You're acting like a goddamned girl."

Jake tried to clear yesterday's cobwebs from his weary mind as he approached Woody's Pub. The place had been here forever, an old, white, two-story clapboard building with pine-green trim. The locals hung out here, especially on stormy days like this when they weren't out fishing. It felt good to step into the warmth of the unpretentious bar where men in plaid flannel shirts and baseball caps straddled the red vinyl bar stools drinking beer. They were swapping stories about the fish they caught and colorful tales of the good old days in the Village of Ranier.

"Hey, Jake," they greeted him warmly. He'd become one of the locals, an honor that he relished. Butch, the bartender slid a Leininkugel's beer across the bar to him before he had a chance to order one. A stuffed moose head with a cowbell around its neck hung over the polished wood bar. The walls were covered with photos of customers holding their prize fish and news articles featuring Woody himself, the infamous fishing guide and proprietor of this rustic establishment. There was an assortment of old beer signs and mounted fish on the walls surrounding several wobbly, weathered tables floating on the shifting, well-worn floorboards. A faded black and white photo of former President Dwight D. Eisenhower hung in an alcove beside an ugly mounted catfish. It was as if time had stopped here years ago.

Jake chugged down his beer, half-listening to the conversation around him. When they tired of their fish stories, the conversation shifted to politics. The locals were a self-reliant and independent bunch, descended from pioneer families who had endured many hardships to survive here on what was once the last frontier. They worked hard and they played hard. They disliked laws that limited their freedom. That included restrictive hunting and fishing regulations. Some had never gotten over the National Park Service's controversial acquisition of private land and waterways used to create Voyageur's National Park back in 1975.

"What do you think, Jake?" Someone jolted him from his private world of anguish.

"I'm sorry—guess I was lost in thought. What's the question?" he smiled wearily.

"The park. Was it a good move or a bad one? We can't seem to agree on that." A bulky man sporting a grizzly gray beard shoved another beer at him. "My round," he added.

"Thanks, Bud," Jake took a long swig of his beer. He knew that he wasn't quite himself tonight. He wasn't sure that he was up for an argument. But he might as well jump in anyway. It was an important issue, one that meant a lot to him. All eyes at the bar focused on Rainy Lake's major real estate broker, someone who'd made lots of money over the years selling lake property. Now the Park Service owned much of that land. Surely this would have cut into Jake's profits…

"I support the park. It was an excellent move, I think. We have a moral obligation to preserve our lakes and this exceptional piece of the wilderness for future generations. To provide habitat for our shrinking wildlife population, the bears, moose, wolves…" Jake began.

"You sound like our boy Ober," the bartender reflected. He was, of course, referring affectionately to Ernest Oberholtzer, the pioneer conservationist who'd spent much of his life living on a rocky island in Rainy Lake, just half a mile from the Canadian Border. A legend in these parts and an unsung hero to many, Ober had fought relentlessly to preserve this, one of the last great wilderness areas east of the Rockies. His efforts eventually resulted in the creation of Voyageur's National Park as well as the Boundary Waters Canoe Area Wilderness and Quetico Provincial Park in Canada.

Ober had been a colorful character—a friend of the Ojibwe, explorer, photographer, musician, and scholar whose island library housed thousands of volumes. The gang at Woody's frequently entertained themselves reminiscing about the "little giant," as they called him, and his wilderness adventures.

"When I think of that canoe expedition that he made with Billy Magee, his Indian friend and guide, all the way to Hudson Bay, Canada in 1912," Bud stared into the past. "It's hard to imagine how they survived."

Jake had recently done some reading on this epic journey. "Can you imagine canoeing for two thousand miles, for 144 days, through wild, unpopulated territory that was largely unmapped at that time?"

"And the incredible photos that he took of the natives they met on their journey," the bartender added. "Quite a legend, he was. And his legacy lives on, doesn't it?"

"Sure does—every time I get out there on the lake into the park waters," Jake added.

"Still," one man countered the others, "don't we have individual rights to own and enjoy our own little piece of this wilderness?" It was the same old argument that the locals had engaged in for the past thirty years.

"That's for sure!" another jumped into the debate. "My family's island home is gone now, demolished, thanks to the park. Gone…nothing but memories."

"It needed to be done," someone sided with Jake. "Too much development, too many homes, too many fast boats. My God, what would it be like today?"

"Without the Park Service stepping in with their resources, Kettle Falls would be in ruins," Jake reminded them. "Nobody here had the money to renovate that wonderful piece of our history, or to manage it in a way to preserve it for the future. We still have our privately-owned islands and lakeshore property on the fringe of the park, you know. But I can tell you that it's a wonderful feeling when you enter the park waters and lose yourself in the pristine wilderness. You see wildlife again. You become a part of nature. That's what it's all about."

"Maybe," one younger man conceded. "I do want my kids and my grandkids to enjoy it someday… But you know, the feds are cutting back funding for our national parks. How are they going to be able to keep them all up?"

"That's why I plan to leave some of my money to the Park Service when I die, specifically for Voyageur's…" Jake spoke quietly, aware that he was speaking more freely than he probably should be. He'd never told this to anyone before, certainly not to his wife. It would be a part of his legacy to the world. As much as Rainy Lake meant to him, it was the least that he could do in return. His memories of Sarah, of their wilderness trips together in what was now Voyageur's National Park, brought back some of the best times of his life. And the worst. He still visited Sarah's Island as often as he could.

You could have heard a pin drop as they all turned to stare at him. He managed a weak smile as he stood up to leave, zipping his jacket. "One more round for the house," he called out to the bartender, tossing a twenty on the bar. "I need to head out, calls to make," he excused himself.

"Jake, you all right?" the bartender asked.

"I'm fine, thanks. Just a little tired, I guess, after my trip to New York and all. See you guys later." He headed out into the night, thankful that the wind had died down. The stars were brilliant tonight, illuminating the familiar path back home. Back home where he could be alone with his thoughts. Where he could struggle with his guilt as he tried to figure out how and when to tell Beth the rest of the story.

※ ❦ ☙

It was cold out tonight, but he needed to sit out on the porch for a while, rocking, gazing up at a pitch-black sky sprinkled with orbs of pure white light. He wondered what was really out there beyond the stars, beyond the universe as we knew it… Where was heaven? Where was Sarah tonight? The night sky, despite its mysteries, helped him to put things into perspective. It humbled him to realize that he was, after all, just a tiny speck in a gigantic universe. He was really not that important after all, nor were his little problems. Finally, his old bones began to ache with the penetrating chill of the night. It was time to turn in for another sleepless night. But first, he fired off an email to Seth.

Hello, Seth. Fall is moving in fast. I'd like to have you put up a supply of wood on the island again this year, if you would. This time, of course, it will be for Beth, who plans to spend the winter there. Just send me your bill. I also need to ask a little favor of you. Please keep an eye out for her, will you? She's dealing with some tough stuff right now and I want to be sure that she's OK. Thanks, Seth. Please stay in touch. Jake.

Jake half-heartedly checked his stocks online, somewhat pleased that his recent investments in gold had gone through the roof. He saw gold as a hedge against inflation and the deteriorating value of the dollar. He should be exuberant…

Moments later, an email from Seth popped up on his screen. *Hello, Jake. Yes, I will put up the wood for Beth. And it will be my pleasure to keep an eye out for her. We have spoken and she is quite upset. I trust that she will be all right. She needs time and space to deal with this—a break from both of us, it seems. She knows that I'm here if she ever needs anything. I do think the world of your daughter, Jake. I'll stay in touch. Seth.*

Jake smiled to himself. He had a feeling that something could be developing between his daughter and her neighbor. If that were the case, he would be more than pleased.

"Hope is the thing with feathers
that perches in the soul…"
Emily Dickinson

Chapter Twenty-one

Dog days…that's what Nana had called the last sultry days of summer. Lazy days. Days to *lollygag around,* Nana said. So many *Nana-isms,* Beth thought to herself as she toiled in her vegetable garden, hot and sweaty beneath the sweltering summer sun. Weeding, hoeing, picking vegetables, mending fences. Trying to bury her anger at Jake. The soil comforted her as it sifted slowly through her outstretched fingers. It seemed to reconnect her with the earth. To ground her in reality. She didn't leave the island these days. She needed to be alone, to get a grip on life, to flush the anger—the poison—out of her system. At least Rob wasn't harassing her, thank God. Maybe he really was moving on with his life. A life without his wife of twenty years. With each passing day, she felt a little safer, a little stronger. She no longer checked and double-checked the locks on her doors at night. She no longer woke in the middle of the night to check them once again—just in case. And she no longer anxiously scanned passing boats to be sure Rob wasn't out there, somewhere, looking for her. He had moved on…wasn't that what she wanted?

The only intrusion into her reclusive existence were those calls from her attorney. Bad news, always more delays. It would be a while before the divorce was settled, before she should expect to receive an alimony check, before their home sold.

As her funds dwindled away, she began to get the picture. She couldn't rely upon Rob to help support her, that was for sure. She wasn't about to ask Jake for money. *It's up to me to support myself,* she realized one night as she sat in the gazebo staring vacantly into a black sky filled with glittering stars. A falling star blazed across the horizon, plunging into the lake. She suddenly saw herself, pathetic little Beth, plunging into unknown depths of self-destruction if she didn't take control of her life soon. A spark ignited deep within her soul, smoldering amongst the cold ashes of her life. Finally, flames began to flicker, then to blaze with newfound determination and confidence. *I'll be damned if I ever have to rely on a man again! Never again! I can take care of myself—Nana did, and so can I.*

๑৪৯

She woke early the next morning to the song of birds chirping outside the windows of the eagle's nest. Instead of dragging herself out of bed as she'd done each morning for the past few weeks, she was almost eager to face the day. Determined. Today she would begin going through Nana's drawers and closets.

While it felt strange to be rifling though someone else's possessions, Beth could feel something nagging at her, telling her that it was time to pull her head out of the sand and face the future. The sun peeked cautiously through the windows of Nana's old bedroom, almost blushing, as Beth opened the first drawer of Nana's bureau. Memories of Nana flooded through her mind as she held a frayed navy-blue sweater to her cheek. She remembered Nana wearing it on chilly evenings by the fire. She sorted through faded photos and mementos of the past. Pieces of a life that no longer existed. *Things* that once mattered to Nana. In the big picture of life and death, *things* no longer mattered, Beth realized. Now, it was time to dispose of her grandmother's possessions. She would, of course, keep a few items for herself and for Emily, perhaps a few mementos for some of Nana's friends. Maybe even something for Jake…

In the back of Nana's closet, she discovered a large cardboard box labeled *Property of Beth Calhoun* in Nana's distinctive handwriting. Beth's heart pounded as she carefully opened the box. The first thing she found was a wrapped Christmas present labeled *Merry Christmas to Beth from Nana with Lots of Love.* A teary-eyed Beth wondered if Nana had forgotten to mail it to her last Christmas…or if Nana had been waiting to give it to her when she finally came home again. A pang of guilt pierced her heart as she carefully opened the package. It was a stunning vintage-style necklace. A delicate black onyx cameo was framed in a silver filigree setting with four strands of shimmering ebony and silver beads. It was exquisite—and most importantly, Nana had made it for her.

Beth had forgotten about Nana's jewelry-making business. Years ago, her grandmother had spent long winter nights at the kitchen table surrounded with her beads and tools. While Beth studied by the fireplace, Nana sketched designs for her creations or pored through bead catalogs. Before long, locals and tourists alike were buying *Jewels by Emma.* This had supplemented their income over the years.

Oh, Nana, Beth sighed as she tried the necklace on. She would wear it proudly, wrapped in her grandmother's unconditional love. Not that she deserved it… There was more in the big box—layer after layer of plastic organizer boxes filled with beads and pendants of all kinds. Cameos, turquoise and shell beads, bamboo, crystal stones, aurora borealis rhinestones. Spools of wire, jewelry clasps and fittings, tools, bead catalogs, and a notebook filled with Nana's jewelry sketches. Everything a person would need to start a jewelry business…

The thought struck Beth with full force. The answer to her financial dilemma had been waiting for her in a box in her grandmother's closet. "I can do this!" Beth shouted to the empty house. "Thank you, Nana. *Jewels by Emma* will live on in your honor. And I will never again need to depend upon a man!"

Nana's gift lifted Beth's spirits and filled her with hope for the future. She spent the next few days working on her version of a business plan, doing research on the Internet, studying catalogs, and devouring Nana's design sketches. Beth wondered why it had taken her so long to realize that Nana had been an artistic and talented woman. Nana hadn't become rich with her business. She'd frequently given her jewelry away or priced items low enough for the locals to afford. And her marketing efforts had been largely through word-of-mouth. Today, Beth had access to the Internet. That's how Seth sold much of his work. He might be willing to help her create a Web site for her new business…but it wouldn't be *her* business. It would be *their* business, a joint venture between Beth and her deceased grandmother. *Jewels by Emma* would be a tribute to the woman who had raised her…perhaps a way for Beth to make things up to her.

"The greatest source of experience and inspiration
comes from the seasons of Spring and Autumn
and the transition and motion of life during these seasons."
Gerald Vizenor, Ojibwe writer

Chapter Twenty-two

As the autumn mist cleared over Rainy Lake, Beth grabbed her notebook, a camera, and a mug of steaming coffee. She crunched through falling leaves of red and gold as she hiked out to the gazebo.

Her mother would have been inspired to write a poem today. And that was exactly what Beth intended to do—to try to capture her favorite season in words. She settled into her wicker chair in the gazebo, looking out across the bay to see smoke rising from Seth's chimney. She couldn't let herself think about that right now. Breathing in the fresh, cool air, she let herself go, absorbing the images and feelings that surrounded her. Soon the words began to flow, bubbling into her mind from someplace deep down. Hours flew by as she polished her work. It almost felt like her mother was there, writing with her...

Finally she was pleased with what she now perceived as *their* tribute to fall:

MOTHER NATURE PAINTS FALL
She paints…
boldly splattering buckets of gold
and sun-kissed orange
across the landscape
of summer's end.

With the stroke of a brush,
fiery reds explode with passion,
transforming a lonely maple
into the crown jewel of the forest.
She's dazzling in her brilliance,
breaking hearts as she falls—at last
to the whims of winter's frost.

She paints…
weaving waves of yellow ribbons
along old logging trails,
shimmering in the sunlight,
casting reflections into
rippling puddles of time…

Reflections framed by
rigid rows of pine soldiers
standing erect, on guard,
suppressing displays of mirth
as leaves of color
fall at their feet.

Autumn leaves letting go
of their youth, their dreams…
frolicking in their finery
as they drift lazily
into a multi-colored blanket
crunching…
beneath the weight
of scampering squirrels.

She paints…
just holding on
until it's time
to let go
of the seasons of life.

Thanks, Mama, she grinned to herself as she hiked back down the trail to the house. She was anxious to share the poem with Emily and planned to email it to her this evening. Thank God for email, she thought to herself. Although she longed to hear her daughter's voice, to talk with her, at least they could afford to stay in touch by email.

Beth had been reading her mother's poems and more of her diary entries. They were filled with stories about Beth as a baby, a toddler, a little girl. Stories about Jake. About the things they did together on Nana's island. She'd forgotten about the wooden rowboat that Jake had given her. He'd named it after her, Elizabeth Ann, and painted her name on the stern using the bright red paint that she had picked out. The more she read, the more she began to realize, to remember, that they had been happy together. Almost like a family...

As she read, Beth found herself softening, beginning to understand that Jake had been there for them in many ways. Perhaps she had been too hard on him.

❧❧

Feeling more energized than she had in a long time, she threw herself into preparations for the winter. She canned the last batch of tomatoes from the garden, froze green beans, stored the squash in the cellar, and made beet pickles. She started working on a list of supplies that she'd need to get on the mainland before freeze-up. Kerosene for the lamps, extra batteries, snowmobile gas, farmers' matches, first aid supplies, staples, and a turkey for Thanksgiving since the holiday usually fell before the ice was safe enough to cross over to the mainland.

As she scribbled items down on her shopping list, the phone rang. It was Seth, sounding somewhat hesitant, on the other end of the line. She hadn't talked to him, or to Jake, since her meltdown several weeks ago. It was good to hear Seth's voice today.

"I hope I'm not interrupting anything," he began. "If you're busy, just tell me."

"Actually, it's good to hear from you," she grinned. "How have you been?"

"Busy chopping wood, getting ready for fall. That's why I called. Jake wants me to put up a supply of firewood for you over there..."

"I'd appreciate that. Come on over anytime you like. I've just put up a jar of my beet pickles for you."

"Sounds good...you sound good, too, Beth. Things going OK for you?"

"I'm better, much better. Putting things into perspective again, I guess. It's easy to judge when you don't know all the facts. I'm learning so much from my mother's diaries."

"That's wonderful. Have you told Jake?"

"Not yet....I need to talk with him sometime. Not yet. I may have been a little hard on him, do you think?"

"Want my honest opinion?"

"Yes, please."

"Well, then, yes, I think you were hard on him. He *is* your father, Beth. He deserves your respect, a chance to be your father—and to be a grandfather to Emily."

She smiled softly, a tear sliding down her cheek. Emily's grandfather...the grandfather that she would finally get to know when she came for her Christmas visit.

❧❧

Seth spent the next few days chopping, splitting, and hauling wood on Beth's island. She watched him through the window—his long, lean body swinging the ax with ease. He worked hard, stopping only when she invited him in for a bowl of her homemade chicken noodle soup or a piece of pie. They ate together in the kitchen, comfortable in each other's presence. Comfortable in the silences that often permeated their time together. This could get to be a habit, she thought to herself. She told him about her jewelry business plans. He was almost as excited as she was, and he offered to help her set up a Web site to promote her business—when she was ready, of course. She hadn't needed to ask...he seemed to intuit what she needed.

The last day, as he finished the job, leaving her with a winter's supply of firewood stacked high beside the front porch, he came in to tell her good-bye. He shuffled his feet as though he was reluctant to leave her—or was trying to think of an excuse to see her again.

"Seth? I, ah, thank you so much for doing this for me..." Beth stammered.

"My pleasure, ma'am." He tilted his hat toward her, grinning that irresistible smile of his.

"I was thinking that I owe you dinner sometime."

"I'd love that. Just tell me when. I was also thinking—you once told me you'd like to learn more about my people and our history." Watching her eyes brighten with interest, he went on, "I'd like to invite you on an expedition with me if you're interested. Every fall I take my boat out to explore some of the sites where my people lived years ago. When the water levels go down in the fall, I sometimes find artifacts near the old villages and burial grounds. I can show you pictographs on ancient rock formations."

She was surprised but pleased that he was offering to share his private journey with her. "I would love to go with you."

"Then, it's a date...or, ah, an exploration expedition. Say, next Saturday morning, weather permitting?"

"You're on. And again, thank you, Seth," she impulsively threw her arms around him. He hugged her back, reluctant to let her go.

∽৩৬∾

The entire northland was soon immersed in preparations for winter. Chainsaws buzzed and whined around the lake. Stores on the mainland ordered in extra supplies. The islanders would soon be stocking up on staples before freeze-up when they'd be temporarily stranded on their islands. Gardens were cleared and produce put up for the winter.

Evelyn O'Connell was busily pruning and mulching her flower gardens. It was time to prepare for the winter frosts ahead. After all, International Falls wasn't nicknamed the "Ice Box of the Nation" for no good reason. Armed with a thermos of hot apple cider heavily laced with brandy, she took numerous breaks to let the warm liquid seep through her veins. She no longer felt the chill in the air. In fact, she didn't feel much of anything as she flourished her gardening shears in the air, twirling and stomping through the frost-bitten mums like a Spanish dancer. Staggering now and then, she began to laugh, to howl, dancing through her secluded gardens as she clicked the shears. Beheading one flower after another with a wicked gleam in her eyes.

"Beth!" she addressed one faded peony bloom, slashing it to the ground. Next was "Sarah," another victim beheaded by her shears. And finally "Jake, *you bastard*," as she mutilated a drooping Black-Eyed Susan, shredding it into smaller and smaller pieces. It would not survive the winter. It would die slowly, painfully, a little each day—just as she had over their many years together.

"The three of you—you've destroyed my life. How stupid do you think I am? But you will pay—you will all pay," she promised as she slunk to the ground. She pounded the earth with her fists as bitter tears began to fall. Tears of regret for that which once was…for that which had never been—and would never be.

"If we can somehow retain places
where we can always sense
the mystery of the unknown,
our lives will be richer."
Sigurd Olson

Rainy Lake

Chapter Twenty-three

Seth was pleased with himself, at his offer to take Beth with him on his annual pilgrimage. This had always been a private time for him, a sacred time when he reconnected with his ancestors and his history. A time to lose himself in memories of the past, sometimes to embrace visions of the future. He'd never shared this with another living soul. Not until today.

It was one of those perfect fall days, the kind that poets had waxed over for centuries past. The world was alive, bathed in brilliant reds and golds that sparkled in sunlight. The lake was calm, lazily drifting around emerald islands scattered endlessly across the horizon of Rainy Lake. The lake was a part of him, just as it had been a part of his people for thousands of years. The lake was a giver of life. It was the place where his people had fished, traded, celebrated, and mourned.

Beth came running down the path when she heard his boat pulling into the dock. She waved a paper in her hand, grinning with delight. Her divorce was final—and this paper confirmed it. Rob had finally let her go. The terms weren't nearly as good as she'd hoped—but it was a small price to pay for her freedom from this man.

"Well, we have something to celebrate, don't we?" Seth hugged her as she climbed into the boat beside him. He gunned the motor, and they were off, skimming across the lake, back into the days when the landscape was dotted with Indian villages. He had places to show her today, places that were too far away for paddling his canoe. They were headed to Kettle Falls and beyond, into Canadian waters.

Their first stop, just beyond Kettle Falls, was Oak Point Island, where Seth killed the engine so they could drift slowly along the shoreline of this large Canadian island. He did not speak at first, gazing solemnly at the land. Beth followed his lead, not wanting to intrude on his private moments. It was enough just to be here with him. Enough that he had allowed her to accompany him this far into the world of his ancestors.

"Try to imagine this land, this island, two thousand years ago," he finally spoke, still gazing into the distance. "My people lived here in a village of teepees, part of the Ojibwe Bois Forte band. My grandmother was born here, Beth, in 1886—the one in my painting? My people chose this location because it was close to Kettle Falls where they could spear sturgeon, close to the Rat River where they harvested wild rice. This once was prime country for hunting moose and other big game, for fur-trapping, and of course, gathering berries of all kinds. My people were self-sufficient, a way of life that they greatly valued. A peaceful people, quiet, laid-back, self-controlled. And they loved their children very much..." his voice trailed off, far away into a distant past.

She listened intently but did not speak.

"My ancestors learned the habits of the birds and animals, studied the plants. They believed that man is a part of nature, that all living things have spirits—animals, trees, even rocks and bodies of water. They all possess souls and shadows that should be recognized and respected. It was about respect, respect for all living things. It still is...

"All things die, Beth," he turned to look into her eyes. "I believe that all things have a purpose in life, but also in death. Take a tree, for example. When the tree dies and falls, it allows more sunlight to filter down, providing warmth for the animals. Its dead branches and decaying leaves become a breeding ground from which saplings and moss begin to grow. It is the nurturing of life by the dead." He paused, his gaze again focusing on the land.

"To me, death gives life its passion. It's a friend, not an enemy. All things die…but their souls are reincarnated again and again. What was once dead returns to life. You see, it's really a circle of life that cycles on forever." His tone was hushed, reverent.

She was struck by the profound words spilling forth so eloquently from his lips, words that touched her personally. She'd always wondered where her mother was now…and Nana…and Papa. While she'd never thought much about the possibility of reincarnation, it certainly held out a beacon of hope for the future. Perhaps it provided meaning and a greater purpose for one's life than spending an eternity in heaven. She knew that she would not take Seth's words lightly. Coming from him, they held a great deal of credibility in her eyes. Still, reincarnation was a difficult concept to grasp. It seemed to fly in the face of all the traditional religious teachings she'd been exposed to…

She nodded silently when he finally turned to look at her.

"Consider these things, Beth. This is what I believe, what my people have believed for thousands of years."

"I will. Please tell me more."

"OK, back to History 101," he attempted to lighten the mood. "Sometime in the 1600s, my people, after living here by themselves for thousands of years, were shocked to see other people on the waters of Rainy Lake. Pale faces. They were the French-Canadian voyageurs who turned this region into an important part of a vast fur-trading empire. My people began to trap and trade furs to the voyageurs. The voyageurs would paddle their fur-laden canoes from these Canadian waters all the way to the East Coast, where they shipped the furs to Europe. There, they were made into beaver hats and fur coats to meet growing demands. We also traded our hides, wild rice, maple syrup, and berries for their tools, traps, rope, cloth, blankets, sugar, guns, ammunition—and for rum…"

Seth's eyes clouded over. He paused. "My people began to lose their independence. Worse yet, the rum became a problem since we were unaccustomed to alcohol and its effects. The white man's trading posts sometimes took advantage of this—providing unlimited quantities of liquor to secure provisions from the Indians—very cheaply. It's a sad story, one that we don't like to dwell upon…

"Am I talking too much?" he grinned at her as the boat drifted in closer to Oak Point Island.

"Never. I find this fascinating," she grinned back at him.

He carefully docked the boat and they got out to hike on the island. She walked beside him as he searched the earth for a sign from the past. Today, the island was overgrown with shrubs and pine trees—as if Seth's old Indian village had never existed. As they walked, he told her of artifacts that had been found here and at other Rainy Lake sites. Shards of Indian pottery, arrowheads, pipes, crude brass kettles, axes, beads, and ornaments made of bone. Old Indian burial mounds had also been discovered at Mound Point and other sites along the Rainy River. Here, the deceased were brought to places of sepulture where their bodies as well as their spiritual and worldly possessions were placed on these mounds of sacred earth. Clay pots, stone tubes, shell beads, and bone ornaments were scattered about beside the bodies to ensure that souls of the departed were properly launched into the hereafter. Over the years, these mounds grew. This practice stopped about three hundred years ago.

"Can we still see the burial mounds?" Beth was intrigued.

"Unfortunately, there's not much left of them on the U.S. side," he lamented. "But someday I'll take you into Canada, just beyond Fort Frances, where we can see one of the most spectacular mounds, still intact, at the Kay-Nah-Chi-Wah-Nung Historical Center. It's incredible, Beth," his dark eyes lit up, "the largest mound, overlooking the Rainy River, is about 113 feet in diameter and 24 feet high."

"I'd love to see it someday."

Seth suddenly became quiet, very quiet, as he stopped at what was once a clearing overlooking the lake below. She waited as he closed his eyes, breathing deeply. When he finally opened his eyes, they were misted over. "It's my people, my ancestors," he whispered. "I feel their spirits here. My grandmother…"

She longed to touch his hand but decided that he needed his space at the moment. Following him back to the boat in silence, she wondered where his people were now—the descendants of those who'd lived here on the island.

"Most of my people live on the Nett Lake Reservation, where they've been since the 1930s," he suddenly announced.

Seth maneuvered his boat through the Canadian Channel, through Stokes Bay, winding around island after island until Beth was sure that they would be lost in the big lake. He swung into a sheltered cove lined with ancient rock formations. Lifting the motor, he paddled around one jagged rock into a hidden nook. At the end of the narrow inlet, a massive rock protruded from the face of the cliff as if it was suspended in time. Weathered with age, it had been gouged and carved by the forces of nature into something that resembled the head of an Indian chief. The sun's slanting rays played upon the smooth face of the rock, highlighting the chief's eyes and cheekbones.

"Oh my God!" she exclaimed.

"You see it?"

"It looks like the head of an Indian chief!"

He smiled, pleased that she could see it, too. "There's more. We are moving in closer. Please do not speak. This is a sacred place."

As they paddled into the hidden cove, the shifting rays of light exposed painted images upon the rocks—faded red and brown drawings of what appeared to be stick men or spirits, a moose, an overturned canoe. Together, they sat in silence. Time stood still as they stared at the ancient images. They were surrounded by prehistoric rocks that held untold secrets unfolding over the past 2.7 billion years. They soaked it all in, lost in another time, another place. Finally, Seth arched his eyebrows at her in a questioning manner. She nodded. It was time to leave.

Seth broke the silence after they'd paddled out of the inlet and back around the jagged rock guarding the entrance. "That is my Dreamer's Rock," he began wistfully. "It is the place where I, as a young boy, was left to experience my first vision quest. Do you know what a vision quest is?"

"No, I'm afraid not."

"Well, my people believe that by the time a child reaches the age of twelve, it is time for that child to connect with his spirit guide. We each have our own guide out there in the spirit world, someone to guide and protect us, to serve as a bridge between a child and Gitchi Manidoo, the Great Spirit. Our elders arrange for each of us to venture out on a vision quest. We must withdraw from the world for several days. We fast. We pray for a vision, a dream to guide us on our journeys through this life."

He paused, floating back in time to his first vision quest. "I'll never forget it…three days in the wilderness, alone. No food, no water. Just a blanket. It was a lesson in self-control and discipline. I came back a man. A man with a vision for my life and a connection to my spirit guide."

As he spoke, she could see shadows of the past playing across his face, softening his facial features.

He took a deep breath, pulling himself back to the present. "Without the distraction of bodily needs and with total solitude, I found that I could tap into a greater reality than I'd ever known. You see, dreams are the language of the soul, as my people believe. It is through our dreams and visions that we make contact with other spirits, including those who have passed on. Some people believe that the world of dreams has more truth in it than waking experiences. I know…it's a lot to think about, eh?"

"Yes, it is," she smiled. She needed time to think this through. "Thanks for sharing this with me, Seth. Can you tell me more about your dreamer's rock and the images?"

"What you saw was a pictograph that one of my ancestors painted on that rock long ago. Remember that the rock has a spirit, right? Well, many prehistoric groups viewed the surface of rock cliffs as veils between our world and that of the supernatural. As they penetrated the rock surface with paint affixed to their hands, they entered and interacted with the supernatural world."

"How could they produce paint that has lasted for hundreds, maybe thousands of years?"

"As I've been told, they mixed sturgeon oil with powdered iron oxide, plant juice, blood, animal fat, and urine. They applied it with their fingers, feathers, and sticks. They also used chipped stone tools, antlers, and bone implements to carve and incise these images into the cliffs."

"What do the images mean?"

"That is a question that archeologists have struggled with for many years. There is no living Indian who can interpret these ancient drawings. They probably represented dream symbols involving layers of meaning fully understood only by the deceased rock artist. They may have represented spirits and mythical beings or supplications to the Manitou that they called upon for help. Some of the images probably illustrate actual events in their lives and stories handed down to them by their ancestors. During my fast, I ran my hands over the images on that rock again and again, trying to get the rock to speak to me…"

"Did it?"

"Not literally, of course. But I could feel its spirit and that gave me strength. I was not meant to learn more then. And I must respect that. I remember the words of Fred Pine, a highly respected Ojibwe elder and shaman…he said, 'Never let the spirit go out of the rock. These are the dreams of my ancestors. My dreams. Your future.' Those are powerful words, I think…"

"Yes, they are. It's all so mysterious," she sighed, her thoughts drifting to Seth. He had a depth to him that she'd rarely encountered before. "You do a lot of reading and philosophizing, don't you?"

"I do. It's a part of who I am, of what I need to do to try to preserve what is left of our vanishing culture."

"You have given me much to think about. And I can't tell you how honored I am that you have shared all of this with me, Seth." She couldn't help herself from reaching for his hand.

Holding her hand gently, he looked deeply into her eyes. "*I have walked on the edge of the world, alone, yet guided by the voice of the land.* The words of Thor Conway, an expert in Native American rock art."

"Oh, yes," she whispered, her eyes misting over and melting into his.

"Hey, I'm starving." Seth broke through the intensity of the mood that encompassed them both. "Do you know that it's almost dinner time? We never even stopped for lunch." He turned on the boat's ignition, heading for one of Rainy Lake's bays where fishing was always excellent.

It was only minutes before he landed a big walleye, just before she reeled in an even bigger one of her own. He had been planning to make her a shore lunch today. Her job, he told her, was to find a nice spot for their meal.

"But I have no idea where we are," she protested. "So many islands…I guess I never ventured much beyond Kettle Falls when I lived here."

"Canada has some wonderful spots, too, eh? Just go wherever your spirit leads you. I'll follow," he grinned as she scanned the horizon.

"That way!" she ordered him, and he obeyed. "Turn here. Now go right."

"Where are you going?" he laughed.

"No idea—just where my spirit leads me. Now, head in closer to shore so I can find the perfect spot."

He complied, nosing the boat in an easterly direction across Pound Net Bay, around Breezy Island, to the shoreline just north of McKenzie Point. "That's it!" she exclaimed, feeling as if she was mysteriously drawn to this secluded beach surrounded by rocky points winding out into the big lake. What a perfect camping site, she thought to herself, although she had not camped in years.

Seth hauled his portable cooking stove out of the boat along with a can of baked beans, onions, potatoes, and a few pans. While he quickly cleaned and filleted the fish, Beth started a fire and retrieved her picnic basket from the boat—the old wicker basket that Nana had used to take her on picnics years ago. The basket contained a bottle of wine, cheese and crackers, and several slices of homemade chocolate cake.

Like most of the local fishing guides, Seth had his own recipe for shore lunch. He coated the fresh fillets with flour and his secret spices, then flipped them into hot oil that sizzled in his blackened cast-iron fry pan. Potatoes were sliced, mixed with diced onions, and fried in hot oil. The beans simmered in a little pan. It smelled heavenly after a long day on the lake.

As the sun slunk lower in the sky, dressing the horizon in swirling shades of pink chiffon, they sat together on the beach devouring their meal, accompanied by a few glasses of wine. The lake shimmered in the day's fading light, casting a surreal spell upon the soon-to-be-sleeping world. It was getting late. They should be getting back home. But did it really matter? After all they had shared today, did anything as insignificant as getting home before dark really matter? How, Beth wondered, could one night even begin to compare with more than two billion nights that the Dreamer's Rock had been there, silently watching the world coming to life?

"This fish is incredible," she complimented the chef.

"Not as incredible as you," he casually put his arm around her bare shoulders. "Sharing this day, my journey, with you is one of the best things I've ever done. It means a great deal to me. As do you..."

"Oh, Seth," she sighed. "What can I say...except that this has been one of the most memorable days of my life? A day I will never forget. You need to know that you have become an important part of my world. I don't know what that means yet, and frankly, it scares me...I only know that I really enjoy being with you. Is that so wrong?"

"No, it's not wrong. I feel the same way and I'm scared, too. The reason I showed you the things I did today is that...I needed to. I don't know why. I've never shared these things with anyone else. But you…you're different…you're special. My spirit knows you, Beth…"

"I feel as if I have always known you," she sighed, "it's very strange."

"Maybe it's not so strange at all…but I do think a toast is in order, a toast to your divorce, eh?"

As they clinked their glasses together, she was suddenly transported back to the harsh reality of her previous life with Rob, to the fact that she and Seth were celebrating the end of an era. It was over, all over. The good, the bad, and the ugly. A finished chapter in her life. While it was cause for celebration, it was also a reminder of failure. Of her failure to make it work, of his, of theirs. Tears began to well in her eyes as she toasted her new friend.

"Are you OK?" He was confused at her reaction. At forty-two years of age, he'd never been married, never been divorced, never really been in love—not until now. He wasn't sure what she would be feeling at a time like this. "Beth, are you OK?"

"I think so. It just finally hit me that it's all over, that I failed…"

"That perhaps it was never meant to be. That you deserve so much more than what he was able to give you. You need time to work your way through this. Time heals."

"But I need you," she collapsed into his eager arms. He held her close, their eyes locked together. Despite his better judgment, his lips met hers with a sense of urgency, of recognition, as if they were long-lost lovers finally rediscovering each other after many lifetimes apart. Breathlessly, they collapsed on the beach beneath the light of the rising moon. Clinging to each other. Gently caressing, exploring. Losing themselves in the moment. Beth finally broke loose from his embrace and stalked off down the beach, trying to clear her head.

"Beth? What is it?" He pulled himself upright, fire surging through his body. *What was I thinking? This is not the time, damn it! What's wrong with you, Seth?* Only the Great Spirit, Gitchi Manidoo, knew how much he wanted this woman. He'd known her before, many times before. And he knew that he had to wait. Still, wasn't she the one who'd fallen into his arms, telling him that she needed him? She apparently didn't know what the hell she wanted…and he'd need to remember that. It wasn't her fault, he finally decided, watching her slender silhouette walking barefoot along the beach. Dipping her toes in the water as she looked up at the moon. *Maybe we both need time…*

"Beth, wait up," he jogged down the beach toward her, his heart heavy in his chest. She stood at the edge of the lake, staring out into space as the shadows of the night flickered across her pale face. *God, she's beautiful,* Seth whispered to himself as he stood beside her. Finally she turned to him, her eyes pleading with him to understand.

"I'm sorry," she finally spoke softly. "I don't know what's wrong with me. I know what I want…but I'm so scared. Not of you. I'm scared of my feelings for you. I'm overwhelmed, I think."

"You're sorry?" He was startled. "I was coming to apologize to you…" He touched her hand cautiously, his eyes smiling. "So how about if we call it even and forget this ever happened?"

"Yes," she heaved a sigh of relief. "How about if we just remember this wonderful day that we've shared together?"

"It's a deal. Time to go."

Quietly, they made their way back home, skimming across the black water by the light of the moon. It was just a kiss that lingered on a little too long, a caress, nothing more, they each tried to convince themselves. But their hearts knew better. As their thoughts mingled together, unspoken, it became clear that their destinies were somehow entwined. Perhaps they always had been…

"The pain passes,
but the beauty remains."
Pierre Auguste Renoir

Chapter Twenty-four

*Q*ue sera sera... whatever will be, will be; the future's not ours to see, que sera sera. Nana's familiar little tune played over and over again in Beth's head. She could almost hear Nana singing again, singing in the white pines that dipped and swayed to the rhythm of the winds. Words to live by, Nana had always told her. Perhaps she had been right. For now, Beth needed to clear her mind, to focus on finishing her mother's diaries. The afternoon flew by as her mother's entries warmed her heart. Early childhood memories flooded back into her consciousness. There had been some good years, very good years. Finally she read her mother's last entry.

September 16, 1974
Dear Diary,

I'm so excited! Jake and I are going camping together for a few days, all alone. Mama will be taking care of Beth, of course. Jake has some special places to show me. We're even crossing into Canadian waters where we will find a secluded campsite on the lake. The plan is that we will motor to Kettle Falls where we will leave the boat, unload the canoe, and paddle the rest of the way. The weather should be perfect for our trip. The fall colors are already peaking.

We don't get a chance to get away together very often. It's still the same old problem—hiding our relationship from the world. All because Jake's wife refuses to give him a divorce. I can't wait for the day that I will be his wife, that our little girl will have the father she deserves. Jake has a new plan to move ahead with the divorce as soon as we return from our trip. This time it will work, he says. For now, I'm not going to worry about it. Our time together is too precious to dwell upon things like this. It's going to be a wonderful getaway. Have to pack. When I return in a few days, I will have glowing reports for you, dear diary! Until then...

Until then… Beth's eyes brimmed with tears. There was no glowing report about the camping trip. There was nothing more, not a word. It was *The End.* Her mother never returned from the camping trip. She had mysteriously drowned in the lake that she loved.

But—she'd been with Jake! That was not the story that Beth had been told, not the story that the rest of the world had heard. Jake was supposedly the one who found her and tried in vain to save her life. He had been at Kettle Falls with some of his New York business clients for a few days, negotiating the sale of several choice islands. Early one evening, he took a break, alone, to go fishing. He was trolling in the Canadian Channel when a freak storm kicked up out of nowhere. Heading back toward Kettle Falls in the blinding rain, he encountered an overturned canoe bobbing on the waves, drifting in toward shore. An empty canoe. Maybe it had broken loose in the storm…but just in case anyone was in trouble, he'd motored in. There he'd found an unconscious Sarah washed into shore by the angry waves. He'd performed CPR, done everything that he could possibly do to save her life. It was too late. Jake had been devastated, had never forgotten, never really forgiven himself for not being able to save her. So the story went. Nobody ever knew what Sarah was doing out there by herself, canoeing alone. Some had speculated that there may have been another party involved—someone who had mysteriously disappeared. No additional bodies were ever recovered.

The story? Beth was shocked. Was that all that it was—lies? Perhaps a convenient way for Jake to hide the truth about his affair with her mother? Just when she was beginning to accept the fact that he was her father, to forgive and forget—*now this?* She needed to know the truth. She had a right to know what really happened to her mother on that fateful day. Jake was the only one who knew—and he'd apparently hidden the truth from the world for more than thirty-five years. Trembling, she dialed his phone number.

"Hello?" his voice came across the line.

She was unable to speak.

"Hello?" he tried again. "Who's there? I can't hear you."

No response. Quietly, she hung up the phone. She didn't know what to say. Didn't trust the words that could come hurling from her mouth. Worse yet were the uncontrolled sobs, the ones that were now heaving from her gut.

Later, when the churning cyclone within had exhausted itself and ebbed into an empty sea of nothingness, she decided to email Jake instead. *Jake, I need to know what really happened to my mother. Despite the stories I've always been told, I know that you were with her that weekend, camping with her. You owe me an explanation. Please come out to the island. Beth.*

This would not be the tearful reunion with her father that she had recently begun to anticipate. Until she read that last entry in her mother's diary, she'd been feeling guilty about the way she had treated Jake. She'd learned more from her mother's diaries about the love they had shared, about his intent to divorce Evelyn and marry her mother—finally. But now...*now* another lie—a huge lie that seemed to change everything.

❦

Jake slouched onto Beth's porch just a few hours later, head hanging as if he had been whipped, defeated by life itself. He looked tired, Beth realized, as she opened the door and curtly nodded at him to come in. He stood before the fire, warming his hands, not sure how to proceed. There was no easy way. No way but the truth. It would be a relief, in some ways, to finally get it out in the open. But having to relive it again...God, the pain never ended.

"All I want is the truth, Jake," she finally broke the silence. She no longer felt like hurling vases or screaming at him. She was too stunned, too emotionally drained.

"I promise you, that, Beth. I've tried to spare you from the pain in the past. But you do have a right to know, no matter how much it will hurt us both. I will take you back there with me, back...exactly thirty-four years ago today. Yes, September twentieth precisely. God, that makes it all the worse, or maybe all the more appropriate. Today is the thirty-fourth anniversary of your beautiful mother's death." He wiped a tear from his eye.

She sucked in her breath. "Thirty-four years *today?*"

"Thirty-four years, and not a day has gone by that I have not missed her. I love her so..." His aging eyes clouded over with memories. "And I always will..."

That much was true, Beth realized. Whatever had happened or not happened, the truth was that this man, her father, had never ceased loving her mother. He'd never forgotten her, not after all these years. Pain radiated from his eyes, from every pore of his body. He was her father. She was his daughter. They were bound together by memories of the woman they'd both loved, by the pain they shared. She impulsively reached out, wiping a tear from his cheek. "I know. I know how much she loved you, too. Still, I need to know what really happened."

He sat beside her on the sofa, staring into the glowing embers of the fire. Although he'd never spoken of that day, he had lived with it forever. He had replayed it over and over again in his mind, playing the *what if* game. What if he had done something different, something that would have saved her life? What if they had stayed one more day at their campsite? What if they'd paddled back along a different route? He had tortured himself for years, unable to forgive himself, unable to change the devastating ending. He had always wondered why God didn't take him instead of her. He had prayed for that as he'd worked to save her life. God had not answered his prayer. Jake had not gone back to church since.

He took a deep breath, his hands clenched. Bracing himself, he dug down into the past. It was time to tell Beth the truth.

"Though nothing can take back the hour of
splendor in the grass,
of glory in the flower,
we will grieve not
but rather find strength
in what remains behind."
William Wordsworth

Chapter Twenty-five

*T*hirty-four lonely years suddenly disappeared in time as Jake transported himself back to 1974.

❦❦

It had been a crisp, sun-drenched fall day when he'd pulled his boat
up at Nana's island. Little Beth came running down to the dock. "Uncle
Jake, can I come? Please can I come with you and Mama? I'm big
enough, you know, almost *growed up*! I'm six, you know." She jumped
into his arms.

"Sorry, Pumpkin. This time, it's just Mama and me. You're going
to have fun with Nana. We will be back in a few days, and then we will
have a special surprise for you." He kissed her on the forehead.

"Like what?" The little girl wrapped her arms around his neck.
"What kind of a surprise, Uncle Jake?"

"Hmmm…it wouldn't be a surprise if I told you now, would it?
You'll like it. Mama and I will find something very special for you on
our trip."

"Promise?"

"Promise." He hugged her closely before handing her off to Nana.
"Love you, Pumpkin."

"I love you, too, Uncle Jake. Mama, too," she said as she gave them
both a big hug good-bye. "Don't forget my surprise!" she called after
them as their boat disappeared into a bank of fog hovering over Rainy
Lake.

Sarah was radiant that day, thrilled to be off on this wilderness adventure with Jake. She wore a soft, bright-red jacket that set off her
long auburn hair flying wildly in the breeze. Jake held her hand, so
much in love with this woman, the mother of his child.

At the Kettle Falls landing, they unloaded the canoe and began paddling up the Canadian Channel toward Pound Net Bay. The lake was smooth as glass. The blue sky and billowy white clouds were reflected perfectly in the water surrounding the canoe. They paddled together quietly, in perfect rhythm, watching the seagulls, the loons, an occasional otter splashing in the lake. They were getting away together to spend a few days in each other's arms and to explore the Canadian wilderness. Fall was their favorite time of the year. The colors were magnificent. Their world was alive with passion, brighter than usual— because they were together at last. She couldn't quit smiling at him.

He found the perfect camping site for them on the eastern shore of Pound Net Bay, just north of McKenzie Point. A sandy beach was tucked away, sheltered by massive rock formations that jutted out into Rainy Lake. Looking west, they'd have spectacular views of the sun setting over emerald islands. They pitched the tent, set up their cooking pit, hung the groceries high in a tree to prevent bears from stealing their supplies. Jake carried his pistol, just in case they encountered any unfriendly bears in this wilderness area.

Finally, they were alone, part of the vast wilderness, wrapped in each other's arms on the beach that night. The sun slipped into the lake in a blaze of glory, bold fingers of gold streaking across the sky.

"I have never been happier in my life," she beamed at him, running her fingers through his thick black hair.

"You could, and you will be—soon," he dug into his pocket, producing a tiny box which he settled into the palm of her hand. "Open it."

Carefully, she opened the box, discovering a sparkling diamond ring. She gasped, "But, Jake…"

"Will you marry me, my darling?" He got down on one knee in the sand, silhouetted by a full moon climbing above the horizon.

"But…" She was puzzled. He was, after all, still married.

"I know. I know. I'm very late and I'm sorry. I've found a way to get my divorce and it will be soon. This may be premature in some ways, Sarah, but I can't wait any longer. Our little family can't wait any longer. We will be married the day after my divorce becomes final. This is my promise to you, the only woman I have ever loved. I will always love you, my darling. We won't be rich, not financially, after the divorce. You need to know that."

Tears of happiness streamed down her face as she hugged him tightly. "I'll be the richest woman in the world once I'm your wife."

"So, will you marry me and make me the happiest man in the world?" He put the ring on her finger, watching her eyes dance with pleasure as she gazed at the diamond sparkling in the moonlight.

"Oh, yes, my darling, a thousand times yes! I will love you with all my heart, all my soul. Always."

They made love on the beach that night, and again in the tent as they listened to wolves howling in the distance, to waves lapping gently on the shore. They slept. They canoed, fished, hiked, and explored the nearby islands. They read poems to each other—Rumi, Browning, Lord Byron, Dickinson, Shelley, and Emerson. At night they sat around the campfire talking about their future together. About their plans for Beth, about having another baby—a little sister or brother for Beth to grow up with.

One night about midnight, Jake woke to hear a commotion outside. Grabbing his pistol, he slipped out of the tent into a starlit night that took his breath away. Casually hiking along the shoreline, a young bull moose scavenged for food, digging roots and moss from the shallow lake bed. He woke Sarah to see the moose. She threw her jacket on and stumbled out into the night as the moose snorted and lumbered off into the woods.

"What a magical night," she murmured, stoking the glowing embers of the campfire. "Let's sit out here a while and watch the stars…they're twinkling at us, you know."

Jake threw another log on the fire, shook the sand from their blanket, and settled down beside his wife-to-be. They didn't need to talk. Just being together was enough. Their thoughts whispered wordlessly between them. She finally dozed off in his arms. He held her against his chest, feeling her heart beating in sync with his own. He sat there late into the night, unaware of the passage of time, becoming a small part of the universe that surrounded them.

His eyes were finally getting heavy with sleep, his head nodding. As he was about to carry her into the tent and crawl into the sleeping bag beside her, the sky began to shimmer with dancing lights. The aurora borealis blazed and swirled across the horizon. Spikes of emerald green waltzed with ruby slippers, their reflections dancing across the water.

He shook her awake. "Sarah, it's our dancing lights. Our waters of the dancing sky."

She gasped, watching the spectacle unfold across the heavens. Remembering how the northern lights had danced for them the first time they made love on the beach by her cabin in Ranier.

He knew exactly what she was thinking, what she was feeling, as he pulled her into his arms. "A good sign perhaps. They're dancing for us, again, a wedding dance this time…"

She smiled. They'd had such a wonderful weekend together it was difficult to think about leaving the next morning. About returning to the *real world,* a world in which they did not really belong to each other…not yet…

∽৪৯৹

The next morning, they waited until the sun had burned through the bank of fog stretching across the lake. Mist rose from the water, a sign that fall was moving in. The lake was calm, the sun warming them as they paddled back toward Kettle Falls. A perfect day for canoeing. Still, they decided to stay fairly close to shore as they crossed Stokes Bay and headed into the Canadian Channel. Especially in the fall, it was best not to underestimate the fickle moods of Mother Nature.

They were paddling without a care in the world, absorbed in the solitude of the wilderness, when the sky suddenly turned black. The wind howled down the length of the channel as the lake began to chop, building into angry waves that changed direction with the whims of the wind.

"What the hell?" Jake bellowed into the wind as they paddled toward the nearest shore with all the strength that they could muster. But the fierce winds kept spinning the canoe in widening circles, driving it farther into the middle of the lake. Bolts of thunder echoed across the lake, crashing like cannon balls. Cold rain began to pelt the boat, freezing into sheets of sleet.

Sarah was pale as a ghost, her huge eyes filled with terror, as she struggled to paddle, to hear the orders that Jake was barking above the relentless wind.

"Left! Paddle left! Hold on, hold on tight! Use your knees. Brace yourself. It will be OK, honey. We can do this," he tried to reassure her, despite the fact that he had serious doubts about their plight. He'd never seen a storm like this, coming out of nowhere on a perfectly calm day. If they could just keep the canoe upright…

Rolling waves began to crash over the canoe, one after another. The lovers were helpless as a gust of wind flipped the canoe over, throwing them both into the icy waters of Rainy Lake. They had life jackets on as always. She surfaced first, spitting out water. "Jake," she screamed over and over again, terrified, unable to find him. Moments later he surfaced, grabbing her and shoving her ahead of him toward the capsized canoe. If they could just reach the canoe and hold on, just hold on…but the wind pushed the canoe farther and farther away. As the pounding waves continued to wash over them, it was impossible to see shore. Jake was able to retrieve one of the paddles before it floated away. Finally, the wind whipped the canoe back toward them. They swam for it with all their might as the wind tossed it back and forth, teasing them, taunting them. Just beyond their reach.

Sarah began to cry, shaking uncontrollably in the freezing water as the sleet turned to hail. "I can't, Jake, I can't do it," she cried. Another wave crashed over her head as a bolt of lightning flashed across the sky. She sputtered when she came up once again, her lips beginning to turn a strange shade of blue.

"Yes, you can. You must. We cannot give up. I love you, sweetheart. Do it for me, please do it for me, for Beth!" He grabbed her, pulling her along with him, trying to decide if they should forget the canoe and swim for shore. But he could no longer see the shore, either shore. He had no idea which way to go. Shaking from the numbing cold, he knew that hypothermia would get them both if they didn't get out of the lake soon.

"Keep moving!" he shouted over the waves, as the canoe disappeared into the storm. Now, their only hope was reaching shore. He dragged her along with him toward what he hoped was the shoreline. Exhaustion was setting in. *I have to save her,* he repeated over and over again as she began to go limp in the churning water. "Hold on, Sarah. Can you hear me? I need you. Beth needs you, and Nana."

Dear God, he prayed silently, *please save her, please. Take me if you must, but save her*!

The storm finally let up momentarily, just long enough for him to finally see land ahead. They were heading in the right direction, and getting close. "We're almost there, honey, hold on," he shook her shivering body, shoving her ahead of him as he swam with all his strength. A surge of adrenaline kicked in, breaking through his exhaustion.

Finally, the fickle wind began to cooperate, washing them in toward shore. Jake touched bottom, shrieking with delight. He ran up onto the beach, dragging Sarah with him. Settling her into a sheltered cove beneath the trees, he shook her frantically. "Wake up! Wake up!" She was pale, her lips blue, eyes closed. "Damn it, wake up!" Tears streamed down his face as he began CPR, trying to revive her. There was no response. He kept trying for what seemed like hours, exhausted, unwilling to accept the reality of what was happening.

"Dear God, please, please save her! Tell me what to do!" he screamed into the clearing skies.

She was cold, so cold. He covered her with leaves, with sand, with anything he could find to insulate her from the penetrating cold. He could not find a pulse on her. He held her close, trying to share whatever body heat he could generate. He talked to her, rubbed her arms and legs. He tried more CPR. She did not move, did not open her eyes. She had to wake up, he told himself. She had to be OK. He'd lie down beside her and hold her tight until she did.

Much of the rest of that horrible day would always remain a blur for Jake. He was numb, disoriented, shivering on the edge of hypothermia. Sometime later he awoke, his body still wrapped around his sleeping Sarah. The storm was over, the sun providing some greatly needed warmth, just as if nothing had happened, as if the freak storm had never occurred. He knew that he had to get Sarah back to Kettle Falls, back to the mainland and to the hospital. He knew that he needed to move, to clear his foggy head, to see if there was any sign of the canoe. The lonely paddle that he had salvaged was still on the beach. And thankfully, the battered canoe had washed ashore not far from where they had landed. He couldn't wake Sarah so he carried her to the canoe where he laid her gently in the bottom, wrapped in his jacket. He paddled furiously down the channel and back to the Kettle Falls landing where several fishermen were working on their boats.

"I need help!" Jake screamed across the water as he approached the landing. "I need an emergency helicopter to get this woman to the hospital now, right now!"

One burly young man with a bushy beard ran up the hill toward the lodge, promising to get an emergency message out immediately. The other, an old man with a weathered face, was waiting at the dock to help Jake land. He shook his head sadly when he saw Sarah. "Doesn't look good, poor thing," he crossed his heart.

"She'll be OK, just needs to get to the hospital." Jake scooped her into his arms and began running toward the clearing where the helicopter would be landing.

The old man followed, shaking his head. The beautiful young woman was dead...he was sure of it. He'd seen things like this before. "What happened?"

Jake stopped to think…what had happened? "Bad storm out there. I…ah…was out fishing. Found her after her canoe capsized." That was the first of many lies. The beginning of a web of lies and deceit that had haunted him for the rest of his life.

"That her canoe? Where's your boat?"

"Lost mine in the storm. I'll find it later. Right now, I need to get her to the hospital. Tell them up at the lodge that I have her at the helicopter pad. And, if there's a doctor there…"

"Got it." The older fisherman headed up the trail toward the old hotel, leaving Jake alone with Sarah.

"Oh, Sarah, I'm so sorry. I love you, honey. Please come back to me," he rocked her lifeless body in his arms, tears streaming down his face. Miracles do happen, he reminded himself. So what if it didn't look good, like the old man said. Sarah would never just leave him like this…although he probably deserved it. She'd waited for him all these years. They were finally going to be married. No, she wouldn't leave him like this. And she'd never leave Beth or Nana.

The old man glanced over his shoulder, watching Jake cradling and whispering to the young woman that he held in his arms. He knew there was more to this story. But that was none of his business or anyone else's.

Moments later, the emergency helicopter buzzed Kettle Falls and landed. "I love you, Sarah," Jake whispered to her as the paramedics came running toward them with a stretcher. They tried to find a pulse, a puzzled expression upon their faces.

"Sir, I'm afraid that it may be too…"

"Damn it! Get her to the hospital!" Jake exploded. "She needs a doctor now!"

They loaded her onto the stretcher and into the helicopter, a look of pity in their eyes. The poor man was in denial. Whoever this young lady was, she must have been important to him.

Jake jumped into his big boat and took off at full speed for his place in Ranier where he got into his truck and sped to the hospital in International Falls. He prayed all the while, like he'd never prayed before.

❦

"And who are you, sir?" the hospital attendant asked politely as Jake came rushing through the doors asking for Sarah's room.

"Jake O'Connell, a close family friend. I'm here on behalf of the family. Please, where is she?"

"Have a seat, sir. The doctor will be with you shortly." Her eyes were sad, sympathetic.

He paced up and down the length of the room, waiting, just waiting. Finally, a young doctor walked in with *that* look on his face. "Jake?"

"Yes. How is she?"

"Sir, I'm very sorry but she did not survive. She consumed a great deal of water and hypothermia set in. She was dead on arrival."

"Oh my God." Jake collapsed into a chair. The doctor sat beside him. Jake couldn't remember what the doctor said or what he told him. Nothing mattered anymore. Sarah was gone. And it was all his fault, he told himself. He should have been able to save her…he should have been allowed to die in her place.

It was his job to tell Nana and to try to tell Beth in a language that she would understand. It became his job to arrange for Sarah's funeral. His world had ended. But he needed to go through the motions of living for the sake of their daughter and for Nana. He would take care of them both for the rest of their lives. It was the least that he could do.

"Beauty is composed of many things
and never stands alone.
It is part of horizons blue in the distance,
great primeval silences,
knowledge of all things of the earth.
It embodies the hopes and dreams
of those who have gone before,
including the spirit world."
Sigurd Olson

Chapter Twenty-six

*N*either father nor daughter could speak. They sat side by side, staring into the flames, lost in their own thoughts. Darkness descended upon the island. The room seemed to come to life with shadows of the past, spirits that were finally coming into focus.

"Jake?" Beth finally turned to him, wiping her eyes and falling into her father's arms. He held her close, stroking her head, trying to comfort his little girl. She would always be his little girl.

"I'm so sorry, Beth. I would do anything to change what happened…but I can't. All I can do now is to try to make it up to you in some small way…"

"It's not your fault that she died, Jake. We all do the best that we can in life. Sometimes it's not enough. Sometimes life deals us cruel blows that are beyond our control." He had punished himself long enough, she finally realized. He had lived with the pain, the regrets, without support or understanding from anyone.

"Thank you for understanding. You are my daughter—so much like your mother… Do you have any idea how happy she'd be to see us together like this?"

"I do now, after reading her diaries. She loved us both…she'd want us to be together. I know that. But…" Shadows of doubt began to seep through her soul once again.

"But?" he encouraged her to continue.

"But, why couldn't you have married Mama sooner? Why did you wait so long?"

"Because I was stupid and weak, afraid to rock the boat by getting divorced. It was always something—Evelyn's nervous breakdowns, my father threatening to strip me of my inheritance. I kept waiting for the right time. You have no idea how long and how badly I've regretted waiting—waiting until it was too late."

She tried to digest his words as she thought about his proposal to her mother, the ring he finally gave her, on their fatal camping trip. "What about your divorce after Mama died? What happened to that?"

"I dropped it," he sighed with regret. "It no longer mattered. Nothing mattered then. If I couldn't be with Sarah and you, why bother with the hassle of a divorce? I was too shattered, Beth. I barely had the strength to get through each day. I just retreated into my own world. It was all I was able to do."

She was silent as she got up to stoke the dying fire, trying to sort through her conflicting emotions.

"Beth?" he pleaded with her. "Please try to think about the love we all shared, about the good times. I spend a lot of time thinking back on the good memories. They help me to get through the rest of my days on earth. I try not to dwell on the bad ones, on the things that I should have done differently. Can you try to remember the good times?"

She turned to face him, tears in her eyes. "Part of me understands the love you shared, your happiness together, and as I read Mama's diaries, it did bring back old childhood memories…good ones at that. When bad things happen, that doesn't have to erase all the good, does it?"

"No, it doesn't," he breathed a sigh of relief. If only she could find it in her heart to forgive him, to really forgive him.

"I need to be alone for a little while," she suddenly announced.

"I think I'll take a walk down to the gazebo." He, too, needed to be alone, to sit by Sarah's grave, to talk to her. When he returned to the cottage beneath a canopy of brilliant stars, he found Beth rocking in her chair on the porch. Waiting for him. He folded his large frame into the chair beside hers.

She rocked slowly, silently.

"I'm sorry," he began once again. "Sorry that there never seemed to be a right time to start being a *real* father to you. To tell you that I was your father and what really happened. And then it was too late…you grew up. You didn't need your Uncle Jake anymore. Soon you were gone. It was too damn late."

"It's never too late, Father." She stroked his wrinkled hand. "We can start again, can't we?"

"Yes, oh yes," he wiped his eyes. "Thank you for giving this old man another chance." His semi-smile faded as he noticed another question lingering in her emerald eyes. "Beth, what is it?"

"There's a couple of things we need to talk about if we're ever going to have a real father-daughter relationship," she began slowly. It had been a tough day for both of them, and she didn't want to make it any worse. Still, she had lingering issues that needed to be dealt with.

"Go ahead. This seems to be the time to get through all of this." He began to tense up. He didn't want to blow it now, not when she was so close to forgiving him.

"OK. What about Evelyn? Where did she, does she, fit into all of this?"

He thought long and hard before he tried to answer this difficult question. The truth was that he still wasn't sure how his wife of more than forty years fit into his life. It would not have been an issue if he could have married Sarah so many years ago. Evelyn would have had to move on with a life of her own. But now, it was too late. They'd grown old together, yet apart. Creatures of habit. They lived very different lives, usually in separate houses. She had her organizations and club meetings, her travels, her tea parties, or whatever the hell she did with her days. He had his real estate business, his own friends, fishing and boating on Rainy Lake. They pretty much tolerated each other, going their own ways. Ignored each other most of the time. But she'd changed recently, he realized. She was drinking more and was angry, unreasonable, blaming him for everything. There had been no intimacy between them for so many years that he didn't remember the last time they'd slept together.

"To be honest, I'm not sure. I do know that we would have divorced, despite the consequences, if I could have married your mother back then. No doubt about that. Evelyn would have had to get over it and move on with her life. But…"

"But?"

He sighed deeply, hoping that he wasn't heading into dangerous territory. He sure as hell didn't want to compromise this volatile father-daughter bond that he so desperately wanted to nurture. Still, he felt that he needed to tell her the truth as he understood it.

"But?" she repeated her question.

"Evelyn is a troubled woman. She has some psychological issues. Lately, she seems to have become addicted to alcohol and she's not easy to get along with."

"I assumed that."

"She's been my wife, legally, for more than forty years now. I feel nothing for the woman—well, maybe a little pity, a touch of sadness when I look back at the past. As years droned on, our so-called marriage became a habit. Neither of us had the courage to break it. The fact is—and I think you know this—I'm still in love with Sarah, Beth. I can't help that. I always will be. Still, I hope you can understand that I feel some sense of responsibility for Evelyn. The poor woman has nobody but me. No kids, no family members who are still speaking to her. I'm afraid she'd fall to pieces if I just walked out of her life."

"How can you just pretend, Jake? You're living a lie. What kind of a marriage is that?" Not that she was an expert on relationships, to say the least.

"An unusual one, dysfunctional as they say." He stared out into the night. It was perfectly still. "I pretty much live at my place in Ranier, you know. I love it there…but I do stay at Evelyn's when I feel that I need to. I try to help. She needs my financial support now since she has foolishly blown everything that she had of her own. She still needs someone to call when her demons come out in the middle of the night. Guess that's me…"

Beth waited for more, merely nodding her head as she tried to understand this strange relationship.

"I'm getting to be an old man, Beth. I have more money, more real estate investments than I know what to do with. My work became an escape after your mother died. I pretty much ignored my loveless marriage. I blamed Evelyn for holding me hostage within our farce of a marriage, for preventing me from marrying your mother. Now, I wonder if some of the fault wasn't mine as well… Anyway, I feel obligated to use some of my wealth to support her for the rest of her life. Your mother always wanted me to be fair to Evelyn, to provide well for her in the divorce settlement. The rest goes to you. It will be more than you will ever need…"

"Thanks, but you need to know that I'm not looking for anything from you, nothing but your love and being here as my father. And one more thing," she said, looking directly into his eyes.

"Anything, Beth, if you will just forgive me."

"I want you to acknowledge me as your daughter, Jake, finally. You owe me that," she spoke with determination. She would not back down on this.

He sucked in his breath, thinking of the possible ramifications. Of Evelyn's wrath. To hell with it, to hell with what anybody else thought. It was the least he could do. It was about time the world knew of his love for Sarah as well as their daughter. "I will do that. I promise you." He met her gaze solemnly.

"Then I forgive you. I think it's time for me to let go of the anger and bitterness. All that does is eat a person up inside. Sometimes you just need to let it go. So do you, Jake."

He didn't get it at first. "Me? I have nothing, nobody to forgive. This is all my fault, you know."

"You need to forgive yourself, Jake, for the mistakes you've made, for the fact that my mother drowned. Until you do, you won't be free. Think about that."

Words of wisdom coming from his own daughter. He'd never thought about it like that before. Maybe she was right. Suddenly it dawned on him that Sarah would have said the same thing, perhaps used the same words. "My God, you are the spittin' image of your mother. Maybe you're right. You're both right."

"So how is Evelyn going to handle this?" Beth puzzled out loud.

"God only knows, but I will deal with it. It's time."

"She dislikes me, that's pretty obvious. What does she say about me, about the fact that I'm your daughter, about my mother?" she blurted out the questions that had been troubling her.

Jake scratched his head. "We really don't talk about it, Beth. The subject is pretty much off-limits, has been for many years. Hell, we don't talk about much of anything. Never have. I don't know that she dislikes you…maybe she's afraid that I'll leave everything to you. Maybe she realizes I'm still in love with Sarah…"

"Does Evelyn still love you?" she couldn't resist asking the question.

His mouth dropped open as if he'd never considered this. "Hell no! This has nothing to do with love. You need to understand that."

She was not about to challenge his perception. Her father didn't think like a woman—and she couldn't expect him to. He didn't understand what Evelyn, as a rejected spouse, might be thinking and feeling—even after all these years. Beth had been there, done that. She still remembered the sharp pain shooting through her heart every time Rob had fallen in love with another woman. At least she'd moved beyond that. Maybe Evelyn never had…

"What about years ago? Did she love you then? Did you love her? Why did the two of you ever get married in the first place?" She blurted it all out, then waited. Yes, she was putting him on the spot. But there had to have been something there once, and she wanted to know what it was. What made a person fall out of love with one person—and in love with somebody else?

"Those are tough questions. I'll tell you what I think. I have no idea how she would answer your questions…" He began to pace along the front porch, gazing out at several deer bathed in the moonlight. They seemed to be waiting, just like Beth was.

"I've always thought of our marriage as one of convenience. You see, our parents strongly encouraged us to marry—for their own selfish financial reasons. She once was a very attractive woman, I must admit. We got along well enough in those days. To be honest, I guess we both thought it was love. Little did I know then what love really was…" his tone of voice turned bitter. "I almost backed out of the deal the night before the wedding. Something seemed to be missing. My father was furious, told me that I was a fool to expect more of any marriage, any relationship. So, we married. We had a few good years together. The turning point, I think, was when she refused to have children. She'd always known how badly I wanted a family. But she aborted my baby…"

"I'm sorry."

"Love, Beth? I sure as hell didn't have a clue what it was—not until I met Sarah. Not until you were born…" He drifted off into the past, crumbling into the chair beside hers as he wiped his moist eyes with the back of his hand.

She reached over to squeeze his hand. "Life gets complicated, doesn't it?"

"I guess it's all about living and learning, huh? One more thing, while we're on this difficult subject. If I had one wish, it would be that you and Evelyn could find some common ground. That you could get along. I won't be around forever, you know. She's all alone."

So he does care about her in a way, Beth thought to herself. *And perhaps he should*. Still, she was not ready to make a commitment to get along with this woman, the one who stood between her parents. If

Evelyn's alcoholism was making life difficult, maybe it was time for Jake to do something about it. "I have a suggestion for you. Why don't you put her into treatment for her alcoholism? It's up to you, you know. Think about it."

He felt like he'd been slapped in the face once again. This time it was with a cold gust of reality. Beth's fresh eyes saw something that he'd been denying. Just because Evelyn was able to confine her drunken episodes to her home, hidden from the world that she wanted to impress, it did not mean that she would get by with this forever. In fact, her drinking seemed to be getting worse with age. She could no longer handle it. It had to be destroying her health, although Jake had no knowledge of that. If he had been ignoring her symptoms simply to punish her for preventing him from marrying his true love—well, maybe it was time to let it go. Maybe that was not fair. Life sure as hell wasn't fair.

It was too late for an emotionally exhausted Jake to venture out onto the lake that night. He decided to spend the night. Besides, he had a special place that he wanted to show his daughter the next morning. He'd named it Sarah's Island.

Beth warmed up her homemade chili for a late dinner. As Jake sat down at the table across from her, he pulled a little box from his jacket pocket and handed it to her.

"It's your surprise—a little something to make up for the one that we promised to bring home to you after our camping trip years ago," he smiled wistfully.

It was the diamond ring—Sarah's ring—the one Jake had given her thirty-four years ago on the beach at Pound Net Bay. The one he had tenderly removed from her lifeless hand just days later.

Beth was stunned as she placed the ring on the third finger of her right hand. It fit perfectly. Her mother's ring, a symbol of the love that her parents had shared. "Shouldn't this have been buried with her?"

"She would have wanted you to have it. I've saved it for you for years, for the right time. I think this is it."

"Thank you, Father," she threw her arms around him. *Father?* The word didn't feel quite right to her as she struggled to integrate it into her vocabulary.

"How about Dad, just Dad?" he grinned at her.

"I love you, Dad."

"And I love you, my long-lost daughter."

⚜

Early the next morning, Beth woke to the smell of coffee. *Dad* was an early riser and he was anxious to take her to Sarah's Island today. They took off in Jake's big boat shortly after sunrise, following what had become a familiar route by now. First to Kettle Falls, then through the Canadian Channel where her mother had drowned. Jake slowed down reverently and stopped to point out the spot, the precise place where his life had also pretty much ended.

From there, they crossed Stoke's Bay and swung around McKenzie Point, where he idled the boat at the exact spot where Beth and Seth had shared their first kiss just last week. She was stunned. Something had mysteriously led her to this place last week, the place that she now learned was the campsite where her parents had spent their last weekend together. What were the chances of landing at the same spot on this vast wilderness lake which encompassed 212,000 acres, close to 1,600 islands, and stretched twenty miles into Canada?

"You've been here before?" Jake tuned into the shocked look of recognition upon her face.

"Yes, Seth and I stopped here just last week. Something led me here, Dad."

"Perhaps it was your mother's spirit. She loved it here," his voice trailed off as it often did when he replayed the memories that he and Sarah had once shared. "Perhaps it was the seagull…" he added as a lone gull drifted overhead.

Then he had to grin to himself. Seth and Beth—here together? He hadn't missed the look in his daughter's eyes. It was the same look that he'd seen in Sarah's eyes when she had looked at him, when she'd talked about him.

Directly across from the campsite, he stopped at a small rocky island, pulling the boat up onto the shore. "Welcome to Sarah's Island," Jake said as he gallantly helped Beth out of the boat. They hiked up a trail covered with pine needles and years of fallen leaves crunching beneath their feet. The trail wound through the dense forest, climbing higher and higher until it emerged into a clearing where the sun was once again visible in the sky. Father and daughter stood together, in awe, on the top of a rock formation with an incredible view of the lake and islands scattered throughout the bay.

"Wow!" Beth exclaimed. "What a view!"

"Your mother found this place. She wanted to buy the island. Of course, it's not for sale. The Canadian government owns it. If it had been for sale, I sure as hell would have bought it for her, no matter what it cost. Anyway, we used to sit here on this rock for hours. We read poems to each other. We talked about the future, our future. You know, she used to joke that this was as close to heaven as you could get. She told me that if she died before I did, this was where she wanted to be."

Beth could almost see her mother sitting on the edge of this ancient slab of granite, gazing out at the world below. Writing poetry. Always on the edge of life.

"So," he continued, "since her death, I've always thought of this as Sarah's Island, in her honor. I come here whenever I can. I sit by her, talk to her, read her poems."

After taking a few moments to catch his breath, he shuffled slowly to the edge of the rocky cliff hanging out over the lake. Quietly, almost reverently, he gazed across the horizon as if he was waiting for something. "Shhh," he cautioned Beth as she came up slowly from behind.

Together, they sat in silence. She basked in the view of Rainy Lake while he drifted into the past.

He sighed. "This is her place, Beth, right where we are sitting. I feel her spirit here. I can almost feel her arms around me sometimes, holding me, waiting for me. Other times, she…wait, we need to be quiet, very still."

It wasn't long before a lone seagull circled closer and closer, finally perching on the cliff beside Jake. He did not move, nor did the seagull. The white gull fluttered her wings, moving closer to Jake, closer to Beth.

Beth watched her father's eyes mist over with tears, yet they sparkled with a radiance that she had not seen in years.

Solemnly, he pulled a tattered book from his jacket pocket, the words of local environmentalist and nature writer Sigurd Olson. "Your mother loved the words of this great man. We used to read them as we sat here together," he whispered to his daughter.

Flipping through the book, he began to read aloud. As the seagull soared once more, circling high above them, Jake closed the book and tucked it back into his pocket. A look of serenity illuminated his face.

Beth watched the sleek white gull with its striking black accents rise effortlessly above the waters below. She could not take her eyes off the bird as it dove down into the pristine lake, then spiraled back up into turquoise skies that hovered above the ancient cliffs. Happiness radiated from its wings. Something very strange seemed to be happening here, but it made no sense. It could not be real. It was nothing more than a figment of their shared imaginations.

As if he could read her thoughts, Jake tried to explain, "I know that I may sound like a senile old man to you. But what I believe, what I sincerely believe, is that this is a sign of your mother's love. She's here with me sometimes. And sometimes…sometimes, she manifests herself in physical form, as a seagull, her favorite bird…"

Beth's heart went out to him. The poor man, she sighed. He loved my mother so much that he can't let her go. He wants, he needs to believe that she's still with him. How sad, how tragic…after all these years.

"I know this doesn't make sense to you, Beth." He saw the skeptical reaction that she was trying to hide from her grieving father. "But I know you felt it—I saw it in your eyes." Jake's matching green eyes pleaded with hers. "I understand this doesn't fit what you've always believed. All I'm asking is for you to be open to the possibility that life, and relationships, do not end with death. Death, I believe, is just another form of existence, a new beginning on the other side of life. I know personally that it *is* possible to bridge the gap between life and death. Your mother and I—we still communicate with each other, Beth. We still love each other through the veil that separates our worlds. And someday we will be together again…"

"I…I don't know what to say," she stammered. "Of course, I will be open to all things. But this is strange. Sometimes when people grieve over a tragic loss, they see things that may not really be there…things they want to believe…"

"I know what I know." He pulled himself up, turning his back to her as he gazed out over the horizon once more. Of course she didn't understand. Someday she would.

Then he led her back down the path, breaking off into a secluded clearing surrounded by several large boulders that had been tossed onto this landmass by the ancient glaciers. Here he proudly showed her the bronze marker that he'd bolted onto the smooth face of a granite boulder. Here, it would not be found or disturbed by other hikers on the island. It was simply inscribed, *Sarah, My Love Forever.*

As they hiked back down the trail, Jake stopped and turned to her, his eyes very serious. "I have one request when I die. I want a marker placed here beside your mother's. Will you do that for me? Promise me?"

"I promise you, Dad. You will be here beside Mama—forever."

"Let us be silent
that we may hear
the whispers of the gods."
Ralph Waldo Emerson

Winter Wonderland

Chapter Twenty-seven

Winter blasted across the northland with a vengeance one early November night. Beth woke to the howling of the winds in the white pines. The rickety old shutters of the eagle's nest rattled in the wind. Wrapping herself in a blanket, she tiptoed to the window seat, where she spent the remaining hours of the night watching the first winter storm of the season. Heavy, wet snowflakes swirled against the frosted window-panes. She always marveled at the fact that of all the snowflakes falling over the sleeping earth, no two were alike. Each had its own intricate shape and design. Just like people, she thought to herself. In her hand, she held the flashlight from her bedside table, just in case.

By morning, the storm had subsided. The world had transformed itself into a winter wonderland—pure white, dazzling in its brilliance. The pines were decked in fluffy blankets of snow, their limbs dipping to the ground. The open waters of the lake churned and frothed, trying to prevent winter's freeze-up from silencing its energy.

Shortly after sunrise, Beth slipped out into the wonder of the season's first snowfall. Into cozy memories of past winters. As a child, she'd been thrilled with the first snowfall. Too excited to eat her breakfast before running out to taste the snowflakes, to make snow angels that Nana told her were the prettiest ones she'd ever seen. Memories of warm hand-knit mittens and hot chocolate by the fire. She'd never outgrown that childish delight. In fact, she was tempted to flop down into the snow this morning, spreading her arms and legs, making a snow angel for Nana…

Today, however, she found heavy banks of snowdrifts around the house, making it difficult to open the door. She shoved her entire body weight against the kitchen door, finally cracking it open far enough to wiggle out, grab her shovel, and begin clearing a path. She needed to be able to get to her pile of firewood which was, thankfully, protected beneath a plywood roof that Seth had built for her. There had to be several feet of snow on the ground, she realized, but it was hard to measure with all of the drifting that had taken place across the windswept open areas. She would not be going anyplace for a while.

Finally, exhausted but exhilarated, she kicked the snow off her boots and went into the kitchen to warm up with a cup of coffee. Her answering machine was blinking. It was Seth. "Beth, just checking to be sure you're OK. Lots of snow out there. If you haven't heard, there's a winter storm warning, more snow moving in and blizzard conditions for the next twenty-four hours. Call me."

She dialed his number immediately, realizing how nice it was to have him close by. He was her only year-round neighbor within at least five miles.

"It's going to be a bad one. Do you want me to come over?" he asked, hopefully.

"No, I don't want you to chance it, Seth. I'm fine, really. I've been through storms like this before."

"Be sure you have lots of wood in the house. We may lose power, you know. And be ready to get that generator going."

She smiled to herself, amused at the twinge of disappointment in his voice. He was, she realized, anxious to assume a caretaking role over her life. He had, however, underestimated her survival instincts and knowledge. The old Beth was beginning to surface. She did not need help…not even from this man.

Abruptly terminating her coffee break, she lit the kerosene lamps and started a fire in the fireplace. The portable generator was ready to go. As she hauled her last load of firewood into the house, the wind began to howl like a pack of hungry wolves. Blinding snow mixed with freezing sheets of sleet ravaged her from all directions—so violently that it almost knocked her to the ground. It was a total whiteout. The short distance from the woodpile to the front porch was almost impossible to navigate. She felt her way along the side of the house to the porch and up the steps, understanding how people became disoriented in a blizzard like this. With the storm churning in all directions, it would be easy to go in circles forever, never finding your destination.

She slammed the front door shut, collapsing beside the fireplace, her pile of logs scattered around her on Nana's faded rug. Suddenly, the electricity went out.

She grabbed the phone, wanting to hear Seth's reassuring voice. But the phone was dead, of course. *That's OK*, she told herself, *I'm fine. I don't need anybody*. Deciding that she didn't need the generator yet, she warmed herself by the fire, throwing more logs into the dancing flames. By flashlight, she selected a good book from Nana's vast library—something to keep her company, to divert her attention as the storm raged on.

As she and Nana had done so many times before, she turned on the old battery-operated ham radio to check on weather conditions. It crackled with static electricity generated by the storm, but she could still make out the latest weather warnings. Dangerous conditions. No travel advised. Be prepared to take cover, stay away from windows. Dangerous conditions on the lakes. Again, no travel advised whatsoever.

Emanating from Fort Frances, Ontario, Canada, station CFOB 800 had long been the only station to tune into for weather reports in this wilderness region. They even broadcast messages three times a day for isolated islanders with no other means of communication. She tuned in again at 7:05 p.m. that night, just in case there were any messages for her. If nothing else, it was fun to hear the messages being relayed around Rainy Lake. A source of entertainment for stranded islanders when there was not much else to do.

"Message for Beth Calhoun," the radio station's announcer said, tearing her away from the pages of Flaubert's *Madame Bovary.* "Dad will be out to the island as soon as the storm lets up. If you need help before then, wave a red flag from your gazebo." *Dad*? She smiled to herself at Jake's first attempt to acknowledge her as his daughter. He obviously had no clue that the whiteout was severe enough to prevent her from even finding the gazebo. This was not your average winter storm.

She sighed, stoking the fire. She knew that Seth would also be tuned in to CFOB, listening to Jake's message. The message was also meant for him since he was, after all, the only one close enough to see a red flag waving from her gazebo. The men in her life did seem to be there for her these days. Her father, and Seth…

As the storm raged on, whistling through the drafty log walls of Nana's beloved home and shaking its foundation, Beth dragged her sleeping bag downstairs to sleep by the fire. It should be over soon, probably by sometime tomorrow. And if it wasn't, she would deal with it.

❧ ❧

The next morning, Beth woke to a world encrusted in layers of ice. The frosted pines shimmered in the early morning light, bowing to the ground with the weight of the ice adorning their limbs. She strapped on her snowshoes and ventured out to assess the damage from the storm, the work that needed to be done. Rainy Lake tossed and tumbled in angry shades of grey, unwilling to give in to the whims of winter. Soon the lake would begin to freeze—shifting and groaning until it was transformed into a thick slab of ice. Island residents would be stranded until the ice was thick enough to support skiers and snowshoers, then snowmobilers. Finally, the plow trucks would cautiously venture out onto the lake, plowing a network of ice roads. Beth heard that one of the plows had gone through the ice last winter. The driver escaped, but recovering the truck had been quite an operation. One of their neighbors on the mainland always plowed a road from the Tilson Creek Access, past Ober's Mallard Island, beyond Roberts, Stop, and Jackfish islands to the remote cluster of islands where Beth and Seth lived.

Beth knew that she would not be leaving her island until freeze-up. Neither would Seth… She had books to read, snow to shovel, sales catalogs to pore over, Christmas presents to order. And, she excitedly reminded herself, a jewelry business to launch. Her kitchen table now looked like Nana's had years ago. It was covered with boxes of colorful beads, cameos, tools, and jewelry designs. She planned to spend her days of winter solitude making jewelry. Nights would be spent by the fire going through Nana's jewelry designs, creating her own patterns, and developing her Web site. By spring, she hoped to have a supply of vintage costume jewelry ready to sell on her Web site and through several gift shops on the mainland. Every time she thought about her new business adventure, her heart smiled. She was growing, learning, finding herself. Her pride swelled with a newfound sense of independence—one she'd never before known.

As the snow pack settled, she snowshoed around the island almost every day. She'd arrive at the gazebo around noon, where she'd look across the bay toward Seth's island. He was usually down by his dock, waving at her. Now that the phones were back up, they talked regularly. Between the phone and email, she was connected to the outer world—considerably different than it had been in years past when islanders were totally isolated from the rest of the world.

⋘✥⋙

By Thanksgiving, the bay was frozen solid enough for Seth to ski over to Beth's island for dinner. The ice wasn't safe enough yet for snowmobiles. The large expanse of Rainy Lake was still open, making it impossible to travel across the lake by boat, car, or snowmobile. This meant that Jake, who had planned to come out to the island for Thanksgiving, was unable to get there.

So it would be just the two of them—Beth and Seth—celebrating her first Thanksgiving on the island since she'd been a child. *Our first Thanksgiving together,* she thought to herself as she basted the turkey, then abruptly dismissed the silly thought. A fire blazed in the fireplace. The aroma of turkey and pumpkin pie filled the house once again. The table was set with Nana's white linen and the elegant Bavarian china that she had reserved for holidays and special occasions. Beth had made the Thanksgiving centerpiece herself—a gold candle surrounded by pine cones and artificial fall leaves.

She couldn't resist trading her uniform jeans and sweatshirt in for a long black skirt and a creamy white Victorian blouse that clung to her slender figure. The black cameo necklace that Nana had made for her shimmered seductively against her skin. Her fiery hair was swept up in a classic style. She dabbed a bit of Obsession perfume behind her ears and on her wrists—something she hadn't bothered with since she'd moved back to the island six months ago.

She anxiously watched for Seth through the frosted window panes. It had been a long time since she had seen him. Finally, she caught a glimpse of him gliding across the frozen bay on skis.

She flung the door open when she heard him stomping up onto the porch. He was radiant, his dark eyes alive with the fresh air, the excitement of his journey. But there was something more in those eyes—an earthy blend of appreciation, desire, recognition. She felt like she was being drawn deeper and deeper into those mysterious, yet familiar eyes.

"Wow," he swooned as his eyes moved up and down the fascinating vision standing before him. "You are incredibly beautiful," he murmured as he threw his snowy jacket on the floor and held his arms out to her.

She slipped into his arms as if she belonged there. "I've missed you, Seth," she whispered, as he held her close.

"I can tell," he grinned, teasing her as his heart pounded. Stepping back, with his broad hands still resting on her shoulders, he smiled down into her emerald eyes—eyes that had held him captive since the day they met.

"And?" Beth inquired.

"I must admit that I've thought of you once or twice." His eyes sparkled with mischief.

"That's all?" She impulsively ran her fingers up and down his spine until his lips found hers, consuming her, filling her with a passion that she'd never before known. *Please don't stop, don't ever stop,* her heart pleaded silently.

But Seth wasn't ready this time. And he was quite sure that she wasn't either. Not really. He remembered the time they almost lost it on the beach at Pound Net Bay. He wasn't going to let that happen again. Reluctantly, he released her and walked to the fire. He stood there warming his hands, his back toward her. "I'm sorry, Beth. I don't know what comes over me when I'm with you. It's all I can do to resist, to wait until the time is right for us."

"How do you know when that is, when the time is right?" Her voice was low and sexy.

"Look, I respect you too much to rush into something. I can't deny my feelings for you, that's pretty obvious. But what does that mean for us, for the future? I don't know how to live with someone else, Beth. I've always been alone. And you, you haven't been divorced all that long. How do you even know what you want in life, in a man?"

"My heart tells me. Besides, it's not like we're making a lifetime commitment, is it?"

He turned abruptly to face her, a glint of anger flashing in his eyes. "Yes, it is. To me it is. I don't take something like this lightly—not with a woman like you."

She paused—startled at first, then pleased. "Neither do I," she assured him.

"Well then," he breathed a sigh of relief, "the only reasonable thing we can do is wait until we're both sure… That turkey smells good enough to eat," he said, and headed for the kitchen.

Despite the rocky start, it turned out to be a memorable Thanksgiving. After dinner, they settled by the fireplace where they played a game of Scrabble, talked, and enjoyed each other's company. Before dark, he hugged her good-bye, carefully respecting the boundaries that had been set.

She watched him skiing, powerfully, back across the lake to his island. He was a good man, just like Jake had told her. One who respected her and refused to play with her heart. One who was at least thinking about the possibility of a future together. As intriguing as that sounded, it was also scary. Once upon a time, she had believed in a future with Rob. How could she be sure of anything anymore? Perhaps Seth was right. Maybe she wasn't ready, but would she ever be? Would *he* ever be ready, she wondered? Perhaps he was content with his solitary life just the way it was. Without her.

⊷ঌঌ

The chill of winter finally silenced the energy of the open lake. Layers of ice grew thicker and deeper. The world slept, cradled gently in snowy blankets of white that drifted and swirled slowly into obscurity. It slept beneath the shimmering light of a silver moon casting shadows upon long winter nights.

"My favorite time of the year," Seth sighed as he and Beth sat late one night on the shore of her island. Winter stars blazed across the pitch-black sky. Huddled together, they sat in silence, a tiny part of the star-studded universe.

They tried to absorb as much solitude as they could, knowing that it was temporary. This was a window in time before snowmobiles began whining across the lake and through the woods. The ice would soon be safe enough to transform the untouched winter wonderland into a frozen landscape dotted with cross-country skiers, snowmobilers, and ice fishermen.

❧ ❧

It had been weeks since either one of them had been able to get to the mainland. Their mail was accumulating at the Ranier post office. Once they heard the first wave of snowmobiles roaring down the lake, they decided that the ice was safe enough to snowmobile to the mainland together. Bundled in their snowmobile suits and helmets, they were off one clear morning, skimming across the frozen lake. She followed behind him, allowing space for the snow that his machine kicked up in its wake. It felt invigorating to be out on the lake again after being stranded on their islands for so long.

The village of Ranier was decorated for the holidays. Fresh evergreen wreaths, red candles, and twinkling Christmas lights framed the windows of the village's cottages and businesses. After retrieving their mail at the post office and stuffing it into their large backpacks, Beth and Seth split up to do some Christmas shopping at the local stores. They were limited to small items, things they could easily fit onto their snowmobiles for the trip home.

Beth bought an engraved gold pocket watch for Seth—to replace the old one that no longer kept accurate time. For Jake, a warm hat and gloves. A set of beautiful, locally made American Indian jewelry for Emily. Remembering Dorothy, the woman she'd met at the Lakeside cabins where her mother once lived, she picked out a framed sketch by local artist Bernie "Spike" Woods. Hoping to find Dorothy home, she hiked over to her place in the fresh snow.

Beth passed her mother's old cabin, now closed for the winter. She knocked on Dorothy's door and waited. After a few moments, she heard footsteps moving slowly toward the door. Dorothy cracked the door open and broke out in a huge smile when she saw Beth standing there in her snowmobile suit.

"Come in, my dear. How good to see you! Please come in."

Beth wiggled out of her snowmobile suit and gave the old woman a hug. "It's great to see you again. I've wanted to come in for that cup of tea you offered me. But I've been stranded on my island until today."

"Tea, it is!" Dorothy put on a kettle of tea and sat down at the kitchen table across from Beth. "I've thought of you out there all by yourself…you know, you could move into town for the winter. Some folks do. I could even put you up here in one of my winterized cabins."

"Thanks, but I'm fine out there. And I have a wonderful neighbor within sight, a good friend."

"Seth?" The old woman smiled knowingly, a gleam in her eye.

Beth's eyebrows shot up in surprise. How and what could Dorothy possibly know about Seth? "Why, yes, Seth. I'm surprised that you know of him…"

"It's a small town, honey," she chuckled. "Everybody knows everybody else's business—and then some. I do need to tell you that I think a lot of that young man. You could do much worse in picking out a…a good friend, shall we say?"

"I like him a great deal," Beth found herself confiding in this old woman, her new friend. Dorothy reminded her so much of Nana.

"I can see that in your eyes," Dorothy said softly. "I wish you the best, both of you. You need somebody like Seth. There aren't many men like him these days, you know. Now, if I were younger…" Her eyes crinkled in laughter.

They shared a cup of tea as Dorothy told her some of the local news. Beth sought her advice about gift shops that might be interested in handling her jewelry. Dorothy was excited about her new business venture and offered to contact several of the gift shops. Time slipped by as it does when friends share moments of their lives. Glancing at her watch, Beth realized it was time to meet Seth and Jake for lunch at Grandma's Pantry. First, she wished Dorothy a Merry Christmas and presented her with the sketch.

"Oh, this is lovely!" the old woman beamed. "I've always loved Spike's work. And this sketch in particular—Houska's Point. I see this place every morning when I get up and look out my window. It has a fascinating history. And Spike really captures the feel of it, of life here in a simpler time. Thank you so much, my dear."

As Beth zipped up her snowmobile suit and bid her good-bye, Dorothy called out after her, "You'll find a little something from me also, once you get caught up on your mail. Just a little wish for a Merry Christmas and new beginnings up here in God's country, as I call it."

❦

Beth was still grinning to herself when she arrived at the restaurant and found Seth and Jake at a table in the corner, deep in conversation over mugs of steaming coffee. She gave Jake a warm hug and joined the two men in her life. The three of them had logistical plans to make for the rapidly approaching Christmas holiday. Emily was flying back from Paris, coming *home* for Christmas. Jake agreed to pick her up at the International Falls airport on the morning of Christmas Eve while Beth and Seth snowmobiled to the mainland to meet them. Beth would bring an extra snowmobile suit and warm boots since Emily obviously wouldn't have appropriate clothing with her for snowmobiling out to the island. Seth would bring a sled and tarp to haul Emily's luggage back to the island behind his snowmobile. And Beth would remind her daughter to pack light, very light.

It was going to be a wonderful Christmas with Emily here. Jake would also be spending the holidays with them. He had finally placed Evelyn in a treatment center in Duluth. She wouldn't be home for Christmas this year. He would drive to Duluth to visit her tomorrow—for the first time since he'd dropped her off there. That had not been a pretty scene. "I hate you!" she had shrieked at him, pounding her fists against his chest, when she was taken away. "I wish you were dead!" her final words to him echoed down the halls. Hopefully she'd have settled down a bit since then. At least she'd be sober.

Christmas would not be complete without Seth, as far as Beth was concerned. This would, however, be the first time that Emily met him. Of course, her daughter would love him. Beth had no doubt of that. She hoped with all her heart that Emily was ready to accept the fact that her mother had a new friend—a very special friend.

"The future belongs to those
who believe in the beauty of their dreams."
Eleanor Roosevelt

Chapter Twenty-eight

A bleary-eyed Emily stumbled off the commuter plane in International Falls, Minnesota, on the morning of Christmas Eve. Her enthusiasm over coming home to her mother's for the holidays had temporarily ebbed with the rigors of the trip. It had been a long overnight flight from Paris to New York. She almost missed her connecting flight from New York to Minneapolis/St. Paul. That plane was packed with holiday travelers. And it had been her misfortune to be sandwiched in between two very large individuals—both of whom kept trying to engage her in conversation. All she had wanted was to catch a few hours of sleep. And now, after yet another flight on this miniature airplane from St. Paul to International Falls, she was looking forward to some badly needed rest before the Christmas Eve celebration.

Jake was waiting to pick her up at the airport. It seemed strange to think that his role in her life had suddenly changed. He was no longer her mother's uncle—he was now her Grandpa Jake. She'd been rather shocked at the news, of course, but she'd taken it in stride. She'd always liked him when he came to visit them in Chicago. She'd loved his stories and jokes. But they'd never had much time to get to know each other. Things would be different this time, she realized. He would be spending the holidays with them. She was looking forward to getting to know her grandfather.

"Emily," he called out, when he saw his beautiful granddaughter walk through the security gate. She looked so much like her mother...and like Sarah, the grandmother she would never know. He held out his arms and gave her a big bear hug. "How was your trip?"

"Fine, but what a hassle. I'm just glad to finally be here. Exhausted, but happy," she smiled up at him. "It's good to see you...*Grandpa*. Can I call you that?"

He started to choke up with happiness. This was almost too easy. "Yes, you can. It's music to this old man's ears, you know. Thank you,

Emily. I…I want you to know how proud I am to have you for a grand-daughter. My only grandchild…this means a lot to me."

"Thanks," she mumbled, suddenly aware of the tragic loss of nine-teen years that they could have spent together. Her entire life. It dawned on her that this must be her father's fault. She remembered his hostility toward Jake every time he came for a visit. She remembered the arguments she'd overheard between her mother and father about her mother's wishes to go home to Rainy Lake for a visit. It was like her father had tried to isolate them from Mom's entire side of the family. Why, she wondered, had her mother given in to the bastard so often? I will never let a man run my life the way she did, Emily vowed silently. And I will get to know my grandfather whether Dad likes it or not. "Where's Mom?"

"She's waiting for us at my place in Ranier, with the snowmobiles."

"Snowmobiles?" Emily was puzzled.

"Ah, yes. You did get your mother's letter about arrangements to get out to the island?"

"What letter?" Her weary eyes reflected concern.

"I'm sorry if this will be a surprise to you, after your long trip and all. But we will need to snowmobile out to the island. The ice is safe, I assure you, for snowmobiles—just not thick enough yet for cars or trucks. They can't even plow the ice roads yet."

"I feel like I've just fallen off the edge of the world," she sighed, too tired to protest. What were her choices? She had known this was going to be an experience in wilderness living, but this was almost too much. "What about my luggage?"

"No problem. We have a sled to haul it back to the island. Ah…how much did you bring?"

"I was limited to only two medium-sized bags. So that's it."

Thank God, Jake mumbled to himself. He hoped they would fit onto Seth's sled. If not, he'd tow his sled out there with the second bag. Damn mail, he continued to mutter to himself. The poor girl was going to be in for more surprises than she expected. He didn't know how much Beth planned to tell her.

Beth waited with Seth in Jake's office, running to the door every time a vehicle came past. Finally, Jake's truck pulled up. She ran to greet her daughter, tears flowing down her cheeks. "Oh, honey, I'm so happy to see you. It's been so long. We're going to have the most won-derful Christmas together!"

Emily hugged her mother. She hadn't realized, until now, how much she'd missed her mother. If only she lived in a civilized part of the world so she could see her more often. If only she didn't have to travel by boat or snowmobile to get to her home. Emily was a city girl. She'd never before ridden on a snowmobile, never walked on a frozen lake in her life. But she'd always been an adventurous type, especially when it came to traveling the world. She could do this, she reminded herself. Then, she would catch up on some badly needed sleep.

Seth stood in the background waiting, touched as he watched this mother-daughter reunion. Finally, Beth grabbed his arm and pulled him with her to meet Emily.

"Let me guess…Seth, right?" Emily smiled at this ruggedly handsome man. She'd heard enough about him in her mother's letters to know that he was becoming a good friend. She liked him from the moment he smiled at her. His eyes were kind and gentle.

Beth grinned, gazing up at Seth, as she formally introduced him to her daughter. Emily didn't miss the look in her mother's eyes. Mom had never smiled that way at her father…but why should she, given the way he'd treated her for years? Still, it was a little shocking to see her middle-aged mother acting almost like a teenager. And so soon? What would Dad think? Not that he had a right to think anything, Emily reminded herself. Look what he'd done. Her mother's eyes glowed with happiness, enough to begin warming Emily's skeptical heart. Emily needed time to process all of this.

❧❧

It took two sleds to transport her luggage, plus her carry-on bags that were overflowing with beautifully wrapped Christmas presents. Emily stuffed herself into an unflattering snowmobile suit, her head concealed within a hard helmet and goggles. Wearing totally unfashionable boots, she climbed onto the back of her mother's machine. She held on for dear life as her mother slowly accelerated, picking up more speed as her daughter's comfort level increased. Seth and Jake followed on their snowmobiles, pulling their sleds across the frozen lake.

Emily breathed in the fresh, cold air, feeling better already. Invigorated. This certainly was a different world than the one she lived in. She'd only been back to her mother's childhood home a few times in her life. It had been summer and she'd been too young to remember much of anything.

When she walked into her great-grandmother's cozy, old-fashioned cottage, she felt like she was stepping back in time. It was her mother's home now. Seven red and green stockings were hung by the fireplace—the old ones that Nana had knit for Sarah, Beth, Papa, and herself years ago. Beth had worked late into the night the last few weeks to knit matching stockings for Emily, Jake, and Seth.

While Beth put the finishing touches on their Christmas Eve dinner, Jake and Seth went out to cut a Christmas tree. Emily unpacked and settled into the upstairs bedroom, falling asleep instantly when she laid down on the big bed beneath her mother's faded blue comforter.

It was almost dark when Emily woke to the strains of "Silent Night" floating up the staircase. She hadn't planned to sleep so long. Downstairs, a large white pine stood in a corner of the great room. Boxes of old ornaments and lights were scattered around the tree. Seth stood on a chair, placing Nana's star at the top of the tree while Jake worked to untangle cords of Christmas lights. Emily and Beth joined in the fun. When the tree was decorated, they shut off the lights and sat around the tree drinking steaming cups of hot apple cider. Then, Beth served dinner on Nana's good china. She'd made the usual Swedish dishes that Nana had made every Christmas. The meal included Swedish meatballs, Swedish rice pudding, and lutefisk in a cream sauce.

"Lutefisk? What is this?" Seth asked before he bravely tried it for the first time in his life. Beth laughed, her eyes sparkling, as she explained that it was cod fish that had been soaked in lye, then boiled.

"Lye?" he almost choked. He cautiously looked around the table to see the others enjoying this traditional Christmas dish.

"That's how the Swedes process it. People either love it or hate it. It's OK if you don't like it. You don't need to clean your plate, Seth," she teased him. But he did, deciding that it wasn't bad after all—just different. He'd get used to it after a few years, he figured. *A few years? What was he thinking?*

☙ॐ

After dinner, they gathered by the fire to open presents. Emily brought souvenir gifts from Paris for all. When the gifts had been opened, Seth disappeared out onto the porch. Moments later he reappeared with a large present for Beth.

He sat beside her on the floor, carefully watching her face, as she opened the package. She gasped, unable to speak, tears filling her eyes. Jake and Emily gathered around, also stunned. It was a painting of Beth sitting beside the fireplace in her long black skirt, silk Victorian blouse, and Nana's black cameo necklace. It was Beth exactly as she'd looked on that Thanksgiving day she'd shared with Seth. He had captured her perfectly—right down to the diamond ring that sparkled on her right hand. Sarah's ring. The most stunning part of the portrait, however, was the love that burned softly in her emerald eyes, the tender look upon her face. Seth had worked hard to capture the essence of this woman, and the way she had glowed as she'd looked into his eyes.

"Oh my God, I don't know what to say." Beth threw her arms around Seth, hugging him close.

"This is like incredible," Emily, an artist herself, said as she stared at the painting. "Who did this?"

"I did. It's what I do," Seth replied humbly.

"Wow! You do amazing work, Seth. That's my mother all right. It's like her inner beauty shines through, reflected in her eyes. I had no idea you could paint like this!"

"Thank you," he smiled, "if you're interested, I'll take you over to my studio some day while you're here. You too, Jake. Maybe we'll even let Beth come along, eh?" They all laughed, breaking the intensity of the moment. Tomorrow, they'd snowmobile over to his island together.

Jake's heart was warmed as he watched his daughter with Seth. Their feelings for each other were clear. He sighed deeply. If he could have one wish in the world, perhaps a Christmas wish tonight, it would be for the two of them to find happiness together. Forever. *Sarah, Nana, Papa,* he thought to himself as he glanced at their stockings hanging over the fireplace, *if you're here with us tonight, please help make my wish come true.*

⋘⋙

Christmas Day dawned sunny and calm. A perfect day for a snowmobile excursion, they all decided. After breakfast, they dressed in their snowmobile suits and headed down to the lake to get the snowmobiles gassed up and ready to go.

Emily wandered into the shed beside the boathouse where the helmets and other seasonal items were stored. She found an old desk, dock sections, wheelbarrows, tools, even crates of old books and antiques. She was busily exploring when Jake walked in.

"Grandpa?" The word came out of her mouth naturally. She was anxious to spend time with him, to learn from him.

Jake grinned at her. "Find anything interesting?"

"What in the world is that machine back against the wall?"

"Oh, that is a real antique, a piece of history that you should know about." He led her over to a dusty machine that looked like a cross between an ancient snowmobile and a little airplane on skis.

"Tell me about it."

"Well," Jake began, "you're looking at one of the first wind sleds ever built. Your great-grandfather built this shortly after World War II ended in the mid-1940s. That was before the days of snowmobiles. Anyway, there was a surplus of aviation engines after the war, especially used ones that were damaged. You could buy them cheap. So your great-grandfather and some of his friends decided to try building a machine to get around on the frozen lake during the winter. And it worked. Even if there was deep snow or heavy slush on the lake, this Continental 65-horsepower engine was powerful enough to build up enough speed to get through it. Quite an ingenious idea, I would say."

Emily listened intently as he explained how the engine was mounted at the rear and designed to push the sled with the propeller. There was an elevated fuel tank and a cockpit which was big enough for two, plus a baggage area. All of this was mounted on a frame of steel pipes and three long homemade skis—two at the back and one in the front for steering and stability.

She was curious and had lots of questions. There was so much that she wanted to know about her family's history. She realized how special it was to spend time with a grandfather who shared these family stories with her.

Emily and Jake continued talking closely, getting to know each other. Beth watched from the doorway of the shed, grinning to herself. She hated to disrupt the bonding that was taking place here in the old shed, but it was time to head out. The snowmobiles were ready. Seth had even packed a picnic lunch for them all.

Jake led the group today, determined to show Emily some of the unique sights on the lake. Their first stop was an old commercial fishing camp near Lost Bay. The buildings were still intact, preserved by the National Park Service.

"Harry Overson's old place," Jake announced as they hiked through the knee-high snow to get a better look at the ice house on the edge of the lake. "You won't see anything like this again, Emily. Commercial fishing was once an important part of our economy. Now, it's a piece of our history."

Emily listened intently as Jake explained how huge blocks of ice were cut from the lake in the winter, sometimes fourteen inches thick and weighing close to four hundred pounds. The ice harvest, as they called it, was a social event. Neighbors turned out to help cut the ice cakes and slide them up into the insulated ice house with the help of a horse and pulley. The ice house had thick double walls that were insulated with wood shavings and chips. Once the ice blocks were stacked high and packed tight, sawdust was dumped on top and around the edges to keep the ice cold. The ice was used to pack and preserve the fish that the fishermen netted during the fishing season.

"As soon as the lake opened up in the spring, old Harry would be out there on the lake by dawn to set his nets," Jake recalled. "Later in the day, he'd head out to lift the heavy nets, yard by yard, dumping the day's catch into the boat. He'd unload the fish and haul them to the filleting house over there," he pointed to the building beside the ice house. "After he cleaned the fish, he'd store them in the ice house. Later, he'd pack them into big wood-planked boxes and haul them to market. In the early days, the fish boats would pick up crates of fish from fishermen around the lake and transport them to Kettle Falls for fish auctions that attracted hundreds of buyers from around the country. Those days are gone, of course. So are the commercial fishermen… Of course, the recreational fishermen and fisherwomen still fish here. Rainy Lake is one of the greatest fisheries in the world," he bragged. Jake had caught more than his share of fish on this lake over the years. Some pretty nice fish at that, and he was damn proud of it.

History lesson completed, they set out again on their snowmobiles. They'd traveled quite a ways when Jake turned off into Anderson Bay with its breathtaking views of rocky cliffs and islands. There, he stopped at the foot of the granite cliffs. "What do you think?" he smiled at Emily as the other machines pulled up beside him.

"Wow, it's like a postcard. Let's stop here a while."

"Looks like a perfect spot for lunch." Seth pulled a backpack off his machine, pouring its contents onto the frozen lake. He had dry wood for a fire which he started with a farmer's match. They warmed themselves by the fire, silently enjoying the tranquility of the winter landscape. They roasted hot dogs and washed them down with cups of hot chocolate.

"A hot dog tastes so good out here on the lake over a fire," Emily proclaimed as she devoured another one. "My compliments to the chef," she saluted Seth as she began snapping photos of the winter wilderness that surrounded them. As if she was a tourist in a foreign land. Perhaps she was. Beth was pleased and relieved to watch her daughter enjoying their adventure. For a city girl, she was doing great.

After lunch, they snowmobiled back to Seth's island, where he showed them his studio. Emily was entranced with his work, soaking it in, asking questions. She and Seth talked enthusiastically about art while Beth wandered back to stare at his grandmother's portrait. Jake settled his weary bones on the sofa beside the fire. He was beginning to feel his age. As he stared into the glowing embers, he sighed deeply, more content than he'd been in years. Spending the holiday with his daughter and granddaughter was the best Christmas present he'd ever received.

As the winter sun set over the lake, they all returned to Beth's island for a late Christmas dinner. They agreed that it had been a wonderful holiday. They'd become a family of sorts, together for the first time. Making new memories. Quietly remembering past holidays with those who were no longer physically present.

"The best and most beautiful things in the world
cannot be seen or even touched.
They must be felt with the heart."
Helen Keller

Chapter Twenty-nine

After the holidays, Jake and Seth returned to their homes. Beth and Emily had close to a week alone together. Time to catch up on all that was happening in their lives, time to sit by the fire reading and relaxing. Emily entertained her mother with animated stories about her life and travels in Europe. She loved Paris. She felt at home there.

"I think I'll have to make a trip to Paris someday soon," Beth announced one afternoon as Emily was showing her photos of the city and surrounding countryside. "I can see that your heart lives there."

"Oh yes, Mom. I would love that. I'll show you all the sights," Emily beamed, shuffling through her photos. She suddenly hesitated, sucking in her breath, as she fingered the last photo. Almost as if she was trying to decide if she should share it with her mother or not.

"What is it?" Beth caught a glimpse of a chubby baby boy. "Who's this?" As she studied the photo, Rob's nose began to come into focus. *Oh my God...Rob's son? The little brother I always wanted for Emily? The one he refused to let me have. And now...now, he has a baby boy with that little tramp who broke up my marriage?*

"My baby brother, Mom..." Emily whispered, her jaw clenched. "I'm sorry if this is a shock, but I thought you'd want to know. I'm shocked too, and embarrassed to death, if you want to know the truth. I don't know how to feel. I mean, this innocent little baby didn't ask to be born into this mess, you know. He deserves to have a family that loves him and is good to him. And what did he get? A lying bastard for a father—an old man having a midlife crisis, and a young slut for a mother. Who will take care of this baby? They're not even married. I don't even know if they're still living together. But this little guy—he *is* my baby brother..."

"I always wanted a baby brother for you, Em..."

"But not like this, Mom. My God!"

"No, not like this," Beth continued to stare at the photo. Chubby little fists, a dimple on his chin, a hint of a smile spreading across his face. "But he's here. He is adorable, I must admit. What's his name?"

"Jason Robert Calhoun."

"Jason," she repeated quietly, lost in her own thoughts. The color drained from her face as she clutched the photo.

"Mom, are you OK?"

"It just feels strange, almost surreal to me. That's all. I feel betrayed, I guess. As for your father—it's totally over between us. You know that. It's time for both of us to get on with our lives. So that doesn't bother me. But it is hard to believe that your father is a father again, at his age…"

"But what kind of a father will he be, Mom? Will he even be around to raise this child, or will he take off with someone else?"

"I don't know…" Beth's eyes clouded over with doubt. She knew Rob too well. How could he be so damn stupid? So irresponsible?

∘⑥⑨∘

As the week flew by, Emily watched her mother closely. She'd worried about her during the divorce, after she ran away to the far end of the earth. Now, she could see her mother blossoming, happier than she ever remembered seeing her. Her mother seemed to have put together the missing pieces of her past, to have found a life of her own. She seemed to have found something else, too—a man. Emily wasn't quite sure how she felt about that yet. This was *her mother,* after all…

"Mom?" Emily broached the subject one afternoon as they snowshoed out to the gazebo. Beth wanted to show the family graveyard to her daughter as well as the gazebo that she had restored to its former splendor. Seth's island loomed just across the bay. Staring at his place, hoping that she'd see him there today, Beth realized how much she missed him.

"Mom?" Emily clumsily snowshoed up behind her mother who was gazing off into the distance. "I want you to know that I like Seth a lot. He is so right for you…"

Beth sighed. She could feel the *but* hanging heavily in the air between them. "But?"

"Well, it's just that…how could you get involved so soon, Mom? You're hardly divorced! Like, what's Dad going to think about this?"

Beth felt her long-suppressed anger surging through her body. "My God, why should I care what your father thinks? Look what he's done! You don't know half of it. Why would you even care what he thinks?"

"Maybe because he's my father? Sometimes I hate him…other times, I feel sorry for him, I guess. I'm not sure what I feel anymore. I feel like I'm being torn in two sometimes. Maybe it's not so much about him…maybe it's just that you're *my mother!* And it doesn't feel right for my mother to have a…a boyfriend."

"Emily, we're just good friends for now. I'm not ready to make any decisions about my life—not yet. But he is a wonderful man and he's been very good to me. I enjoy his company. Is that so wrong?"

Emily slumped down beside her mother on the snow-covered steps of the gazebo. "No, I guess not. Looking back, you should have left Dad years ago, Mom. He treated you like shit much of the time. Like what you had wasn't really a marriage. I don't even know what a good marriage looks like or feels like. I worry about that sometimes."

"I'm sorry I couldn't provide a good role model for you, honey. I always thought it was best to stay together until you were grown—for your sake, so you didn't come from a broken home. At least you had a father…" Beth's thoughts trailed back to her own childhood.

"I know you meant the best for me. But I wish you'd left long ago—with me, of course," she smiled. "I wish you'd met someone like Seth years ago. I think. I'm not blind. I see the way you look at each other. So I guess I should be happy for you—and I am. I just don't want you to jump into anything."

"I promise you that I won't jump into anything." She pulled her daughter into her arms. Emily was entitled to have mixed emotions as she struggled with her parents' divorce. As worldly and well-traveled as Emily was, she was still a little girl at times.

"I know you won't." Emily leaned into her mother's arms. "And I don't want you to be alone forever either. It must get lonely out here all by yourself…"

"Being alone isn't always bad. I'm actually enjoying being in control of my own life, doing what I want, when I want to do it." *Like not having to walk on eggshells,* she thought to herself, recalling her life with Rob. "It feels like I'm finally becoming my own person, not just a shadow of somebody else. And that feels good."

"Yes, but, it can also be lonely, you know. Especially if you're isolated out here in the middle of nowhere."

Beth stopped abruptly, surprised at her daughter's remark. "I thought you liked it here, Em."

"I do—for a vacation. It's beautiful, a wonderful break. But this isn't the real world. It's like you're hiding from something. Don't you go slightly crazy knowing that you are stuck on this island? Like, what if you have a medical emergency? What if there's a bad storm and you are stranded? What if a bear breaks into the house—or a burglar? You have no police protection close by. No doctors. No fitness center. No malls to shop in or movies to see. No restaurants. You used to love dining in Chicago, and all the museums." She finally paused to catch her breath.

"I have everything I want or need on the mainland," Beth said simply. "I know this isn't Chicago, and there are some things that I miss about life there. Look at my hair! Do you know how long it's been since I went to a beauty salon? I used to have my hair done every week back in Chicago. Here, I've learned to make lists so I can get all my supplies and run my errands when I go to the mainland. It's not so simple to run to the store for a quart of milk. But...no place is perfect. Chicago is too busy, too much traffic and noise. You can't see the stars at night or listen to the loons. I love it here..." She breathed deeply as delicate flakes of snow began to fall around them.

"But what if you can't get to the mainland? What if you need help right away?"

"I have a good neighbor close by, one who will be here for me anytime I need help," Beth began cautiously.

"Seth, of course," Emily sighed, then smiled. "Yes, he would be here for you. That's pretty obvious. I don't mean to be critical of your lifestyle...but I worry about you out here, especially by yourself. There's so much more to life than this. You'd love Paris, seeing the world."

"I will see Paris and I will see the world. But wherever I go, I will love coming home to the solitude, the beauty of Rainy Lake. It feels more like home than anyplace I've ever lived. Maybe because it was home for me as a little girl..."

"It's your life...when you were my age, did you like living here, Mom?"

Beth burst out laughing, remembering how much she'd hated it here as a teenager. "The truth? I hated it here then and couldn't wait to get away. I wanted to see the world, to live in the big city."

Emily grinned, sticking her tongue out to catch a lacy snowflake. "Maybe we're more alike than we think."

"Cherish what is dearest
while you have it near you,
and wait not
till it is far away."
Thomas Carlyle

Chapter Thirty

Jake had just dozed off on the sofa at his Ranier home one gloomy winter evening when the phone began to ring. He decided to ignore it. But it rang again and again. Some people don't give up, he grumbled to himself as he finally picked it up.

"Jake, it's Butch," the bartender at Woody's spoke in a hushed tone. "You've gotta get over here. There's a stranger in here askin' questions about Beth and how to get to her island. Lookin' for a guide and a snowmobile to rent."

"What's he look like?"

"Big city dude. Fancy clothes. Rolex watch. Don't belong here, I tell ya."

"Thanks, Butch. I'll be right over." Jake grabbed his jacket and jumped into his truck, heading for Woody's. It couldn't be Rob, Beth's ex-husband, could it? That would not be good news.

As he pulled up by Woody's, a man in an expensive, long wool coat strode out of the bar. He began hiking down the street in his slippery city shoes toward a big, black Lincoln. Not the kind of car that folks around here drove. Not the kind of clothes that tourists or seasonal residents wore up here in the winter. Obviously the big city dude. Jake drove past him slowly, craning his neck to get a good look. A chill ran up and down his spine. His worst fear was confirmed. It was Rob. No doubt about it. He watched Rob slide behind the wheel of the Lincoln with its Illinois license plates. He followed him from a distance until Rob headed out of the village onto the highway and turned right toward International Falls.

What was the bastard doing nosing around here? The last thing Beth needed was an unexpected visitor out there all by herself. Rob couldn't be trusted. If he'd come all this way to find Beth, he wasn't going to give up and go home without accomplishing his mission—whatever that may be. Jake suspected that he would be back.

He raced back home, trying to decide if he should snowmobile out to the island to deliver the news in person. He didn't want to upset her. She was finally getting over the fear and nightmares that had haunted her for so long. Someone should be there with her, he decided. Who could get there the fastest? And who had the strength to overpower Rob if he became violent? Seth, of course.

Jake dialed Seth's number. "Seth, sorry to bother you so late. But we may have a problem here and I need your help." He went on to explain the situation to him.

"I'll get over there right away. I'll take care of her, Jake, you know that."

"I do. But listen, you need to stay there with her—until we're sure that Rob is gone. Will you do that?"

"If she'll let me…" Seth sighed. "On second thought, I'm staying whether she likes it or not. I'll sleep on the sofa. I don't want her there alone any more than you do."

Jake chuckled. "Thanks for looking out for her. Now, get on over there and keep me posted. I'll do some sleuthing around here to see what more I can find out." He hiked back over to Woody's to talk with Butch over a beer.

∽৽৽

Seth stuffed a few things into an overnight bag, grabbed his pistol, and set out for Beth's island. Before he left, he gave her a quick call so she wouldn't worry when a snowmobile showed up on her island. "Beth, I'm coming over. We may have a problem and I need to be there if you need any help."

She froze. "Seth? What kind of a problem? Seth?" she repeated into the dead phone. Seth was already on the way. She could hear his snowmobile roaring across the well-worn path between their islands. She stood on the porch shivering in her robe when he came running up the path.

"What in the world?" She followed him into the house where he immediately bolted the door behind him and checked the kitchen door as well.

"Look, we're probably overreacting, Jake and I. But you need to know that your ex-husband is in town looking for you, wanting directions to get out here."

"Oh my God." She slunk down onto the sofa.

He sat beside her, his arm around her. "He may not mean any harm, Beth. We don't know what he wants. All I know is I'm not leaving you here alone." He pulled his pistol from his jacket pocket and set it on the table beside them. "Just in case."

She shuddered. "How do you know it's him? Are you sure?"

"Jake saw him and has no doubt whatsoever. Rob was heading toward the Falls twenty minutes ago. We think he might come back…"

"Of course he will. Rob never quits until he gets what he wants." She continued to shiver as Seth held her close.

"Look, I'm staying here tonight and as long as it takes. Orders from Jake. No arguments from you, OK?"

"None," she managed a weak smile as she cuddled up in his arms. "You can stay in Nana's bedroom down here."

"Precisely my thoughts," he sighed. Well, not exactly, but close, he realized as he scolded himself for his foolish feelings.

They sat by the fire for a while—until she was sleepy and calm enough to go upstairs to bed. Seth is here, she reminded herself. I have nothing to worry about. Finally she drifted off to sleep.

Seth, meanwhile, paced through the creaking old house in the dark, peering out the windows anytime he heard a sound. There would still be snowmobilers on the lake, he reminded himself. They'd be closing up the bars, buzzing back home across the lake. He was starting to yawn and decided to call it a night when two snowmobiles suddenly came roaring up onto the island.

Beth heard it, too. She threw on her robe, tucked Nana's ancient pistol into her pocket, and came running down the stairs. Someone was at the door, knocking loudly. She and Seth stood side by side, waiting. The knocking became louder, more aggressive. Their guest had no intention of leaving.

"Beth, I know you're in there. Open the door. We need to talk," a familiar voice from the past called out. It was Rob all right. Beth's eyes filled with terror as she moved closer to Seth.

"Listen, I'm not here to hurt you in any way. I'm sorry about coming out so late. But I really need to talk with you. It's important. We just got an offer on the house—a great offer. I need your original signature on this offer to purchase or we lose the deal. The offer expires at noon tomorrow unless we both sign it and get it back to the realtor by then. He sure as hell wasn't going to come all the way up here on such short notice—or find a guide and a snowmobile to get here. Beth?"

She wasn't sure what to think, what to do. They'd waited a long time for a reasonable offer. She didn't want to blow a deal that would finally release her equity in their home. Was he telling the truth? She raised her eyebrows toward Seth, looking for some guidance.

He shook his head firmly. He didn't know this man or what he had done to her. But he didn't trust him. He fingered the pistol in his hand, wondering what Beth would decide to do. Pangs of déjà vu suddenly consumed him as he watched her twist a strand of auburn hair around her finger.

"Please, Beth. You have nothing to be afraid of. We just need to get this business taken care of. Then I'll leave. I promise. My guide is waiting for me," Rob continued to plead in his most persuasive voice.

Finally, Beth whispered to Seth, "I need to find out what this is all about. Stay in the bedroom. It's best if he doesn't see you here...but keep your ears open, all right?"

"Are you sure?" Seth snapped back from his trance, searching her eyes. He didn't like this. She nodded as he reluctantly tiptoed back into the bedroom, cracking the door just enough so he could keep an eye on things.

Cautiously, she walked to the front door, trying to control the fear that surged through her body, trying to appear confident and unafraid. She unlocked the dead bolt and inched the door open.

Rob was smiling, tentatively, as he slowly pushed the door open and walked in. "Thank you, Beth." He couldn't take his eyes off of her. "You don't need to be afraid. Please...I really need to talk to you. I've been such a fool, such an ass...God, I've missed you..."

She slowly backed away from him as he moved closer. His penetrating gaze was making her uncomfortable. "We have nothing to talk about, Rob. This is business. I'll sign the papers. And then I want you to leave immediately as you promised to do."

"First, there are a few things that I need to tell you." He casually plopped himself down in an old rocking chair while she stood, unsmiling, arms folded across her chest. His charm seemed to be lost on her, he realized, but he went on. She would soften. She always used to. Most women did.

"I was wrong, Beth, so wrong in the way that I treated you. It wasn't until you left that I realized...that I realized you are the only woman in this world that I want to be with. I'm asking you to forgive me. I swear to God, I'm done chasing. I just want you back, back home with me in Chicago where we belong. I'll make it up to you. Whatever you want, it's yours. Anything. You name it. Remember how you wanted to see Sweden and research your ancestors? Well, we can do that—together. We can stop to see Emily in Paris on the way home."

Beth was too stunned to speak, too skeptical to believe the words that flowed like maple syrup from his polished tongue. Even if she could believe him, it no longer mattered. She felt nothing but ice chilling her veins. She wondered what had happened to his latest love, the young mother of his new baby son.

"Beth, sweetheart?" He held his arms out to her—as if he actually expected her to fall into them. His eyes were filled with remorse— pleading with her to love him again, to forgive him one last time. He was looking at her, once again, the same way he had when she'd fallen in love with him years ago.

But it was too late. She remained rigid, her eyes hard as steel. "We are divorced, Rob. It's over. All I want is for you to leave, to get out of my house. Where are the papers?"

"Papers?" His condescending laugh erupted once more. "*What papers*? Well, it got me in the door, didn't it?"

"You bastard!" she shouted as he began to approach her slowly.

"I asked you nicely. I tried. I'll give you one more chance."

"Leave, now!" Her voice began to shake as she backed away from him, one step at a time.

"Not until you come with me." His voice was firm, confident. Rob didn't take no for an answer—not from anyone. He never had. "I'm taking you back to Chicago with me. Please, baby, I need you. Someday, you will thank me for rescuing you from this hellhole. Now, where's your jacket, your boots? Leave the rest. I'll buy you new clothes in Chicago, anything you want."

"I'm not leaving. But you are!" She stood her ground as he advanced. Images of that horrible night in Chicago, the night he almost raped her, suddenly flashed through her mind. She gripped the pistol inside her pocket. Trembling, she wondered if she could really pull the trigger—if she had to. But Seth was here—where was he?

Just as Rob attempted to pull her into his arms, the door of the bedroom flew open and Seth stormed into the room, his eyes shooting daggers. "You heard the lady. Now get the hell out of this house."

Rob stood there speechless as Seth approached him, practically breathing fire.

"I said *now*," Seth growled as he moved in closer, his hand in his pocket. He was ready.

Rob began to laugh hatefully, anger flashing in his eyes. "Now, I get it. So you're already sleeping around? My God, Beth, use your head. What can this guy give you that I can't? He's nothing but a loser—a half-breed at that," he sneered. "You're coming with me," he ordered her.

"Oh, no, she's not," Seth pulled his pistol, cocking and aiming it at Rob. There was no doubt in anyone's mind that he'd use it. "Out, now!" he ordered Rob, who began backing slowly toward the door. "Do not *ever* come around here again. Do you hear me?" As Rob stumbled out onto the porch, Seth slammed the door and bolted it securely. He pulled a trembling Beth into his arms. Together, they stood by the window, watching her ex-husband disappear into the night.

❦

"Crazy bastards!" Rob grumbled to himself as he ran for his snowmobile. He fumbled with the key, dropping it into a snowbank. Frantically he pawed through the snow on all fours. Finally, he found the key and started the machine. He took off, veering erratically through the ghostly trees, dodging an imaginary barrage of bullets.

"No woman is worth this, not even Beth," he reminded himself as he shot past the stunned guide who'd been waiting for him by the edge of the lake. "She's *my wife*—and she's sleeping with another man! Whores, they're all whores…just like my mother. But why couldn't it have been different with Beth? Why won't she give me one last chance?" One lonely tear slipped down his cheek—probably the only tear that Rob Calhoun had ever shed in his life.

❦

Once Rob was gone, the horror of the night finally washed over Beth in sickening waves. *If Seth hadn't been here, what would have happened?* She crumbled into his arms, unable to support her own weight. He carried her to the sofa where he wrapped her in a blanket, propping her head on his lap. They sat together by the fire as he held her hand.

"Do you want to talk about it?" he finally asked, gently massaging her tense shoulders.

"Hmmm? Talk about what?" Her eyes were glazed, unfocused, as she tried to hide herself from a cruel world that seemed to barrage her with blows from all directions. It was safer to hide, to bury her feelings.

"Your feelings? I'm not a mind reader, Beth. I don't know what you're feeling. I feel helpless. I've never been there, never been married, never been in love…not until now. But you, after all these years of being married to this man, what?"

She sighed. "My feelings are numb. I feel nothing for that man. If he was serious, which is debatable, well…it's just too little, too late. It's over." She paused, trying hard to tap into her feelings. Was there anything, she wondered, still buried in that vault where she'd hidden her true self for so much of her life? But all she could think of were Seth's words, "*never been in love…not until now.*"

Seth got up to stoke the fire, somewhat reassured by her words, but troubled on a deeper level. "He still loves you," he finally spit the words out.

"What?" she gasped.

"I said, this guy loves you and he will apparently do anything to get you back." He turned back to the fire, trying to mask his reeling emotions. Trying to hide his fear of losing her.

"He's a pathological liar, Seth. He loves what he can't have. He loves the chase. As soon as he gets what he wants, he falls in love with someone else. It goes on and on. I've lived with it for twenty years."

"I'm sorry," he softened, returning to her side.

"It's over, Seth, believe me," she tried to reassure him as images of Rob's visit began to resurface in her mind. Rob backing her across the room, determined to take her back to Chicago. The gun in her pocket. Seth bursting into the room, ready to defend her any way that he had to.

She shuddered. "Thank God you were here tonight, Seth. I don't know what would have happened without you. You saved me…saved my life." Her tears finally began to fall. "Hold me, Seth, please just hold me," she whimpered.

He pulled her into his arms, holding her close, stroking her back as she cried in his arms. "I will always be here for you," he whispered.

She breathed a heavy sigh of relief, feeling that she'd finally found a man she could trust. When her tears were spent, he tucked her into her bed in the eagle's nest before retreating back down the stairs. He tossed and turned, alone, in her grandmother's bed that night.

❦

She made him breakfast in the morning. Tired but content, they lingered over their coffee as they watched the deer scampering in the snow, feasting on moss and winter berries.

"What are your plans today?" she finally asked him.

"Nothing that doesn't include you. I'm not going anyplace unless you come with me." He flashed that irresistible grin that made her heart do cartwheels and somersaults all at once.

"I'm fine. I'm not afraid to be here alone, you know," she half-heartedly protested.

"Maybe I'm the one who is afraid. I've promised your father, and I'm not leaving you alone."

She couldn't help smiling back at him, almost relieved. She enjoyed his company. And at least until they felt comfortable that Rob was gone and not coming back, maybe it wouldn't hurt to have him stay here. "You win. But don't you have work to do?"

"As a matter of fact, I do. I'd like you to come over to my place with me for the day. You can read a book, sleep, putter around, even watch me paint if you like. Then I'll come back home with you."

> "All that we see or seem
> is but a dream within a dream."
> *Edgar Allen Poe*

Chapter Thirty-one

And so their unusual living arrangement began—as a result of Rob's visit to the island. By the time they had proof that Rob was back in Chicago, it had become a habit. A habit that neither Seth nor Beth were anxious to break. Gradually, as the endless winter began to show hints of spring, they felt comfortable enough to create a little more distance in their relationship. Seth would frequently go home to his place in the morning to spend the day working alone, balancing himself with the solitude that his soul craved. She spent her days making jewelry and developing a business plan. He'd be back to her island before dark. She'd have dinner ready for him or they'd cook together. He was always anxious to get back home to her. *Home*? Where was home? What did it mean?

Seth wasn't always working when he was alone on his island. He was struggling, trying to sort out his feelings. Sometimes he spent an entire day sitting in the woods meditating, seeking wisdom from his spirit guide. Sometimes, on sunny winter days, he sat instead on an upside-down five-gallon bucket beside a hole in the ice, fishing. If he was lucky, he'd bring some nice fish back to Beth for dinner.

Sometimes, as sat on his ice bucket, he became so deeply engrossed in thought that he didn't notice his red and white bobber disappearing beneath the ice. The *future* question loomed larger and larger over his relationship with Beth. He'd always seen himself as a bachelor, an intellectual, philosopher, and artist. An American Indian who was proud of his heritage and dedicated to preserving the cultural traditions of his people, to sending as much money as he could spare back to his people on the reservation. He was one of the few who had decided to strike out on his own.

Now his future was in limbo. His heart ached to hold this woman in his arms every night for the rest of his life, to care for her. But he also craved solitude and independence. Sometimes he even thought about children—and grandchildren. While he and Beth were probably too old to think about having any of their own, he could see himself as a surro-gate father to the lovely Emily, as a grandfather to the children that she would have someday.

He struggled to adhere to the boundaries that he and Beth had set. He continued to sleep alone in Nana's downstairs bedroom while Beth slept upstairs. Each was acutely aware of the other's presence—so close, yet so far away. It had become harder and harder to tell each oth-er good night. It was all about respect, he told himself—respect laced with fear. When he was honest with himself, he realized that he was also afraid—afraid of commitment, of losing his identity and solitude—but also afraid of losing her.

❦❧

One winter day Seth sat silently beneath a tree in the woods on his island. Sunlight flickered through the pines as squirrels scampered around him. Closing his eyes, he drew deep breaths, trying to open himself to the wisdom of the universe. Trying to find the answers, to understand the lessons he needed to learn.

Warmed by the sunlight, he found himself getting drowsy. Slipping back into another world—another time, another place. The year was 1849. He was racing across the western plains on a horse. His long black hair billowed behind him, adorned with white eagle feathers. His bronze chest gleamed with sweat. He wore buckskin pants, decorated with beads. His face was painted in the traditional style of the Shoshone tribe. He was one of a band of braves, kicking up a cloud of dust as they rode toward a parade of wagon trains lumbering across their land. White men! The braves stopped on a hillside to watch them pass through the valley below. He was curious about these strange people and what they were doing here. Were they friend or foe? His was a peaceful tribe, although he carried his bow and arrow with him at all times—primarily for hunting.

"Indians!" a cry echoed throughout the valley below. The covered wagons hurriedly formed a circle as pale-faced men began scrambling to and fro with long black objects that made loud, booming noises. Fire and smoke exploded into the air as foreign objects whined across the prairie. These were not friendly people, the braves decided as they be-gan to retreat. As they did, one of them fell to the ground, blood oozing from his chest. He was dead. With that, the braves pulled out their bows and returned the fire with their arrows. A white man or two fell, then another of his tribe.

The last thing he remembered was a piercing pain in his back. When he came to, he was alone on the hillside except for his faithful horse grazing nearby. Shooting pains radiated through his body as he pulled himself into a sitting position. Now he could see the bodies of his friends lying in pools of blood. Not moving. Dead. The wagon train was gone. His horse came to his side, nuzzling his face, waiting for him to mount. Gritting his teeth, he forced himself to stand and mount the horse. Half-sitting, half-lying, he held onto her neck as she galloped across the plains. He prayed to Gitchi Manidoo to lead them to help, to home. His world suddenly went black once again.

It could have been hours or days later that he opened his eyes to find himself lying on a soft, blanket-covered bench in a room made of fallen trees. He could smell bread baking. He felt a wet cloth gently stroking his forehead. Somebody was here with him… Focusing with all of his strength, he looked up into the eyes of a young pioneer woman—a white woman. She twirled a lock of auburn hair around her little finger, a worried expression upon her face. He could not understand her words, but he knew her spirit. Her hands were soft and gentle, full of love and compassion. She spent several months lovingly nursing him back to health in the little log cabin that her husband had built for her before he died a year ago. She'd been all alone since then—until she found a wounded man lying near her chicken coop one late summer day. His horse stood nearby, neighing into the wind. She'd led the horse into the ramshackle barn and fed her grain from the garden that she had tilled and planted herself.

They'd fallen deeply in love and learned to communicate with each other. It was as if they'd always known each other—despite the fact that one was white and one was Indian. As his strength finally returned and he was prepared to ask this woman to marry him, she'd grown weaker and weaker from some mysterious illness that swept through the western plains. He did his best to nurture her back to health…but she died. He buried her beside her husband behind the log house. He never forgot her, and he never loved another woman.

❧☙

One hundred and fifty-nine years later, Seth awoke on his Rainy Lake island. He shook his head, trying to come back to the present time, trying to understand where he'd just been. All he knew was that his vision had been real. He felt it deep within his soul. It was almost as if he'd flashed back in time to a previous lifetime—one he'd shared so briefly with the woman he'd loved. His future suddenly became perfectly clear.

He was late getting back to Beth's that night. The sun had already sunk low in the sky, leaving the world in semi-darkness. When she greeted him on the porch with a relieved hug, he held her close as if he would never let her go. Someday, when the time was right, he would tell her about the amazing things he'd just learned.

He helped Beth with her business Web site that evening. But he was very quiet, trying to digest the experience he'd just had. Beth was also quiet, trying to sort through her feelings. It was all that she could do that night to break away from their traditional goodnight kiss and climb the stairs to her lonely eagle's nest. Sleep came slowly and sporadically those long winter nights, interrupted by ghosts of the past, fears, and thwarted desires that burst forth, uninvited, into the world of her dreams.

Tonight, as soon as she dozed off into a fitful sleep, she finds herself floating on her back in Anderson Bay, basking in the warmth of the sun. She is watching Seth as he builds a fire on the rippling surface of the lake. Together, holding hands, they stroll across the water. They roast hot dogs, devouring every bite, before they fall into each other's arms. They float together on the surface of the eerily still lake.

As they shed their clothes and he finally enters her, swirling ghosts of the past surface from the depths of the lake. Rob's flaming eyes of red-hot steel zap her, paralyzing her. His arms, dripping with blood, tear her away from Seth, dragging her down into the icy, black waters of the lake. She cannot breathe. "Seth!" she cries as Rob drags her deeper and deeper into a sea filled with creatures that are circling around her, slashing their fangs, moving in closer and closer. She cannot move, cannot get away, cannot find Seth. Rob's mouth roars, growling, snarling, moving in for the kill. Then, her limp body drifts with the waves, wrapped in seaweed. "Seth!" she screams silently into the night. "Seth, help me! Seth!"

✖✖

"Seth," she continued to scream, finally finding her voice.

Within minutes, Seth stormed up the stairs to her bedroom, clad only in his shorts. "Beth, what is it? Beth?" He froze when he saw the look of stark terror in her eyes. "Beth, it's me, Seth. It's OK."

She stared vacantly, still lost in the horrifying world of her dreams, unable to see the man standing at her bedside.

He shook her gently. "It's me, Seth. It's OK," he repeated over and over again. Jake wasn't kidding about her nightmares. What was he supposed to do?

Her eyes blank, disengaged, she began to thrash about, striking out in all directions. He tried to hold her, but she became more agitated. He backed off. Finally, after what seemed like an eternity to him, she opened her eyes and looked into his. "Seth?"

He scooped her up into his arms. "You've had a bad dream. I'm here, Beth." He held her in his arms, like a child awakening from a bad dream.

She buried herself in his naked arms, sobbing. "Stay with me, Seth. Please stay with me," she pleaded as she threw her bedcovers open, inviting him to climb in beside her.

"Only if you agree to marry me, Ninimosche," he whispered huskily, finally giving in to their destiny as he crawled in beside the woman that he'd always loved—for as many lifetimes as he could remember.

"Ninimosche?"

"My love—the one I always have and always will love."

"Yes, I will marry you, my love," her heart spoke for her as she welcomed the love of her life into her bed. Wrapped in the heat of each other's arms, layers of fear and doubt began to shrivel and peel away like the skin of an onion. All that was left was the naked core of their beings, souls that were starved for the warmth of each other after being apart for so long.

As he caressed every inch of her body, slowly and lovingly, she opened herself to him, needing him more than she'd ever imagined. Finally, throbbing with years of pent-up passion, he entered her. Their bodies and souls merged in an explosion of eternal recognition and love that could no longer be denied. Two became one.

"Always
I think of you
when the day is ending –
my dreams hold the memory
always."
Kay Karras

Northern Lights by Steve Henry

Chapter Thirty-two

ndless winter days finally began to stretch slowly, like a rubber band warmed by the sun, teasing the weary world with promises of spring—a sunny daffodil breaking through receding splotches of snow only to be buried by the next spring blizzard. Jake called to let Beth know that the seagulls had returned to Ranier on schedule. This was alleged to be the first sign of spring, although their return was usually followed by at least three additional winter storms. Not that anyone was counting. Not much else to do when the ice on the lake turned black, shifting and groaning, breaking up into floating burgs of rotting ice. The locals were more than ready for the next change of seasons. That's why they lived here, after all.

As pools of open water began creeping outwards from the shore-line, the islanders were unable to get to the mainland until the spring break-up process was completed. Beth and Seth were settled into her place, although Seth still liked to spend his days working in the studio on his island. As the ice began to deteriorate, he traded his snowmobile in for skis or snowshoes. Toward the end, he slid his canoe beside him, ready to jump in if the ice began to crack and give way beneath his feet. He gave that up and stayed at Beth's the last week.

Jake kept them posted on the progress of spring on the mainland. The white pelicans had returned to Lake Kabetogama, just south of Rainy Lake. He missed his frequent trips to the island and was looking forward to taking the two of them out for dinner at the Thunderbird as soon as the lake was open again. Beth and Seth planned to announce their engage-ment that evening. She couldn't wait to tell Jake the news. They hadn't set a wedding date yet, although they'd decided to wait until summer when the lilacs and lady slippers were in full bloom. It would be a simple ceremony in the gazebo on her island. They planned to honeymoon in Paris, paying a visit to Emily as well. Life was good, almost too good…

≪≫

Finally, the Canadian geese returned to the islands, honking as they glided across the growing expanse of open water. The same geese re-turned year after year, in pairs. They mated for life. It was sad to see a lone goose fly in, having lost its lifelong mate.

Patches of green grass finally began to emerge through the shrink-ing piles of dirty snow. The forest took on brighter shades of spring green as new growth sprouted from the trees, reaching upwards toward the warmth of the sun.

Early one morning Beth and Seth awoke in each other's arms, to the sound of waves frolicking on the rocky shoreline. Spring had come to the islands. Their world had opened up once more. The boats were ready to go. The snowmobiles were winterized and back in the shed. Tonight, they would meet Jake at the Thunderbird for dinner. It had been almost a month since they'd seen him and they missed him.

As Beth scrambled eggs for breakfast, Seth came up behind her, wrapping his arms around her. "I have something for you. Close your eyes." He spun her around to face him. When she was allowed to open her eyes, she found him on one knee in the middle of the black-and-white checkered kitchen floor, a tiny box in his outstretched hand. "I want to do this the right way. I love you with all my heart, all my soul. Will you do me the honor of marrying me?"

"You know very well that I will. I love you, Seth. And I always will." Opening the box, she found an intricately carved sterling silver ring with a green turquoise stone glimmering in the center. "It's stunning...it looks like a family heirloom?"

"It is. It belonged to my grandmother. It was given to her by her husband, who probably got it for her on his travels. You see, he was a French-Canadian fur trader. She was the first one in our Bois Forte band to marry an outsider, something that probably caused a stir in those days."

"I think you're a lot like your grandmother," she teased him. "Tell me more."

"We think the ring was crafted by an Indian tribe from the southwest. She felt that it had spiritual powers, that it protected her and guided her. She wore it every day of her life. When she died, the day I was born, she asked that it be passed on to me. It was her wish that I pass it on someday to the woman I love—as a blessing from her. And that is what I am doing...I never dreamed that I'd find a woman special enough to give this to, but I finally have. Perhaps she's the one who led me to you..."

Beth's eyes filled with tears as she slid into his familiar arms. "I accept, and I will make your grandmother proud. I will use her blessing to make you the happiest man in this world."

"I already am," he whispered in her ear as their eggs fried to a crisp on the stove.

∽ঌ৯∽

Jake was waiting for them in the dining room of the Thunderbird Lodge. They sat together at a table by the wall of windows, enjoying the view of the lake that stretched into the wilderness. Seagulls chattered, soaring over the marina, as a lone eagle swooped low over the water in search of a fish for dinner. Spring had arrived.

"What?" Jake asked, watching the two of them sitting across from him. They were unable to contain their happiness. "Looks to me like you're bursting at the seams to tell me something."

Beth slowly moved her left hand toward him, her ring gleaming in the candlelight that danced in the center of their table.

"I am so happy for the two of you…" Jake began, a tear dribbling down his wrinkled cheek.

"Wait," Seth interrupted. "I should do this properly. I'm sorry that I could not wait, Jake…but I do want to ask you now for your lovely daughter's hand in marriage. I promise to love and to care for her for the rest of my life."

"You've got my permission, Seth. I think you know that. You are the man that I would choose for my daughter. Congratulations!" They shook hands as Beth ran around the table to give her father a hug.

The restaurant was suddenly still. Waitresses and customers alike were watching, smiling. Suddenly, they burst out in applause. "Looks like a toast is in order here. Here's to the happy couple," an older gentleman in an expensive suit stood, raising his glass into the air. "Round on me, please, bartender, for everyone in the house."

"Thank you," Jake acknowledged the man's kind gesture, trying to place him. He looked familiar…

"You're welcome, Jake. My best to you all," he smiled knowingly.

Jake hated it when he struggled to remember names and faces—something he was doing more of these days. But this was no time to dwell on that. He stood proudly, raising his glass, and his voice. "To my daughter, Beth, and my future son-in-law, Seth…" He hesitated a moment, trying to find the words that he needed to say. Slowly, they came to him. "May your lives be blessed with the special kind of love that I found with Beth's lovely mother, Sarah. Today, we—Sarah and I—stand together to wish you the very best that this life can offer." He settled into his chair as Beth's eyes filled with tears. She and her mother were being recognized at last.

A hush fell over the restaurant. Once the other customers drifted back into their own conversations, including whispered messages related to Jake's bold confession, Jake decided that it was time to order dinner. He'd have his usual—the Filet Mignon, medium-rare. Beth debated between the Walleye Almondine and Deep Sea Scallops while Seth opted for the Steak Oscar house specialty. The Thunderbird had a reputation for some of the finest dining in the North Woods. Tourists were always amazed to find a place like this up here on the outer edge of the civilized world.

Once they'd ordered, Jake decided he had some business that needed to be taken care of. He produced a large manila envelope from the seat beside him and handed it to Beth. "This is for you. I want you to have it now, to file it away in your safe deposit box."

"What is this, Dad?" She was puzzled as she glanced at the official-looking papers inside.

"No need to look at it now, Beth. It's the deed to the island. I've executed and recorded it, so it's legal. I'm trying to take care of some paperwork—deeds, wills, the kind of thing that we should all be doing at my age, you know. I don't want all of this tied up in my estate some-day."

"Well, thank you so much. I don't know what to say."

"The island has always been yours, Beth. It belonged to Nana. Just so you know, there's a second deed in there also. I'm turning my place on Houska's Point over to you. You may want a place on the mainland someday—someday when you're old like me," he managed a weak smile, "or anytime you want to get off the island for a while."

"But…" she stammered, "I can't accept that."

"You have no choice. I've already registered the deed. Look, I want you to have it. All I ask is that you think of me, and of Sarah, when you spend time there, OK? It was a special place for us, Beth. All the mem-ories…" His voice cracked with emotion.

"Does Evelyn know?"

"She will soon. There's more than enough for her. It won't be an is-sue—especially now that she has completed treatment. She's back home and doing much better. You can almost hold a conversation with her these days. I think we're all going to see some positive changes in her…" he drifted off, trying to find a way to get an important message across to his daughter. "Beth, I probably don't have a right to ask this of you, but I need to."

"I'm listening, Dad," she reached out for Seth's hand beneath the table, catching her breath as Seth squeezed her hand and held it firmly in his own.

"It would please me if you'd give Evelyn another chance," Jake whispered, his eyes pleading with hers. "She's going to need a friend like you someday."

"Yes, I'll give her another chance," Beth's words almost surprised her. "She's not my enemy just because she's your wife, you know."

Seth was a little puzzled. Why, he wondered, as he vowed to sup-port whatever decision Beth made about all of this, were relationships, marriages, and divorces so damn complicated? Jake was still married to one woman although he'd loved another for many years—even after her death. And Beth was supposed to forgive and befriend his wife...the one who'd kept her parents apart? He didn't get it.

Still, it turned out to be a memorable spring evening—one that would live on in Beth's heart forever. A silver moon danced upon the dark waters of Rainy Lake to the rhythm of a gentle breeze. The boats at the pier swayed to nature's symphony as the three of them walked out onto the deck of the Thunderbird. Jake lingered as if he didn't want this evening to end.

"How about a nightcap?" he suggested, settling into an Adirondack chair on the deck.

As they sat together in the dark, sipping Irish coffee, Jake seemed to have things on his mind, things that he needed to share with them. Things like how much it meant to him to have a daughter like Beth, a granddaughter like Emily, and a son-in-law like Seth. How grateful he was that Beth had forgiven him, that they were a family again. He reminisced about his life—the good and the bad.

He talked about Sarah and how much he loved her. "She's still with me," he sighed, "I want you to remember that. Death is not the end. It's just a different state of existence. A new beginning. Someday, we will all be together again..."

Finally, they called it a night, hugging each other good-bye. Jake held onto Beth as if he didn't want to let her go. "I love you, Beth. Always remember that," he reminded her as he left them at the pier. As he walked slowly toward his car, he glanced over his shoulder one last time. He watched the lovers holding hands, sharing a lingering kiss in the moonlight before climbing into the boat for their trip back to the island. His mission was complete. His Christmas wish had come true.

❧❦

The walleye were biting, Jake discovered when he made his way to Woody's the next morning for a cup of coffee. "Where's everyone?" He glanced around to find most of the regulars gone.

"Fishin'. Some nice walleye comin' in, Jake. Wish I was out there," Butch lamented as he wiped down the bar, sipping his muddy coffee. That's the way he liked it, the way he made it every morning. The regulars got used to it.

Jake had been waiting all winter to get out fishing. He wasn't into ice fishing these days—too cold—but he loved to spend his summers on the lake. He gulped down his coffee and hiked back to his place, a definite spring to his slowing gait. His boat was waiting at the dock, already loaded with his fishing gear. He'd put in a new fish locator this spring. He was ready to go. He tossed a half-loaf of bread, a jar of peanut butter, and a few bottles of water into the boat. He started the motor and was untying the boat from the dock when he realized he'd forgotten his jacket. Damn, he mumbled to himself, as he made one more trip up to the cabin. Only a fool would venture out onto that lake without a jacket—especially in the spring when weather could be unpredictable.

Finally, he was off for a leisurely day on the lake. Sometimes he'd cast. Sometimes he'd troll. And sometimes he'd explore the endless bays and open stretches of water, looking for a good fishing hole. He could almost taste fresh walleye. When the first one hit his line, he set the hook. His eyes sparkled as he reeled it in and flipped it into the boat. *Nice fish,* he congratulated himself on his first catch of the season. What a day to be out on the lake, he thought to himself. It didn't get much better than this. Fluffy clouds floated in a brilliant blue sky. It was warm, calm, with just a hint of a breeze. He watched an otter at play, loons diving beside the boat, ducks flying overhead. Butch was right—they were hitting good today. He filled his limit in no time at all. Time to head back and clean the day's catch.

ക⁹⁹

Jake fished almost every day for the next few weeks. He had more fish than he knew what to do with, so he decided to bring one into the Falls for Evelyn one evening. She seemed surprised to find her husband standing there on her doorstep in his smelly fishing clothes. But she invited him in.

"Let's sit in the garden," he suggested, realizing that he still had fish blood and slime on his jeans. He didn't fit into Evelyn's fancy house—never had.

"Good idea," she laughed as she put the fish into the refrigerator and led him out into the garden. She was curious, wondering why he'd suddenly decided to pay her a visit. Now that she was off the booze, he stopped over now and then. Just to talk—something they'd rarely done for years. She enjoyed his visits now. Before…when she was drinking, she'd been the one to call him on the phone—drunk, demanding, insisting that he come over for one reason or another. He'd come, reluctantly, ready for an argument, counting the minutes until he could escape back to Houska's Point. Things had changed. It almost felt comfortable between them now—almost—despite the skeletons that lay buried at the core of their marriage.

He seemed lost in thought as he gazed at Evelyn's garden. Her peonies were in full bloom, their fragrance wafting through the garden. "Nice garden, Evelyn. You do have a magic touch, you know."

"What?" She was shocked to receive a compliment from her husband. It had been a long time coming.

He shuffled his feet, staring at the ground, needing to tell her something.

"What is it, Jake?" she asked softly.

He cleared his throat. "Ya know, we did have some good years, some good times together. Some bad ones, too, I'm afraid. But all in all, I'll remember the good, Evelyn. I hope you will, too."

She was too surprised to respond. She simply nodded her head as he pulled himself up from his chair. His back must be bothering him, she thought to herself.

"Well, gotta run. So…" He stood clumsily in front of her chair, waiting for something…for what? When she stood, he awkwardly hugged her good-bye, then turned and left. He never looked back. He couldn't—his eyes were watering for some odd reason.

Evelyn dropped back into her chair, stunned. He had not hugged her in so many years that she could not remember the last time. Why now, she asked herself?

∽✞✞∾

The next evening, Jake brought fish out to the island for Beth and Seth. They made a shore lunch down by the lake. Jake was quiet that evening, perhaps a little tired. Too many long days on the lake, too much sun and water. He'd feel better after a good night's sleep, he decided. As the sky began to swirl into pink streaks, the sun climbed down a ladder of gold-tinged clouds—finally slipping into the lake. He hugged them both good-bye and took off for home in his boat. "I love you both," he called out as they waved to him from the dock.

The memory of Sarah filled Jake's heart and mind as he skimmed across the silent lake. God, he missed her tonight. He could almost see her beside him as she'd been so many times before, so many years ago. He could almost feel her hand holding his as they enjoyed the beauty of the night together. He sighed wistfully as he landed the boat and headed for his dark, lonely cabin. At times like this, he liked to get Sarah's pic-

232

ture out of his safe, to hold it close as he rocked in his favorite chair on the deck overlooking Sand Bay.

Tonight, he once again held her close, rocking back and forth, back and forth. The steeple of the old Canadian Indian mission church across the bay glowed eerily beneath the light of the moon. He searched the horizon for a gull, for a sign that Sarah was with him tonight. It was quiet, so quiet, not a gull in sight.

His eyes were getting heavy. His bones ached. No sign of Sarah. *Sarah, sweetheart,* he thought with all of his might, *our mission is accomplished. Beth has found her way—and the love of her life. I think it's time for me to come home to you. Please give me a sign...*

As he began to doze off in his chair, the northern lights suddenly exploded in jagged sheets of red and green. Throbbing with passion, they danced wildly through the heavens. Glowing red rockets streaked across the sky, diving down into the depths of the bottomless lake.

Jake had never seen such a spectacular demonstration. As he watched, his eyes were drawn to an image that took his breath away. An iridescent form emerged through the veil of the dancing lights. A beautiful woman floated across the water toward him, holding out her arms, calling to him. Love radiated through her flowing hair, from her fingertips. As she came closer, she glowed brighter and brighter.

Sarah, oh, my darling... Sarah, I'm coming home! He clutched his heart as he slumped in his chair.

"Death is the golden key that
opens the palace of eternity."
John Milton

Chapter Thirty-three

*B*eth and Seth also watched the aurora borealis lighting up the winter sky that night. Huddled together on her dock, they were captivated by this mysterious phenomenon. Never before had they seen the lights dance so boldly, so passionately, across the shimmering lake. Dressed in brilliant shades of red and green, the northern lights swirled and twirled, waltzing with the stars far above the planet Earth.

Beth sighed deeply, feeling more content than she'd ever been in her life. Whatever demons she'd faced in the past, they no longer mattered—not within the big picture of the universe of life. The man she loved sat beside her, holding her hand in his.

"It's a mystery, isn't it?" Seth whispered, almost breathlessly. "Do you know what this means?"

"The northern lights?"

"Yes. My people believe that the northern lights are spirits from beyond the grave who have come back to gather recently deceased spirits. They're here tonight to help others cross over to the other side of life."

The spiritual beliefs of his ancestors intrigued her. They opened up new worlds, new possibilities. Jake also had a strong belief in life beyond this world. He believed that her mother was still with them. Was Beth the only one struggling with things that she could not see, could not prove? She remained silent, lost in the magic of the night.

"Someone is crossing over tonight, Beth," he continued. "It was a night like this when my grandmother went to the light…at least that's what they tell me."

"I'm sorry, Seth," she said as she pulled him into her arms. "Your grandmother meant a great deal to you, didn't she…even if you never really got to know her?"

"She's always meant a lot to me. She's here for me, always has been." His gaze was transfixed upon the dancing lights. "When I see the northern lights, they comfort me. I hope they comfort others to-night, that others realize their loved ones are going home, escorted by the spirit guides who have watched over them for many lives." He paused to brush his lips across her forehead. "When Grandmother comes back for me someday, I know I will go to the light..."

Many lives? Beth stroked the ring on her finger, his grandmother's ring. Trying to understand, trying to tap into the ancient wisdom that this ring represented within the culture of the man that she was about to marry. *The circle of life,* Seth had told her. It's all about the circle of life.

◈◈

Seth could not sleep that night. Early the next morning, he untangled himself from her arms and crawled out of their warm bed to start breakfast. He threw another log on the fire. Something was wrong. He didn't know what it was, but he had some suspicions. Despite the cold drizzling rain that splattered against the window panes, he decided that he needed to head to the mainland as soon as the sun broke through the sleeping world.

"Seth?" A bleary-eyed Beth stumbled into the kitchen to find him sitting at the table in the dark with a cup of coffee. "What are you doing up at this hour?"

"Can't sleep, honey. I need to head into town first thing this morning."

"Can't it wait? It's raining. It's cold, even here in the house." She shivered, wishing that he'd crawl back into bed with her.

"No, I need to go," he was firm, very serious. He threw more logs into the fireplace, watching the red-hot coals disintegrating into ashes.

"What is it? Something's wrong?"

"I hope not, but I need to make sure."

"I'm going with you." She disappeared to get dressed in warm clothes and grab her rain gear.

As the pre-dawn stillness merged into a dreary day, they donned their rain suits and fired up the boat's engine. Shivering in the chilling rain, they did not speak as they headed for the mainland. A growing sense of apprehension hung heavily in the air between them—like a suffocating blanket of fog.

Seth headed for Jake's place, tying the boat up at his pier. He strode ahead of Beth toward the house, stopping dead in his tracks when he reached the porch. "Oh my God," he cried out when he saw Jake, eyes glazed over, slumped on the porch in his rocking chair. He ran to his side, searching for a pulse, for a sign of life. There was none. He began CPR as he heard Beth's footsteps running up behind him.

"Seth, what is it?" She gasped when she saw her father. "Dad, wake up! Dad!" she screamed. He did not move when she touched him, when she hugged him. He was cold, so cold. A picture of her mother was still clutched in his stiff hand. "You can't leave me—not now…come back, Dad," she collapsed in sobs.

Seth continued CPR, trying to save the old man. There was no response whatsoever. Finally, he slunk to the ground, defeated. It was too late. Jake was gone. All he could do now was try to comfort Beth. "Honey, he's gone…" Seth folded her into his arms, their tears mingling together. Jake had gone to the light. He'd already said his good-byes—in his own way. Seth held her close, stroking her head, suddenly flashing back into an eerie déjà vu experience when he'd stroked her head just like this…

She suddenly stopped crying for a moment, looking up at Seth in amazement, as if she'd just had the same strange recollection. Shaking her head in disbelief, she began choking with sobs once again. "He…he can't just leave me, Seth! We just found each other. I finally had a father of my own, and now…now, he left me again!"

"He's still with you, honey. He still loves you. It was his time to cross over. You need to believe that." His mind drifted back to their dinner with Jake at the Thunderbird, how pleased Jake had been with their engagement. He must have known his time was coming soon and he had, in fact, passed his daughter into Seth's care. "We need to remember the good times, Beth," he began softly, "Christmas together, the snowmobile ride he took us on, the way he proudly showed us landmarks of Rainy Lake."

She smiled through her tears. "Yes, I'll always remember that special Christmas we all shared together," she sighed, recalling how her father had bonded with Emily, his only grandchild, how she'd listened to his stories in the old shed. She needed to call Emily to tell her the tragic news, even if it wasn't possible for her to come for the funeral.

"Did you know," Beth whispered, "that he bought me a rowboat when I was a little girl and named it after me? *Elizabeth Ann…*"

"He's always loved you, Beth. That's what you need to remember," Seth murmured, stroking her back.

Finally, her river of tears dried to a trickle. She released Seth so he could make the necessary phone calls while she sat beside Jake's body, her hand covering his. A lingering mist drizzled over her world. It didn't matter. Nothing mattered. The lake that her father loved lapped mournfully around Houska's Point. The fog rolled in, enveloping her in a cloud of gloom. Her mind floated through memories she'd made with Jake—as a little girl, as his finally-recognized adult daughter. She barely acknowledged the funeral director when he intruded on her private world. He'd come to take Jake away.

Seth walked her back into the house and settled her beside him on the sofa. They sat in silence until Beth had recovered from the initial shock. "I need to call Emily." She reached for the phone and began dialing. As usual, she woke her sleeping daughter halfway around the world. Once Emily answered, Beth broke down in sobs once again, unable to speak.

"Mom, what's wrong? Mom? Are you there?"

Beth handed the phone to Seth, turning the responsibility over to him. He did his best to tell Emily what had happened, to try to reassure his soon-to-be stepdaughter, and to remind her how much Jake had enjoyed spending Christmas with her. He wasn't sure what the hell to say—was there any good way to relay news like this? Finally, Beth took the phone back from him and cried together with Emily.

Beth knew that Emily hated funerals and felt that you could tell someone good-bye without attending a formal funeral. Still, Emily was more than willing to come back for her grandfather's funeral, to be there to support her mother. Beth knew it would be a hardship for her and released her from feeling obligated to come. "I will be OK, Emily, I have support here...Seth is with me. I don't want you to come for my sake. I know how you feel about funerals."

"If you're sure, Mom..." Emily breathed a sigh of relief. "Mom? I'm glad you have Seth with you...I think I'm going to like having him for my stepfather," she finally had to admit.

Beth's heart smiled as she squeezed Seth's hand and told Emily good-bye. "Do we need to do anything else, call anyone?" she asked him quietly.

"The funeral director has already called Evelyn," he cautiously broached the subject, "but we need to call your father's attorney. I found his card on Jake's desk—along with an envelope marked *Funeral Wishes of Jake O'Connell*. There's a sticky note on it, asking you to call this Mr. Fryberg if and when something happened to your fa-ther…do you want me to do it for you?"

"No, I can do it. I need to do it." She moved to her father's desk, run-ning her hand along its smooth surface. She sat in the heavy leather chair where her father had spent many hours of his life. With trembling hands, she opened the envelope that contained Jake's final wishes. He had ap-pointed his attorney as the executor of his estate. It was time to make the call, she decided, time to inform him of Jake's death. Her voice crackled with emotion when she tried to speak into the cold, black telephone.

"I'm so sorry. Jake was a wonderful man, a good friend as well." Mr. Fryberg didn't sound completely shocked at the news. "I assume this is his daughter, Elizabeth Ann, or Beth, right?"

Beth was stunned at first. "Yes," her voice squeaked. Of course, Jake had seen to it that she'd be taken care of. His attorney would know the whole story.

"I'll dig out my copy of his will and take care of whatever needs to be done. I'll be in touch with you and am anxious to meet you. I've heard so much about you, Beth."

"Thank you," her voice began to choke up once again.

"If there is anything that I can do personally, as a friend, will you let me know? I mean that sincerely." He hesitated, for a moment. "Will you be in touch with Evelyn about the funeral arrangements?"

"I'm not sure how to handle that," she confessed, looking for guid-ance from someone. It might as well be Jake's attorney. "Evelyn and I have not had the best relationship…"

"I understand," he quickly assured her. "That's one reason why Jake left a document relaying his funeral wishes."

"I have it here," she glanced down at the document. It was all so fi-nal…his final words, his final wishes.

"Good. Now, this document is quite detailed—right down to the songs he wants sung at the funeral, his wish to be cremated, everything. It's all prearranged with the funeral home. The only thing that is not completely clear is the assignment of responsibility for someone to work with the funeral home to execute his final wishes. He has given this responsibility to 'family members.'"

"Evelyn then?"

He paused. "You are his daughter, Beth. He wanted you involved. To be honest, I think it was his hope that you and Evelyn could some-how work together on this. That's why he left it vague."

Now she understood. She recalled Jake's comment at the Thunderbird several weeks ago. He'd asked her to give Evelyn another chance. And she had promised him that she would. Jake must have known that he had little time left, she now realized. He was trying to prepare them all. *And I was so blind, so focused on Seth, that I missed all the signs,* she chastised herself.

"Beth? Are you there?"

"I'm sorry. I'm not exactly myself."

"I understand. I won't keep you, but I suggest that you pay Evelyn a visit—perhaps offer to assist her with funeral arrangements. If you can do that, it would please your father. Again, my deepest condolences to you, Beth."

Mr. Fryberg was right. Evelyn had, of course, already been informed of Jake's death by the funeral director. Now it was up to Beth to make good on her promise to her father. At least she would try. This was something she needed to do by herself, she realized, without Seth.

❧❧❧

Slowly driving into the Falls to pay Evelyn a visit, Beth thought about her family graveyard on the island. She wanted to bury an urn of her father's ashes there, beside her mother. Jake's funeral document specified the burial of his ashes in the traditional cemetery in International Falls—in the family plot beside Evelyn, of course. *But he really belongs by my mother*, Beth lamented. Yes, she would place a plaque for him on Sarah's Island, beside Mama, as Dad had requested. But what about Beth's family graveyard? He belonged there, too…

She cautiously parked her SUV in Evelyn's driveway and walked to the front door. The shades were drawn. Holding her breath, almost hoping that she wasn't home, she rang the doorbell and waited. Finally, as she was about to leave, the door cracked open. She could feel eyes peering through the gap, watching her. But nobody spoke.

"Evelyn?" Beth came closer. "It's Beth," she croaked, as tears once again began to spill down her cheeks. Through her tears, she watched the door creak open, framing a distraught old woman. Evelyn wore a navy-blue bathrobe, no makeup. Her puffy red eyes stared without seeing. She stood there as if she was in shock.

"Evelyn, I'm sorry. So sorry. Are you all right?"

The old woman nodded absently, then retreated back into her house, leaving the door ajar. Beth wasn't sure if she was being invited in—or asked to leave. She followed Evelyn into the sitting room, where

253

they sat silently across from each other. The only sound to be heard was the ticking of the grandfather clock marking time, time that somehow marched on while loved ones slipped away into timelessness.

"I don't want to disturb you," Beth began slowly. "I just came to tell you how sorry I am—and to…to help you with funeral arrangements. Or, ah, anything else that you need. Jake would want that."

No response, so Beth continued. "I have his funeral wishes here. It's all set—except somebody needs to contact the funeral home and work with them. If you're not up to it…"

Finally Evelyn spoke, slurring her words as if she'd taken a strong tranquilizer. "I don't need your help. I can do it myself…but if you insist, you can at least call them and set up an appointment."

Beth found the phone book and made the call, pleased that she could help in some small way. The appointment was set. Evelyn sat motionless, slumped in her chair, lost in her private thoughts. She did not speak, seemed to be unaware that she had company.

"Evelyn," Beth tried to get her attention, "is anyone coming to be here with you?"

"I don't need anyone. I'm fine."

"Have you eaten anything?"

"I don't want to eat." End of conversation.

Beth headed for the kitchen, rummaging around for something to feed this grief-stricken woman. *Jake's wife…* She returned to the sitting room with tuna fish sandwiches and coffee. Evelyn had not stirred.

"You need to eat something before our appointment," Beth told her, setting her lunch on the table beside her. Finally, Evelyn began pecking away at her food as Beth managed to eat half of her sandwich. Beth steered her into her bedroom so she could get dressed and comb her hair. She had to knock on her door several times to remind her that it was time to leave for the funeral home.

Finally, Evelyn emerged from her room. Her bright red lipstick was smeared, her hair uncombed. She wore a hot pink blouse over a long red skirt that floated above her green vinyl garden clogs. "Where are my car keys?" She shuffled into the kitchen, opened the refrigerator, and began rifling through the vegetable crispers. "Not here," she sighed in frustration.

"No need for your keys. I'll drive my car." Beth had taken over out of necessity.

"You'll what?" Evelyn began to protest.

"Are you wearing those garden clogs?" Beth asked cautiously.

"What?" She glanced down at her feet in surprise. "Of course not," she snapped, "I was just going to change." She put on a pair of black pumps and meekly followed Beth out to her car.

⤙⤚

Beth was also in charge at the funeral home since Evelyn sat there in a daze through most of the meeting. When asked for her opinion, she'd blankly reply, "That's fine."

They looked at cremation urns, selecting one that seemed to suit Jake. Beth finally spoke up at that point, asking for a second urn of his ashes, just a small one that she could keep. "That's fine," Evelyn repeated her words once again.

Beth was surprised when the funeral director produced an obituary that Jake had already written for himself. Clearing his throat, the man in the black funeral suit asked Beth to review it. Slowly, she began to read the words that her father had written, her mouth suddenly dropping open.

"Is something wrong?"

Nothing was wrong, she assured him, tears once again welling in her eyes. Nothing except that Jake had, through his obituary, recognized her as his surviving daughter. Emily was also listed as his granddaughter. Even more shocking, he had listed Sarah Peterson as a *special beloved friend* who had preceded him in death. Tears came to Beth's eyes. Dad had made good on his promise to recognize her and her mother. She glanced over at Evelyn, wondering what her reaction would be if this was published and made public to the world.

The man in black watched her knowingly. He understood that this was an awkward situation. Awkward as hell for him also. He cleared his throat again.

"I don't know what to say. I'm just not sure that Evelyn would be comfortable with this. There are some things here that other people may not know..." She spoke quietly, not wanting to upset Evelyn at a time like this.

"I understand. Of course, this is your decision. You are his daughter, Beth." He leaned in closer.

She sucked in her breath. Did everyone know? Was Evelyn able to admit it and finally recognize her?

His kind eyes focused on hers. "May I speak to you on a personal level?"

She nodded.

241

"These are your father's words, his final words to the world. He wanted to recognize you, your mother, and your daughter. I know that for a fact. As for Evelyn…" He glanced over at the silent woman who seemed to have tuned them both out. "Let me speak with her."

The funeral director scratched his head, walked over to Evelyn, and sat down beside her. "Evelyn, I need your permission to publish the obituary that your husband wrote. Can you hear me?" He laid a copy of Jake's obituary on the table in front of her.

"I'm sorry. I'm a little distracted." She seemed to be listening more intently than she had all afternoon.

"That's all right. I understand. Now, we need to make sure that we're not missing any information here, any surviving or deceased family members that should be recognized." He waited for her to read the obituary that her husband had prepared. She merely glanced at it, then turned away.

"What I need to know is if there are any other surviving family members, anyone except for you? Any children?"

Beth was shocked when the old woman looked up at her, nodding slowly. She seemed to be recognizing her as Jake's daughter.

"Just to be clear, are you telling us that Beth is his surviving child?" he asked gently.

Evelyn nodded, staring at the floor, as Beth breathed a silent sigh of relief.

"Are there any additional children, living or deceased?" the funeral director continued.

Evelyn shook her head, her hands trembling in her lap. Remembering her own unborn child. Wondering if her marriage would have turned out differently if—if she hadn't aborted the child Jake had wanted so badly. So many *ifs* in life, she thought to herself.

How long, Beth wondered, had this woman lived with the fact that her husband had a child by another woman? Had she always known?

"All right, then. Just so we all understand," the funeral director's voice droned on, "the obituary will list you and Beth as surviving family members. And a granddaughter, Emily. Is that correct?"

"A granddaughter?" Evelyn's eyes lit up. "How wonderful! I never had a daughter or granddaughter of my own, you know…not until now." She wiped a tear from her eye, the only one that Beth had seen her shed all day.

Once again, the funeral director cleared his throat nervously, as he reviewed the names of those who had preceded Jake in death. Evelyn nodded in agreement as the names of Jake's mother, father, and siblings rolled off of his tongue. "And finally, we have Sarah Peterson, special beloved friend," he spoke softly, watching for Evelyn's reaction. Beth held her breath at the far end of the mahogany table, almost feeling sorry for the old woman.

Evelyn tensed up, her mouth a thin, tight line. *Special beloved friend?* She began to drum her fingers lightly over the table, trying to decide how to respond. She'd tried so hard to hide this, all of the shame, for so many years. Now, her husband was letting it all out of the bag. Did it really matter anymore, she wondered? She was too exhausted to deal with this. He'd always loved Sarah, she knew that. And she knew that the others were waiting for some response from her.

Finally, she looked up. "Fine," she mumbled. "She is Beth's mother, after all."

ॐ ॐ

Beth decided to stay with Evelyn until the funeral was over. She slept in the guest room upstairs. The house was silent, filled with ghosts of the past, as the two surviving women in Jake's life crossed paths only as needed. Strangers passing in the night, they rarely spoke. Each mourned silently beneath the same roof—the roof of Evelyn's house. Jake had spent little time there over the years. It was difficult for Beth to understand why Jake's death had hit Evelyn so hard. They had lived separate lives for so many years. Why now?

ॐ ॐ

The old stone St. Thomas of Aquinas Church in the Falls was filled to capacity for Jake's funeral. Beth sat in the front hand-carved wooden pew between Evelyn and Seth, holding her head high. She was Jake's daughter, finally recognized by the world. Her heart smiled, knowing that Jake would be smiling down upon them all today. Sunlight streamed in through the stained glass windows of the old church, warming her soul, comforting her. She gazed up at the life-sized stained glass replica of Saint Theresa of the Little Flower, the one she'd loved as a child when Nana had taken her to church here. Saint Theresa's angelic face glowed in the light. She held red roses in her arms, roses that she mysteriously distributed in answer to prayers from those who believed in her. Saying a little prayer to Saint Theresa, Beth tucked her hand into Seth's. There was something about the way he squeezed her hand—something so familiar.

෯ඏ

After the funeral and lunch at the church, Beth took Evelyn back to her house. They talked about the funeral as a fitting tribute to Jake. They even shared a few details about their lives, things that neither knew about the other. Exhausted, they went to bed early. Beth would leave the next morning, free at last to go home to Seth. He would be picking her up in his boat at Houska's Point.

Evelyn had coffee made the next morning and was up to tell Beth good-bye. "Beth, I want to thank you for all that you've done here," Evelyn told her as they stood awkwardly at the door. "I don't know what I would have done without you. It's a strange situation for both of us...one that I'm just learning to live with, but..."

"It's what Jake would have wanted."

"I know that," she sighed. "Now, you have your young man to get back to...and I have things to take care of. But... I'd be honored if you would accept my invitation for tea some afternoon. Will you?" She seemed to be holding her breath, waiting for the answer that she wanted.

Beth's eyes widened in disbelief. Death seemed to have a way of turning surviving relationships upside down, of shifting them into strange new patterns. "I'd love to," she replied sincerely as she gave her a hug good-bye. As the words slipped from her tongue, a pang of guilt pierced her heart. *How would my mother feel about this? Would she understand?*

෯ඏ

As she pulled into Jake's place on Houska's Point, she suddenly remembered a strange request he'd once made of her. He'd asked her to open his safe immediately if anything happened to him. She'd forgotten, but she did have the safe's combination tucked away in her purse. Letting herself into his house, her house now, she found the safe and carefully entered the code. She held her breath, wondering what her father had left for her, and why it was so important that she get into the safe right away. Maybe she'd find his journals, old family photos, a farewell letter perhaps? The lock clicked and released. Still holding her breath, she eased the door open, peering into...an empty safe.

Seth found her with her head in the safe, searching for a false bottom, for a hidden drawer. There had to be something here, something that her father had wanted her to find. But there was nothing. The safe was barren. The treasures or secrets that it once held would remain a mystery.

"To err is human;
to forgive, divine."
Alexander Pope

Chapter Thirty-four

*T*rue to her word, Evelyn called Beth several weeks later, inviting her for tea. She waited for Beth in the glassed-in breakfast nook, gazing out into her gardens. They had sprung back to life after a long winter's rest. This was a season of renewal after all, she thought to herself—a fresh beginning for all forms of life, even for relationships.

Her breakfast table was littered with an assortment of papers, photos, and journals that she'd been sorting through during the past week. Someday, she decided, she might share some of this with Beth. But for now, it was hers—perhaps the only way she'd ever understand the stranger she had married so long ago. Now, he was gone and this was all she had left of him. She cleared the table, dumping it all into a cardboard box that she stashed beneath the sink.

Dressed in a long, sky-blue dress that billowed softly around her ankles, she stepped out into the sunshine and began strolling through her garden, through the memories of her life. Her crystal pendant shimmered in the sunlight. Her white hair was perfectly coifed, fresh from the beauty shop.

Beth soon arrived to find this image of elegance in her garden. The old Evelyn was back. They walked together along stone paths that wound through the flowers and circled the fountain. Beth admired the peonies that were in full bloom. Delicate rosebuds were beginning to open, surrounded by hostas and daisies. The fragrance of lilacs filled the air. A variety of birds sang and chirped, dipping themselves into the pool at the base of the bubbling fountain.

Evelyn had set the patio table with a white linen cloth, a vase of freshly cut lilacs, and delicate Bavarian china cups and saucers that she had purchased in Europe years ago. They had tea together along with fresh raspberry scones that Evelyn had baked that morning.

Beth admired the floral design on the fragile tea cups—soft pink roses floating across shimmering ridges of translucent ivory, trimmed with a delicate band of gold. "They are lovely," she sighed.

"My spring china," Evelyn smiled. "One of my obsessions, I must admit. I've collected china and crystal for every season of the year. Even a Christmas set—rather gaudy but festive with snowmen and decorated trees. I have more sets of china than I will ever need..."

"Well, these are exquisite, one of the most beautiful patterns I've ever seen."

"Would you like them?"

"What?" Beth almost dropped her teacup.

"I want you to have this set, Beth. It suits you perfectly. And someday, when I have the privilege of meeting your daughter, I would like her to pick out a set for herself."

"I...I don't know what to say. I can't accept something like this."

"Listen to me, young lady." Evelyn leaned across the table, her voice serious. "I am trying to make up, somehow, for the past. I've treated you horribly—and I'm sorry, Beth. I tried to run you out of town, you know. I tried to destroy your reputation, as well as that of your mother. I tried my best to sever your ties with your father, your own flesh and blood. And... I refused to release him into the arms of your mother, the only place that he ever wanted to be. I know that now. I am ashamed of myself, so ashamed."

Beth could not speak, but she listened carefully.

"I've done a lot of thinking, especially since Jake died..." Evelyn choked up with tears.

"I know it was hard for you."

"He hurt us both, you know, and your mother, too. He thought he could have it all, he couldn't give any of it up. A part of me will always blame him for what he did—to all of us," she stared into the distance.

"He made some mistakes, Evelyn. Maybe we all have..." she whispered.

"Oh my, yes. I made mistakes all right." She wrung her hands in her lap. "Maybe that's why this has been so difficult for me. You see, it's worse to lose someone when you have regrets—regrets for the things that you did or didn't do. I punished my husband during most of our life together. Do you know why?"

Beth shook her head, surprised that Evelyn was opening up to her like this. Perhaps she needed to vent, needed someone to talk to.

"I punished him because he could never love me the way that I wanted him to. He loved someone else—your mother, of course. That never changed, not ever, not even after she died. Her ghost has always lived with us, between us. I punished him for that, Beth. Maybe it took his death to make me see things a little differently." She paused, taking a deep breath before she was able to continue. "I finally understand that Jake and your mother were meant to be together. It was their destiny—something I could not change or control. Perhaps it was my destiny as well, something I needed to learn in this lifetime…" She wiped her eyes with an embroidered lace hankie.

"Evelyn, he cared about you, too. He asked me to look after you," she tried to extend a bit of comfort.

"And I've always cared about him in my own way. It's just that…do you have any idea how it feels when the one you love loves somebody else?"

Oh, yes, Beth thought to herself, it was the story of her life with Rob—over and over again. "Yes, I do, believe me, I do."

Evelyn's eyes widened in surprise. "Really? Well, I never thought…but that's not any of my business. I will tell you that I've decided it's time to forgive my husband. It's time to let go of my bitterness. I could blame him forever, but that would only hurt me more. I'd be stuck, poisoned by my bitterness, you see."

"There's more to life than that. I understand completely."

"It's also time for me to make amends to those I've hurt…please let me do that, Beth." She reached across the table and took Beth's hand in hers. "You and I, we have one common bond. Jake. He's gone now and I have no other family. Your mother and father are both gone. I would be honored if you could find it in your heart to think of me as a part of your family."

Beth's heart was torn with conflicting loyalties. She had to turn her gaze away from the tear-filled eyes that stared into her own, pleading with her. This was the same woman who had stood firmly between her parents. The one who had prevented her mother from fulfilling her dreams and Beth from having a real father in her life. She'd tortured Jake, holding him prisoner in a loveless marriage, hadn't she? Or had she? Perhaps Jake bore some responsibility for all of this. Why had he stayed all these years if things were so bad?

Her mind reeled, playing the *what if* game of her youth. What if Sarah hadn't died and the three of them—Jake, Sarah, and Beth—had become a real family? Then, Evelyn would have been the one alone and devastated. As it was, she'd remained his wife but had still spent her years pretty much alone and unhappy. There was no solution that could have made them all happy. And now, Beth realized, the others were gone. It was just the two of them—and Emily. Jake had brought them together through his death. Maybe it was time for his surviving heirs to find a way to get along. A way to honor his memory, thereby also honoring the memory of her mother. Wasn't that what her mother would have wanted?

As Beth looked up, her heart went out to this lonely woman. "Yes, Evelyn, I want you to be a part of my family," she stammered as she circled around the table toward her with outstretched arms. Evelyn rose and fell into her arms sobbing. It was the first time that she'd allowed herself to cry since Jake died. Beth stroked her back as Evelyn unleashed the bitter tears that had consumed so many years of her life.

When her tears finally ceased, Evelyn sighed, "I can't tell you how much this means to me…"

"It's going to mean a lot to Emily and me also—to have you in our lives," Beth smiled, speaking the truth.

"I have one more piece of unfinished business." Evelyn regained her composure. "I need to go to the cemetery. Do you want to come along?"

Thunder suddenly boomed over the Rainy River as raindrops began to fall. Typical summer weather here in the northland with its sudden shifts between sun and rain, laughter and tears.

"It's raining. Are you sure?"

"I have two umbrellas. This is important." Evelyn grabbed the vase of lilacs and hurried inside to retrieve two black umbrellas. Beth carefully carried the china and tablecloth into the kitchen.

They drove, windshield wipers racing back and forth, to the International Falls cemetery. With its long history, stately stone monuments, and beautifully manicured grounds, it was impressive. The Rainy River flowed peacefully just beyond the last row of burial plots. The river—a symbol of life, of death, of rebirth.

Beth drove through the cemetery to get as close as she could to Jake's fresh grave. The last of his funeral flowers were beginning to wilt. His memorial stone wasn't completed or erected yet. The rain suddenly began to pour down from the heavens. "Let's wait until it lets up," Beth suggested.

But Evelyn had her own agenda. "No, I need to go now, alone for a few moments, please." She wrapped a long black cloak around herself. Clutching the vase of lilacs in her hand, she stepped out into the rain and opened her umbrella. With a look of determination upon her face, she marched almost defiantly through the soggy grass. Lightning flashed through the black sky. She did not flinch.

Beth watched her disappear into the fog that was now drifting in over the river. Concerned, she quietly got out of the car with her umbrella, following Evelyn from a respectable distance. Another bolt of lightning sizzled, providing enough light for Beth to catch a glimpse of a ghostly image sprawled over Jake's grave. Evelyn's black cloak and umbrella billowed around her as the wind whipped across the graveyard, across the hopes and dreams of those long gone.

Evelyn's tears mingled with steely drops of rain that splattered to the ground. She gently stroked the muddy ground with one hand while holding onto her umbrella with the other. "Jake, I forgive you, and I'm asking you to forgive me, too. I finally understand…and I release you to Sarah. Remember that I love you too, in my own way…" She prayed silently that he could hear her, wherever he was.

"Rest in peace," she continued, whispering into the wind. "I will take care of Beth. She's with me, you know. You have a wonderful daughter—and a granddaughter who I am anxious to meet."

The sun suddenly poked through the clouds as the rain retreated. Evelyn pulled herself up from the pile of ordinary dirt that covered the ashes of her husband. Smiling through her tears, she carefully rearranged the lilacs in her cut-glass vase, propping it up at the head of the mound of dirt.

"There is a land of the living
and a land of the dead
and the bridge is love –
the only survival,
the only meaning."
Thornton Wilder

A Seagull Soars by Anna Merritt

Chapter Thirty-five

Seth waited for Beth at the Thunderbird marina, pacing back and forth. His boat rocked with the rhythm of the waves, with the rhythm of the universe. The skies had cleared. It was going to be a perfect day for a trip to Sarah's Island, a perfect time to place Jake's plaque beside Sarah's, to bid them both farewell from the place they had loved.

He scanned the horizon. Where was she? There still were times, he had to admit, that he worried about the future, about committing himself to spending a lifetime with another human being. Was love enough? Would it last forever...and what if it didn't? Not that he could imagine living without Beth. But he thought about the deadly love triangle that had haunted Jake, Sarah, and Evelyn for most of their lives. He shuddered to think that anything like that could happen to him.

Finally, Beth's mud-splattered SUV splashed into the parking lot. She ran down to the marina, her auburn hair flying in the wind. Jake's Irish eyes lit up the sleepy harbor. She flung herself into his arms. "I've missed you," she said, nuzzling herself into his chest, into the warmth of the man that she was going to marry.

He sighed deeply, holding her close, erasing any doubts from his mind. This was meant to be.

"Let's go home," she whispered in his ear as they took off into the open waters of Rainy Lake.

"After we pay our respects to Jake and Sarah. We're on our way to Sarah's Island. I have Jake's plaque with me."

She showed him the way—the same trip that her father had taken her on last fall, the same route that her mother and father had followed on their fatal camping trip so many years ago. She shivered at the thought.

"Are you OK?" Seth held her hand, the same way that Jake had held Sarah's hand long ago.

She nodded silently. With Seth at her side, she would always be OK. Her father knew that. She wondered if her mother did...and if they were together again, at last. It was a comforting thought anyway...

Sarah's Island was quiet, elegant in its early-summer wardrobe of velvet green. Lady slippers crept through the shady nooks, their delicate petals perched upon dainty white slippers that were streaked with swirls of pink. They wound their way up the wooded trail to the secluded clearing, where they mounted Jake's memorial plaque beside Sarah's. Together, they stood in silence, listening to the birds and the waves lapping against the shore below.

Then they hiked up to the rocky ledge where Beth sat with Jake last fall. This was the place that Sarah had loved, where Jake had spent so many hours of his life after she died. Hours spent searching for Sarah, reading poetry to her, trying to feel her presence.

Staring out over the lake and the sea of emerald islands that glittered in the sunshine, Beth settled upon the ancient rock. Seth sat beside her silently, holding her hand, waiting for something...

Beth remembered the seagull that had perched beside Jake on this rock last fall. He'd believed that it was a sign from Sarah. She remembered his words, the serene look upon his face. Today she waited, fool-ishly hoping for a glimpse of that sleek white gull.

They scanned the horizon in silence. Suddenly, a pair of pure white gulls circled overhead several times—then landed beside them. Beth held her breath as her tears began to flow. Letting herself go, she felt waves of love and peace flowing through her like a river with no be-ginning, no end. The female gull stared into her eyes, mesmerizing her, as images of her mother flickered through her mind.

Time seemed to stand still—until the gulls finally soared back up into the brilliant blue sky, into the universe of life. Together at last.

"The circle of life…" Seth whispered as he pulled Beth into his arms.

"Of love," she sighed, as long-forgotten images of other times, oth-er places, began to flash seamlessly through her soul. A river of lives cycling again and again. "I've always loved you, haven't I?" she sud-denly realized.

"Always," his spirit answered hers. "Always."

I AM NOT GONE
by Janet Kay

I am not gone
for I live on
in another time
and place.

When you think of me,
I will be there…
as seagulls soar o'er
waters of the dancing sky,
when a gentle breeze
caresses your face,
in the magic of moonlight
shimmering softly
'cross the lakes I loved…

Look up at the moon
and tell me "good night,"
tell me about your day.
For this I know…
I am not gone,
I'm just away
until we meet
again
someday.

Rainy Lake Resources

To learn more about this unique region of the world, check out some of the following:

RESOURCES

Kettle Falls Hotel	www.kettlefallshotel.com	218-240-1726
Thunderbird Lodge	www.thunderbirdrainylake.com	800-351-5133
Voyageurs National Park	www.nps.gov/voya	218-283-6600
Voyageurs Nat. Park Assn.	www.voyageurs.org	218-283-6600
National Park Foundation	www.nationalparks.org	202-354-6460
Rainy Lake Visitors Bureau	www.rainylake.org	800-325-5766
International Falls Chamber of Commerce	www.ifallschamber.com	218-283-9400
Koochiching County Historical Museum	International Falls	218-283-4316
Kay-Nah-Chi-Wah-Nung Historical Center	Stratton, Ontario, Canada	888-992-9949

Waters of the Dancing Sky Scenic Byway	www.watersofthedancingsky.org	
Mike Williams, Rainy Lake Resource	mandmwilliams@frontiernet.net	218-286-3591
Bois Forte Ojibwe Heritage Center, Nett Lake	www.boisforte.com	218-753-6017

BOOKS

Kettle Falls, Crossroads of History	www.vogageurs.org/links-and-resources/books	218-283-2103
Voyageurs National Park	www.voyageurs.org/links-and-resources/books	218-283-2103
Ojibwe Tales	www.voyageurs.org/links-and-resources/books	218-283-2103
Reflections from the North Country by Sigurd Olson	www.voyageurs.org/links-and-resources/books	218-283-2103
Toward Magnetic North -Oberholtzer 1912 canoe trip	www.eober.org/pages/store or Borealis Books, Chicago	800-621-2736
Keeper of The Wild, The Life of Ernest Oberholtzer by Joe Paddock	www.eober.org/pages/store Oberholtzer Foundation or MN Historical Society Press	800-647-7827
Ranier, MN, My Hometown by Bernie "Spike" Woods	www.ranierbookandprints.com	218-324-0180

About The Author

Janet Kay lives and writes on a lake in the woods of Wascott, Wisconsin. Drawn to nature since she was a child, she sees its wonders as a source of renewal, reflection, and connection with something greater than oneself. Her lifelong passions include creative writing, photography, travel, and spending time with family.

Waters of The Dancing Sky is her debut novel. Due to numerous requests from her readers, she is planning a sequel which will be set, again, in the Rainy Lake, Minnesota region. She is currently working on another novel that will be set in the antique country town of Walnut, Iowa and the old western ghost town of Virginia City, Montana. Next up is a paranormal novel set in Galveston, Texas.

For more information, check out her website at http://www.watersofthedancingsky.com. It includes a photo gallery, her blog, and opportunities to enter her promotional contest. Her blog, Janet Kay's Journey, can be found at http://watersofthedancingsky.blogspot.com.

She hopes to hear from you!

COMING SOON!

AMELIA 1868 by Janet Kay

What if a restless spirit comes back to life seeking revenge for her murder in a previous lifetime?

She's a bored farm girl growing up in the little town of Walnut, Iowa. Commitment-phobic, she stands her fiancé up at the altar and heads west. A mysterious force drives her to the old western ghost town of Virginia City, Montana.

Why does she finally feel at home in this strange place, recognizing old historical landmarks? Flashbacks begin to rack her soul. Roaming around a cemetery nestled in the mountains overlooking the town, she discovers an overgrown gravestone inscribed simply "Amelia 1868." No last name, no date of birth. For some reason, it chills her to the bone.

Obsessed with discovering who this long-forgotten woman was, Rose finds herself flashing back and forth between two very different realities – her current sheltered life in Iowa and that of a hurdy-gurdy dance hall girl struggling to survive in the saloons of the Wild West.

Her strange journey becomes more complicated when a love interest materializes and throws her off balance. Their relationship becomes a bizarre dance twisting and turning between love and hate. Can she still accomplish her mission? Does it matter?